"Imagine never having anyone touch you— never touching anyone else."

Krista thought of his hard hands, gentle despite their size, craving the feel of another person's touch. "I thought I'd never touch a woman again," his low-pitched voice raised goosebumps on her skin, the ache in her belly turning to something different at the heat emanating from his body.

He reached out and caught her hand in his.

"Never feel smooth, warm, skin under my fingers."

Heat coursed through her. Common sense screamed at her to pull away, get out while she could, but nothing could drown out the fact that she wanted *him*. And call her crazy, call her stupid, but she wanted to touch him, give him this, as though it could make up in some small way for her part in what had happened to him.

"Do you have any idea how that would make you crazy? How it would make you ache?" He closed the distance between them. Yes she could imagine the ache. It was consuming her right now.

His mouth came down on hers, hot and fierce. It was almost scary, her body's reaction to him, of all people. A spike of fear broke through the heat of desire, a voice warning her to pull back before she went plummeting over the edge, past the point of no return.

As though sensing her hesitation, Sean tightened his hold...

PRAISE FOR *BEG FOR MERCY*

"4½ stars! Top Pick! Alden's emotionally gripping *Beg for Mercy* makes readers beg for mercy, too…this is a high-caliber romantic suspense—exactly what the genre should be!"

—*RT Book Reviews*

"An exhilarating investigative thriller…never slowed down…Filled with action, but character driven by the heroine, sub-genre fans will appreciate this taut suspense…and look forward to Slater's follow-up case."

—GenreGoRoundReviews.blogspot.com

"The chemistry between Megan and Cole was absolutely mouth-watering. You could *feel* the sizzle when they were in the same room…I'm really looking forward to the next book in the series."

—TheRomanceaholic.com

"The sexy, heated love scenes leave the reader eagerly awaiting more, as they were well placed and a great catalyst for the ultimate showdown. I am waiting most impatiently for the next book in this series."

—TheRomanceReadersConnection.com

"Five stars! Flawless! This novel was nothing like anything I have read to date…The twists are crazy good! Not only that but the sexual tension and encounters were phenomenal!…[Cole Williams] is sex personified!…What a rush!"

—ShamelessRomanceReviews.blogspot.com

HIDE *from* EVIL

Jami Alden

FOREVER

NEW YORK   BOSTON

Copyright © 2011 by Jami Alden
Excerpt from *Run from Fear* © 2011 by Jami Alden
All rights reserved. Except as permitted under the U.S. Copyright Act of 1976, no part of this publication may be reproduced, distributed, or transmitted in any form or by any means, or stored in a database or retrieval system, without the prior written permission of the publisher.

Forever
Hachette Book Group
237 Park Avenue
New York, NY 10017

www.HachetteBookGroup.com

Forever is an imprint of Grand Central Publishing.
The Forever name and logo are trademarks of Hachette Book Group, Inc.

The publisher is not responsible for websites (or their content) that are not owned by the publisher.

Printed in the United States of America

First Edition: November 2011
10 9 8 7 6 5 4 3 2 1

ATTENTION CORPORATIONS AND ORGANIZATIONS:

Most Hachette Book Group books are available at quantity discounts with bulk purchase for educational, business, or sales promotional use. For information, please call or write:

Special Markets Department, Hachette Book Group
237 Park Avenue, New York, NY 10017
Telephone: 1-800-222-6747 Fax: 1-800-477-5925

To Gajus, sexier, funnier, and smarter than any hero I could imagine, and thankfully minus the emotional baggage

Acknowledgments

As usual, I owe a huge thanks to my writing buddies who have helped me through every single book since I started this crazy writing adventure. First to Monica McCarty, for the daily sanity checks and accompanying ego boosts or ass kicks, depending on what I need that day. I love our shared brain. And to Bella Andre/Bella Riley/Lucy Kevin, without whom this book would not exist! If you enjoy *Hide from Evil*, thank Bella, because if I'd had my way Sean would have never had his own happily ever after. And most especially thank you to my readers, for reading my books, enjoying them, and letting me know it! Nothing gets me through the tough spots and plot snags like knowing you are out there eagerly awaiting my next offering.

Chapter 1

Y ou ready to go?"

Krista Slater looked up and nodded at King County Prosecuting Attorney Mark Benson, who stood in the doorway of her office, briefcase in hand and an over-stuffed accordion folder under his arm. She gathered the notes she'd made on the witness statements she'd taken in the past month, trying to summon up that hungry feeling that used to overtake her every time she prepared for court.

Come on, Slater, eye of the tiger, she told herself as she shoved her files into her briefcase. She needed to be on her A-game today. No room for self-doubt or mistakes, not when they were facing off against a slick fish like Roman Karev and his team of five-hundred-dollar-an-hour attorneys. Karev, a restaurant owner with known ties to the Russian mob, was accused of murdering a local businessman and his wife.

Today was the pretrial hearing, and while she was damn sure their case was rock solid, she knew any mistake, any slipup could and would be used to get crucial pieces of evidence thrown out. She couldn't afford to be distracted by anything, especially not—

The phone on Krista's desk buzzed, and she pushed the button on the intercom. "What is it, Lisa?"

Her paralegal's voice sounded on the speakerphone. "Ms. Slater, I have a phone call for you. He won't say who he is, only that he was told to call you—"

As casually as she could, Krista punched Lisa off speakerphone and picked up the handset. She shot Mark an apologetic look, praying her elevated pulse rate and the twist of anticipation in her belly didn't show on her face. "I have to take this."

Benson looked pointedly at his watch. "We need to be there in ten minutes, and I need to go over some last-minute details."

"Two minutes, I promise." Krista ignored Benson's impatient sigh. "Put him through." She glanced up, stifling a grimace when it became clear Benson had no intention of leaving.

Krista swiveled her chair, turning her back to Benson, a thousand questions racing through her mind in the seconds it took for Lisa to put the call through.

"Is this Krista Slater?" asked a hoarse male voice.

"That's me," she said. "Who's this?"

"This is Jimmy, Jimmy Caparulo."

"I'm so glad to hear from you. I've been waiting for you to call."

"Uh, yeah," the man replied, his confusion at Krista's borderline flirtatious tone evident.

Her heart thudded against her ribs. Jimmy Caparulo, the man Nate Brewster had tried to frame as the Slasher before Nate had been caught and killed. "I'm really glad you called," Krista said. "My friend mentioned you might be in touch."

The "friend" was private investigator Stew Kowalski, whom Krista knew through his work on several cases with the prosecuting attorney's office. But this time Stew wasn't working in any official capacity, so she was careful not to mention him by name in front of Benson.

Krista had hired Stew a couple of months ago to look deeper into the Nate Brewster case. Even though there was no doubt Brewster was guilty of killing seven women, including Evangeline Gordon, some things about him just weren't adding up. Too many gaps of information, too many things screaming at her that what happened to those women didn't begin and end with Nate Brewster.

But everyone from the FBI agent in charge of Brewster's case to Krista's own boss seemed content to let it go. The Slasher had been caught. They had incontrovertible proof in the form of video that he'd killed all seven victims—eight in total if you included Evangeline Gordon, the victim whose murder Sean Flynn had been sent to death row for. Flynn had been exonerated, freed, and generously compensated, and now everyone seemed content to put the entire embarrassing episode behind them.

Except for Krista, who couldn't let it go. When it became clear there was no way to keep the investigation active, she hired Stew on her own dime to find out the real story behind Brewster and the prostitution ring he'd run out of one of Seattle's most exclusive nightclubs. Up until now, he hadn't been able to find anything. The trail was cold, and Krista realized she needed to resign herself to the fact that sometimes the bad guys got away.

Flynn was free. She should be happy about that.

Then, a few days ago, Stew had made contact with Jimmy Caparulo. Krista told herself not to get her hopes up. Even so, this call from Jimmy sent her back on high alert. "I told Stew I would only talk to you. I knew the way you helped Sean. You're the only one I can trust with this," Jimmy said, his words coming out in a rush.

"I wish you'd called sooner." Krista injected a pouty note into her voice and snuck a glance at Benson. His expression was one of disbelief.

"I knew they would hurt my aunt if I ever said anything," Jimmy continued, unable to stop himself now that the words had started. "But now Nate's dead and she's gone too. I can't keep it in anymore. I should have said something sooner. I should have helped Sean—"

Krista cut him off before he got rolling. She couldn't completely focus with Benson tapping his foot and giving her the *wrap it up* sign, and she didn't want to miss a word. "I really want to talk to you more, but this isn't the best time. Can I call you later, or better yet, why don't we go out?"

"Go out? Yeah, this will be better in person. Where do you live?"

"Wow, you don't waste any time!" she said with a little laugh. "How about we at least meet for a drink before you invite yourself over?"

"What on earth are you doing?" Benson whispered incredulously. "We have to leave, now!"

Krista held up a finger and mouthed *Sorry*, as she grabbed a pen to write down the name of a coffee place near Jimmy's aunt's house. "Tonight at eight. It's a date," she said before she hung up.

She gathered her things, avoiding Benson's eyes as she

braced herself for the scolding that would begin in five, four, three, two...

"What was that all about?" Benson said, exasperated, his footsteps echoing off the hard floors of the corridor that connected their office wing to the courthouse. "Ten minutes before we face off against Karev is not the time for a personal call."

Krista bit back a smart-ass response. Relieved as she was that Benson had bought her performance, it galled her that he really thought, after working with her for over seven years, she would be that frivolous. Still, he'd be furious if he knew she was investigating Brewster after he'd told her to drop it. "I know, and I'm sorry. But I made a commitment to myself to give a little more balance to my personal life, and my friend has been trying to connect me with this guy for months now, and I've been really excited to meet with him."

At least that part was true. Ever since the truth about Sean's innocence had come out, Krista had wondered if Jimmy had known all along that Nate was guilty. When Jimmy had testified against his friend Sean, had he known he was covering for Nate Brewster?

To date, Jimmy hadn't given any indication that he knew more about Brewster and his activities than he'd let on. Even when Brewster had tried to set Jimmy up as the Slasher, Jimmy wouldn't say a word other than that they'd become close friends in the army but had lost touch over the years. Nothing new, nothing Jimmy's aunt, who Jimmy had cared for during the last years of her life, couldn't tell them.

But now... *I knew they would kill my aunt if I ever said anything.*

Her heart skipped a beat. *They.* So she was right. Nate Brewster hadn't been working alone.

It looked like Jimmy had something to say after all. It took all of her restraint not to share the news with Benson, but she needed to play her cards close to the vest until she had something concrete to go on.

Then all bets were off.

Benson paused and stayed Krista with a hand on her arm. "You know Rae and I would love nothing more than to see you settled down and happy. But really, Krista, couldn't you have had Lisa take a message and called him back?"

Krista forced a smile. "Aren't you the one who always told me to seize an opportunity as soon as it presented itself? I'm not getting any younger, and Lord knows I've given enough of my life to the job these past few years. I need to find some kind of a balance, especially after..." She let her voice trail off.

Mark frowned down at her, his face creased with paternal concern. "I know the last few months have been hard on you, and I know it's hard to drive forward after a mistake like that."

She couldn't suppress her indignant squawk. "A mistake? Mark, what happened to Sean Flynn was a catastrophe. And we were the engineers."

Mark gave her arm a gentle squeeze. "We did the best we could with the evidence we were given. No prosecutor would have acted any differently."

Nothing but cold comfort, Krista thought. She couldn't just shrug off her guilt.

Mark rubbed his thumb over the crease between his brows. "Mistakes were made. It happens in this job. But you learn from those mistakes, move on, and do a better job the next time."

Krista swallowed hard. She knew he was right, that the cases they prosecuted were rarely black and white, cut and dried. She did the best she could with every case, but she couldn't afford to agonize over every case that didn't go exactly the way she wanted it to.

Even though months had passed since Flynn's release, she still couldn't put it behind her. It was starting to take its toll, and it showed.

As though reading her thoughts, Benson said, "You've lost that fire, that passion that got you to where you are, and where I know you want to go."

Oh, Jimmy's call had lit a fire all right, but it had nothing to do with advancing her career with the prosecuting attorney's office.

"This is a big deal," Benson continued, "being part of the Karev case, and I put you on it because I know you're the best. This is your chance—our chance, to put the whole Sean Flynn disaster behind us."

"And I appreciate that," Krista said. She truly did. She knew Mark, her mentor who had hired her straight out of law school, was handing her a great opportunity to get her career back on track. But she wished he wasn't quite so eager to nail the lid shut on the Brewster/Flynn case. Was he becoming so embroiled in the politics that surrounded his position that he no longer cared about seeing justice done?

No, she knew Mark better than that, Krista thought as she shook off her cynicism. Mark was a good man, and he had also been shaken to the core after the events of the past few months. He had every reason to be cautious when it came to dealing with such a high-profile case.

Exactly why she needed to keep her little side investigation to herself until she came up with something concrete.

And just because they'd messed up royally with Sean Flynn, that didn't mean the whole system was broken. There was still good to be done, criminals to get off the street. Especially those who might have been working with Nate Brewster behind the scenes.

The mere thought of it was enough to make her blood simmer.

She made herself focus that fire, channeled it into the here-and-now as she walked into the courtroom. Roman Karev's mud-green stare raked her from head to toe, his greasy smile making her yearn for a shower.

I'm going to nail you, asshole, she thought, picturing the bodies of Aurelia and Nico Salvatore clinging together after Karev and his thugs had beaten them to death for reasons that changed depending on whom you talked to.

Some said it was because Nico had failed to pay back a loan he'd taken out to keep his trattoria running when business slowed to a crawl. Others said it was because Nico refused to let Karev's men use the apartment of the restaurant as a holding area for stolen goods after Nico had already taken payment.

Either way, Nico made a fatal mistake when he decided to do business with Karev, and now it was up to Krista to prove it.

As hard as it was to follow Benson's lead and let go of Flynn's case for the time being, right now she had to focus on the big picture. For her, this job was all about doing right, making sure sleazebags like Karev got their due, and on the rare occasion that she fucked up, doing everything she could to make sure the truth came out.

Forty-five minutes later, Krista gathered up her files, her gut churning at the debacle that had just occurred. "I can't believe it," she murmured again. "Without Baker's eyewitness account, we're screwed." In a move that had blindsided them, the judge had granted the defense's motion to make their key witness's testimony inadmissible in the trial.

"It's a blow," Benson replied.

"It's more than a blow," Krista hissed low so the other side wouldn't hear. "All we're left with is circumstantial." The chances of getting a jury to convict were now hovering somewhere around zero, and Karev and his sharks knew it.

"Keep your head," Benson warned. "We'll regroup back at the office."

Krista nodded, gathering her composure around her like a protective force field. *Never let the defense see your cracks.* It was one of the first lessons Benson ever taught her. No matter what, never show anything but supreme confidence to the enemy.

She slung her briefcase over her shoulder and stormed out of the courtroom. Mark followed a few steps behind. Karev and his team were standing outside, shaking hands and patting backs. Karev's lead counsel, Matt Swanson, shot her a sympathetic look and shrugged as if to say, *Better luck next time.*

Krista ignored the friendly gesture from the man she'd known nearly half her life, wanting nothing more than to get away from them before she completely lost her cool.

"Roman, congratulations," a masculine voice boomed. A wave of dread paralyzed her. As if this morning could get any worse. "Matt, I heard you did a great job. Sorry I couldn't be there myself, but, well, there are certain conflicts."

Krista looked up to see a pair of familiar grayish-green eyes on her. "So why are you here, Dad?"

"I came down to observe. I wanted to see how everything went." He leaned down and kissed her on the cheek, and Krista forced herself not to wipe it off.

She didn't even need to ask how he felt about the outcome. They may have shared the same eye color and light-blond hair, but that was where the similarities between Krista and her father, John Slater, ended. While Krista had focused her career on using the system to make sure criminals got what they deserved, John Slater cared about one thing: winning.

And today his partner at the highly regarded law firm of Slater, Swanson, and Miller had scored a major victory against his own daughter.

Decades of disappointment and disdain roiled in her stomach, and underneath that the sharp ache that never failed to assault her whenever she saw her father. Mark, who knew her history with her father, gave her a sympathetic look and she did her best to keep her turmoil from showing.

"Mark, good to see you," her father said, reaching past Krista to shake Mark's hand. The two exchanged pleasantries and Krista felt like her head was going to explode. She started to move past them.

Her father caught her by the arm. "Will I see you at the Maxwell luncheon on Friday?"

Krista gave her head a curt shake. "Political fund-raisers aren't exactly my thing."

"David has been a friend for years." Her father's scolding tone made her feel about five years old.

Krista refrained from reminding him that just because someone paid your firm hundreds of thousands in legal fees didn't make them your friend. "I have to work." Then, because she couldn't resist: "Not everyone can take off in the middle of the day to spend a thousand dollars for a plate of rubbery chicken."

"You could if you wanted to," her father said quietly. "You know I always have a place for you."

He still didn't get it. After everything that had happened, he couldn't accept that she would never be like him.

Murk shifted uncomfortably beside her and murmured something about getting back to the office.

Before they could go, Karev spoke, his English thickly accented and dripping with arrogance. "I would hire you. You come work for me, you never have to worry again." The smug grin he exchanged with her father made her jaw lock.

"Don't think this is over," she said, hitting him with an icy glare that had felled better men than him. "You may have slithered your way out today, but I'm going to nail you for what you did to the Salvatores."

Karev's smile pulled into a sneer and he stepped close enough for her to pick up the cloying scent of hair gel. "You can try. But I will give you some advice. Think of today as a bullet you dodged and quit while you're ahead."

* * *

Six hours later, Krista's gut was still churning as she entered the coffee shop where she was supposed to meet Jimmy Caparulo.

Though she'd dismissed Karev's threat for the macho posturing that it was, what had happened today had left her with a bad taste in her mouth. She'd faced down hundreds of lowlifes in the courtroom, but it wasn't often that she left the room feeling so contaminated by the people she came in contact with.

Now that boil on the ass of society was going to walk free unless she could come up with another witness to put him at the scene when the Salvatores were killed.

And her own father had shown up to rub her nose in it. She supposed she should be grateful her father had recused himself from the case and let his partner handle it. No doubt he was still working behind the scenes in an anonymous advisory role, pitting himself against her.

Trying to demonstrate, yet again, that Krista's quest for justice was not just misguided, but ultimately futile. Waiting for the day when she finally tucked in her tail and admitted Daddy was right, that she was wasting her life in a thankless government job when she could be making millions as the daughter and protégé of one of the top defense attorneys in the Pacific Northwest.

The mere thought made her skin crawl. It was one thing to take money from wealthy businessmen like Maxwell to protect them from lawsuits. It was another to help a scumbag like Karev get away with murder, and God knew what else.

She ordered a latte and forced herself to stop brooding over today's failure and instead focus on how she was going to salvage the case.

Jimmy was late, so she pulled out Karev's case files to review while she waited. Her irritation escalated as eight turned into eight-thirty, eight forty-five, and finally nine o'clock passed, and still no sign of Jimmy Caparulo.

Two phone calls at the number he'd given her dumped straight into voice mail, and her texts went unanswered.

She swore under her breath as she looked up Jimmy's address from the report Stew had given her. Jimmy was not the most stable person in the world, with documented PTSD and a history of alcohol and drug abuse. Most likely he had gone on a bender and either forgot about their meeting or passed out before he could meet her.

Which also made whatever information he provided less than reliable, she reminded herself as she walked the short distance to the house where Jimmy lived with his aunt.

Still, it was a start, and maybe if it wasn't all bona fide he'd give her something—

Her inner monologue stopped short as she registered the flashing blue and red lights in the driveway halfway down the block. She bit back a swear when she saw it was Jimmy's house.

As she got closer, she could hear the voices popping over the radios and the murmurs of the small crowd gathered on the front lawn.

A woman was sobbing inconsolably against the shoulder of another woman. "It was awful, so awful. Thank God Angie wasn't here to see it."

Krista recognized one of the uniforms controlling the perimeter. "Roberts! What happened in there?"

Roberts looked at her in confusion. "What are you doing here?"

"I was supposed to meet with Jimmy Caparulo about an hour ago," Krista admitted. So much for keeping their meeting secret until she'd built up her case, but with her number popping up all over his cell phone in the last hour, there was no way to keep a lid on it. "When he didn't show I decided to come by."

Roberts let out a mirthless laugh. "Guess he was too busy blowing his brains out to keep your date."

Krista's stomach bottomed out at the news. "He killed himself?"

"They're not gonna call it right now, but from where I'm standing, there isn't much question he ate the business end of his Glock."

She swallowed back a surge of bile. "Who found him?"

"Neighbor," Roberts said, indicating with his head the direction of the sobbing woman. "She found him about fifteen minutes ago and called it in."

"How'd she get in the house?"

"She has a key. She was a friend of Jimmy's aunt, and since she died a couple weeks ago, they've been taking turns bringing him dinner. Came over to deliver a plate of enchiladas and got one hell of a surprise."

"Neighbors didn't hear anything?" The houses on the Caparulos' street were close together. "Seems like someone would hear a gunshot."

"It's an older neighborhood," Roberts said, and as Krista took a closer look at the crowd milling on the lawn she saw a lot of white hair and hunched backs. "The lady next door says she might have heard it but at the time she thought it was the TV."

"She say what time?"

"About seven-thirty."

Krista pulled her wool coat tighter around herself. All that time she was waiting for Jimmy at the coffee shop, and he was already dead.

And he just happened to kill himself on the day he was supposed to meet you.

A shiver that had nothing to do with the damp spring night slithered down her spine. "Okay if I go inside?"

Roberts frowned. "The M.E.'s still in there and they haven't even moved him yet—"

Krista cut him off with a wave of her hand. "I've seen worse."

Yet Krista could see a thousand bloody crime scenes and nothing would ever prepare her for the smell. She was brutally reminded of that the second she stepped into the small one-story house. She flashed her ID at a uniform and didn't bother to ask where Jimmy was.

It was all too easy to follow the odor of violent death. Sickly sweet, metallic blood and excrement mixed with an indescribable stink, like she could smell the body already rotting though he'd been dead for less than two hours.

She followed the smell and sounds of activity down a short hallway, past a bathroom on the left, and through the second door on the right. Like a homing beacon, her gaze skipped right to the headboard of the double bed and the wall above. A wall that was painted white now displayed a splatter pattern of blood punctuated with the occasional pieces of gray brain.

Despite the cavalier attitude she'd shown Roberts, Krista's knees went a little wobbly and her vision started to tunnel. She leaned carefully against the doorjamb and took a deep, quiet breath as she kept an iron-clawed grip on her composure. She'd worked for the prosecuting attorney's office for seven years, dealt with some of the bloodiest crime scenes imaginable, and had never shown even a hint of weakness. She wasn't about to start now.

She forced herself to look at the scene analytically. She knew the crime scene guys would do a thorough investigation, but she wanted to take her own look around and see if there was anything going on here that would indicate it was anything other than a gory suicide scene.

Jimmy was flopped back on the bed, his booted feet resting on the floor, knees bent over the edge of the mattress. His right hand was flung out to the side, and there was a chalk mark on the bed to indicate where the gun had fallen.

Flashbulbs popped as the techs took pictures of the scene and she recognized Medina from the coroner's office leaning over Jimmy's body. She greeted him, and immediately regretted it when he straightened up, giving her a good look at Jimmy's face. What was left of it anyway. Her stomach lurched and she pinned her stare to a blank spot on the wall until she was sure she wasn't going to hurl up the coffee she'd drunk.

"This guy wasn't screwing around," Medina said as he snapped off his gloves and dropped them into a biowaste container. "We'll need ballistics to confirm it, but judging from the way it took off half of his skullcap, Mr. Caparulo used a hollow point, which expanded on impact."

"Roberts said the Glock was registered to him."

Medina nodded. "I guess so—that's for these guys to figure out." He gestured at the crime scene techs.

"You're sure he did it himself?"

Medina frowned like the question confused him. "I need to do a full postmortem, and the forensics will have to confirm it, but he has powder residue on his hands."

A cold breeze wafted through the room, providing momentary relief to the suffocating stench. The shade flapped against the window frame. "The window is open." Krista lifted the shade and saw the screen was still in place. She turned to one of the techs, an Asian woman wearing wire-frame glasses who was dusting Jimmy's desk for fingerprints. "Was it like that when you got here?"

"I'm not sure. You'll have to ask whoever was first on the scene."

Krista started to ask who that was when her gaze snagged on a silver-framed photo on Jimmy's desk. She recognized Jimmy Caparulo, dressed in army fatigues. He looked younger, smiling into the camera with his arms slung over the shoulders of the two other men in the photo. Her breath caught as she recognized the other two.

Flanking Jimmy on the left, looking like a fallen angel with his dark hair and piercing eyes, was Sean Flynn, the man whose face had haunted her, waking and sleeping, from the day she'd watched him walk out of the courtroom a free man.

But the man in the picture wasn't the Sean Flynn she knew. Gone were the deep, grim lines in his cheeks, the tight mouth, the eyes dark with anger.

In the picture was a Sean that Krista had never seen. Eyes sparkling with humor, mouth wide open and laughing, his teeth bright white in contrast to his sun-baked skin. So happy and gorgeous it was hard to believe she'd ever thought he was a murderer.

And on Jimmy's right, Nate Brewster, the epitome of an American hero, his flawless blond, blue-eyed perfection hiding the well of evil at the root of his soul. Evil that had ruined the lives of the men who considered him a friend.

Now Jimmy was dead, just as he was about to reveal the secrets Brewster had killed to keep.

Despite Medina's assessment, Krista knew in her gut it was no coincidence. "Make sure you check the window outside for signs of forced entry," she said to the tech dusting for fingerprints, who looked confused by the order but nodded in agreement.

Who else could be hurt by the information Jimmy had? What was she missing?

Before she could ponder the question further, her phone rang. When she recognized Stew's number, she ducked out of the bedroom and into the bathroom across the hall, closing the door before she picked up.

"Jimmy Caparulo's dead," she said.

"I know," Stew said. "The late local news already picked it up. They're saying he killed himself after the trauma of being framed for the Slasher murders."

"Conveniently on the same night he was going to meet me," Krista said. "I don't care how the ruling ends up. I don't think this was a suicide."

"I'll look into it. But that's not why I called you. I think I found something."

"Yeah?"

"I've been tracking Brewster's financials and I think I've found something. Could be something big."

Chapter 2

Krista went through everything one last time before she headed for Benson's office. She wanted to make sure all of her ammo was in order.

She hadn't been surprised in the least when he'd left a message last night at midnight asking that she meet him first thing. By then he must have found out about Jimmy Caparulo's alleged suicide and about how Krista showed up at the scene after her number popped up on Jimmy's phone about half a dozen times.

Benson was understandably curious. Curiosity that would be followed shortly by anger once she told Benson she was meeting Jimmy Caparulo as part of an independent investigation into a case that he considered emphatically closed.

He didn't disappoint. "What part of 'drop it' don't you understand? Nate Brewster is dead, Sean Flynn is free, and we don't have the time or the resources to waste on some theory you have that Brewster wasn't working alone."

"We have every reason to believe there were others involved. There are witnesses who are willing to give statements to that effect."

Benson cocked a skeptical brow at her. "Witnesses? Don't you mean witness? One that has disappeared off the face of the earth?"

Krista forced herself not to drop her gaze like some timid teenager. "Talia Vega could have important information." Unfortunately the prosecution's star witness in Sean's original trial had disappeared almost immediately after she'd been rescued, along with Megan Flynn, from Nate Brewster's brutal clutches.

"And you only know that secondhand, from Sean Flynn's sister. Hardly a reliable source."

Krista's eyes narrowed. "I consider Megan a reliable source, and even if I didn't, you know as well as I do that Detective Williams is solid."

Benson replied with a skeptical grunt.

"And you can't tell me the files deleted from Brewster's computer don't raise a red flag," Krista continued.

"Yes, they do, but with nothing else to go on, our hands are tied."

"And yesterday Jimmy Caparulo turns up dead, right after he tells me he has information about Brewster. You don't think that's a little too much of a coincidence?"

Benson's thick gray eyebrows raised above the wire rims of his glasses. "He was a disturbed young man struggling with serious PTSD and addiction issues. I imagine you'd have to take any information he provided with a huge grain of salt."

Krista opened her mouth to protest but Benson silenced her with a raised hand. "We've been through all of this, and I keep telling you, there's not enough to go on—"

"What about this?" Krista had been waiting for the right moment to break out the new information Stew had discovered. She slid the paper across Benson's desk and perched on the edge of her seat as she waited for his reaction to her bombshell.

"What am I looking at?"

"A bank statement, from one of Brewster's offshore accounts. One we just found, under a dummy corporation."

"He had several, including the one he used as a holding company for Club One. What makes this one different?"

"There are three ten-thousand-dollar deposits: one on May fourth, one on October sixth of last year, and one on March third this year."

"So?"

Krista kept her jaw from dropping. Benson was only in his early fifties, and she had never known him to be anything but razor sharp. Was it possible that edge was starting to dull? "March third was when Bianca Delagrossa was murdered." She'd been found in a trailer park, tortured, raped, and murdered in the Slasher's signature style. "And at least one of the other deposits coincides with when he murdered another victim."

"Which means what?"

"Which means it's possible someone was paying Nate to kill those women." She sat back and folded her arms, waiting for Benson to congratulate her on her insight.

Instead, Benson leaned back in his chair, slipped off his glasses, and rubbed his eyes. "Krista, you have got to stop spinning your wheels on this. I think you've gotten so close to this case you've lost all perspective."

"What do you mean? What if someone was paying him to kill those women?" She knew her theory was radical, but when dealing with psychotic minds you had to allow for all possibilities.

"Brewster was sick. He killed several women. He also ran a very successful *legitimate* computer consulting business. Don't you think it's possible that a customer might have happened to pay him on the same day one of the murders occurred?"

This time Krista couldn't keep her jaw from falling open. "I can't believe what I'm hearing. Why won't you even consider that he wasn't working alone—"

Benson slammed his palm to his desk, sending a stack of files to the floor. "Because we have a backlog of three dozen fucking cases, we're going to lose at least three people because of budget cuts, and one of my best pros-ecutors is wasting her time on a case that was closed months ago!" He snapped his mouth shut and closed his eyes. When he spoke again, his voice was calmer, but the lines of tension around his mouth were still there. "I'm sorry. I shouldn't speak to you like that." He rubbed his eyes tiredly and when he looked at her again, it was with a paternal smile edged with exasperation. "Krista, your thoroughness and your commitment are things I appreci-ate most about you, but I'm asking you, please. Let this go. For both our sakes, I need you to turn your focus to something that really matters."

Krista could barely see through the red fog hazing her brain. She couldn't believe the man she'd looked to for ad-vice on everything from whom she should call on as an expert witness to whether she should buy a house or a condo was dismissing her suspicions out of hand. "Sean Flynn was sentenced to death and Jimmy Caparulo is dead along with seven other women because we went after the wrong guy. Now I come across evidence that Nate might not have been working alone and you think that doesn't matter?"

"There's a difference between information and evidence, Krista. I can't open an investigation based on what you've given me." He reached down to gather the files he'd knocked to the floor. "Now, we need to find another angle in the Karev case. We need to think about..."

Krista barely heard a word as he droned on about his strategy for the investigation. He really expected her to drop it. Just tuck her tail between her legs and ignore the fact that she was sure Brewster hadn't been working alone. When she'd first been hired fresh out of law school, she would have shrugged aside her suspicions and trotted obediently away.

But that was before she'd encountered Sean Flynn.

"I have a lot of vacation days piled up," she blurted out in the middle of Benson's speech.

"What?" he said, startled. "You can't. After today's setback we have to completely rebuild our case against Karev—"

"Chandler can take it," Krista said. "He's dying to get in on Karev's case." Luke Chandler had been hired three years ago, and he was hungry for a big case to beef up his profile.

"I don't want Chandler on this case. I want you."

Krista shook her head. "My head isn't in the game, not like it needs to be. You said so yourself. Just give me a couple weeks to get it straightened out. Let me see this through."

"You're on the fast track here, Krista," Mark said, not unkindly. "If you take off in the middle of a case like this, you could be risking everything you've worked so hard for."

Krista didn't have the heart to tell the man who had

taken her under his wing and fostered her from the very beginning that, after the last few months, she wasn't sure she wanted to be on any track in this office, fast or not. "I understand," she said. She rose from her chair and gathered her printout of the bank statements.

"Leave that here," Benson said. Krista shrugged and handed over the copy. Maybe if he took more time to study it he'd finally see what she did.

Mark Benson waited until Krista had shut his office door behind her before he reached into the bottom-right-hand drawer of his desk. He grabbed the bottle in the back without looking.

He kept the bottle of fifty-year-old Macallan to commemorate his greatest victories, like the day Sean Flynn was pronounced guilty and Krista had knocked back two fingers with him in celebration. At the time they'd been flush with the triumph of nailing a sadistic killer to the wall.

He also kept the bottle for the days when things went to utter shit. Like when, two years later, Sean Flynn's conviction had been overturned and the whole thing had blown up in their faces, and the open-and-shut case had revealed itself to be more complicated than anyone ever could have imagined.

When he'd gone for the death penalty, he'd believed with every fiber of his being that Flynn was guilty. He'd had no idea that conviction would land him in a quagmire of shit with no visible way out.

The public relations nightmare that had ensued after they'd sent an innocent man to death row had been hell. The Seattle PD and the prosecuting attorney's office were painted as a bunch of bloodthirsty incompetents, and even Krista's work to make sure Sean was cleared of all charges hadn't done much to repair their reputation.

If only that was the worst of it. But right now his image issues were the least of his problems. And Krista's unrelenting crusade to discover the truth about Nate Brewster threatened to send it all erupting to the surface, spewing forth like lava, destroying everything. Destroying the lives and careers of countless others.

Others who understood that sometimes people had to die to keep their secrets safe.

Damn it.

Despite their efforts to make it look like the murders and the prostitution ring began and ended with Brewster, there were too many loose ends for Krista to track down and tie together.

Now they were calling on Mark to stop her, to help them get this mess cleaned up before the whole world found out how deep the rot really went.

He wished he could tell them they had nothing to worry about, that Krista would never find anything, that they were safe. He squeezed his eyes against the burn of tears. Krista, damn her, was one of the only people smart enough, relentless enough, to piece together the truth if she wasn't stopped.

And she wasn't going to stop on her own. She'd made that clear when she walked out the door.

He stared at the phone. Maybe he should play dumb. Pretend he had no idea what Krista was up to, act blindsided when she went public with her accusations. As soon as the notion crossed his mind, he dismissed it. If Krista wasn't stopped in her tracks, the fallout would be immeasurable. Starting with him, destroying his family before it spread like a virus until the whole damn city fell apart.

It wasn't even nine in the morning yet, but he knew he needed the whisky's bracing effects to handle what he needed to do next.

He poured himself half a glass of scotch and swallowed it in two gulps. The next glass he sipped more slowly, thinking about Krista and the way she'd come out of law school, figurative guns blazing in the name of truth, justice, and the American way.

Young and fresh with her startling, old-Hollywood ice-princess beauty—not that she'd ever tried to use her looks to get ahead. A real ballbuster, but with a heart of gold and an unshakeable core of integrity under her no-nonsense attitude. Making her way in the boys' club with a no-bullshit demeanor that had the toughest gangbangers reluctant to face her in the courtroom.

She reminded him of himself thirty years ago, full of zeal and passion. Before he'd learned the compromises and tradeoffs he'd have to make to climb this high. Before he'd realized who really controlled the system of so-called law and order in which he worked.

He swallowed the last of his scotch, his hand shaking as he reached for the phone. The liquor churned in his stomach like acid and he hesitated. Maybe there was another way. Maybe he could throw her a bone, let her carry on her investigation while making sure she was fed enough misinformation...

No. They wanted her stopped. They'd made that clear. And he knew Krista too well. He could toss her all the false leads he wanted, but as long as she was digging, she was bound to discover something.

He'd had his chance to stop her and he'd failed, and in the meantime she'd already discovered too much. Brewster had done a damn good job moving his money around, but Krista had easily connected the dates with the deposits. It was only a question of when, not if, she figured out who had been paying him and why.

Now Mark needed to man up and accept the fact that a woman he looked on as a daughter would be lost as collateral damage in the aftermath of Brewster's death. That was just the way it needed to be.

He picked up the phone and dialed. "It's me. I tried to get her to drop it, but she won't let up."

"I'll see it's taken care of. I'll call you when it's over."

"Wait," Mark said before the other man hung up. "Promise me they won't...hurt her." Images of Brewster's victims flashed through his head and his throat burned with bile. The other people they used were capable of equal brutality.

"I make it a practice not to micromanage," the man said. "You'll know when it's taken care of."

The line clicked. Mark barely got his head to the trash can before the scotch came spewing back up.

Thunk. Crack. Thunk. Crack. Krista followed the rhythmic sound as she picked her way down the rutted driveway to what she hoped was Sean Flynn's cabin. When Megan Flynn, Sean's sister, had told her Sean was living in their family's hunting cabin outside the blink-and-you'll-miss-it town of Winton, it had only taken a quick call to Stew to track down the address.

Problem was, about an hour out of town the GPS on Krista's phone had crapped out, displaying an endlessly spinning pinwheel instead of the designated route. Luckily, it didn't take too long for her to find someone in town familiar with Sean to direct her to his cabin.

At first, the man working behind the counter in the combination gas station, grocery store, and post office had eyed her with suspicion. "What do you want with Sean?" he'd asked when Krista asked if he knew where she could find his cabin.

"I'm a friend of his," she lied. "He's expecting me." Also a lie, though to be fair she had left him four voice mails in the past two days, explaining that she urgently needed to talk to him about what had happened to Jimmy Caparulo. If Sean didn't want people showing up on his doorstep, he should return their calls and tell them so.

"Go around the south side of the lake and take Forest Service Road Twenty-Two," the man working at the gas station in Winton told her. "About a mile in, there'll be a fork in the road. You'll wanna go left. Follow the road up the hill until the paved road ends, and about five miles in you should see a red mailbox. That'll be the Flynns' place. And as long as you're goin' up there, give him this." The old guy handed her a pile of mail neatly stacked and bound together with a rubber band. "This is all that came in for the week."

She took the woodworking catalogs, a couple of bills, and offers for credit cards and tossed them on the front seat of her Toyota. She followed the old man's directions exactly, but eight miles past where the paved road ended there was still no sign of the red mailbox. Her low-slung sedan had threatened to bottom out half a dozen times on the rutted road, and Krista was about to give up and head back down the hill. Then she spotted a rusted-out box balanced precariously on top of a rotting wood post. There were about two square inches of red paint still visible on the side, but it was the closest thing to a mailbox she'd seen in miles.

The driveway was deeply rutted and after only a few yards she knew her car wouldn't make it without severe damage to the undercarriage. She'd pulled her car over and grabbed Sean's stack of mail from the passenger seat.

Now she winced as her big toe slammed into an unseen rock and a couple of magazines slipped off the pile. She snatched them up, cursing as she wondered why someone would live like this, all alone in the middle of nowhere, at the end of a dirt road that probably closed down after the first big storm of the winter.

A nervous flutter settled in her belly as she made her way down the drive. She didn't kid herself that Sean felt anything but hostility for her.

As the driveway curved, the woods gave way to a grassy meadow and Krista gasped, her anxiety forgotten for a moment. Okay, she wasn't exactly outdoorsy, but she couldn't deny the stunning view of the lake in the distance. The mountains still topped with white in late spring rose up like sentinels from the lake bed. Even she could put up with the boondocks for a few days if she got to look at that view every morning.

There at the end of the drive was Sean's cabin, a small but sturdy looking log structure with a porch that wrapped around it, with seats on the east-facing side to take advantage of the breathtaking view. A stream of silvery smoke piped up from the metal chimney on top.

On the other side of the cabin was a huge metal shed with an ancient blue pickup truck parked out front. She followed the *thunk-crack* sound to the back of the shed, and as she rounded the corner she stopped dead as Sean Flynn came into view.

The *thunk-crack* was from the ax he wielded as he split firewood on top of a thick stump. Impervious to the chill of the mountain air, he'd stripped off his shirt, and Krista's mouth went dry as his muscles rippled and bunched with the steady swing of the ax. The tattoo on the inside of his right forearm undulated as his big hand gripped the handle. The skin of his back and shoulders was a deep burnished tan, and as Krista took a step closer she tracked a bead of sweat as it rolled down the deep groove of his spine to the waistband of the jeans hanging off his narrow hips.

Oblivious to her presence, he tossed the wood onto the growing pile and bent to grab another thick log. Krista couldn't stop herself from staring at the hard line of his glutes flexing against the soft denim.

Heat curled in her belly and rose in her cheeks. She forced an image of Jimmy Caparulo's bloody headboard into her brain. She was here to talk to Sean, not ogle him, and hopefully get some much-needed answers in the process.

She cleared her throat to get his attention, and it was hard not to gape all over again when she was hit with the full force of Sean's piercing green stare. He really was an amazing specimen of masculine beauty. Krista had been struck by it from the beginning, but it was easy to ignore when she believed he was guilty of brutally raping and murdering a woman.

Then, his chiseled features and black Irish beauty had made him all the more repulsive, as she'd convinced herself he'd used his good looks to charm Evangeline Gordon into trusting him, paving the way to her doom. Now that she knew beyond a reasonable doubt he was innocent... she was anything but repulsed.

After several seconds she realized his full lips were moving and she forced herself to focus.

"What the hell are you doing here?" he said, dark eyebrows drawn tight over the bridge of his nose.

Krista kept her gaze locked on his face, not on the arrow of dark hair that bisected what had to be an eight-pack ridging his abdomen. She held out the stack of catalogs. "Mail call."

The green eyes narrowed, and Krista could feel the hostility radiating off him. "You didn't come all the way here to deliver my mail." His grip tightened around the ax handle, and Krista's skin prickled. She knew in her gut Sean wouldn't hurt her. Still, she was out in the middle of nowhere with a man who hated her. And he was holding an ax.

Krista took a step back and rolled onto the balls of her feet in case she needed to run. Maybe cornering Sean on his own turf wasn't such a bright idea after all.

Her tension uncoiled a notch when Sean leaned the ax against the stump and reached for the shirt draped across the back of a plastic lawn chair.

Krista bit back a sigh when the muscles disappeared under a layer of blue-and-black flannel. "You're right. I wanted to talk to you."

"You didn't need to come all the way out here."

"I called. Several times."

"Maybe you should have taken the hint when I didn't call back."

He turned his back and started stacking the logs against the side of the cabin, underneath the overhang of the metal roof.

Krista moved closer and picked up the scent of clean sweat and wood smoke emanating from him. "I assume you've heard about Jimmy Caparulo?"

Sean froze for a second and then resumed stacking. "Megan called me right after it happened." He shook his head. "Goddamn crazy Jimmy," he muttered, but Krista could hear the catch in his voice.

"What if I told you I'm not sure it was a suicide?"

He straightened and pinned her with a hard stare. "What are you talking about?"

"I spoke to Jimmy the afternoon before he died," Krista said. She was close enough to see the bump on the bridge of Sean's nose from where it had been broken. She didn't remember him having it during the trial. It must have been another souvenir from prison. She watched him closely, gauging his reaction to her news. "He told me he had information about Nate Brewster, but he couldn't tell anyone before because Nate threatened to hurt Jimmy's aunt if he told. I was supposed to meet with him Wednesday night, but he never showed. When I went to his house, I found out he was dead."

"And you think someone killed him to keep him quiet?" Sean raised a skeptical brow.

Krista shrugged. "It seems like kind of a crazy coincidence, don't you think?" She could read nothing in Sean's stare. "Any idea what he wanted to tell me?"

Sean shrugged. "I have no idea."

"When he talked to me, he said he should have said something sooner, that it would have helped you."

His mouth pulled tight, and Krista fought the urge to smooth the deep lines that grooved his cheeks. "He sure as hell could have helped me by not testifying at my trial, but he's a good three years too late for that." He blew out a frustrated breath. "Jimmy was messed up. He saw some things... We all saw some things..." Sean's voice trailed off and his gaze blurred, became that thousand-mile stare. The look of a man who was there but not there, too caught up in the horror replaying in his head to see what was in front of him.

He shook his head to clear it and ran a hand through his dark hair. It had grown beyond the short buzz he'd worn in prison, long enough to wave a little as the sweat dried. "I'm sure Jimmy thought he knew a lot of things, but I guarantee it was just paranoid ramblings. Now if you'll excuse me, I have some work I need to finish up."

Krista reached out and grabbed his arm as he went to turn away. Corded muscles rippled under her fingers, the heat from his skin singeing her palm. She snatched her hand back as an electric buzz pulsed through her body. "I don't think Brewster was acting alone when he framed you and killed those women," she said.

Sean folded his arms across his chest. "One phone call from Jimmy told you that?"

"No. But Brewster's computer was tampered with after he was killed and before the police seized it. We could tell files had been deleted, but so far no one has been able to restore them." She pulled out another copy of the bank statement Benson had blown off. "And two days ago the investigator I've been working with found this."

Sean's eyes narrowed as she pointed out the correlation between some of the large deposits and the other murders.

"Nate was a sick bastard, and who knows, maybe he was working for hire. But even if that's true, what does that have to do with me?"

Krista drew back. Even when she'd been convinced Sean was evil incarnate, she'd never thought him thick. "Other people might have been involved in covering up for Nate after he framed you for Evangeline's murder. Doesn't that matter to you?"

"I'm out of prison and the man who tried to kill my sister is dead. That's all I care about." But the cold, closed look on his face was that of a man who didn't care about much of anything at all. "If what you think is true, I'm sure the cops are more than capable of getting to the truth of it." Was that a note of sarcasm in Sean's voice?

"They're not investigating, and that's the problem," Krista said, irritated that she had to tilt her head back so far to look him in the eye. "You're the only link I know of between Nate and Jimmy, and if there's any chance—"

Sean cut her off. "I don't know anything. And even if I did, the last thing I want to do is dig all that shit up again. Now, I'd really appreciate it if you'd leave."

Krista shook her head like she wasn't sure she'd heard him right. "If I'm right, the people working with Brewster are still out there, getting away with it, getting away with hurting Jimmy—"

"People get away with shit all the time," Sean said coldly. "And innocent people take the heat for things they don't do. You know that as well as I do."

That arrow hit her straight in the chest and exploded on impact. "Then you should want to make this right as much as I do."

Sean shook his head. "If you need to clear your conscience, that's your problem. I just want to get on with my life and forget the last three years ever happened."

Ignoring her protests, Sean turned his back and walked to the shed. Krista followed after him, cursing as her foot hit a stray log that hadn't made it into the woodpile. "Sean, wait." She tried to catch him as he went through the door. The door slammed in her face with a metal *clank*, followed by the snick of a bolt sliding home.

She tried the door. Sure enough, the bastard had locked her out. She pounded the metal wall with her fist, cursing as pain radiated up her arm. A second later she heard the high-pitched whine of some kind of power tool surging to life.

She knocked and kicked for several more minutes but got no response.

She gave the door one last kick and slumped down onto the stump, weighing her options. Sean Flynn thought she'd give up so easily? He must have forgotten who he was dealing with.

Chapter 3

Sean regretted slamming the door shut almost immediately. Not because he felt bad for how he'd treated Miss Deputy Prosecuting Attorney—she could pound on the damn door till her knuckles were raw and he still wouldn't give her the time of day. But the closed-up shed made his chest tight and his heart pound. If he didn't get a breeze going through here pretty soon he'd be in a cold sweat and feeling like he was having a heart attack.

Mild cleithrophobia, the shrink had said. Unlike claustrophobia, where someone was scared of tight spaces, Sean got antsy if he felt like he was confined, even if the space was a mostly empty forty-by-fifty-foot work shed. He'd refused the anxiety meds they'd offered and discovered that as long as there was a door or at the very least a window open, he could keep it all in check.

When he'd bought the prefab shed to use as a woodworking shop, he'd special ordered a model that had oversize windows along one side. He slid three open and took a deep, bracing breath of the cold, clean air. He picked up a hickory two-by-four and slammed it onto his table saw.

He could hear Krista outside, stomping around in the

gravel, and he hoped to hell she was heading back to her car to haul her ass out of here.

There were a lot of people he had no interest in seeing—ever—and she was right there at the top of the list for a lot of reasons. Coming around and stirring up shit he wanted nothing more than to leave behind was the least of it.

He clenched and unclenched his hands, willing himself to relax, to stop shaking. If he wasn't careful he was liable to lose a finger working on the handmade rocking chair.

He slid on a pair of safety goggles to protect his eyes from sawdust, picked up his iPod, pushed his earbuds in, and cranked the music up loud. Loud enough to muffle the sharp whine of the saw, loud enough to drown out the questions buzzing in his mind, questions he didn't want to think about, didn't want to answer.

Krista Goddamn Slater. Couldn't she just leave him alone? He shouldn't have been surprised she showed up unannounced, but her appearance had hit him like a hammer to the chest. He had hoped she'd get the point when he hadn't returned her calls. Damn stubborn woman.

Why couldn't she just leave it alone? Leave him alone? He just wanted a little peace, for fuck's sake. He was still getting used to life on the outside, something he was afraid was going to take a lot longer than anyone could have anticipated. The two years in solitary with minimal contact had left worse scars than any wound he'd received in combat. And then at the end, facing the certainty of his own death...

In order to survive he'd checked out, shut down, and months after he was freed he was still struggling to emerge from the numbing fog.

Things were piercing through it though, things like Jimmy's suicide. Their friendship had ended ugly even before Sean's arrest, but the news of Jimmy's death made him feel like he'd lost a limb.

They'd once been closer than brothers, seen each other through shit straight out of a nightmare. And now Jimmy was dead. Rather than face his life for another day, he'd decided to eat the business end of his Glock.

Sean could relate to the feeling. So much so he'd left his handgun back in Seattle in a gun safe in his sister Megan's closet.

There were a few too many nights by himself, one shot of Jack too much, when he craved the taste of the gunmetal. When it got bad, he kept the urges at bay by telling himself that if he just kept moving forward, just made it through one day and then another, eventually the pain of the past few years would fade and he'd start to feel normal again.

But now Krista had to show up and blow everything to hell. Calling everything into question one more time, even Jimmy's death. Making him wonder if Nate, the third brother, their betrayer, had somehow reached beyond the grave to cause Jimmy's death.

Questions, still so many questions unanswered, questions Sean had managed to force from his head. He had his own suspicions about Nate and whether he'd been working alone. But now that he was out, Sean only wanted to move forward, to put the past away for good. Too much blood had already been shed, too much pain had already been caused.

Christ, he'd nearly lost his own life. Worse, his baby sister had nearly been killed proving his innocence.

Didn't he deserve to get on with the future, free and clear? He carefully guided the plank against the blade, let the hum of the saw calm him as he felt the machine's vibrations rumble through his hands and up his arms as he held the plank steady.

He tried to focus on the project, lose himself in the process of taking raw lumber and turning it into something else.

What if Jimmy really was murdered? Don't you care about your friend?

His hand jerked, jogging the plank to the right. The plank spit out a chunk of wood, and only the safety shield kept his fingers from being pulled into the blade.

He swore as much at the ruined lumber as at Krista for barging into his life with all of her questions about stuff he'd just as soon let die.

Like Jimmy died.

Guilt twisted in his gut as he tossed the wood aside and went to work on an armchair that needed a final sanding. What if Jimmy had been murdered? What if it had something to do with Nate and the people who might have helped him cover up not only Evangeline's murder but the other murders as well?

Goddamn it, he did not want to think about it.

Maybe someday he'd want answers, but not now. Right now it was all he could do to hold his own shit together. And even if they had gone after Jimmy—much as it made him sick to think about it—it had nothing to do with Sean. He didn't know anything about what Jimmy and Nate might have been up to, and as long as he kept his head down and minded his own business, Nate's mysterious colleagues seemed content to leave him in peace.

Exactly like he wanted. And if that made him self-centered and uncaring, too bad.

And if Krista Slater wanted to go looking under rocks for slugs, that was her damn business.

He was content here, alone, working on his furniture and hitting town once a week or so to have an in-person conversation. He'd had enough trouble in the past few years. The last thing he was going to do was go chasing it.

Yet as he sanded the final rough spots from the wide armrest of the chair, he couldn't get the damn woman out of his mind. What was it about her that got so far under his skin? It wasn't just that she was beautiful. Sean had been with lots of beautiful women in his life, and no one ever gave him that grabbed-by-the-balls feeling that had overcome him at the sight of her standing in his driveway.

She wanted to make things right, did she? Right now he could think of about a thousand different ways she could make a lot of things right in his world.

He ran his hand over the smooth maple of the armrest, oiled and polished to a high sheen. Her skin would be even smoother, he thought. And the color of cream instead of the warm gold of the wood. Warm and giving under his hand.

He snatched his hand away, felt his face warm along with the rest of his body as he realized he was getting a hard-on.

What the fuck?

He'd chalk it up to needing to get laid, which given that he hadn't had sex since before his arrest would make sense. Three years and counting.

Problem was, he wasn't exactly plagued with unfulfilled lust. Despite his longest dry spell since the time

Mary Hinky had given him a blow job under the bleachers sophomore year in high school, his balls weren't tightening up for anyone. Not for Wendy, the pretty single mom who ran one of the two bed-and-breakfasts in town. Not for the attractive travelers passing through town—though granted this time of year the pickings were pretty slim.

Lack of prospects was no excuse, or it hadn't been in the past. Sean had had some dry spells during his years in the Army Rangers. And while he wasn't proud of it, his standards had gotten a little compromised after a six-month deployment with nothing but a bunch of smelly guys and his own right hand. At that point, any girl in a bar with a pretty smile and a pulse would have done.

But in the months since he'd gotten out, his body had barely reacted to a woman. And if it had, he quickly lost interest when one of two things happened: The woman would recognize him and get a look on her face that said she was scared shitless, or worse, even more turned on that she was about to score with a convicted felon. And if she didn't recognize him, Sean would have to explain what the fuck he'd been doing in the three years he'd been out of the army. He could skirt around the issue as much as he wanted, but Sean wasn't a liar, and he wasn't about to keep his prison time a secret just so he could get laid.

And nothing killed the mood like telling a woman you'd been on death row.

Then there was that damn numbing wall he couldn't break through. Wasn't sure he wanted to. But it was deadening his body along with his emotions, and he knew that if he didn't figure some way out of it, it would eventually kill his soul.

So he should take it as a good sign, he thought bitterly, that the blood was running thick and hot through his veins and he was as hard as a spike behind the fly of his jeans. And he would have, if it had been for anyone but her.

What kind of sick fucker was he that the only woman who could make his dick stand up and say hello was a woman who had once wanted him dead? Granted, once she'd realized her mistake, she'd done everything in her power to make sure he was released from prison and his name was cleared.

But that couldn't give him back two years of his life— three if you counted the agonizing year of the trial. Couldn't take back the suffering of his sister, both from the emotional pain of Sean's trial and conviction and the physical danger from Nate, the sick fuck who'd been walking around free. Free to foster his obsession with Megan. Free to torture and kill helpless women.

And what if he hadn't been working alone? What if Krista was right and there was more to the murders than just Nate getting his fix and covering his tracks?

Sean shoved the thought aside. Don't borrow trouble. He'd learned it the hard way when he'd tried to help Evangeline Gordon and ended up framed for murder and gotten within days of the death chamber.

And regardless of his body's perverse reaction to her, every cell in him screamed that Krista Slater was nothing but trouble. He took out his earbuds. It took a few seconds for his eardrums to recover from the scream of Alice in Chains. He heard nothing but the rush of wind through the birch and pines and the squawk of birds.

She had to be gone by now.

He checked his watch and saw that he had enough time

for a run to siphon off some of the energy surging in his veins and still get the finished chair delivered. The run wouldn't be nearly as satisfying as a long, lusty fuck with a certain prosecutor, but it would serve to take the edge off, not to mention be infinitely better for his sanity.

He cleaned the shop, vacuumed up sawdust, and put the tools away in their proper places, a process that had been drilled into him first by his father and then reinforced in his years in the army.

He stepped outside and reflexively lifted his face to the sky and sucked in a deep lungful of fresh air. Like his brain wouldn't accept he was outside until he looked up and saw the sky. The soles of his work boots crunched on the gravel driveway. The air smelled like wet dirt and pine needles, and through it the cold bite of winter still clinging to the mountain air.

He grabbed an extra armful of firewood as he walked past the pile. Even though it was mid-May, he'd have to get the wood-burning stove cranking before bed if he wanted to stay warm tonight. He pushed open the front door of the cabin and was greeted by the familiar smell of the cedar paneling and wood smoke.

There was something else underneath it, a hint of something that didn't jibe with the smell he'd always associated with the cabin. Something kind of flowery and soapy and...

Exactly like Krista Slater, who was perched on his leather couch, wearing his green fleece pullover and holding a cup billowing steam like she owned the fucking place.

He closed his eyes, hoping it was a lust-induced hallucination, but nope, she was still there when he opened his eyes, a sheepish smile and an apologetic look in her eyes. "What the hell are you still doing here?"

Her smile slipped and he could see her cup shake a little as she set it carefully on his slate-topped table. "My car won't start."

His eyes narrowed. "Really? What a coincidence."

She rose from the couch. "What? It's not my fault the roads around here beat the hell out of my Camry."

"You shouldn't have come up here in the first place," he pointed out.

"I would have called a tow truck, but I couldn't find your phone."

His boots thumped across the wood floor as he walked into the kitchen to wash the sawdust from his hands. "That's because I don't have a landline." He splashed water on his face to get the worst of the dirt off.

Her eyebrows, two shades darker than the butter-colored hair that hung past her shoulders, drew together over her nose. "What number did I call?"

"My cell."

"I don't get any service up here," she said, flashing her phone at him.

"Neither do I."

"Then how do people get in touch with you?" she asked like she couldn't comprehend a world where people weren't available twenty-four/seven.

He dried his hands and face on the kitchen towel next to the sink. "There's a spot about a mile down the road where I get reception. A couple times a day I take a walk, pick up messages, and return calls if I feel like it."

Her blue eyes narrowed. "And you didn't feel the need to call me back."

"Getting the hint yet?" He grabbed her purse off the table and fished around until he found her keys. "Let's go take a look at your car."

She followed him through the doorway and out to the driveway. He ate up the distance in long strides, and he could hear her breath speeding as she struggled to keep up in the higher altitude. The soft panting did nothing to quell the tight ache in his groin. He walked faster.

Undaunted, Krista trotted beside him as they neared the end of the drive. "I don't understand why you won't just listen to what I have to say. What happened to you didn't start and end with Nate Brewster. There are still people out there messing with people's lives—"

Something in him snapped. A red fog flooded his brain and he turned on her, grabbing her by the shoulders and lifting her bodily off the ground. "And now you want to mess with mine? Whatever they were doing, it has nothing to do with me, and I want to keep it that way. I just want to be fucking left alone. Don't you get it?"

Her eyes were wide in her pale face. This close, he realized they were not blue as he'd always thought, but a grayish-green color, the color of the ocean on a stormy day.

They were also filled with fear. And what woman wouldn't be scared, in her position? Dangling in the air like a rag doll in the hands of a man nearly a foot taller and at least a hundred pounds heavier, his face no doubt flushed with rage as veins bulged in his forehead and pulsed in his neck.

He set her down with a soft curse, but didn't apologize. Maybe if she was scared she'd take a goddamn hint and get out of here. She wrapped her arms around herself and licked nervously at her lips, and Sean had to fight back the unfamiliar urge to give her a comforting hug.

She was mercifully silent as they reached her car. While she stood outside, he slid into the driver's seat and tried the ignition. Nothing. He popped the hood. He wouldn't put it past her to disconnect the battery or pull a hose just to have an excuse to keep pestering him.

Krista leaned close to peer over his shoulder. He tried not to notice how the scent of her perfume mingled with the wood smoke smell that clung to his fleece pullover that hung off her slender frame. "I took a look, but I don't know much about cars."

Sean grunted and did a quick check of the engine and didn't see any obvious signs of tampering. He got back into the car and checked the fuses for the ignition and the fuel pump under the dash. It would take a lot more mechanical know-how to mess up the car that way than she claimed to have, but she was a lawyer, after all. In his experience, lying was like breathing to them.

The fuses were still in place. He swore. "If I had to guess, there's something wrong with the electrical system." Definitely beyond his capabilities. He got out of the car and sighed. "I'll take you down the hill to call a tow truck."

He looked at his watch and swore. It was already three-thirty, and a Friday to boot. The chances of her getting her car repaired before the garage closed up for the weekend were nil. And that was assuming Frank Halfer who ran the one garage in town had the parts on hand to fix something that wasn't an American-made pickup truck. "Wait here," he told her as he went back down the drive to get his truck. A few minutes later she climbed into the truck and slid across the wide bench seat.

He drove until his cell phone had a few bars and then he gave her the number to call. "He said he'll be here in twenty minutes," she said after a brief conversation.

Sean drove back up the hill, and while Krista waited outside for Frank, Sean took the opportunity to clean himself up. He stepped into the shower and adjusted the faucet to just above freezing, shuddering under the icy spray as he willed his body back to the numb state it had existed in until this afternoon. Fifteen minutes later his lips were blue and his balls had crawled up into his abdomen for warmth. He was as prepared as he'd ever be to face Krista once again.

He found her back on the couch, skimming through a back issue of *Field and Stream*. He had a few seconds to admire the clean line of her profile before she noticed him.

"Frank says it will take at least until Monday to get the parts, assuming he can figure out what's going on."

"That's what I figured," Sean replied as he grabbed his jacket from a hook by the door and scooped up his truck keys. "Let's go."

"Where are we going?" she asked as she rose. How could a woman look so appealing in jeans, running shoes, and a way oversize fleece coat? But even in the sloppy clothes she somehow managed to look elegant and put together, her classic beauty radiating through even though she did nothing to enhance it. Tempting him to move in for a closer look to see if she was as flawless as she appeared.

"I have to deliver a couple pieces to a customer, and after that I'll drop you in town. There are a couple B and Bs where you can stay until your car's fixed."

A little wrinkle appeared at the top of her nose. "I'm not really a B and B person."

What the hell was that supposed to mean? "Winton doesn't have a Holiday Inn, so it will have to do."

She was quiet for a second, her gaze darting around the small cabin. She swallowed and straightened her shoulders as though steeling herself. "I could stay with you. It would give us a chance to go over everything—"

"That would be a really bad idea," he snapped. Jesus. A weekend alone in his cabin with Krista Slater confined to one thousand square feet. It sounded like heaven and hell and everything in between.

A suspicion confirmed when after just five minutes her presence in the cab of his truck with him was enough to undo the freeze job he'd done on his cock. When had he become part bloodhound, he wondered. Even with the windows rolled halfway down to let the fresh air in, her scent seemed to permeate the cab and saturate his nostrils. He was attuned to the warmth radiating from her, the fluttering of her pulse along the delicate line of her throat. Christ, he was barely going to survive an hour alone in the truck with her without doing something colossally stupid.

All he had to do was get her down the hill and out of his truck, and then send her on her heroic quest for the truth. As far as he was concerned, if he never saw Krista Slater again it would be far too soon.

Carl Grayson felt the subtle vibration in his pocket and quickly excused himself from the man he was talking to. He wove his way through the dining room of The Georgian restaurant at the Fairmont Olympic Hotel, packed full of Seattle's wealthiest and most influential citizens, where they were wrapping up the "informal" five-thousand-a-plate fund-raiser for his mother, Margaret Grayson-Maxwell, who was making a run for the state senate seat.

The luncheon had gone long. Margaret looked a little weary as she and her husband, David Maxwell, flashed him a questioning look as he passed their table, though their tablemates would never notice the shift in their attention. He gave his mother a subtle nod, and her pasted-on smile got so stiff he was afraid her cheeks were going to crack.

Carl and David had tried to dissuade her from making her run this election season. There were still too many loose ends to tie up in the wake of Nate's death, too many land mines still waiting to blow at any time. All it would take was one person to find the thread of connection and to give it a tug and their whole damn world would unravel. This was not the year for her to make a big splash on the political scene.

But Margaret had insisted. This was the point of everything they'd done, wasn't it? All the money they'd gotten—more important, the influence they had over anyone of any importance in the state? They had their claws sunk in so deep, now was the time to get her branch of the Grayson family back into the realm of legitimate, political stature. No more of this shadow play, controlling from behind the scenes. That might work for her husband, but for Margaret, power was meaningless unless the rest of the world bowed to it. No way in hell was she going to wait another four years.

Carl was in his stepfather's camp. You could get a lot more done flying under the radar and leveraging the right people, gaining advantage before anyone even realized that you held the key to their success— or failure—in your hands.

Now everything they'd built was at stake. The situation with Nate had left them vulnerable, and while Carl wasn't afraid of any of the clients talking—people in their positions had too far to fall—they hadn't had time to do as clean a cover-up as they would have liked. Nevertheless, Margaret had insisted that this was the year, and damned if she'd wait another four before she made her run.

Up until a couple days ago, Carl had been feeling better about the situation than he had been immediately after Nate's death. Then it had been all triage, trying to keep the truth from bleeding out as they scrambled to keep their tracks covered. Waiting with bated breath to see if any other players came forward to reveal the rotting foundation holding up one of Seattle's most prominent families.

Then they'd all breathed a sigh of relief when everyone seemed content to believe that everything—the murders, the framing of Sean Flynn, the high-end prostitution ring—started and ended with Nate Brewster.

Carl knew it was too good to be true, knew there were too many questions and sooner or later someone was going to want answers. It was up to him to make sure no one ever found them.

This phone call should provide another dose of reassurance. He waited until he was out of the dining room to answer his phone, a disposable pay-by-the-minute model that he would ditch after this call. "Is it taken care of?"

"Not yet," the voice rumbled in answer. "She left town earlier today and it took me few hours to pick up the trail."

"So what's the issue? Take care of it."

"She went to visit Sean Flynn."

Carl absently ran his finger down the scar bisecting his right cheek and sighed. "You'll have to do both of them then." He'd known it might eventually come to this, but he'd hoped not to take care of Sean Flynn so soon after Jimmy Caparulo. The connections between the two of them and Nate were too well known. All three of them dying violently in quick succession would raise too many red flags.

But Krista Slater had forced his hand, and now he had to make the best of it.

There was a second of hesitation on the other line. "Are you sure that's necessary? Flynn has kept to himself. I don't think he's a threat— "

"We don't pay you to think. We pay you to do," Carl snapped. "If you don't want the work, tell me now so I can make other arrangements."

"That won't be necessary, sir."

"Good. Do it as clean as you can—make it look like an accident if possible."

"It will cost you double."

"I'm aware of that," Carl snapped, swiping at the sweat beading on his upper lip. "You'll get the balance when I get confirmation."

He pressed at the headache taking root at the base of his skull, hiding his pain with a smile for the mayor of Seattle as he ducked back into the dining room.

Goddamn Nate. Dead for nearly five months, and he still threatened to ruin everything.

Chapter 4

Krista snuck a glimpse at Sean's profile and huddled deeper into the borrowed fleece for warmth. The already cool spring air was downright frigid as they traveled at forty miles an hour with the windows rolled down.

Sean seemed impervious to the cold, his hard jaw tense, his gaze fixed on the road as he whipped around the curves.

Loud rock screamed through the speakers, so Krista had to practically yell to be heard. "Do you mind rolling up the windows?"

"Yeah."

She couldn't have heard that right. "I said, do you mind rolling up the windows?"

Sean reached out and turned down the stereo. "And I said yeah, I do mind." He pinned her with a glare that was a good ten degrees frostier than the air whipping through the truck.

"But I'm freezing," she said, pointing to her chattering teeth for emphasis.

"Tough shit. Not my fault your goddamn car broke down." The music went back on full blast, making any further conversation impossible.

She scooted down in her seat in an effort to keep herself out of the wind and stared out the window to avoid Sean's suspicious gaze. He still wasn't convinced she hadn't sabotaged her car herself.

And he was right. Not that he, or even the mechanic, would find proof unless he knew exactly what to look for. Still, anxiety knotted her belly when she thought of what his reaction might be. Given his reaction to her, he'd probably push her out of the moving car and onto the side of the road and leave her to fend for herself.

Come to think of it, he looked like he might be contemplating that move anyway. So she cranked up the heat and kept her mouth shut against the millions of questions swirling in her brain, even when he pulled off the road to a miles-long driveway that led to a beautiful, custom-built log home.

He switched off the car and her ears rang in the sudden silence. "I have to deliver a couple pieces," he said.

Krista was shocked he bothered to explain at all. "Anything I can do to help?"

He stared at her a minute, as though looking for an ulterior motive. His broad shoulders inched up and down. "I suppose you can carry the footstool."

She climbed down from the truck and stamped her feet, which had gone numb, as she circled around to the back. She blew on her hands before stuffing them back into her pockets as Sean unlocked the tailgate.

He reached in to pull out a gorgeous, hand-carved mission-style chair and set it on the ground beside her. Next was the matching footstool, which he handed to Krista.

Krista couldn't help but be impressed at the way he lifted the chair, which had to weigh at least a hundred pounds, without any visible effort and walked it up a short set of stairs to a sprawling front porch. The footstool, made of the same dense hardwood, was considerably lighter but still had her huffing a little by the time they made it up the steps.

"Do we just leave it here?" Krista asked, indicating the porch.

"I'm going to set them up inside. I don't want them out in the weather." He punched a code into the panel beneath the doorknob and the dead bolt slid free.

Though the air in the unheated house was only a few degrees warmer than outside, it felt almost tropical as it washed over Krista's chilled skin. Sean flipped on a light, and as she stepped in, she saw the inside was as impressive as the outside, the massive great room decorated with authentic Northwestern tribal art and a huge flat-screen television and state-of-the-art sound system adorning one wall. "That's a trusting customer to give out the combination to a place like this."

Sean's chair thumped onto the wide-plank hardwood floors as he spun around. "You think I'd give them a reason not to trust me?"

Krista jumped back, almost losing her grip on the stool. "God, no, that's not what I meant. I didn't mean it personally about you. I just meant in general. If you have a nice place, you don't want to just let anyone come in any time..." She closed her eyes, felt her cheeks burn as she realized she was digging herself in deeper. Though she hadn't meant it, of course Sean, who had been wrongly accused and was still viewed with suspicion by some, would take it personally. "I'm sorry," she said lamely. "I'm not exactly known for my sensitivity."

Sean blew out a breath. "I'm sorry too." His apology surprised her. "I'm a little oversensitive about some stuff."

"Yeah."

He picked up the chair and carried it to the far side of the great room, placing it in front of a massive picture window that offered a breathtaking view of the Cascade Mountains erupting up to the sky. He reached out for the footstool. "And I'm sorry about the windows in the car," he said as he placed it on the floor. "Ever since I got out of prison, I can't stand being in a totally enclosed place."

"Claustrophobia?" Krista's stomach rolled with guilt. This scar, too, was partly her fault. All the more reason she needed to make everything right.

He shook his head, the lines of his shoulders and back tense as he stared out the window. "It's not a small space thing. It's a no-way-out thing. Like this room is huge, but if the door closes and I don't get a window open quick, it's, like—bam—full-on panic attack. The therapist calls it cleithrophobia."

"That sounds like a fear of something else," Krista snorted before she could stop herself. She bit her lip, as shame washed through her.

Sean turned, his startled laughter sounding rusty as it erupted from his chest. "No, I'm definitely not scared of that."

Krista's guilt fled at the expression on Sean's face. His smile alone, which she'd never seen before in person, would have been enough to knock her flat. It transformed his hard features. Green eyes glowed with warmth and crinkled at the edges, bright white teeth flashed against tan skin.

But it was the heat in his eyes as he ran them down her body and back that made her leg muscles go suddenly weak. *I'm definitely not scared of that.* No, he wasn't, and the look on his face said he was thinking pretty hard about proving it to her.

Then, as though he realized what he was thinking and who he was thinking it about, Sean shook his head. His eyes went cold, and his mouth pulled into a grim line. "We better get into town," he said, heavy boots thumping as he stormed past her. "The sooner I get you out of my hair the better."

Krista lagged behind, not in any hurry to be shut in the close confines of the truck with him. On the bright side, the freezing air would certainly cool the blood pulsing through her veins. What was it about Sean that could get her blood simmering with nothing but a look?

It was nothing she couldn't ignore. In her profession, she'd had to learn to keep a tight rein on her emotions, never let even a flicker of sexuality enter her interactions if she wanted to be taken seriously. She needed to deal with Sean like she'd dealt with him in the courtroom: coolly, professionally, never giving any hint to the confusing, contradictory tangle of emotions that erupted from just being around him.

Sean seemed determined to do the same, barely grunting at her when she joined him on the porch. He locked the door and stormed down the steps, not bothering to see if she followed. He climbed into the cab and the truck roared to life, and once again the stereo deafened her as she got in through the passenger door.

Hot air blew from the vents as Sean cranked up the heat and then reached behind his seat to grab something.

Wordlessly, he leaned over and tucked a thick down coat around her. It was huge, covering her from her neck to her knees, and it smelled faintly of wood shavings and soap.

Like Sean.

"Thanks," she said.

Either he didn't hear or he didn't care, but his gaze locked forward.

She snuggled deeper into the folds of the jacket, puzzling over the man sitting next to her. The memory of his smile washed through her; his small courtesy of turning on the heat and giving her the coat warmed her from the inside. No matter how much he resented her presence, he couldn't let himself be a complete inconsiderate ass.

Guilt knotted her stomach as she remembered something Sean Flynn's sister, Megan, had said in the days leading up to his trial. *Sean always looks out for the little guy. He takes care of people. He would never let a woman be hurt, much less hurt her himself.*

Krista felt like she'd seen a tiny glimpse of that man today, the core of him still lurking beneath the angry, closed-off person he'd become.

It hit her like a brick in the chest, so obvious she felt like an idiot for not realizing it before. Then again, maybe in her guilt, she hadn't wanted to see it.

The realization that the years on death row had cost Sean so much more than time.

Sean parked his truck in front of Frank Halfer's garage, located on the south end of Winton's Main Street. It was a lost cause he knew, but as he climbed out of the cab he couldn't help but pray that by some miracle Frank had fixed Krista's car so she could be on her way tonight.

After the past few hours, he wasn't sure he could stand the idea of her staying in town for a weekend, even if she was cozied up in the little B&B a couple blocks down from Frank's shop. He was afraid of what he might do, that a few miles wasn't nearly enough space between them to prevent him from doing something stupid.

Like punch through the brick wall he'd built around himself and give in to the sudden, desperate urges to touch, to taste, to feel. Krista Fucking Slater. Of all the women in the world, why was she the only one who managed to remind him he was still alive in a way no one had been able to in three long years?

A way he *didn't* want to feel, goddamn it. He'd lost any meaningful connection with everyone except for his sister, and that was just fine with him. No emotional tangles, no obligations to anyone but himself. No worrying about hurting anyone or getting hurt back.

But now she had to come storming in, yanking his body back to life and ripping the cover off a tangle of emotions he'd been content to keep on lockdown for the past three years.

At least she was mercifully silent, having gotten the hint that there was no way in hell he was going to go digging through his memories, no matter what she thought was at stake.

Sean ducked under the half-closed garage door and heard the soles of Krista's running shoes squeak against the concrete floor as she followed. The tinny sound of a country song on a radio echoed through the room.

"Hey, Frank," Sean called. Frank looked up from the battered, paper-strewn desk tucked into the back corner of the garage.

"Hey, Sean. Ma'am," he said, nodding at Krista.

"Any chance you've gotten her car started?" Sean asked, fingers crossed inside his coat pocket.

Frank shook his head. "Damndest thing," he said. "Entire electrical system is fried. I should be able to get parts Monday—"

"Do you work with a lot of imports?" she interrupted as she doubtfully scanned the garage and attached lot populated by early-model American trucks. Sean's shoulders tightened at her condescending, know-it-all tone—the one he'd grown to hate in the courtroom.

Frank's eyes narrowed. "This may be the country, but it ain't Mayberry. I have all the latest diagnostic software and my suppliers are the same that sell to your mechanic back in Seattle. I know what I'm doing."

"Of course you do," Krista said, raising a slender hand. "I'm sorry if I offended you."

Sean wanted to roll his eyes at the way Frank seemed to melt under Krista's smile. He turned to her with a frown. If she thought she was going to get to him with this new, charming side of her, she was seriously mistaken.

"Did you figure out what was wrong after getting a closer look?" Krista asked. Sean's ears pricked up at the nervous undercurrent in her voice.

Sean's eyes glazed over as Frank launched into a litany of possible reasons for the electrical failure and then concluded, "But honestly, it's almost impossible to tell at this point."

Was it just him or did Krista breathe a little sigh of relief? It froze in her chest when she caught him looking. "Well, thanks, Frank. I'll guess I'll check back in with you Monday."

"Guess I'm stuck here," Krista said as they walked down the street. Though she was fairly tall—Sean would guess about five seven or five eight, and those damn legs of hers started somewhere up around her armpits—she had to practically run to keep up with him as he rushed to Wendy Trager's bed-and-breakfast.

"Do you know how much this woman charges? It's not going to be really expensive, is it?" Krista said, slightly breathless in a way that filled Sean's head with all kinds of ways he could make her breathe fast.

He shook the images out of his head. "You're a lawyer. I thought you'd be rolling in it."

She gave a snort. "I work for the government and it's a recession. They spent more to keep you alive on death row than they pay me."

He almost tripped over his own feet as he shot her a startled look. There it was again, that flash of inappropriate under that perfectly buttoned-up surface.

"I'm sorry," she said, clapping her hand to her mouth. "That was totally out of line."

"It's okay," he said, stifling a chuckle.

It should have offended him, just as her making fun of his diagnosis should have offended him. But the fact that she blurted it out without a thought, like her internal editor went out for a quick smoke, made her seem actually human underneath the controlled professional she showed to the world. Made her appealing.

Likeable, even.

Oh fuck, he didn't even want to go there. He was startled from his thoughts as his shoulder slammed into someone who let out a loud grunt on impact. "Excuse me," Sean said. He looked up and registered two men, dressed similarly to him in plaid flannel shirts, boots, and jeans. But there was something about them, the flat look in the eyes of the blond guy in particular, that made Sean's neck prickle as they walked by.

He looked at them over his shoulder, but they didn't look back as they continued down the street.

"What?" Krista said.

Sean shook his head. "Nothing." But the prickle wouldn't go away, that nagging sense that the enemy was close, crouched behind the next rock waiting to take him out. He kept his eye on the two men until they rounded the corner and he shook his head.

He was just paranoid, he told himself. That's what happened when your best friend betrayed you and everyone who knows you is willing to believe you're a monster.

And the woman next to him, the one he couldn't seem to block out, had her own part to play in that. Sean seized on that resentment, shoving away any feelings of attraction or, God forbid, affection as he reached for the door of the B&B.

And found it locked. He knocked a couple times and then ducked his head to look in one of the glass panes that framed the hand-carved door. "Shit. She must have gone out." He straightened up. "I'll go get your bag and you can wait over at Marty's until she opens up."

"Wait, you're just going to dump me off? What if she doesn't come back?"

Sean wanted to tell her it wasn't his problem. Wanted to tell her it was too damn bad, that it would be no less than she deserved for coming up here uninvited and trying to force him to dredge up a part of his life he had no interest in revisiting.

It was the shiver that did it, barely perceptible beneath

the bulk of the borrowed down coat that hung almost to her knees, as she braced herself against the rapidly cooling breeze.

He muttered a curse under his breath and grabbed her by the arm, tugging her across the street. "Let's go get something to eat while we wait."

The scents of beer and fried food greeted him as they walked into Marty's pub and Sean braced himself. Fortunately, the place was relatively empty during the low season, and the customers were mostly people he knew, at least by sight if not name. No tourists to do the double take, the *Isn't that?* and then bend low to whisper over their hamburgers and fries, followed by another assessing look as they wondered if maybe he hadn't gotten away with murder after all.

"Sean, darlin'," Nancy McFee, the late Marty's wife, called as she rushed across the restaurant to greet him. Pushing sixty, Nancy was still holding it together with her dyed red hair and busty figure that flirted with matronly plumpness. Her arms were flung as wide as her smile as she rushed to greet him. Sean fought not to choke on her cloud of perfume as he suffered a tight hug and a kiss on the cheek. "It feels like an age since you've been here. It's not good for a man as handsome as you to keep all to himself up in that lonely cabin of yours."

"I've been busy," he said, grimacing as Nancy rubbed at his cheek with a red-tipped thumb, scrubbing away at the smear of lipstick she'd no doubt left on his chin.

"But I see you have someone with you—" Nancy's bright smile faded abruptly as recognition set in. "You're her—you're that prosecutor."

"Deputy Prosecuting Attorney Krista Slater," Krista

said and held out her hand. She didn't react at all when Nancy gave a sniff of disdain.

"Can't imagine what you're doing here with her. What she did to you was unforgivable."

"No argument here," Krista said softly.

"To be fair, Nate Brewster was the one who framed me," Sean said, the words cutting him as deeply as ever. He had no idea why he felt the urge to defend Krista, but his mouth moved almost without his consent. "Krista was doing her job."

"Well, if you ask me, she was doing a piss poor job of it. How anyone thought you could be capable of murder is beyond me. Known him all his life, I have, and I never believed it, not for a minute."

Yes, she had. But Sean didn't bother to remind her of what she'd said to the reporter from the *Seattle Tribune* after his conviction, about how you thought you could know someone and never see the evil lurking inside. Let her have her false memories and her overdone affection if it made her feel like she was making up for thinking the worst of him. "Thanks, Nance. I see my regular table's empty. Be a sweetheart and bring us a couple of pints."

He led Krista to the corner booth next to the window, nodding at the handful of other patrons. Many of them he'd known since childhood. They all gave him the same overeager smiles and friendly waves, as though that could erase the fact that all of them, like Nancy, had at one point believed he was capable of raping and murdering a woman in the most brutal way imaginable.

He slid into the booth and cracked open the window. "You don't have to," he said as Krista leaned over to the window on her side to do the same, but he felt the tension in his shoulders unravel a degree as the cold breeze blew across his face. "You're going to be cold."

"I'm fine. The heat's cranked up so much I need to strip off a few layers."

Jesus, he wished she wouldn't use words like *strip*.

The menu had barely changed in twenty-five years, but Sean studied it like his life depended on it, wondering how a woman could be sexy stripping off a parka that made her look like the Michelin Man.

"We're causing quite the stir," Krista said after a few minutes. Sean looked up. Sure enough, the handful of regular customers were sneaking glances at their booth, informed by Nancy of Krista's identity, if the glares were anything to go by.

"Not every day a former convict has dinner with the prosecutor who put him on death row," he bit out, angry with himself that he hadn't anticipated this. Shit, he should have ignored her woeful look and left her in front of the B&B to freeze, but no, he had to be the nice guy and take her someplace warm, keep her company. You'd think he would have learned, especially after what had happened with Evangeline Gordon, that his stupid fucking chivalrous streak never brought him anything but trouble.

Now it got him here, across the table from a woman he wanted despite all logic and common sense, trying to ignore curious stares that made his skin crawl.

Nancy came by to take their order herself, her glare never leaving Krista's face.

"If looks could kill," Krista muttered.

"You'll get used to it," he lied. "I did."

"I get a lot of dirty looks in my line of work." Krista slumped against the leather cushioning of the booth.

She was quiet for a few minutes, staring out the window at the light traffic on Main Street. Their food was delivered quickly. Krista smiled and thanked Nancy, never even flinching when her bowl of scalding hot chili threatened to teeter over in her lap. Krista calmly steadied the bowl and picked up her spoon. "You've been coming here all your life?" Her blond eyebrows arched as she lifted a spoonful of chili to her mouth.

Sean nodded and swallowed a mouthful of battered cod before he answered. "My grandfather built the cabin back in the fifties. I came up every summer for at least a month until my sophomore year, and I had football camp starting in late July."

"Why come back here?" she asked, indicating the mix of curious and hostile stares glued to their booth. "Why not a fresh start?"

Sean shook his head. "It's the closest place to home I have," he replied. He didn't want to delve into the details, how after his parents' death and moving in with his grandparents he'd felt the need to hang on to the one place that was a constant, the one place where he'd known nothing but happiness. After he'd been released from prison, ping-ponging around Seattle and trying to get a handle on his life, he'd come back here in an attempt to regain some sense of belonging.

He didn't say any of it, but the way Krista was looking at him it was as though she knew.

"Anyway, there's no such thing as a fresh start for me."

Krista's mouth pulled tight. "No, I don't suppose there is." She finished off her chili, sat back with a sigh, and picked up her beer. "So you played football," she said with a faint smile. "Why am I not surprised?"

"Not just played," Sean said, unable to stop himself from smiling back. "Captain."

Krista laughed and took a sip of her beer and then trailed her finger down the damp glass. Sean forced his eyes to stay locked on her face and not on that slender finger sliding up, down, up, down. She took another sip, her pink tongue chasing a droplet of beer across her bottom lip. Sean shifted, his pants suddenly two sizes too small in the crotch. "Did you play sports?" he said in a desperate effort to distract himself.

But her sly smile just made him harder. "I was a nerd. Braces. Glasses. The whole nine yards. My dad thought sports would be good for me, but I was too uncoordinated to do anything but run track."

"No hurdles," he smiled.

"Or javelins. I would have lanced the mascot."

Sean was shocked to find himself for the second time that day laughing at something she said. He looked around and caught the stares and realized how they must look. Like any other couple. Talking. Laughing. Flirting.

Like a normal date, the kind he hadn't had—hadn't even wanted to have—in over three years.

For a split second it felt so good he was almost ready to give himself up to the illusion of normalcy.

Except the whole thing was completely ab-fucking-normal, starting and ending with the woman sitting across from him. Jesus Fucking Christ, what the hell did he think he was doing? What the hell did he think *she* was doing—flirting, acting all interested so she could lure him out, get him to help her on this misguided need for the truth? As if that would ever help anyone.

"So football, that's how you got to be friends with

Jimmy Caparulo, right? Before you joined the army together and met Nate?"

And just like that she confirmed his suspicions. "Damn, I gotta give you credit. You're good. Subtle. You almost made me believe it."

To her credit, she didn't bother to pretend to not know what he was talking about. "Look, I get it. You want nothing to do with my investigation. But before he died, Jimmy said he should have told you something—he should have helped you. If you can think of anything, no matter how random, maybe it will help me figure out the truth—"

Sean threw a couple of bills on the table and stood up. "I told you. I have no idea what was going on with Jimmy and Nate." Except that he had trusted both of them, loved them like brothers. "Whatever it was, it didn't involve me." He snatched his coat from the booth and headed for the door.

"Except for the part where Nate framed you for murder and involved Jimmy in the cover-up," she called after him.

Sean's stomach twisted, the fish and chips sitting like a bowling ball in his gut. "And now they're both dead, so I guess they got what they deserved." The other diners were staring, transfixed. Sean kept his gaze on the door, careful not to make eye contact with anyone.

As he looked through the pub's front window he could see that the B&B was still dark. "Nance," he called. "Do you know when Wendy will be back?"

Nancy looked up from the cash register. "I believe she's back next week."

"Next week?"

Nancy looked up, startled at the menace in his voice. "Yes, she went to Seattle to visit her sister like she always does this time of year."

"Then who's running the B and B?"

Nancy frowned at him. "It's closed for the season."

Oh, shit. "Closed," he parroted like an idiot.

"We don't get enough people in the shoulder seasons."

"What about the place farther out on Highway Two?"

"They're not opening up until Memorial Day. No one is. If you need a room, you should be able to find something in Wenatchee."

Sean nodded curtly, grabbed Krista's arm, and yanked her out the door.

"Wenatchee is nearly twenty miles away," Krista protested. "How the hell am I supposed to get back to my car?" she said.

"Not my problem, just like this whole fact-finding mission isn't my problem. You're lucky I'm feeling generous enough to give you a ride."

They reached the truck and he climbed inside. She rapped sharply on the window until he unlocked her door. She flung herself into the seat with an irritated huff. She opened her mouth, but before she could utter a sound he gunned the engine and turned on the stereo full blast, the roar of Alice in Chains drowning out any questions.

Krista reached out and snapped off the stereo and did her best not to shrink under Sean's menacing stare. She'd definitely caught glimpses of a nice guy lurking underneath, but Sean could turn on the mean like few people she'd ever encountered. And in her line of work that was saying something.

But despite the real, justifiable rage she could feel simmering through his blood—toward her, toward the friends who had betrayed him, toward the friends who'd lost faith in him—she trusted him not to hurt her. Trusted that he was the kind of man who wouldn't use his far superior strength against a woman.

If only she'd had that insight years ago.

"I came a long way to talk to you, and I'm not going to leave without something—"

His hand flashed out and turned the stereo back on. She switched it off. "God, do you have to be so juvenile? I just want to talk a little bit—"

"I don't have any answers," he snapped. "I don't know how to make it plainer."

"Did you know we traced the ownership of Club One back to a dummy corporation linked to Nate?"

Sean's gaze flicked in her direction. "So Jimmy worked for him?"

Finally, a response. "No, at the time Jimmy was contracted through a company called West Hall Security. Apparently that's where they got most of their security staff up until recently." Jimmy had quit West Hall shortly after Sean's arrest and had worked as a private contractor until his death.

Sean's hands tightened on the wheel and Krista's stomach dipped as the road made a steep decent down the mountainside. "That's right. Jimmy tried to recruit me, right after I got back to town."

"Before you had your falling out?" Krista kept her gaze pinned to Sean's face as she tried to ignore the sheer drop-off on her side of the road. She wasn't usually a nervous passenger, but the guardrail along the highway was little more than window dressing against the hundred-foot fall.

A curt nod was his only response. Krista started to press him, but the words caught in her throat as they saw the sharp curve coming up. "Uh, maybe you should slow down?"

"I'm trying," Sean said through gritted teeth.

"Try harder!"

The engine screamed and the smell of burning clutch permeated the truck cab. Just then, bright lights flooded the interior. Krista looked back and saw the outline of a dark SUV looming inches from the truck's bumper. "Holy shit, they're going to hit us. You need to get out of the way!"

Sean pulled the car over to the left, riding the yellow line so the SUV wasn't directly behind them. The other side of the road was thickly forested with old-growth evergreens but Krista would take a head-on with a tree trunk over going off a cliff any day. Krista closed her eyes, praying another car wasn't around the next corner. Though at the speed they were going, it wasn't likely they were going to make it. "Why aren't you slowing down?"

"Accelerator's stuck," Sean said, his eerie calm doing nothing to slow her heartbeat. The SUV thumped up against the bumper and sent them hurtling toward the guardrail and then it screeched to a halt just before the curve.

Krista swallowed hard, unable to take her eyes off the scene of her own death. She hoped she would pass out before they hit the ground.

"Brace yourself," Sean said.

Brakes squealed and the scent of burning rubber invaded her nostrils. The seatbelt threatened to cut her in half at the waist as she was flung forward toward the dashboard. Pain exploded as her forehead made contact with the dashboard and then was wrenched to the side and into the window. Krista wasn't sure if it was her head or the truck that was spinning.

Metal crunched and the truck shuddered to a stop. Krista blinked her eyes. The sun was almost down, but she could see the front of the truck crunched around the thick trunk of a pine tree. For several seconds, all she could hear was the sound of her own heartbeat pounding in her head, the harsh echo of her own breath.

A big, masculine hand curled around her arm. She looked over at Sean. His face was grim, and he had a cut over his eyebrow that was streaming blood that looked black in the dim light, but from what she could tell, he wasn't seriously injured. Relief washed through her so intensely that it took her several seconds to register the fact that his lips were moving.

She shook her head to clear it, wincing as the movement shot a spike of pain through her skull. "What?"

"Are you okay? Can you move?" His voice was quiet, but she could sense the anxiety.

"I think so," she said, unbuckling her seatbelt and carefully sitting up as she took stock of her injuries. Her head was ringing, and when she put her hand up to her forehead she could feel a goose egg that was tender to the touch. But somehow, miraculously, she seemed otherwise okay. "You're bleeding," she said, reaching with a shaky hand toward his face.

Sean leaned over to look in the rear-view mirror and lightly fingered the cut. "Nothing a Band-Aid can't help," he said. He unclipped his seatbelt and reached behind the seat, wincing as the motion pulled at some unseen injury. He had a bottle of water and a bandana in his hand, which he soaked and used to dab at the cut on his head.

"Nice driving," she said.

"Thanks," he said with a half smile. "I was first in my class when we did defensive and evasive driving techniques. Never thought they'd come in handy like this."

"You saved our lives," Krista said, feeling her muscles start to tremble as the enormity of what had almost happened hit her with the force of a truck. "I thought they were going to run us off the road. I thought we were dead for sure." Her heart raced and her teeth started to chatter, her body shaking so hard it felt like her muscles were going to detach from the bones.

She heard the sound of a car door opening and shutting, and a few seconds later her own door opened and she was being pulled out of the truck. Her knees started to buckle and he wrapped his arms around her to hold her up.

Krista instinctively wound her arms around his waist, up under his jacket, burying her face against the rock wall of his chest, seeking relief from a cold that had taken hold of every pore.

"You're okay. We're okay."

Screaming engines. Screeching tires. The guardrail hurtling at them, and after that, the abyss... "Oh God, we could have—"

"Stop." His command was firm, but gentle. She wondered how he could possibly be so calm. "Don't let your mind go there. Don't think about what could have happened."

Big hands smoothed up and down her back, and she swore she could feel the heat of his palms through the bulk of the parka. She didn't think it was possible, but she felt her body calming, the tremors subsiding, her breath easing as her pulse rate slowed to merely double time.

As the chill eased and the adrenaline faded, she became aware of several things. The subtle shift of muscle under the soft flannel fabric of his shirt. The smell of woodchips and soap that pierced through the oily burn of tire rubber and clutch fluid. The way his muscled arms wrapped all the way around her, how his hand was big enough to span her back.

How his other hand had come to rest on the top of her hip, his thumb riding the dip of her waist as his fingers curved down.

Was it just her, or did his body temperature jump a good five degrees too?

She lifted her head, licking her lips nervously when she saw him. It was too dark to read his expression, but she could feel the intensity of his stare.

Her breath caught in her chest and her heart started a steady thrumming in a way that had nothing to do with fear.

"I better call the police," Sean said, dropping his arms and stepping away quickly, then cursed when she stumbled a little at the abrupt motion.

She held up a hand to signal she was all right. Once again her brain cluttered with images. Bright lights flooding the cab. The SUV roaring up behind them as the truck sped uncontrollably toward the side.

This was no accident. Her stomach bottomed out at the realization. "They need to know what they're dealing with so they can investigate properly," she was amazed at how calm she sounded. Sean paused, phone in hand. "They're coming to the scene of an attempted murder."

Chapter 5

Goddamn it, I knew the second I laid eyes on you there was going to be trouble," he muttered as he thumbed the DISCONNECT button on his phone before the 911 call could go through.

Dread coursed through him at the idea that these assholes had anything to do with Krista.

He didn't want to believe, didn't want to think for a second that this had anything to do with her investigation into who or what might have been involved with Nate Brewster.

He wanted to dismiss the idea as crazy, even though every instinct was screaming that she was right.

"Goddamn it," he muttered again, casting her a side-long glare. "You are really something else. I was happy enough just minding my own business, and now I have people trying to run me off the road."

Even in the rapidly dimming light, he could see guilt mingled with fear in her wide eyes. "What if they come back?"

Sean shoved aside his anger. Right now he needed to focus on keeping them both alive. He listened, but there was no sign the SUV was returning. "We're far enough off the road that we'll have time to get out of here if we hear someone coming."

She nodded and wrapped her arms around her waist, steadying herself. Pissed as he was at her for dragging him into this mess, he had to fight the urge to go over and hold her. What had started out as a comforting gesture to keep her from sliding into shock had turned into something more way too quickly. By the time she warmed up to him and was looking at him with those big eyes, every sense had kicked into high gear and he was using every ounce of restraint to keep his hand from sliding down the slim curve of her butt.

His fingers still twitched at the memory of the way his hand settled into the dip of her waist, making him wonder if he could wrap his big hands all the way around. The way she'd burrowed into him, her breath hot against his chest, making him kick himself for covering her up with the bulky parka that kept him from feeling the soft press of her breasts against him.

"The accelerator got stuck," she said. "When did you realize it?"

"Right about the time we started down the grade and I couldn't slow the truck," he snapped.

"How did the pedal feel?" she asked as she opened the truck door and started rummaging around.

He struggled to remember. "I'm not sure. Why?"

"Do you have a flashlight?"

He leaned over her and grabbed a duffle bag that contained emergency supplies, including a Maglite.

"What are you doing?" he asked as Krista went around to the driver's side and bent over to stick her head down by the floor.

She ignored him. "Did it feel like it totally gave under your foot and got stuck there, or did it give and come back like normal but the accelerator stayed engaged?"

He crouched down next to her and tried to figure out what she was looking at. "Like it gave and stuck there even when I took my foot off."

"Huh. Well the accelerator can get stuck for a lot of reasons. Sometimes it's carbon buildup on the throttle bore; sometimes it's friction; sometimes it's just a floor mat getting stuck."

"Frank serviced the truck about a month ago and cleaned out the fuel injection system, so that rules out buildup. And I don't have any floor mats."

"Another way to get it to stick," she said as she straightened, "is for someone to put something in the throttle body that will hold it open once you get up to speed. But I need to look under the hood for that."

"How do you even know any of this?"

"My uncle is a mechanic. He taught me about cars."

He was a little slow on the uptake after the crash, but his brain finally did the math. "Your car?"

She was silent for several seconds, and then: "I blew the fuses with my jumper cables and a screwdriver."

And he'd fallen for her damsel-in-distress act hook, line, and sinker. "Son of a bitch."

She straightened up. "Do you believe me now that this wasn't an accident?"

Sean stood, grimacing as several aches emerged as the adrenaline wore off. "I don't know what to believe, except for the fact that whenever you show up, you don't bring me anything but a shitload of trouble."

He pulled out his phone and dialed 911.

Krista paced back and forth, rubbing her hands up and down her arms as she listened to Sean report what had happened to the police. "I can't believe it. I can't believe they actually tried to kill us," she said when he hung up.

"Lucky for you they didn't succeed. Now maybe you can take a hint and back the hell off."

She stopped short. "What are you talking about? This proves I'm onto something. We have to find out who's behind this—"

"I don't know about this *we* stuff. Like I keep saying, you want to keep digging up trouble. That's your business. I don't give two shits about anything except being left alone."

"Sean, someone tried to kill us tonight. You think they're going to drop it?"

"I'm pretty sure I can take care of myself if you just leave me the hell alone." He told himself that after tonight, he didn't give a damn what happened to her. She could clean up her own mess.

Krista pulled out her phone and dialed. "Mark? It's me. I've been in an accident."

Mark? Sean curled his fingers into a fist as he realized she must be talking to her boss, Mark Benson. After his release, Sean was determined not to wallow in the past, but he couldn't keep the bitter taste from creeping into his throat at the thought of that man.

Krista had played her part in getting him convicted, but it had been Benson who'd made the call to push for the death penalty. Decided to make an example of Sean to make sure he did well in the polls for the upcoming election.

At least Krista's zeal had stemmed from her desire to punish someone she was convinced was guilty.

"No, I'm fine, because of some miracle and Sean's excellent driving... Yes, I came up to talk to him about what happened to Jimmy Caparulo and the information I found on Nate... Nothing so far, but Mark, someone tampered with Sean's truck. Whoever is behind this, they've targeted us now. I need you to officially open the investigation, show whoever's doing this they can't get away with this—"

She stopped at the sound of an engine approaching. "The police are here so I have to go, but I'll call you later."

Sean took a quick look to make sure it was the police before he called out their location.

Flashes of red-and-blue light from the squad car bounced off the trees. The sound of boots crunching through the brush was accompanied by the wide beam of a flashlight.

"We're right here, officer," Krista called. Sean heard the cop radio in his location as he approached.

"You folks call in the accident?" he said as he approached.

"Yes," Sean said.

"That's just it, officer—we don't think it was an accident. Someone deliberately tampered with the car, causing us to lose control—"

"Now hold on," the cop said, raising a beefy hand. "Why don't you let us do our job and figure out what happened, and you go ahead and tell me how you ended up against this tree."

"With all due respect, officer, I'm a deputy prosecuting attorney with the King County prosecutor's office, and I believe this is related to a case—"

"With all due respect, miss," the cop said, hitting

Krista full in the face with the blinding beam of the flashlight, "you're in my jurisdiction now and I will do my own investigation of the scene."

The cop's attitude put every nerve on edge. Sean had run across dozens of guys like him in prison. He was just like the guards who got their one little taste of power and took every opportunity to shove their authority down your throat. Sean had learned the hard way that the best way to deal with it was just to ignore it, let them have their one moment of superiority in their otherwise pathetic lives, even though every instinct was screaming at him to punch the cop in his doughy face.

When Krista glared back and opened her mouth to rip him a new one, Sean grabbed her by the arm and leaned in to whisper, "Don't. It's not worth making trouble."

He could feel her muscles tense, but she kept her mouth shut.

Sean silently handed over his driver's license when the cop requested it. The cop studied it for a long time. He lifted the light and pinned Sean with the beam. "You're that murderer that just got off, aren't you?"

Sean didn't so much as blink, careful not to give away any hint of the hostility burning through him like acid.

After several seconds the cop gave his license back. "Fresh out of prison, and now you've had a head-on with a tree." The cop took a closer look at the truck, whistling as the beam of his flashlight illuminated the front of the truck. "When you called, you said you didn't need medical attention. You sure about that?"

Sean squinted as the beam hit him in the face. "We're a little banged up, but nothing a couple ibuprofen won't cure."

"Hard to believe, with how crunched up that truck is." He stepped closer and tilted his head up to look at Sean. He made a loud sniffing noise. "You know how they say sometimes drunks don't get injured because their bodies are more relaxed? You been drinking?"

"No."

"I told you, the car was tampered with," Krista burst in, "and then someone drove up in an SUV and tried to run us off the road."

"First you're tampered with and now someone's trying to run you off the road? You better get your stories straight. In the meantime, I believe I'll have to ask you to take a breathalyzer."

He crunched back to the car to retrieve the equipment, and Sean heard him speaking over the radio. "This is Deputy Jensen. I'm at the scene of an accident on Highway-Two, west side of the highway just past mile marker fifteen. I'm going to need a tow truck to pull this old pickup. I'm treating this as a probable DUI."

"This is ridiculous," Krista muttered.

"I agree," Sean said. "But stay quiet and cooperate. Don't give him any more reason to fuck with us."

Krista muttered something about Barney Fife but didn't protest when the cop held out the breathalyzer first to Sean and then to her.

"There, satisfied?" Krista said when the beer Sean had with dinner caused him to blow a measly .02 while she herself blew a .05.

"Breathalyzer only shows alcohol, but I guess you know that, being a big-shot prosecutor. No telling what we'll find when we run a full drug panel."

A siren squawked as another police car pulled up, cutting off Krista's retort. A tow truck quickly followed, adding flashing yellow and orange to the light show.

"Armstrong, what the hell are you doing out here? I didn't call for backup," he said to the broad figure making his way over to the scene.

"Sheriff wanted me to come up here," the other deputy said tightly. "He wants you to stay at the scene while I take them into Chelan to take a statement."

"Why the hell would he do that? This is my scene, and I can take a statement—"

"Don't get all over my ass," Armstrong said tightly. "Call Doyle yourself if you don't believe me."

The other deputy took a few steps away to do that, his mouth pulling tight as the sheriff confirmed Armstrong's orders. "Yes, sir." The man practically spit as he said it.

"Sir, miss, do you mind coming with me?" Armstrong said, motioning them back toward the road.

"I need to get my bag from the car," Krista said.

"I'll get it," Sean said, and leaned though the open door to get Krista's purse and overnight bag from the back. He then turned to follow the deputy out to the road.

The tow truck driver passed them on the way. "Wait," Krista called. "You need to be careful not to dislodge the throttle cable or else you won't be able to see where it was tampered with."

"Ma'am, I really need you to come with me," Deputy Armstrong said. "I'll be sure to take down all the details in your statement."

Armstrong was much more laid back and polite than Officer Asshole, but something about the situation made Sean uneasy.

Then again, maybe he was uneasy because the thought

of climbing into the back of another cop car brought him back to the only time he'd been arrested.

Small wonder he looked at the door of that squad car as his own personal gateway to hell. He fought the urge to flee and swallowed back a wave of panic as he climbed into the back seat and slid over to make room for Krista. He took a deep breath, willing his heartbeat to slow, focusing instead on his anger toward the woman next to him.

For barging into his life and getting him involved in her mess. For putting him in the crosshairs of a killer.

For the way she pierced through his numb shell and made him excruciatingly aware of how beautiful she was, reminded him of how long it had been since he'd touched a woman, the silk of her skin, the wet heat of her body taking him inside.

"I'm sorry," Krista whispered, "for getting you into this."

Sean didn't trust himself to speak. He shoved himself as far away from her as possible and dug his fingers into the vinyl upholstered seat.

As they pulled out onto the road, the car seemed to close around him. It was a patrol car, so of course the back windows didn't roll down. Sean could feel the sweat beading on his forehead, the shortness of breath like an elephant was stepping on his chest.

Suddenly, a slender hand reached across the seat to cover his. Forgetting his anger for a minute, Sean clutched at her, concentrating on the cool softness of her palm as it lightly caressed the back of his hand. "How far out are we?" Sean felt like the words were being wrenched from his chest.

"About ten minutes."

A fucking eternity.

"Do you mind cracking a window? I'm a little shaky from the accident and I tend to get carsick on these windy roads," Krista said.

"We wouldn't want that," Armstrong said with a chuckle. He cracked the front windows a couple of inches.

Sean sucked in lungfuls of the cold, fresh air, stifling a groan of relief.

"Better?" Krista whispered so only he could hear.

He nodded, his relief mixing with humiliation that she got an up close and personal look at how weak and messed up he was. Real fucking tough. A former member of one of the military's most elite branches, and now he couldn't even ride in a closed car.

Still, it took some doing to make himself release her hand when she tugged it free. Damn it, he didn't want to be grateful to her for anything, even something this small. Why couldn't she just stay the same no-nonsense, ball-busting bitch he'd encountered in the courtroom?

But ever since the night she had come to visit him in jail and promised she was going to get him out of there, she'd been chipping away at that image, revealing a woman who was not only beautiful but honest. Decent.

And tuned in to him enough to see the signs of him starting to freak out, and kind enough to do something about it.

Damn it, she was nothing but trouble for him. Tonight had proven that in spades. His discovery of a few redeeming qualities couldn't make him lose sight of that.

"Do you know if they're looking for the SUV?" Krista asked. "The one that rammed us?"

"We're keeping an eye out, but without the license number it will be hard to track."

"They hit me pretty hard. There has to be some damage," Sean said, not holding much hope they would find the car even if they really were bothering to look for it.

"I'm sure they're accounting for that," Armstrong said, craning forward as he slowed the car at the sign for a forest service road.

Sean sat forward as Armstrong turned off the main highway. "I thought you were supposed to take us to Chelan."

"Just making a quick detour."

Sean looked at Krista, uneasy. Every sense went on high alert, just like it had earlier that day when he'd passed the two men in town, every instinct shouting that something wasn't right.

The car rolled to a stop and a foreboding washed through Sean as the deputy got out of the car.

"Wait, what are you doing?" Krista asked, tugging futilely at the door handle. With the doors locked from the outside, there was nothing they could do but wait for what happened next.

Sean braced himself, ready to move at the first opportunity.

The deputy unlocked Krista's door first and motioned her from the car.

Sean gave a resigned sigh when he saw Armstrong had pulled his gun and had it pointed straight at Krista.

"What's going on here?" Krista said.

"You too," Armstrong said. "Out of the car, hands where I can see them."

Sean scooted out of the car, hands up. An unnatural

calm settled over him as he clicked automatically into combat mode, years of training kicking in as though a switch had flipped. He stepped from the car, searching in the rapidly dimming light for anything he could use as a weapon.

"What the hell are you doing?" Krista demanded. "I'm with the prosecuting attorney's office," Krista said. "You won't get away with—"

"Shut up!" Armstrong yelled.

Sean picked up the undercurrent of nervousness in his voice. The guy was shaky. Good. Any way Sean could throw him off balance would work to their advantage. Sean took a step forward and the gun whipped in his direction.

"Don't move! Stay where you are."

"What the hell are you trying to pull?" Krista snapped. The gun went back to Krista and Sean's foot whipped out, cracking against Armstrong's arm and sending the gun flying. The glow of the headlights showed where it landed and Sean dove for it.

Something cracked across his back—Armstrong's nightstick. Sean rolled to his feet and turned just in time to take the next blow across his shoulder instead of his jaw. Sean feinted left and then darted in, catching the baton on the way down and wrenching it from Armstrong's hand.

Krista dove right, scrambling for the gun in the dark as Sean's arm raised to deliver a blow.

The baton came down across Armstrong's shoulder with a meaty *thunk*. Armstrong went down to his knees, scrambling for the Taser on his belt and Sean raised up for another blow.

Footsteps pounded up behind them, the loud crunch echoing in the night. "Freeze," a gravelly voice said. Sean turned in to the beam of a Maglite, unable to see much more than a hulking, shadowy figure and the outline of a semiautomatic machine gun.

What the hell? That was no cop, not with a weapon like that.

"Drop it, bitch, or I'll blow your face off," a lightly accented voice said from just beyond the glow of the flashlight.

He heard a struggle and Krista's cry of pain, and it took every ounce of restraint to hold still and take in the situation calmly when everything in him rebelled at the thought of her being hurt.

He shoved aside the voices yelling at him to react, to protect, to punish. He raised his arms and put his hands on the back of his head and he forced himself to assess the situation calmly, without emotion, and he looked for a way out.

Easier said than done, he thought when he saw Krista's white, terrified face in the glow of the flashlight. Her eyes were wide, pupils mere pinpoints, and he could see her pulse pounding in her neck even from several feet away.

"On your knees." The bastard emphasized his words with a yank to her hair. Her cry of pain lanced through Sean like an electrical current.

"You too," the thug holding the semi on Sean said. Sean dropped to his knees next to Krista, his muscles tense, coiled for action.

Deputy Armstrong didn't seem concerned in the least that two heavily armed civilians had appeared out of nowhere. If anything, he seemed annoyed.

"What the hell took you so long? This asshole could have crushed my skull while I waited for you. I was told they'd be easy to subdue."

"Not our fault you got faulty intel," said the gravelly voiced one. "Now where's your gun?"

"Over that way," Armstrong said and pointed the beam in the direction Sean had kicked it.

"What's going on?" Krista asked, her voice high and shaky. "Who are you working with?"

They ignored her.

"Try to stay calm," Sean said.

"There it is," the cop said as the beam caught the glint of gunmetal against dirt.

"Get it," said the thug trained on Sean.

"How can I stay calm? We have three men with guns on us and we're totally unarmed—"

"Shut up," said the one with the accent, rapping Krista on the head with the muzzle of his gun for emphasis.

Sean's fingers fisted in his hair as he glared at the guy. He couldn't make out much in the spillover of the flashlight beams, but he made the guy as slightly above average height, athletic, and strong looking. His cohort was big, as tall as Sean, and had what looked like a good thirty pounds more weight on him—hard to tell in the dark if it was muscle mass or bulk that would slow him down.

Neither of them was going to be easy to take out.

The deputy, on the other hand, shouldn't be a problem as long as Sean could keep the deputy's hands off that Taser.

"Give it to me," the big guy said and held out his hand. Armstrong handed over his gun and took a couple of steps away from the car, coming to a stop a few feet from Krista.

"Let's do it over here," Armstrong said. "I don't want to get anything on the car." He turned to the side, aiming his shoulder at the thug and turned his head away. "Through and through, right? I don't want this to fuck up my golf game—"

Sean felt Krista jerk, heard her gasp as the shot cracked through the night. Saw Armstrong's eyes bulge and his mouth drop open as the shot hit him not in the shoulder but square in the chest.

He sank to his knees and fell to the side. The ground underneath him darkened in seconds. "You asshole," Armstrong gasped, his breath a wet rattle that Sean recognized. "You were supposed to do it in the arm."

"Change of plans," the big thug said. Another shot, this time in Armstrong's head. The body jerked once and then went still.

"Oh my God," Krista said, and audibly swallowed next to him.

Stay with me, he thought, as though he could calm her by force of will. They couldn't afford for her to freak out, not if they wanted to get out of this.

"Who the hell are you? Who sent you?"

The thug ignored her question and nodded at the guy behind her, who jerked her to her feet.

"Do you realize who we are? If you kill us, you're going to be hunted down like dogs—"

"That's why we're not going to kill you," the thug said simply as he held the gun up to Krista's head. "He is," he said, indicating Sean with a nod of his head. "And then he'll do himself."

Son of a bitch. They were going to make it look like a murder-suicide. The psycho ex-prisoner with a vendetta against the woman who put him on death row. A little melodramatic, but the media would eat it up.

"No one will buy it. They'll know it was a setup when they examine the evidence," Krista said in a rush, struggling against the smaller thug's hold as he dragged her over to the big guy, who kept his semi trained on Sean.

"I think the investigation will go exactly the way we need it to," the big guy said. "Now shut your mouth or I'll make it look like he raped you first."

Krista stiffened as the thugs traded places, the smaller guy covering Sean while the big guy lifted Armstrong's gun and pointed it at Krista's chest.

Chapter 6

In the space of a heartbeat, Sean's years of training and combat experience took over. He inhaled deeply as the world pulled into sharp focus, his brain, his body registering every detail as though the world was moving in slow motion. He could hear his own heartbeat, see the faint tremor in Krista's hand as she stared the thug down with an unwavering gaze. He wanted to reach out and grab her hand, tell her he'd gotten himself out of worse clusterfucks than this, reassure her that he'd keep her safe.

He remained silent, motionless, his muscles coiled as he waited, ready to spring into action at the first opportunity.

"I think we do it anyway," said the smaller thug, who gave a smug laugh and reached down to give his groin a squeeze.

The big guy shot his cohort a nasty smile, and in that nanosecond of distraction Sean launched. He dove at Krista, knocking her to the side out of the beam of light, and rolled after her. The big guy yelled and the spray of the semiautomatic kicked up puffs of dirt on the ground next to him.

A hot sting erupted in his calf. Sean ignored it and

shoved Krista in the direction of the car. He ducked and rolled as another bullet whined past his year. He turned, lashed out with his booted foot, and caught the smaller thug in the chest and kicked his wrist hard enough to snap his forearm and send the gun flying.

The smaller thug lay gasping and Sean dove after his gun, trying to use the smaller guy for cover as more gunfire peppered the air. He just managed to hook his finger on it when a booted foot caught him in the ribs.

"Don't even think of it, asshole." Sean grunted in pain as the boot pressed into his hand, grinding the bones together as the guy reached down to retrieve the gun and then tucked it into his waistband. He pointed the guns at Sean. "On your knees. Hands where I can see them."

Sean obeyed, half blinded by the beam of the flashlight, and prayed he'd hear the sound of the squad car starting up as Krista made her escape. Come on, what was wrong with her? He was most likely a goner, but she could get herself out of here.

The night was silent except for the smaller thug's groan of pain as he breathed around cracked ribs, and the elevated breathing of the bearlike thug as he closed in for the kill.

"Hard to make it look like a murder-suicide if you hit me with that," Sean said.

"Don't worry, asshole. We always have a plan B. And a C and a D if that doesn't pan out."

Suddenly Sean saw something, a shadow of movement behind the guy, but in the glare of the flashlight it could have been a trick of the light. Sean gave away nothing. Silently and quicker than he would have imagined, a hand came up and hit the thug with something on his neck. His body jerked and convulsed.

Sean rolled to the side as the thug squeezed the trigger convulsively, firing wildly into the air until he fell backward to twitch on the ground like a dying fish.

Taser, Sean realized as he reached down to take the semi. He heard a yelp as Krista hit the smaller thug with seventy-five thousand volts and stifled a laugh at the way she said breathlessly, "You like that? Do you?"

Sean searched both men for ID and came up cold, but he took the cell phone clipped to the big guy's belt. He would have loved to wait for them to come to and ask more questions, but the way the night was going he wouldn't be surprised if another wave of assholes showed up to make sure the job was done. Right now they needed to clear out and regroup.

"Come on," Sean said, and he grabbed Krista by the arm. "Let's go." He pulled her to the car, pausing to pick up the second thug's gun and the deputy's sidearm.

"Wait," Krista said, tugging at his grips. "They just killed the cop and tried to kill us. We need to report this and wait for the police."

Sean yanked her to the squad car, opened the door, and half threw her inside. "Are you fucking insane? That was a cop who just tried to kill us. A cop who just set us up."

"But there has to be someone we can call," Krista sputtered as Sean walked around to the driver's side. "We can't just leave the scene like this."

Sean slid into the seat of the cop car and gave a mental thanks to the universe for making Deputy Armstrong negligent enough to leave the keys in the ignition. He started up the engine and peeled out over Krista's protests, and it was only when they were on the highway that he spoke.

"You need to get it into your head. Whatever you did,

whomever you set off, they have connections to the system, to the police, to the people you think are supposed to help us. As of this moment, all bets are off."

Krista sat numbly in the passenger seat of the squad car as Sean's words and the reality of the night sank in. He was right. A cop had tried to kill them. An unassuming, small-town deputy whom she'd trusted on sight, and he'd tried to lead them to their death.

A wave of nausea rolled over her as she remembered the blood pouring from his chest, the wet sound of his breathing before they shot him in the head. "Pull over," she said tightly.

"We shouldn't stop—"

"Pull over!" she shouted, barely waiting for the car to roll to a stop before she staggered out, her stomach heaving up the few bites of the meal and the beer she'd consumed—God, had it been only a couple hours ago? It felt like a lifetime.

Sean rubbed her back with a surprisingly gentle stroke. Krista closed her eyes and tried to spit the vile taste from her mouth. The nausea faded, leaving the sting of humiliation in its wake.

"Sorry," Krista said. "I'm not usually this squeamish. Not like I've never seen a dead guy before."

"It's a different deal when you actually see them die," Sean said quietly, his hand maintaining that firm, even pressure as it stroked up and down her spine. "Not to mention when that gun gets pointed at you."

Krista nodded and climbed back into the car. She felt marginally better, but still unable to focus on the tangle of questions whipping around her brain.

Suddenly the radio squawked to life. "Attention all units. We have just received word of an officer down. Deputy Armstrong has been shot and killed off Forest Service Road 14. Armstrong picked up Sean Flynn and Krista Slater after an auto accident. We believe Flynn seized Armstrong's gun and has stolen his squad car. It's unclear whether Slater is an accomplice or a hostage, but at this time Sean Flynn should be considered armed and dangerous. Approach with caution and use lethal force if necessary."

"That didn't take long for the guys to call in their story," Sean muttered as he reached out and switched the radio off. Krista's stomach rolled and she was afraid she might be sick again. What the hell had she gotten them into? "I'm sorry," she said for what felt like the thousandth time since she'd visited him in prison all those months ago. "I can clear this up," she said without conviction. "Just drop me in town and I'll tell them it's a mistake."

"If I really believed for a second that that would work, I'd do it," Sean snapped. "But even I'm not enough of an asshole to throw you to the wolves to save my own ass." Krista couldn't tell if the anger in his voice was aimed at her or himself. Either way, the relief that he wasn't going to dump her on the side of the road to fend for herself was only barely edged out by the guilt over having dragged him into this mess in the first place.

"I don't suppose you knew either of those guys," Sean said as he pulled back onto the highway.

She shook her head. "I didn't get a good look, but I don't think so. You?"

"No." Sean was quiet a few seconds. "You notice the smaller guy had an accent?"

She hadn't. In the moment, she'd been too focused on the gun pointed at her face. But now that Sean mentioned it, in the few words the thug had said, there had been the distinct pronunciation of an Eastern European accent.

Could he work with Karev? Oh, God, what if none of this had anything to do with what she'd been digging up about Nate and had everything do to with that warning Karev had delivered? The warning she'd dismissed as empty posturing.

There was no good reason for Karev to come after her, but since when did the Russian mafia need a *good* reason to kill someone? If they thought she posed any risk at all, that would be enough of an excuse to take her out.

But all of this on the heels of Jimmy's supposed suicide and her investigation into Nate's past being exposed—it was too much of a coincidence. It had to be related.

"Did you ever hear anything about Nate being involved with the Russians?" she asked, not really expecting Sean to answer.

"Not that I know of, but then again I haven't exactly kept in close correspondence in the past few years. Hell, he was dealing in high-end hookers. Anything's possible."

Krista pondered it for a moment. Nate was involved in prostitution and the Russians had their hands all over human trafficking in the Pacific Northwest. She grabbed her purse and fumbled around until she found her phone.

Sean reached out and snatched the phone from her hand before she could dial.

"What are you doing?" she asked, as he turned the phone off.

"What kind of a dumbass move is that?" Sean retorted.

"I need to call Mark and tell him there's been a mistake about what happened with the deputy and then I want to call the investigator I'm working with to see if he can find any connection between Nate's business and the Russians. Why are you looking at me like I'm an idiot?"

"Are you insane? They can track you through your phone. You of all people should know that. You have to have used it as evidence in a case."

Krista closed her eyes and shook her head, calling herself a hundred kinds of idiot. Of course he was right. The combined trauma of the last hour and a half had mucked up her thinking so badly she hadn't even considered how easy it would be for someone to get a bead on them through the cell phone's GPS technology.

And whoever was after them had a long reach, far enough to get into the local sheriff's department within half an hour of their crash. More than long enough to triangulate the signal and track their progress away from the murder scene.

"Give me my phone."

Sean handed it back with a warning look. She rolled the window down a few more inches and tossed the phone outside. "Better?"

"Much."

Krista's stomach clenched as they came around a corner, half expecting the black SUV to come roaring out at any moment. Even if no one was tracking them through GPS, there were only two directions they would have been able to take the car. Now that the deputy's body had been discovered, it was a good bet they would run into either the cops or the thugs before they reached town.

As though reading her thoughts, Sean pulled the car over to the side of the highway. He picked up the deputy's handgun. "You know how to use one of these?"

Krista nodded. "I took a gun safety course when I joined the prosecuting attorney's office."

Sean checked the safety and handed over the gun, along with another clip he'd taken off the deputy. Krista took the gun and gingerly tucked it into her waistband, her skin recoiling at the cold bite of metal. She stuffed the extra clip into her pocket.

She stuffed her purse into her overnight bag as Sean took up the extra guns and the flashlight and got out of the car. Krista followed silently, not bothering to ask what his plan was.

His quiet, take-charge attitude went a long way toward soothing her frayed nerves. It was something she had sensed in him, even when she'd faced him across a court-room. At the time, she'd read it as arrogance. Now she saw it for what it was: an innate confidence that made him a born leader. She could easily imagine him leading his fellow soldiers into the fray, fighting alongside them, and watching over them, leaving no one behind.

Just as he refused to leave her behind even though he had every right to. Her own personal knight in shining ar-mor.

She gave herself a mental slap. God, she must have hit her head harder than she'd realized if she could imagine Sean Flynn as the hero of her private fairy tale.

Still, despite Sean's anger and resentment toward her, Krista instinctively trusted him to keep her safe. Roman-tic delusions aside, tonight that made him a hero.

He kept the light off as he started down the shoulder of

the road. His quick pace had Krista breathing hard. The half-moon cast a silvery glow through the trees, but not quite enough to illuminate the rocks and cracks before Krista stumbled over them.

She sucked in a sharp breath as she nailed her toe on a rock for the third time.

"There's a trailhead into the national forest just up ahead," Sean said, his arm a dark shadow as he pointed. "Once we're on the trail we'll slow down a little bit. Right now I want to get off the road."

Even so, he slowed the pace a degree, enough that she didn't feel like she was rushing headlong just to keep up. Every few steps he looked over his shoulder to check on her and every time she gave him a feeble thumbs-up.

They walked about a hundred more yards, and Sean illuminated a brown-and-gold forest service sign a few feet back from the road that marked the trailhead. "This should dump us out about two miles outside of Chelan," Sean said.

When Sean felt they were safely out of sight he finally turned on the flashlight. Krista didn't let herself fall more than a few feet behind. After about fifteen minutes of steady walking, Sean's voice broke the darkness. "How long has Benson known you've been nosing around Nate's past?"

Krista had to think a minute, redirect some of the energy she was using to keep forward momentum back to her brain. "A couple days."

"Did you tell him you were coming to talk to me?"

"I get where you're going," she said, as everything in her rejected the notion. "Mark hired me out of law school. He's like a second father to me. There's no way he's involved in this."

"It's a pretty damn big coincidence. He finds out, and the next thing you know I'm being set up by Deputy Numb Nuts and two thugs to take the fall for a murder-suicide. Benson would have access, contacts throughout the state..."

Krista shook her head even though Sean couldn't see her. "Benson found out at the same time as just about everyone else in the Seattle PD when I had to explain how I just happened to stumble onto the scene of Jimmy Caparulo's supposed suicide. People might not know the specifics, but it's no secret I had a meeting set up with Jimmy related to an investigation. Anyone familiar with the case could put two and two together."

Sean grunted as he shifted her bag from one arm to the other. "Excellent. So now we can add the entire Seattle PD to our suspect list."

Krista bristled. "Even if that were the case— and believe me, it's not—I think we can safely trust Cole, don't you?" Detective Cole Williams, at the urging of Sean's sister, Megan, had been instrumental in helping catch Nate Brewster, aka the Seattle Slasher, and proving Sean had been framed for the murder of Evangeline Gordon. Not to mention, Detective Williams was now engaged to Megan.

Sean stopped so abruptly Krista walked straight into his back, so big and broad it was like bouncing off a tree. "No fucking way. No way are we mixing them up in this. Megan's been through enough already because of me. You dragged me into this shit storm, fine. I have nothing to lose. But stay the fuck away from them."

Krista let the matter go as he resumed his march up the trail. But if she knew Cole—and Megan for that matter—

once he got wind of what happened, he would be involved up to his ears whether Sean liked it or not.

Two hours later they were following the road into the outskirts of Chelan. "How are you holding up?" Sean asked as he scanned the road for any signs of traffic.

Besides the blisters rubbed into both heels, a stubbed toe she was afraid might be broken, and an ache in the arch of her foot that told her that her running shoes were way past their prime? "Fine," she replied. "Now what?" she asked, leaning forward slightly to stretch out her back.

"How much cash do you have on you?"

Krista had to think for a minute if she had any. She was so used to paying for everything with a card she rarely carried actual bills. Then she remembered she'd gotten cash to pay the lady who cleaned her house every other week. "I think I have about forty dollars."

Sean pulled out a money clip and thumbed through a few bills. "Seventy-two dollars. First thing we do is hit an ATM and get as much cash as we can." He started walking again.

"But they'll be able to track our cards."

Sean didn't pause. "We'll be gone soon enough."

At this hour, downtown was shut up for the night and they didn't encounter anyone. They picked their way along the side roads, careful to stay out of the glow of the streetlights. Even though it was unlikely their pursuers would have tracked them here, with the news reports painting Sean as a cop killer, they couldn't be too careful.

Fortunately, Chelan was small enough and low-tech enough. As far as Krista could tell, they hadn't invested in the traffic cameras and exterior security cameras that had become so common in Seattle.

There was no avoiding the camera installed at the ATM, however, or the cameras installed in the parking lot next to the bank. Sean made sure the semiautomatic was tucked under his jacket, out of view. After they maxed out their ATM withdrawals and credit card cash advances, Sean grabbed her hand and walked quickly back toward Main Street and then turned down a side street and headed back toward the main highway.

After a few minutes they spotted the glow of lights from a roadhouse bar that was still rocking hard after midnight. The muffled wail of country and western music came from inside, and the parking area was crowded with pickup trucks and a handful of Harleys parked near the front.

Sean walked around the gravel lot, out of the glow of the single streetlight in the center of the parking area. He wove in between the rows of trucks, finally stopping at a dark-colored Ford that, as far as Krista could tell in the dark, was about eight years old. "That was a pretty cool thing you did with your car earlier," he said as pulled the semiautomatic out from under his jacket.

The sight of the gun in his hand sent a shock through her tired body and brain. "Don't tell me you're going to shoot me over it."

His surprised chuckle was warm and rich in the cold night air. "No," he said. Krista heard the rustle of fabric and realized he was taking off his jacket. "But I'm thinking your skills might come in handy."

She couldn't see him in the dark, but there was no mistaking the sound of glass crunching as he slammed the jacket-wrapped butt of the gun against a window. Before Krista could so much as gasp, he'd reached in and popped the lock on the driver's side door and slid in.

"No way," Krista said. "I'm not hot-wiring this car for you."

"It'll probably take me twice as long, and we don't have that kind of time," Sean said, a familiar edge creeping into his voice.

Krista took a step back. "I'm a prosecutor. I can't commit a felony—"

"Right now you're a fugitive," Sean said. "And if we're caught, we're as good as dead. I don't know about you, but I don't have plans to die tonight. And since you brought this shit to my door, I figure you owe me one."

Krista got into the car. "Slide over." Sean stood in the open doorway and held the light as she went to work. Cold sweat beaded on her face as she popped the covers surrounding the truck's ignition tumbler. It took only a little over a minute, and with every move, Krista was aware that she was crossing a line.

No matter that Sean was right. They couldn't trust anyone, not even the police, and they had no other reasonable way to stay out of reach of the men who had tried to kill them. She'd heard excuses like that for years in the cases she prosecuted. Heard them and dismissed them out of hand, convinced that there was always another choice that didn't involve breaking the law.

After a lifetime of following the rules, and over a decade of working within the system to take down the bad guys, with this one simple act she was about to join their ranks. If she did this, would she be that much different from the so-called lowlifes she'd worked to put away?

The truck's engine roared to life, and Krista slid over to make room for Sean and stared at her hands.

Sean pulled out of the back of the parking lot, avoiding the front of the bar. "Nice work."

Krista looked over, and in the glow of the moonlight she could see a flash of white teeth and the admiration on his face as he looked at her.

She didn't want to think about what it meant about her that the rush of warmth at his smile went a long way in drowning out her ethical crisis.

He was silent a few minutes as he took the highway just out of town and then turned the truck onto a forest road that forked to the right. "I know this probably goes against everything you believe in, but sometimes you have to break the rules to do the right thing."

Krista looked at the hard line of his jaw, the shift of muscles in his arm, the flex of his big hands on the steering wheel, and she wondered how many rules he'd have her breaking before this was over.

"Relax, baby, you so tense you not letting me work."

David Maxwell stifled the urge to smack the girl across the face with her condescending smile and playfully chastising finger. He grunted and shoved her face back into his lap and closed his eyes.

But nothing, not even the half a Viagra he'd knocked back with his scotch, could get his cock to go stiffer than half-mast.

Olga...Oksana...whatever-the-fuck-her-name was right. He was too tense, his gut a writhing knot of anxiety ever since his nephew Nate's death, ever since that goddamn crusader Krista Slater started shoving her nose in Nate's past.

Ever since *she'd* disappeared. Talia.

Gone without a trace after escaping a brutal death at

the hands of David's own nephew. He hoped she was dead. If he ever found her, he'd make her wish she was.

But God, she'd been good. Gorgeous, smart. And completely at his mercy. Nothing like these dime-a-dozen sluts that came over by the truckload from the Eastern Bloc. The ones they got were top choice, cream of the crop, supermodel beautiful, and desperate enough to do whatever was necessary to protect themselves and their families back home.

But despite their beauty, with their empty gazes, vapid smiles, and broken English, they were indistinct, indistinguishable to the point he might as well have been jacking off into a handkerchief instead of getting a blow job.

No one could ever compare to Talia. She'd loved him at first, so much so she'd practically glowed with it. All starry-eyed idealism, thinking he was going to pull her up out of the 'hood like she was some modern-day *My Fair Lady*.

She'd soon learned how far that was from the truth. And then she'd learned to fear him, because she knew without him telling her what would happen to her and her sister if she ever tried to get away or told anyone about their relationship.

David sighed, a slight smile pulling at his face, his balls tingling at the memory. Love or fear: He still couldn't decide what look he liked better on Talia Vega's face.

He rolled his neck and was just getting into it when the phone on the table next to him rang. His stomach tightened as he picked up. "Tell me it's done."

The second's-long hesitation was answer enough. David's half a hard-on wilted into nothing before Richardson spoke. "They got away."

David shoved the whore's head out of his lap, knocking her onto her ass as he rose from the armchair. "How the fuck did they get away?" He hit the girl with a mean look and made a shooing motion with his arm. She gathered her dress and shoes and hustled from his private suite. He waited until the door clicked shut before speaking. "I didn't expect anything from that goddamn Ruskie but I expect you to make sure these things run smoothly. I had everything set up with the cop. What the fuck went wrong?"

While a car crash would have been an ideal way to get both Slater and Flynn out of the way—a high mountain road, an unstable ex-con driving too fast, maybe trying to kill himself and take the bitch who put him away—David knew better than to bank on it working.

So he'd accounted for some contingencies, made a few phone calls, and called in a few favors to get it done. The deputy had been clear on his mission, eager to get the money to help himself out from being underwater on the shitty little house he'd overpaid on. All he had to do was take a bullet to the arm and tell everyone that Sean Flynn had stolen his gun—wounding him in the process—killed Krista, and then killed himself.

The cop would never see the money, of course, because Richardson knew not to leave any loose ends and David wasn't about to trust anyone he hadn't personally vetted to keep his mouth shut. According to Richardson, Deputy Armstrong had played right along, right up to the part where he took a bullet to the head.

But fucking Sean Flynn hadn't cooperated and somehow managed to get away from one of the most highly trained men on David's personal security detail. Richardson was a goddamn fucking former Green Beret who was supposed to make sure that shit went down smoothly and as discreetly as possible.

"I take full responsibility, sir," Richardson said, his tone echoing back to his military training. David had to give him that—unlike most of the pussies running around today, when Richardson fucked up, he didn't try to spout excuses. "In an effort to make the scene as authentic as possible, I neglected to cuff Flynn or Slater. Flynn got the drop on Gregor, and while I was subduing him, Slater retrieved Deputy Armstrong's Taser from his belt. They then escaped in Armstrong's squad car."

David pressed his thumb and forefinger to his eyes, feeling like the top of his head was going to blow off.

"We spoke to our contact here and they're circulating the report that Flynn killed Armstrong and has taken Slater hostage. Law enforcement across the state is on it. Once they have them in custody we'll be able to take care of it."

"You better hope they pick them up soon." Thank God for small favors. There were a lot of people as motivated as he was to ensure Slater and Flynn didn't unwind the thread that connected him to Nate Brewster.

His phone beeped, signaling another call. He grimaced when he saw who it was. Another interested party who wanted to make sure Slater in particular was taken care of. "I have to take another call," he told Richardson.

He disconnected the call with Richardson and clicked over.

"You told me your man can handle it." The thickly accented voice made David's lip curl. He could picture the big Russian, cigarette smoke coiling around his head, his light-brown hair slicked back from his high forehead. The slightly almond-shaped eyes with a flat, dead expression that reminded David of a snake.

"Yeah, well it sounds like your guy was the one who fell down on the job."

"If you let them just shoot in the head, straightforward like, we wouldn't have this problem. You do this crazy thing, like James Bond movie, too many chances to escape."

David rolled his shoulders and grasped for patience. He'd explained the subtlety necessary in taking out Slater and Flynn. "I told you, now that word is out that she's been investigating Nate more closely, if she and Flynn show up murdered, there are going to be a lot of questions."

Karev made an exasperated sound. "And you have all this power to make sure no one asks these questions, *nyet*? You telling me maybe my business is not as secure as you say?"

"You walked away from a murder charge two days ago," David replied. "Did you forget I'm the one who called the judge?" The Honorable Judge Terence Phillips was more than happy to throw out key evidence in exchange for having a video featuring him being serviced by a beautiful young Asian remain hidden.

"Good, so everything is clear for shipment next week? Is very important."

"Yes," David snapped. Damned if he was going to let this headache with Slater and Flynn interfere with business.

Karev rang off with his usual warning: "If anything goes wrong, I cut off your `*khu i*` and feed it to a pig while your wife watch, *da*?"

David hung up without a reply. Karev's threat might have been humorous if it hadn't been dead serious. He ran his fingers through his hair, grimacing when he saw the amount that came off in his hand. He sank back into the chair, feeling tired and suddenly really fucking old.

Working with Karev was a huge risk. The guy was bat-shit crazy, snake mean, and loyal only to himself. But the last few years of financial turmoil, combined with his wife's determination to buy herself a senate seat, had taken a serious toll. As dangerous as Karev was, the partnership had been immensely lucrative for both of them, and as long as that remained the case, he'd stay in bed with the Russian.

The Russians didn't operate by any rules but their own. *If things go south, you have way more to lose than they do*, his nephew Nate had warned. *They have no loyalty and no qualms about turning on you, disappearing, and letting you take the fall.*

Ironic that Nate had been the voice of reason when he was the one to blame for their current turmoil. David went over to the desk and pulled a picture from the drawer. A brunette woman with big brown eyes smiled into the camera, cheek to cheek with a blond-haired, blue-eyed toddler as she cradled a dark-haired baby girl in her other arm.

David had lost most of his sentimentality eons ago, but his heart twisted as he thought of what had happened to the mother and children in the picture.

His sister Heather, lost to alcohol and drugs, murdered by a boyfriend who abused her and her children. His niece, Sarah, whom he'd only met once, died when she'd accidentally locked herself in the trunk of a car on a hot summer day, hiding from her mother's boyfriend to avoid being raped.

And Nate, the sole survivor, forever twisted from seeing his mother killed and stabbing the boyfriend to death in self-defense.

He knew it wasn't his fault—that his sister made her own bad choices, that leaving his name and his past behind was necessary for him to integrate into the upper echelons of wealth and power.

Still, he never got rid of the guilt over the fact that while he'd been making money hand over fist and marrying into one of Seattle's wealthiest families, the money he'd sent Heather had run out and she was living in that shitty house in a desolate part of eastern Washington, drinking herself to death, dating that lowlife who ended up bringing them all down. So even though he couldn't claim him publicly, David couldn't turn his back on his orphaned nephew.

He'd discreetly supported him, made sure he had a place to live and money for clothes, schools, and anything else he wanted.

And when Nate's bloodthirsty streak had reared its head, David had done everything he could to channel those urges and cover Nate's ass the few times it had been necessary.

This is what he got for trying to do right by his nephew. Sweating bullets as he and his stepson Carl worked to cover the tracks that led from Nate to them. Doing whatever was necessary, including ordering a hit on a prosecuting attorney, in order to keep the dark underbelly of his business hidden, to maintain his hold over everyone who mattered to make sure his business—and Karev's—continued without interference.

Chapter 7

Krista jerked awake as the car slowed to a stop and she instinctively reached out to brace her hand against the dashboard. Her head ached and her heart thudded in her chest as for a split second her disoriented brain replayed the moment Sean's truck came to a jarring stop against the tree.

"Where are we?" she said, blinking as she looked around the parking lot. She looked at the clock. Twelve fifty-two. She'd been asleep for only a little over half an hour, but it felt like hours.

"Walmart," Sean said matter-of-factly. He clicked on the dome light and was writing something down on a piece of paper. When he finished, he handed it to her, along with a baseball cap he'd found crumpled on the floor when they'd first taken the truck from the parking lot of the bar. "I want you to use some of the cash to pick up these supplies. And wear the hat in case someone in there has been watching the news."

Krista's stomach clenched. Before she'd succumbed to the adrenaline hangover and dozed off, she'd heard several more news bulletins alerting everyone within earshot to be on the lookout for her and Sean. As disguises went, a baseball cap wasn't much but it would have to do.

"Wait, why am I going in alone?" she asked. Her eyes narrowed. "You're going to ditch me, aren't you?"

"Of course not!" The offended look on his face seemed real, and he had stuck with her through some pretty hairy stuff tonight, but she didn't know Sean well enough yet to gauge his acting ability. Despite his earlier words of assurance, sending her into the store alone would be the perfect opportunity for him to ditch her to fend for herself.

"Then come in with me."

"I would but I don't think this will go unnoticed, even in Walmart." He lifted his right leg so she could see it in the glow of the dome light. Below his knee, the faded denim of his jeans was stained dark with blood.

Krista started to reach out and then jerked her hand back. "Oh my God, why didn't you say anything?"

Sean shrugged her off. "It's just a graze. The bullet didn't even penetrate—"

"You were shot?"

"Those sure as shit weren't squirt guns those two had."

Krista struggled for calm. Sean didn't seem fazed, and he was the one who'd been shot. Still. "That's a lot of blood. We should get it looked at—"

"Nothing a good scrubbing and some butterfly bandages can't fix. That's why I put them on the list."

Krista glanced down at the rest of the supplies he'd listed. *Prepay cell phones, pants, size 33W x 36L. Butterfly bandages. Antibiotic ointment.*

"I barely know first aid. If we go to a hospital, they can help us—"

Sean cut her off with a curt shake of his head. "They have to report all gunshot wounds to the police. We can't have that."

Krista chewed her bottom lip. "It's the middle of the night. No one knows where we are. It's ridiculous to think they would be able to get to the cops here."

"They managed to get to a sheriff's deputy in bumfuck nowhere in the space of a few hours. What makes you think they haven't sent out the alert all over the state?"

She hated to admit he was right. But there had to be a way to deal with this that didn't leave them so completely to their own devices. "Okay, I'll patch you up and then we'll drive straight through to Seattle. We'll go to Mark's house—"

Sean held up his hand. "Assuming he's not involved, you really want to lead these assholes straight to him? Anyone who helps us now might as well paint a target on his head."

Sean's weary sigh echoed through the car. "Look, you want to take your chances with the cops, you go ahead. But remember, you came to me. You want my help on this. We're on our own until we get a better handle on exactly what the hell is going on here. You just have to trust me on this." Even in the dim light she could see his stare, challenging her.

Krista gave a reluctant nod, her stomach churning. "I trust you."

Something flashed in his face, a softening around his mouth and eyes that was gone so quickly she thought she'd imagined it.

"There are security cameras on these lights," he said, pointing at the parking lights spaced evenly among the rows of cars. "And all over the store. Try to keep your face off them without being too obvious."

Krista nodded. The chances of having been tracked

here so quickly was slim but they couldn't be too careful.

She reached for the door handle and he stayed her with a hand on her wrist. "If I'm not here when you come out, it's because the cops made me and hauled my ass away, not because I ditched you."

Krista flashed him a brief smile.

Krista made it out of Walmart with their supplies without incident. Sean drove another forty-five minutes before insisting they switch cars again. The older SUV's door was unlocked—probably because the owner never imagined the car would be stolen—saving Sean the added step of breaking a window. Krista knew better than to protest, and while she hot-wired her second car of the night, Sean switched out the license plate of the SUV with that of a car parked down the street.

Still, it was hard not to worry about whether she'd have a career after this—assuming they made it through alive. She didn't imagine the people of King County would be willing to excuse one of their prosecuting attorneys from boosting cars, no matter how necessary it was at the time.

Finally, a little after two-thirty a.m. they pulled into the parking lot of a hotel on the outskirts of Richland, about three hours outside of Seattle. Richland was somewhere in between a big town and a small city, just the right size for them to pull into a squat little motel after midnight without causing too much of a stir.

Krista left Sean in the car and went to register. Her stomach knotted as she approached the door. Between her involvement in Sean's high-profile release and the news of tonight's activities, Krista's face was probably all over the news. But so far the police were portraying her as

Sean's hostage, so maybe people wouldn't be on the look-out for her to walk into a place alone.

Krista pulled the ball cap down so the brim shadowed her face. The clerk slowly roused himself at the sound of the doorbell and Krista felt a spurt of relief when she saw the TV above the counter was tuned to a Korean soap opera. Hopefully that meant he hadn't been watching the late local news.

"Sign your name here," the clerk said, passing over the registration card without so much as looking in her direction.

Krista's brain stuttered. Dummy, of course she needed an alias. What was that formula for figuring out your porn name? First pet's name plus street you lived on? She carefully signed the name *Mandy Lockwood* on the card, handed over the cash, and hightailed it back out to Sean before the clerk decided to look up.

Sean parked the car on the other side of the hotel so it wouldn't be visible to the street and carried their stuff to the ground-level room.

He unlocked the door and snapped on the light. Her lip curled as she took in their accommodations. The carpet was dingy, the furniture looked like it had been cycled through Goodwill a half dozen times, and she didn't even want to think about what a UV light would reveal on the avocado-and-orange synthetic bedspreads.

"About what you'd expect from a no-tell that takes cash without questions," Sean said at her disgusted sniff. But she noticed he also removed the bedspread and tossed it on the floor.

"And you're so familiar with these kinds of places?"

"I've stayed in some dumps that make this place look

like the Hilton." Sean's mouth curved in that half smile that got sexier every time she saw it. She mentally scolded herself, telling herself any reaction she had to him was because of the extreme events of the evening, the adrenaline rush and crash that had her thoughts and emotions all over the place.

Sean pulled the phones out of the Walmart bag and plugged them into the wall to charge. Krista eyed the phones, but didn't push it. Sean needed to deal with the wound on his leg. She could push the issue of contacting someone who could help them later.

Next he grabbed the bag containing the first-aid supplies and went to the bathroom. "Come here," she heard him call over the noise of running water.

She joined him in the bathroom, trying her best to avoid brushing against him in the tiny space. "What is it?"

He'd washed the blood from the gash over his eyebrow off his face, but there were dark reddish-brown stains around the collar of his T-shirt. As she stepped around the toilet, he took her chin in a hand that was slightly damp and smelled of soap. She tried not to flinch. Not because his touch was unpleasant but because the opposite was true.

"I want to look at that bump on your head." As he tilted her face up to the light, she fought the urge to rub her cheek against his palm like a cat demanding to be petted.

Krista had never been an especially touchy-feely person, and in her testosterone-laden line of work it was important to maintain physical boundaries. Krista had gotten the *back off* body language so down it was like second nature. It was essential for the job but hell on her dating life as it became almost impossible to let down her guard in front of anyone, even a date.

Sean didn't hesitate to touch her now any more than he had earlier, and it was disconcerting how much she liked the feel of his hands, the way he wasn't put off by any *don't touch* signals she might be sending out.

And if that wasn't a sign of how this night had messed her up and turned everything upside down, she didn't know what was.

He brushed the fingers of his opposite hand over the area above her eyebrow. She winced as he probed against the knot that had formed there.

His mouth tightened in sympathy. "Yeah, you've got a goose egg there but I don't think it's fractured. And I missed this before." In the mirror, he indicated an inch-long scratch on her cheekbone that was crusted over in blood. It was nothing, especially compared to the gash above his eyebrow and the wound she had yet to see on his leg, but Sean took a washcloth, soaped it up, and washed the scratch. Next came a gentle smear of antibiotic ointment and a Band-Aid. "Good as new," he murmured as he studied his handiwork.

"Let me help you," Krista said belatedly as she gestured at the gash over his eyebrow. He was the one with the real injuries.

"I got it," he said, waving her away. "And I'll need some room to deal with my leg so..."

Krista took the hint and got out of the bathroom. Probably better all around, since just the soft brush of his fingers on her face was almost enough to forget why they were stuck in this dump of a hotel room.

It all came back into focus as she grabbed a pair of cotton pajama pants and a tank top from her bag and quickly exchanged them for her sweat-and-dirt-crusted jeans and

T-shirt. She topped the tank with a fleece pullover and sat on the end of one bed, racking her brain as she tried to connect the dots between Nate Brewster, Jimmy Caparulo's so-called suicide, and the men who had tried to kill them tonight.

Someone had secrets to hide, but who? And who could pull the kind of strings it would take to get a cop to turn in less than forty-five minutes? No way they could have set that up ahead of time.

And what if Sean, as he claimed, really had no information to share about Jimmy, Nate, or any of it? No knowledge that put the killer's interests in danger.

The lead ball at the bottom of her stomach got heavier as she became more and more convinced that that was the case. There was nothing Kowalsky had uncarthed, nothing Jimmy Caparulo had said, that pointed her specifically to Sean. Just a gut reaction telling her that maybe Sean, as the third man and the one betrayed by the friends he'd once called brothers, would know something that might shed light on whoever was working with Nate behind the scenes.

So far he'd given her nothing to support that. Yet he'd saved her life and patched up her wounds, ignoring his own until he'd taken care of hers first.

It was a side of Sean she would have never imagined had she not witnessed it herself. And only extreme fatigue and emotional stress allowed her to admit to herself it was incredibly attractive. Krista was used to being in charge, taking care of herself, getting herself out of any hairy situation that might rear its head.

But when the shit came down, Sean had calmly, capably taken charge, kept his head, and gotten them both to safety. Even if his methods had been a bit unorthodox, she thought, wincing as she remembered the cars they'd stolen. He'd stared death in the face and offered himself up as a rock she could collapse against when panic would have floored her before the first gunshot went off.

She knew she couldn't take it personally. She didn't fool herself that he might grow to like her, not after everything that had happened, and not after she had, as he put it, dragged him into this shit storm. But that take-charge, I'll-take-care-of-you-no-matter-what attitude combined with the—call her shallow—intense green eyes and acres of muscles...

Regret burned bitterly at the back of her throat as she realized that had they met under drastically different circumstances, she could have developed a hell of a thing for a guy like Sean Flynn.

"Hey, can you help me a sec?"

Krista snapped her head around. Her cheeks flamed and she ordered herself to calm down. It wasn't like Sean was a mind reader. He had no way of knowing she was out here mooning over him like a hormonal thirteen-year-old.

"I thought I could get it, but I can't quite manage the right angle to bandage my leg properly." His expression was irritated, as though it galled him to have to ask for her help. He'd already closed up the slice above his eyebrow with butterfly bandages that stood out starkly against his tan skin and dark hair.

Krista sprang from the bed, eager to offer assistance, the least she could do after everything he'd done tonight.

"No problem," she said and swallowed hard when she realized that aside from his khaki-colored T-shirt he wasn't wearing anything but a pair of boxer shorts. She forced herself not to stare at his long, heavily muscled legs as he walked over to her with a box of bandages and a tube of antibiotic ointment in his hands.

"I managed to clean it." Sean turned and Krista crouched down so she could get a closer look at the gash that ran diagonally up his calf, starting inside his right ankle and ending just outside his knee. He'd flushed it with hot water and now the furrow was oozing fresh blood. Krista grabbed a gauze pad from the bed and dabbed away the blood. "Sorry," she said at Sean's wince of pain. "I'll be as gentle as I can."

"Don't worry about it. I've had a lot worse than this little scratch."

Krista gave an involuntary chuckle. "You don't have to be tough. And if that's a little scratch, I hate to think of the damage it would have done if it had actually gone through." She'd seen enough bullet wounds and their aftereffects to know that even a small-caliber gun caused serious trauma as its bullet tore through the meat of a large muscle. She took the tube of antibiotic ointment and started to apply it to the wound with a gauze pad, but with the bad light and her awkward, crouching position she couldn't quite do it.

She started to have him prop his foot on the bed, but then that meant she'd be kneeling next to his bent thigh, her face entirely too close to ... She flicked a furtive glance at the front of his boxers.

No way.

"I think this might work better if you lay on the bed." Why was her voice all breathy and nervous like that?

He didn't seem to notice as he stretched out face down on the sheets.

"Be sure to coat the first layer in the antibiotic ointment." She jumped at Sean's muffled voice, grateful he couldn't see the way she blushed as she carefully laid an ointment-smeared layer of gauze over the bottom half of the wound. It took two more sheets to cover the furrow. She secured them with strips of white tape. Damn, the man was in good shape. Of course she'd known he was fit, but his calf muscle was rock hard under her fingers, not a single ounce of fat giving under the skin as she smoothed the tape down.

She stepped back, her gaze guiltily, greedily traveling up his tight hamstrings to the hard curve of his equally tight butt outlined by the soft cotton of his boxers. "I think you're all set."

He grunted and rolled over, flexing and relaxing his big right foot to make sure the bandage didn't pull too tight. Apparently satisfied, he rose to his feet and started gathering up the first-aid supplies and putting them back in order.

Must have been an army thing, she thought as she watched him carefully pack away the supplies and place them on top of the room's dresser. Then he took the bag of extra clothes she'd bought at Walmart, removed and shook out each item, folded them carefully, and placed them in a drawer.

She looked at her own stuff piled next to the door. He'd probably have a heart attack at the way her two extra T-shirts, jeans, and spare undies were balled up and shoved in willy-nilly. And if he ever saw her house...Christ, she'd have to get a bulldozer to clear out the bedroom or he'd run screaming.

Right, like Sean will ever have cause to see your bedroom.

But the idea had more appeal than she wanted to think about. To distract herself, she grabbed the remote and turned on the television that was perched on the dresser next to Sean. And wished she hadn't as soon as she saw the screen. Her image took up the left half of the screen, Sean's the right.

Krista's picture was a headshot from the state employee directory. With her dark suit, hair pulled back at her nape, heavy-framed glasses on her nose, and a bare hint of a smile on her lips she looked serious, professional, and a good five years older than thirty-one. Just what she'd been going for, and a far cry from the scraggly-haired makeupless mess she'd turned into.

She felt her anger rise when she saw the picture they'd chosen of Sean. Of course they couldn't use his formal military portrait, the one with him decked out in his dress uniform looking strong and heroic and handsome enough to make Rosie O'Donnell consider switching teams.

They didn't even use his mug shot from when he'd been arrested for Evangeline Gordon's murder. Instead, they used the picture of him in the courtroom the day of his sentencing trial, hands shackled in front of him, the expression on his face one of pure fury.

In that split second, forever frozen on film, Sean looked like a killer.

Under the pictures was the text *Exonerated murderer shoots cop, kidnaps prosecutor*.

"Huh, the librarian and the beast," Sean said grimly.

Krista switched off the TV before she had to hear the anchor's BS voice-over about what had supposedly happened. But even without his image staring at her, she couldn't get that picture out of her mind.

It was impossible to reconcile it with the man who hadn't hesitated to put himself in mortal danger to save her life today.

That she'd helped put him in prison, sentenced him to an existence so miserable he'd chosen death as a preferable alternative, brought the ever-present guilt bubbling up to the surface.

It bothered her even more than it had before, the idea that Sean had chosen to go the suicide-by-state route rather than keep fighting.

She still wasn't claiming great knowledge, but after everything they'd been through tonight, she just couldn't see Sean as the kind of guy who would just give up, no matter how bad the odds. It didn't fit with anything she'd witnessed today. Sean was so strong, so determined, so capable, so willing to fight even when the odds were stacked against him, it seemed impossible he would just throw in the towel and call it a life.

"I don't get it. Why did you give up?" The words rushed out before she could think about it.

"What do you mean?" he asked.

"When you were on death row, why did you stop the appeals? Why did you want to die?"

Time seemed to freeze with his silence. "Why do you think?" he finally asked. His green gaze narrowed on her.

Krista swallowed hard, forcing herself not to shrink under his hard stare. Alarm bells rang in her head, warning her that she'd walked up to a sleeping tiger and poked it in the eye. Maybe probing Sean Flynn's secrets wasn't such a good idea. "It was a stupid question. I'm sure I can imagine why."

He took a step closer, close enough for her to smell the

soap drying on his skin, the dampness of his hair. It struck her again how big he was, his wide chest blocking out the light, his body seeming to take up all the space in the hotel room. "Really? Then tell me. What do you think made me give up and want to cash it all in?"

He folded his arms across his chest and widened his stance, the muscles in his thighs rippling as he shifted his weight. Her whole body flushed as she was reminded yet again that his lower half was clad only in boxer shorts.

She unstuck her tongue from the roof of her mouth and tore her eyes from the shift of bulging quad muscles under tan, hair-roughened skin. "I guess the loneliness would get to me. The endless waiting, wondering if your appeal would be granted, never knowing if anything was going to pan out." His eyes got a faraway look and grim lines bracketed his mouth as though he was remembering. Funny, she had never once thought about what it would be like to be in prison, much less solitary, other than the vague knowledge that it was a horrible experience. As it should be, in her opinion.

It wasn't like the guilty criminals took their punishment gamely, but how much harder must it have been for Sean and others like him, innocent men locked up. Knowing they'd done nothing to deserve their treatment. The guilt weighed on her like an anvil. Were there others she'd prosecuted who were innocent? Framed like Sean or railroaded by the system?

Innocent men who looked at death as the best option to cope with their misery?

The questions, the doubts plagued her. Calling everything she worked for, everything she believed in, into question.

She shook her head. "It must have been awful. I can only imagine—"

"No, you can't imagine," Sean said, cutting her off. "The loneliness, the waiting—that's the tip of the iceberg. Imagine every personal freedom you take for granted being taken away. Being told when you're going to eat, when you're going to take a shower, when you're going to take your next breath of fresh air. Imagine having nearly everyone in the world you thought were your friends believe you're the kind of monster who could rape a woman and cut her throat."

Krista pressed her fist against the ache forming in her stomach.

"Imagine not hearing another human voice for days at a time. Only seeing someone you love once a week behind a pane of glass."

He took a step closer and Krista's pulse leaped in her throat. "Imagine never having anyone touch you except to push you around, or never touching anyone again."

She thought of his hard hands, gentle despite their size, curled into fists, craving the feel of another person's touch. "I thought I'd never touch a woman again." His low-pitched voice put goose bumps on her skin, the ache in her belly turning to something different at the heat emanating from his body.

He reached out and caught her hand in his. She didn't pull away. He caught her other hand and ran his hands up her forearms, pushing up the sleeves of her pullover so his thumbs could trace the sensitive skin of her inner arms. "Never feel smooth, warm skin under my fingers."

Heat coursed through her. Common sense screamed at her to pull away, get out while she could, but nothing could drown out the fact that she wanted this. Wanted *him*. Wanted to feel those big callused hands on the smooth skin of her shoulders now, cupping her cheeks and skimming his thumbs along the curve of her cheekbones.

And call her crazy, call her stupid, but she wanted to touch him, give him this, as though it could make up in some small way for her part in what had happened to him.

"Do you have any idea how crazy that would make you? How it would make you ache?" He closed the distance between them. Yes, she could imagine the ache. It was consuming her right now, making her blood run thick and hot through her veins, making her clench her thighs against the pulse pounding between her legs.

"Jesus, you're beautiful," he murmured and she felt the warmth of his breath on her face and yes, he was going to kiss her. His mouth came down on hers, hot and fierce. She parted her lips and licked into his mouth, loving the way he shuddered and groaned at the contact.

Her response was fast, ferocious, startling in its intensity. One kiss and she was fired up, more turned on than she could ever remember being. It had been way too long since she'd had a man's hands on her skin, his mouth on hers, but even that couldn't explain the way her body went from zero to sixty in two seconds flat.

It was almost scary, her body's reaction to him, of all people. A spike of fear broke through the heat of desire, a voice warning her to pull back before she went plummeting over the edge, past the point of no return.

As though sensing her hesitation, Sean tightened his hold. One hand fisted in her hair as the other skimmed down her back, chasing away any thought of stopping him in their tracks. They both groaned as his fingers gripped the curve of her ass, yanking her against him until she felt the rock-hard column of his erection against her stomach. A rush of wetness soaked her sex in response.

He released her mouth long enough to pull the fleece over her head and toss it across the room.

She sucked his tongue into her mouth, a little whimper escaping her throat at the feel of his hand sliding up the back of her tank top. She ran her own hands up under his T-shirt, reveling in the feel of smooth, hot skin and corded muscles under her hands.

Sean yanked her tank top over her head, pulled off his T-shirt, and drew her against him. Hot, hair-roughened skin teased her nipples, sending an electric pulse through her body, making her moan.

His answering groan pulsed through her as his arms pulled her close, molding her so tightly to him even a beam of light couldn't have gotten through.

It was too much, too fast, and she knew she should stop it before it went too far. But the tangle of lust, need, and, God help her, affection for Sean was too far gone, off the rails, and she could do nothing but surrender.

Chapter 8

Sean couldn't keep his hands from shaking as they ran over Krista's body. It was like a dam had burst, flooding him with all the sensations that had been blocked away for years. The taste of her, the feel of her, the scent of her coursed through every cell, every nerve, sweeping him away on a wave of total sensory overload.

His lips sucked at hers. His tongue swept in to explore her mouth, absorb the sweet salty taste of her. Her skin under his fingers was beyond anything he'd ever imagined, warm, smooth, giving under his hands as his fingers sank into her silky curves.

The soft weight of her breast in his hand, her rigid nipple against his palm, threatened to send him over the edge.

He cautioned himself to ease up, to not be too rough, but it was so fucking hard not to go after her like some wild animal.

He pulled his mouth from hers to catch his breath and look down at her. Big mistake. The sight of her, cheeks flushed, mouth swollen and red from kissing— good God—her milk-white breasts with their pink-brown nipples peeking through his fingers. All of it was enough to make his cock harden another inch, stretching him so tight he was afraid he might burst through his skin.

But the real kicker, the thing that made him clench his teeth and struggle not to come right then and there, were her eyes. The heated, heavy-lidded look that told him, rough or not, she was ready and willing for whatever he was going to dish out.

He could feel her heart pounding under his hand, see her pulse fluttering in her throat. He bent his head, needing to taste the pulse beat against his tongue, the need so strong he couldn't stop himself from following the flick of his tongue with a nip from his teeth, like a wolf nipping at his mate.

He could taste the salt of sweat on her skin, feel her gasp of pleasure jolt through him like an electric current. He wanted to fucking devour her.

He backed her up until her legs hit the bed and tumbled her back. She bent her knees and pulled him on top of her so his hips nestled perfectly between them.

Any doubts he might have had about how much she wanted this turned to dust as she rocked her hips, grinding against the pillar of his cock so he could feel how hot and wet she was even through the layers of their clothing. His balls tightened and he shuddered, felt a spurt of liquid bead on the tip of his dick and he struggled not to come.

He shifted back to ease the friction and bent his head to capture the tip of one breast in his mouth, groaning as the taste and feel of her exploded in his brain. He sucked, bit, licked at her breasts, barely hearing her moans over the roaring in his head.

Her nipples were dark pink, shiny wet when he lifted his head, and her breasts bore faint red marks from where his stubble had rubbed the tender skin. Krista curved her hand around the back of his neck and pulled his mouth down to hers.

"This is crazy," she panted against his mouth as her hands swept up and down his back and sides, rubbing herself against him like she couldn't get her fill of him any more than he could of her.

No shit, it was crazy, the way the heat exploded between them until he thought he would spontaneously combust.

But nothing was crazier than the fact that it was Krista of all people who would put every sense on high alert, to let loose the rush of lust and bring his libido roaring back to life. Right now his brain wasn't capable of dissecting the fucked-up psychology behind that, analyzing all the reasons why getting in deeper with her on any level was a really bad idea.

Not with all the blood in his body pulsing ferociously between his legs. Not with—holy shit—her hot, smooth palm shoving down the front of his boxers, her fingers curving around his cock to squeeze. Sean let out a strangled groan and buried his face in her neck, sucking at the delicate skin as his hand slid inside the front of her pajamas.

His fingers pushed aside damp silk and slid over the plump folds of her sex. Her clit was a firm little bud, begging to be stroked and flicked. She jumped and shuddered and gave his cock an answering squeeze. He wrestled for control as he slid his hand lower, needing to feel her tight and wet around him. He slid his finger in, and Jesus, she was so fucking wet, drenching his hand in a rush of desire. And tight, her muscles rippling around his finger. So tight he would have to be damn careful at first when he fucked her, easing in slowly to get her used to his size before he rode her hard like he wanted to.

In the next breath, disaster struck. Just the thought of replacing his finger with his dick, combined with the way Krista moaned and stroked his cock in answer, was enough to send Sean over the edge, so fast and furious he couldn't stop it no matter how hard he tried.

His climax thundered through him, and he shuddered against her as his cock pulsed in her hand. His eyes squeezed shut, his whole body clenched as he spilled hotly on the smooth skin of her stomach.

Humiliation rushed through him, chasing away the last wave of agonizing pleasure. He jerked his hand out of her pants and rolled away, yanking his boxers up to cover himself. He sat on the edge of the bed, head bent, unable to even look at her as she lay there stunned.

"It's okay," she said. In the same breath he said, "I'm sorry."

He flinched away from the tentative caress on his back. He shoved himself up on wobbly legs, desperate to get away from her, the harsh panting of her breath, the heat emanating from her skin, the scent of her unfulfilled need.

He stood with his back to her, bracing himself on the dresser across the room, and he heard her swallow heavily and shift on the bed. "I guess I'll go clean up," she murmured, and he felt his face flush with another wave of embarrassment.

He didn't move until he heard the bathroom door click shut behind him. He'd come so hard his muscles were still twitching as he yanked the stiff store-bought jeans up his legs. The rough fabric rasped the gash on his leg and he grasped onto the pain, focusing on it as he cursed himself up one side and down the other for what had just happened.

What the fuck was he thinking? He hadn't, and that was the problem—he'd touched her cheek and—bam— the little head had taken over for the big head and he was a goner. He'd had almost no trouble shutting everything out, shutting himself down in the entire time he was in prison and in the months since he'd been released.

He'd had no trouble controlling his emotions and impulses, had convinced himself they'd all but disappeared.

And then she showed up and proved to him again just how little control he really had. Why? Why of all people was she the only one who could bring the world into sharp focus, make him feel in a way he hadn't been able to feel—hadn't *wanted* to feel in more than three years?

Make him so crazy that even when they were running for their lives, he couldn't resist the temptation to reach out and touch and taste until he was losing control, going off like a horny thirteen-year-old before he could even get inside her.

He wished he could brush off his loss of control as a logical response to three-plus years of celibacy. But that would be bullshit, and he knew it. Convicted felon or no, he'd had plenty of opportunities to break the seal and hadn't had a lick of interest in any one of them. There was something about Krista and only Krista that made her— and his body's response to her—unique.

Special.

He shoved the word aside before it had time to fully form in his head.

His whole body burned as he heard the shower running

behind the closed bathroom door. No doubt she was washing him off her. As humiliating as it was to lose control like that, Sean told himself it was a good thing. Like his body had gotten off a warning shot before he'd succeeded in doing something colossally stupid.

As if nearly being run off the side of a cliff and getting shot at and framed for killing a police officer wasn't proof enough that Krista Slater was trouble, what had just happened here proved that she was dangerous to him in a way he never could have imagined.

Krista stood under the cold shower spray long after the evidence of Sean's release was scrubbed from her belly and goose bumps covered her skin. When she started to shiver uncontrollably, she figured she'd better get out before hypothermia set in, but she was in no hurry to face Sean.

Not that he wanted anything to do with her either, from the way he'd rolled away and jumped off the bed right after he'd gotten off. She could understand that he was embarrassed. He was a guy—and not just any guy. Bigger, tougher, with about double the testosterone of your average Joe and an ego to match. Of course he didn't want to lose control in the bedroom.

And never so dramatically.

Krista tried to ignore the spurt of warmth that flooded her core even as her teeth chattered from her obviously futile cold shower. But there it was—he'd gotten off and she hadn't, and now she was drawn tight as a bow, restless, nervy, like her skin was about two sizes too small for her body.

Almost desperate enough to march out there and demand her turn. And she might have, might have tried to make him forget his embarrassment with her hands and lips and everything else had his embarrassment not been accompanied by something even more powerful, even more devastating.

Revulsion.

She'd felt it like a physical force when he'd flinched away from her touch. Once the fog of lust had died down, he'd realized whom he was with, who had made him lose control in such a basic, primal way, and he was disgusted. With himself, with her.

And goddamn it, even that knowledge wasn't enough to banish the need curled so tightly inside of her that it nearly hurt. She considered taking matters into her own hands, so to speak, but the idea struck her as too pathetic, and in the end she knew it would leave her feeling only more depressed and unsatisfied than before.

She couldn't stay in the bathroom forever, so she pulled her pajamas back on and reminded herself that she faced off against the scum of the earth and their even scummier lawyers every day.

She could stand up against a lone man, even if that man was out there kicking his own ass for touching her.

She strode out of the bathroom with as much poise as a woman who was wearing pajamas and whose teeth were chattering could muster and reached for one of the phones. It was time to take action and get them out of this because God only knew what trouble they were going to get into if they stayed in close quarters for a second longer.

"You can't make any calls until we activate it," Sean snapped. "And even then, I don't want you making any calls. Not yet."

He'd put on pants, she noticed. And though there were ruddy streaks across both cheekbones, his gaze, when he met hers, showed no embarrassment, no remorse, only challenge.

So he was going to pretend the last ten minutes didn't happen. Worked fine for her. "We're stuck in the middle of nowhere with a stolen car and limited cash. Eventually we're going to need help."

"We already talked about this. No calls until I can figure some things out."

At this point Krista was desperate for some information from the outside. "I thought the point of the cell phones is that they're untraceable."

Sean shook his head. "I'm not totally up on cell phone technology, but I think the point is that the phone isn't registered to you. But if whoever's after you is checking the phone records of people you're likely to call, it's possible they could trace the phone back here."

"You don't know that for sure," Krista said.

"After what happened tonight, you really want to take a chance?"

Krista blew out a tired breath. "I know I can't call Mark, but let me call the investigator I'm working with. I didn't tell anyone I'm working with him, and even if someone did know, he's got so many sketchy sources he must get dozens of random calls a day. Our call wouldn't raise an eyebrow even if someone thought to monitor his phone." Sean wasn't arguing so she pressed on. "He's the one who found the information about the bank account. He's the one who got Jimmy to talk to me—"

"And how do you know this guy?"

"I've known him for years, from the time I joined the

prosecutor's office. He's worked on a bunch of cases for us and has contacts in all the departments—"

Sean's eyes narrowed. "So he couldn't be deeper in the system unless he was a cop himself?"

Krista's shoulders slumped as she sagged on the side of the bed. Though she had no doubts about Kowalsky, she could see where this was going. "Actually, Kowalsky worked in narcotics for fifteen years before he went private."

"No fucking way."

Krista tried one more time. "But he's working this case as a favor to me. If he wanted to tip someone off, he could have done it weeks ago when we first started digging. He's the one who found the information about the bank transfers and got Jimmy to agree to talk to me—"

"Jimmy who 'killed himself' "—Sean's long fingers crooked to make air quotes—"before he could tell you anything, and you don't think your friend could have had anything to do with that? Maybe he didn't tip anyone off until he found out there was information worth knowing."

Krista's mouth pulled tight in frustration. She didn't believe for a second Kowalsky could be dirty, but at least Sean was entertaining the idea that Jimmy's death might not have been self-inflicted. "That makes no sense. If Stew didn't want me to find anything, he could have buried the information."

"Or someone could have found out he was working with you and convinced him to spill what he'd found."

His arms were folded across his broad chest, chin tilted at a stubborn angle. He wasn't going to budge on this. No way was he going near anyone who had even a whiff of law enforcement on him. After everything he'd been through, tonight and the years leading up to it, she couldn't say his mistrust of the justice system was poorly motivated.

And the one cop they knew they could trust wasn't an option because Sean didn't want his sister anywhere near this.

Krista couldn't blame him for that either. Which left them in their stalemate. "So we're back to square one. Cops chasing us, limited cash, stolen car, and no one to help us figure out what the hell is going on."

Sean's dark brows pulled into a frown and he reached out to pick up the phone. "I know someone who might be able to help us." But the tight clench of his shoulders and the muscle pulsing in his jaw told Krista this wasn't a favor he was looking forward to cashing in.

"Thought I might be hearing from you. It's been a long time, man."

Tomas "Tommy" Ibarra's familiar raspy drawl crackled through the speaker of the disposable phone, sounding remarkably alert even though it was the middle of the night.

Ibarra had been in the same class in Army Ranger school as Sean, Jimmy, and Nate. Sean hadn't been as tight with Ibarra as he'd been with the other two, not that anyone had been able to call Ibarra a close friend.

Ibarra was a good man and an excellent soldier, but for the most part he kept to himself. He was an expert in communications and navigation and Sean knew he could depend on Ibarra as much as anyone else in his company to have his back. Sometimes he would go out with the group if they had a furlough, but even then he'd sit off to the side, back to the wall, nursing his one drink as he kept a careful eye on the crowd.

When he'd left the army about a year ago, Ibarra had moved back near his family but traded in the family business of sheep ranching for the expertise with electronics and telecommunications he'd developed and honed while in the army.

Now he was living in a house that was rumored to be a virtual bunker, off the grid, developing high-end communication and surveillance systems that were virtually undetectable for his government and civilian customers.

Sean hadn't heard from Ibarra at all until he'd gotten out of prison. But unlike so many of his army buddies who'd crawled out of the woodwork to congratulate him and apologize for not getting in touch sooner—basically saying, without words, *Sorry I thought you were guilty, man*—Ibarra had sent a terse e-mail:

Sorry you got fucked by the system. Sorry I let it happen. If you're ever in a jam again, call this number.

Though Sean had dismissed the e-mail like all the other messages with a mental *fuck-off* to another fairweather friend, something had made him memorize that phone number. Thank God he had, because if anyone knew how to gather intel while staying invisible, it was Ibarra.

Now Sean was hoping he could help them figure out who the hell was behind the hit while making sure he and Krista stayed under the radar of the police and whoever the hell else was involved.

"Got myself in a bit of a situation," Sean said. He was sitting on the end of one of the double beds, trying not to stare at Krista's butt through the clingy fabric of her pajama bottoms as she paced restlessly around the room. She'd been agitated from the second he told her about Ibarra and tried to convince him yet again that they should at least contact Cole before anyone else.

He hadn't even bothered to argue as he'd dialed Ibarra's number.

"Sounds like exciting times in Richland, Washington."

Sean felt the bottom of his stomach drop out.

Ibarra's laugh rasped through the phone as though he could read Sean's mind. "Don't worry, man. I only know because I have specialized equipment, but that should tell you how easy those disposables are to track if you know what you're looking for."

"I figured that if the cops are involved, they might be monitoring people we're likely to call. I don't think you're exactly on their radar."

"I'm not on anybody's radar, and that's the way I like it. Now tell me what you're dealing with."

Sean gave him a quick rundown on Krista's cryptic phone call with Jimmy, the questions about Jimmy's suicide, and everything that had gone down after Krista had shown up at his door.

"Meet me at the gas station just off the Bottle Bay exit on Highway Ninety Five, before you hit the bridge. Should take you about three and a half hours to get here, so call me when you get on the road so I know when to look for you. I'll see what I can dig up in the meantime."

As much as Sean had thought he'd written off his former brothers-in-arms, it felt good to have one at his back again. "Thanks, Ibarra."

"Least I can do. Get some sleep. You're going to need it."

Stew Kowalsky checked his watch as he waited for the files from Nate Brewster to transfer to his online backup service. "Come on," he muttered as he watched the status bar. He was supposed to meet an informant in fifteen minutes, but it would take him at least twenty to get across town, even with the light Saturday morning traffic. It wasn't like Meester would have anyplace else to go, but he'd sounded a little tweaky when he'd called Stew to tell him he had some information to pass on about a case Stew was working on for the PA's office. Paranoid and agitated, Meester would scurry off like a rat at the slightest sign that things weren't going right.

Finally the files finished backing up and he switched off his computer. Normally he would have just left the computer in the office and let the automatic backup happen while he was out, but this whole case with Krista had him spooked. Even though he hadn't found anything that gave them a solid lead, he didn't want to risk losing a single byte of information.

He double-checked the lock on his office and did a quick scan of the empty hallway before he headed out.

At first, he'd been happy to do a little work on the side for Deputy PA Slater. Despite the Slasher debacle and the discovery that Sean Flynn had been framed, Slater was still Prosecuting Attorney Benson's golden child and doing good work for her meant Stew would stay on the short list of investigators contracted by the PA's office to assist in ongoing investigations.

Not to mention, Slater wasn't exactly hard on the eyes, and Stew would be lying to himself if he didn't admit to hoping that maybe one of these times they could have a meeting in person, over drinks or ideally dinner, and move their interaction beyond strictly professional.

But then the shit hit the fan after Jimmy Caparulo's apparent suicide two days ago. Going against all protocol, Caparulo's body had already been released for cremation—without an autopsy. This despite the fact that there were footprints in the dirt outside Jimmy's open window and there was some debate about whether there was enough gunpowder residue on Jimmy's hands to prove he'd fired the gun himself.

Stew had found out all that the morning after Jimmy's death. In the two days since, all of Stew's sources inside the department and the ME's office had clammed up.

And if that hadn't signaled to him that he and Krista were onto something, the news report that Krista might have been kidnapped by Sean Flynn after he'd shot a sheriff's deputy sure as hell rang some alarm bells.

No wonder she hadn't answered any of his calls when he'd tried to reach her with the info about Jimmy.

He wished Krista had talked to him before she'd gone to see Flynn on her own. Stew could have gone in her place, or at least gone with her. Though he smelled something fishy in the story being splashed all over the news, there was no guarantee Flynn hadn't gone off the deep end and taken Krista hostage out of revenge.

If that wasn't the case and the story was a cover for something else, that meant they were onto something big. And Krista was in some deep shit.

And he could be, too, if the wrong people found out Stew was helping her.

So far nothing had happened, but he'd had that creepy tingle between his shoulder blades for the past two days that had him constantly on guard.

Even though he had case files piled up and dozens of clients waiting for reports, something in his gut told him that as soon as his meeting with Meester was over, it might not be a bad idea to head out for an extended vacation in some undisclosed location until this whole thing blew over.

He took the stairs down to the parking garage under his building. On weekends it was nearly deserted. There were only four cars besides his SUV. A sudden wave of paranoia hit him and sent his heart racing. He gave the garage a quick scan, paying particular attention to the shadowy corners, but he didn't see or hear anything. He clicked his key fob to unlock his car and slid his hand inside his jacket to rest on the butt of the Glock 20 10mm he had tucked inside a shoulder holster.

He had just reached his car when he felt the air stir behind him. A hand closed over his throat from behind and before Stew could firm his grip on the gun he felt the icy sting of the blade as it slid in below his sternum.

Chapter 9

Despite her exhaustion, Krista spent a restless night in between the cheap scratchy sheets of the hotel room, too keyed up to sleep.

She couldn't shut off her brain, which raced with questions and scenarios of who was after them and why. Of course it had something to do with the little information she'd uncovered about Nate Brewster, along with whatever else Jimmy Caparulo was planning to tell her before he died. That much was obvious.

It was clear she and Stew had homed in on something, but what? She barely knew anything—yet. What the hell was she getting so close to that it was worth killing not only her but also Sean? Who, she acknowledged with no small amount of guilt, was looking more and more like an innocent bystander in all of this, and not the source of key information that was going to lead her anywhere.

And the even scarier question was, who was behind this? Karev? Maybe. But as powerful as he was in the local mafia, Krista wasn't sure he had the capability to track every move and infiltrate law enforcement, backing them into a corner, ensuring they had nowhere to turn.

She curled herself around the knot in her stomach,

praying Sean's faith in his former army buddy wasn't misplaced.

And her sleep wasn't helped by the fact that she was hyperaware of Sean, only a few feet away from her in the dark, though it might as well have been miles. After he'd talked to his friend, he'd told her that they better get some sleep and turned off the lamp over his bed without another word. Turning his back to her, he pulled the sheet and blanket up over his head, and within minutes she heard his breathing reverberating through the room.

His even breaths were like nails on a chalkboard as Krista lay there, vibrating with unfulfilled desire, itchy and restless. Every exhale, every shift of his big body against the sheets echoed in the room like a gunshot, snapping her awake each time she started to fall asleep.

She finally fell into a fitful half sleep full of dreams that morphed the hotel room into a prison cell where a guard came in to retrieve her only to pull out a gun. Jimmy Caparulo was there, too, saying that he had something to tell her, but before she could get to him, the prison guard was shooting at them both.

Then Sean was there, yelling at her, pulling her out of the way, telling her it was going to be okay.

She jerked awake to find him leaning over her, roughly shaking her shoulder as he shouted at her to wake up. Her hands came up to clutch at his arms and only the realization that this wasn't part of the dream kept her from hurling herself into his arms and burying her head against the warm wall of his chest until her heartbeat slowed down.

He jerked away and told her they were leaving in ten minutes. "It's already almost noon and we need to get moving."

She staggered to the bathroom, splashed cold water on her face, and slipped on her glasses. Even the thought of subjecting her gravelly eyes to contact lenses made her wince. Unfortunately, the heavy frames did nothing to hide the giant circles or the puffy lids.

Three and a half hours later, she wasn't looking any better, she thought as she stared at her pale, strained face in the restroom of the gas station Ibarra had chosen as the meeting point.

She washed her hands, wincing at the icy bite of the water, telling herself it didn't matter how crappy she looked. It wasn't like she was trying to impress Sean. But that didn't stop her from pinching her cheeks and biting her lips to get a little more color in them.

She slid back into the passenger's seat and closed the door behind her. Sean was tuning the radio dial, listening intently through the static. Krista rubbed her hands in front of the feeble stream of warm air blowing from the vents of the stolen SUV.

"Are you sure he's coming?" Krista asked. They'd already been waiting for forty-five minutes. "I thought you agreed on the meeting time."

Sean held up his hand for silence and turned up the volume on the radio. The newscaster's voice popped in and out, so Krista could understand only about every other word. "Flynn...seen...west....Tacoma....dangerous...condition...Slater..."

A faint smile pulled at Sean's lips as he turned off the radio. "Tommy will be here. He already came through for us."

As though on cue, a beat-up Jeep Wrangler pulled into a space two slots down from them. The driver's side door

opened and a man climbed out. Sean opened and shut his
door as he went out to meet him.

Krista frowned. The way Sean had talked about his
friend he'd made him sound like a computer nerd, a guy
who spent most of his time behind a monitor or in his lab
as he developed cutting-edge communication and surveillance devices.

Based on her view from the passenger's seat window,
Tomas Ibarra didn't look like any computer geek she'd
ever seen. Dressed in heavy work boots, worn denim, and
a fleece pullover, he was a couple inches shorter than
Sean but his shoulders were just as wide. Dark glasses hid
his eyes and a dark-brown goatee covered a strong chin.

He and Sean greeted each other with a manly half
hug and slaps on the back. With their tall, rangy builds,
chiseled features, and a don't-mess-with-me attitude surrounding them like an aura, it wasn't hard to imagine
them dressed in fatigues and full combat gear ready to
take any enemy, no matter how fierce.

She felt the tension coiling in her spine ease a degree
as she realized that with these two on her side, maybe she
had a chance of getting out of this mess alive.

Though whether Sean was on her side was still de-
batable if the narrow look he shot at her was any indication. He'd been hostile and close-mouthed ever since
their...incident.

Krista didn't know what else to call it.

But Sean had been avoiding her, as much as it was possible to avoid someone sharing the same tiny hotel room
and within the confines of a car, anyway. Other than their
argument about whom to call and a few words after she'd
woken up late this morning, he'd all but ignored her, as

though he was afraid he'd get contaminated just by talking to her.

Now as she climbed out of the SUV to meet Ibarra and find out for herself how he thought he could help them, she felt Sean's hard stare boring into her. Ibarra slipped off his sunglasses and hooked them over the neck of his fleece, and Krista fought the urge to squirm under the combined intensity of their gazes.

But while Sean kept his look carefully blank, Ibarra's curious stare had a hint of warmth as he studied her. Then, as though he approved of something, he gave a quick nod and took a step forward.

"Tomas Ibarra," he said quietly as his big hand all but swallowed hers up.

"Krista Slater," she replied. She met his stare with her own patented cool gaze, the one she used to make sure no one—not the lowlifes on trial, their smarmy attorneys, not even her colleagues in the PA office who secretly rejoiced in her failures—got it in their head to mess with her. "I hope you can help us. Sean seems to think you can."

Instead of taking offense, Ibarra smiled at her frosty tone. White teeth gleamed against his dark beard and tanned skin, and even as cold, exhausted, and scared out of her mind as Krista was, she'd have to be blind—no, dead—not to notice how attractive he was.

Yet it was the surly man who glared at her and snapped "Mind if we get going?" who made her stomach flip every time she looked at him.

Krista climbed up into the Wrangler, shivering as she braced herself for a cold ride to wherever they were going. Though the afternoon sun beat down on the mountain peaks, at this elevation, a sharp chill hung in the air. Despite the temperature, Ibarra had removed the top of his Jeep, leaving him and his passengers exposed to the elements.

"What about the SUV?" Krista asked, practically yelling over the sound of the engine and the wind whipping around them as he pulled out of the gas station. "Shouldn't we do something before the police find it?"

"You swapped out the plates, didn't you?" Ibarra called to Sean, who nodded.

"Even if anyone notices it here, which isn't likely, by the time the cops bother to check the plates against the serial numbers you two will be long gone."

The whipping wind and roar of the engine precluded any conversation on a drive that was mercifully short. Nevertheless, by the time they pulled off the highway and onto a single-lane dirt road, Krista was shivering so hard her muscles were starting to ache.

Ibarra pulled the Jeep up to a heavy wooden gate and punched a code into the keypad. The Jeep barely cleared the gate before it slammed shut behind them. Ibarra must have noticed her jump. "I have it programmed to shut fast so no one can sneak in behind. My mom hates it," he said and she could see the flash of his grin in the rearview mirror. "The last time she came up here the gate almost took off the back end of her truck."

"Your parents are close?" she asked.

"They're about five miles farther up the road. They still live on the ranch my great-grandfather started when he moved over here."

Within a few yards the wooded drive opened up to reveal a sleek, modern-style house featuring a lot of heavy wood beams, natural stone, and glass. Though it wasn't overly large, it was architecturally stunning, designed to blend in with the mountain scenery even as it was built to take advantage of the natural beauty of the surroundings.

Sean had mentioned something about Ibarra being off the grid, and she noted the solar panels that lined the south-facing slope of the roof. "So you're able to power the whole house on solar?" she asked through chattering teeth.

Ibarra nodded as he led them up the front stairs and typed a code into another keypad to unlock the front door. "Mostly. Part of the reason I always had my eye on this property is the geothermal activity in this area. What the solar panels don't collect, the hot springs and hydroelectric power make up for."

A hot spring sounded heavenly right now, Krista thought as her body gave another violent shudder.

"Can we skip the alternative-energy lesson for the time being and get a cup of coffee into her before she turns into a Popsicle?" Sean snapped as he guided Krista through the door.

"You should be grateful for the fact that all that alternative energy means this place is virtually untraceable," Ibarra said with the bare hint of an edge to his voice.

Nevertheless, within minutes Krista was huddled in front of a woodstove, soaking in the heat it was throwing off. She heard heavy footsteps and looked up to see Sean next to her with a cup of coffee. "Thanks," she said, sighing in pleasure as she wrapped her hands around the hot mug.

Sean grunted something indistinguishable and stomped back into the kitchen. She focused on Ibarra, who was giving her a look that made her feel like a bug under a microscope. Something about his attitude bothered her, an unflappable confidence that danced a little too close to arrogance for her taste. She lifted her chin, hoping a dose of attitude might throw him off his game. "It's great you can use natural resources to fuel the house, but unless you're a full-on survivalist, which you're clearly not, there's no such thing as untraceable. What about property records, taxes, stuff like that? And even without electricity, you're running your own business here. There's no way to do that without phones, Internet, all the other utilities."

Ibarra handed Sean a cup of coffee and poured one for himself. If he was annoyed by her questions, he didn't show it. "The property is registered under an anonymous LLC and as for the other stuff…let's just say it's my business to find ways to work around traditional communication systems." He paused and took a sip of his coffee. "Look, anyone who lives around here knows who I am and where I live, but on the unlikely chance someone tries to connect me to Sean, they're going to have a hell of a lot harder time finding me than most people."

"And we appreciate the fact that you're helping us," Sean said, challenging her with his stare.

"I'm sorry if I sound ungrateful," Krista said, feeling a hot sting of shame. "I do appreciate that you're willing to help us, especially considering that I got us all into this mess and have no idea where this ends."

She hated the pathetic tone in her voice. She had learned early not to show weakness to anyone. But she'd never been through anything like the last twenty-four hours.

How the hell had she ended up here, on the run from the police and God knew who else, her life in the hands of two men she barely knew? One of whom had every reason to hate her.

What happened back in that hotel room notwithstanding.

She squeezed her eyes shut against the sting of tears.

Strong. She had to be strong. Spine straight, chin up, show no weakness or they'll go in for the kill.

Quiet footsteps approached and a heavy hand squeezed her shoulder. She knew it was Sean even before she opened her eyes, recognized the woodsy scent of him even as her body heated at his touch. She looked up, her stomach flipping over as her eyes met his.

The angry unease that had clouded his gaze all day had disappeared. In one look she saw that he knew exactly what she was feeling. As she met his steady stare, she felt a sense of calm flow through her, as though he was transferring some of his strength and composure to her body.

Krista gave Sean a tiny smile of thanks and he moved away to take a seat in a leather armchair across from the woodstove.

Ibarra flipped on the flat-panel TV mounted on the opposite wall. He gave a low whistle. "Damn, they just can't get enough of you two. You're still the lead story on the local news," Ibarra said.

Krista grimaced as yet another reporter regurgitated the cop killer kidnapping angle, and then she felt her stomach flip as the newscaster announced, "Members of Flynn's family refused to comment, but earlier today, Kimberly Stevens from our Seattle affiliate was able to speak to Slater's father, renowned defense attorney John Slater, as well as her colleague, Seattle prosecuting attorney Mark Benson."

Krista's chest squeezed as her father and Mark appeared together on screen. Mark looked exhausted, his face deeply lined, his eyes red-rimmed as though he hadn't slept in days. "We are of course incredibly worried about Krista. All we want is to get her home, safe and unharmed." Guilt assaulted her at the thought of what Mark must be going through. He would be out of his mind with worry. To Krista, the idea of Sean hurting her was preposterous. But as far as Mark knew, she'd been kidnapped by a former convict with a serious grudge.

She watched as Mark stepped aside so her father could speak. His appearance shocked her. In her entire lifetime, she'd never seen him less than perfectly dressed and put together. But today his suit was rumpled as though he'd slept in it, and his eyes, like Mark's, were red-rimmed. And, she realized as she took a closer look, damp? With tears?

"Krista," he said, his voice choking on her name. "If you can see this, know that we love you so much. And we're praying for you to get home safe. And Flynn, if you're watching, I know she seems tough, but she's still my little girl." He broke off and held his hand to his mouth as though he couldn't go on.

There was a queer twisting in her stomach. A cynical part of her wanted to dismiss it as grandstanding for the cameras—Lord knew her father could put on a show for the courtroom—but the grayish cast to his skin and the deep lines carved in his face told her this wasn't purely for show. And to be fair, they didn't see eye to eye on a lot of things, but she knew deep down her father loved her. As much as he was capable of loving anyone, anyway.

"I need to get in touch with them," she said to Ibarra. "Just to let them know I'm okay." She looked to Sean, who was staring at the TV screen, which now displayed his mug shot, his face hard and unreadable. "And to tell them they're wrong about Sean."

Sean's gaze flicked first to her and then to Ibarra. "Do you have a way to call out that won't be traced?"

"Why don't we go in my office," Ibarra said, rising from his chair and motioning them to follow him down a short hallway. The room was all windows on one side, showcasing the view of the mountains and capitalizing on the natural light. A sleek desk dominated the center of the room and three high-definition flat-panel screens were mounted on one wall. One was a news feed, the other a satellite map of the region, and the third was dark.

Several phones were lined up on the desk like an arsenal. Ibarra picked one up, switched it on, and handed it to Sean.

"It's a COMSAT Planet-1," Ibarra explained. "Totally secure, totally untraceable, so well encrypted even the CIA can't hack into it," Ibarra said.

Krista didn't know him that well, but she thought she heard a hint of boastfulness in his tone. Boys and their toys.

Krista nodded politely, trying not to glaze over as Ibarra went through a detailed description of all the tweaks he'd done on the sat phone to boost the connectivity.

Sean's voice jerked her out of her daze. "If your goal is to get into her pants, I don't think the high-tech nerd talk is going to do it."

Krista shot him a glare and felt her face heat with embarrassment. With her pale skin, dark under-eye circles, and librarian glasses she didn't kid herself she was getting second looks from anyone.

"Can't blame a guy for trying," Ibarra replied.

Flustered, Krista quickly dialed her father at home, relieved when no one answered. "Dad, it's me, Krista. I just want you to know I'm okay, and I'm not in any danger from Sean." Not physical anyway, but that was another can of worms she didn't want to open right now.

Mark answered his cell on the second ring.

"It's Krista," she said. Even his cautious hello was enough to offer a small degree of comfort as her life spun out of control.

"My God! Where are you? Are you safe?"

"I'm okay. I'm with Sean. We're—" She stopped short as Sean jerked the phone out of her hand and covered the mouthpiece.

"Don't you fucking dare tell him where we are."

The ferocity in Sean's tone made her take a step back. "What if he can help us?"

"What if he's in on it?" Sean countered. "Until we know whom we're up against, the only person in law enforcement we trust is my brother-in-law. Is that clear?"

Everything in her rebelled at the idea of Mark's involvement. Yet she knew if she went against Sean on this, he'd take it as a betrayal. And since she'd dragged him into this quagmire with him, she owed him her allegiance at the very least. She nodded and reached for the phone. "I'm okay, Mark. That's all I can tell you right now. And Sean didn't kill that deputy, and he didn't kidnap me." Her gaze locked with Sean, who was staring at her through slitted green eyes. "In fact, he's the only reason I'm alive right now."

Krista's words and that steady look in her eyes sent a weird, twisty feeling into Sean's chest. There was gratitude there, and trust. And though he told himself he shouldn't give a shit, something about the idea that Krista truly trusted him to keep her safe, and not just because she had no one else to turn to, mattered. Mattered a hell of a lot more than it should.

Everything about her drew him in as though she had a gravitational pull that worked only on him. He looked at her, searching for a flaw, a glitch, something to turn him off, and came up empty. Even pale and drawn, her face wiped clean of any trace of makeup, the creaminess of her skin and the clean lines of her bone structure couldn't be concealed.

He even liked the heavy-framed glasses perched on her delicate nose.

As he watched, she lifted her hand to stifle a yawn. She had to be exhausted after hardly sleeping the night before. He knew because he hadn't slept either.

Which didn't make any goddamn sense, since his years in the military had trained him to catch sleep whenever he could, regardless of the circumstances. In his lifetime, he'd fallen asleep with mortar fire and gunshots wailing in the background and dozed against a rock as they waited to intercept the enemy.

He'd even managed to sleep in the hell of his twenty-by-twenty cell, despite the harsh twenty-four/seven illumination provided by the fluorescent panels in the ceiling.

But put Krista Slater in a bed three feet away from him and he started at every creak of a bedspring, every shift of the sheets. He'd lain there hoping the deep, even breaths he forced himself to take would cool his overheated blood.

He lay as still as a statue, afraid if he moved so much

as a muscle he'd launch himself across the short span sep-
arating them and finish what he'd started.

The release that had been so powerful it nearly blew
the top of his head off had offered no relief. Even though
the thought of how he'd come in her hand like a thirteen-
year-old getting his first hand job made him sick with
humiliation, his body clearly viewed it as an appetizer,
something to take the edge off before he indulged in the
main course. Which he craved so fiercely he'd spent most
of the night shaking and sweating and reminding himself
of all the reasons he couldn't let his irrational attraction
to Krista go any further.

Something in his wiring had gotten seriously fucked
up.

He shook it off and reached to take the phone from
Krista. "I want to call Cole," he said. "By now he and
Megan have to have seen the news, too, and at this point
someone's going to have to lock her up to keep her from
trying to come after me herself."

His fingers clenched around the phone as he hesitated.
Up until now he hadn't let himself think too hard about
what his sister might be going through, knowing he
couldn't afford the distraction.

Now his gut roiled with anxiety and guilt over the
thought of how stressed out Megan must be. They were
already overprotective of each other. Him, because he
was her big brother and had taken it on as his personal
mission to look after her after their parents died when
Sean was thirteen and Megan only eleven. Though their
maternal grandparents had taken them in, loved them, and
provided for them, their old age and grief over losing
their youngest child meant that Sean and Megan felt like

outsiders, always aware that their grandparents' house wasn't really their home.

Always close, Sean and Megan had bonded even closer together, realizing that after all they'd been through, no one else on the planet would ever know them or understand them like each other, and no matter how close you got to your friends, you could never trust anyone to have your back like a brother or sister.

Yeah, Sean had learned in the most brutal way possible that no matter how much you loved and trusted your friends, no one ever had your back like family.

Megan had been the only one who'd stood by him, publicly proclaiming his innocence and doing everything she could to prove Sean hadn't murdered Evangeline Gordon.

Now in one of life's odd twists, Megan was engaged to Detective Cole Williams, the cop who had originally arrested Sean for murder.

But Sean couldn't really hold that against the man, not when the detective had saved Megan from a brutal killer.

Between that and the fact that Cole loved his sister as much as it was possible for a man to love a woman and was almost single-handedly responsible for putting Megan's smile back on her face negated any mistakes of the past, even a whopper like arresting Sean for murder.

After everything he'd already put her through, it pained Sean to think of Megan wasting a single extra calorie worrying about him. He knew her, knew she had to be going out of her mind with worry, and he hoped Ibarra could help him make contact. He not only needed to reassure her; he had to convince her not to go off half cocked and put herself in danger. After what had happened with Nate, Sean knew there were no limits to how far his sister would go to help him.

As he dialed, he hoped this time Megan would keep herself well away from Sean's mess.

"Williams," Cole answered.

"Cole, it's Sean."

"Hold on. Let me get someplace private." There were a few seconds of silence on the other end. "What the hell is going on?"

Sean gave him a recap of everything that had happened. Cole, to his credit, listened silently and took it all in without interrupting.

"Where are you?" Cole asked when Sean had wrapped up.

"I can't tell you that. But for now, we're safe."

Cole bit out a curse. "You have every cop west of the Mississippi looking for you. They think you killed one of their own and took Krista hostage. Anyone finds you, they're going to shoot first and ask questions later. I can help you. There are people you can trust—"

Sean didn't let him get any further. "No fucking way. I don't want you getting any closer to this."

"I'm already ass deep in it, or did you forget I'm the one who let Talia Vega slip through our net after she admitted she knew more about what was going on at Club One than she let on. I've been trying to work on it behind the scenes, but I've had to be really careful not to let anyone in on it. Missing person or not, there's a lot of pressure to keep this thing nailed shut."

Shit. He should have known Cole wouldn't have let it go, and even if he'd wanted to, Megan would be on him like white on rice to keep digging. "Please tell me Megan hasn't been moonlighting as a detective again."

"Only because I promised her I'd stay on top of it. But she's been out of her mind since she saw the news. She's telling anyone who will listen that it's all a horrible mistake, that she knows Nate Brewster was working with someone else, and that it's all connected."

Sean's stomach dropped to his knees. "Listen to me, Cole, whatever kind of hornet's nest Krista kicked over, these fuckers mean business. I don't want Megan anywhere close to this. I know you're a good cop and you want to get to the truth of this—"

"Nothing takes priority over Megan's safety," Cole said with the kind of conviction that could take down an empire. "I'll get her someplace safe. And keep her there," he said after a minute.

Sean smiled at that. Knowing his sister, Cole was going to be busier than a one-legged man in an ass-kicking contest. "Good luck with that."

"Did Krista discuss the case with anyone else?"

"She's right here. You can ask her yourself." She was hovering off his left elbow, arms wrapped around her waist as she shamelessly listened to Sean's side of the conversation.

She greeted Cole and then explained how she'd started her own outside investigation. "I know. It doesn't make any sense. No one wanted me to look into it either, even though—from what you told me anyway—Talia knew there were other people in on it." A few seconds of silence as Cole responded. "Yeah, I should have called you sooner. But I was getting flack, and I knew you'd already gotten in enough trouble over this case." More silence.

"Anyone who cares to look knows I was on site at Caparulo's suicide. I had to tell them it was related to an investigation. I suppose anyone can put two and two together...No, just Benson, because I was trying to convince him to officially reopen the investigation. And of course the investigator I've been working with...Stew Kowalski? You may know him because he's worked for us in an official—"

She broke off with a gasp and lifted her hand to her mouth. "Oh my God. When? Are they sure?"

"What?" Sean said in a harsh whisper.

Her face was so pale it was almost gray as she turned to him. "Cole said Stew Kowalski was found a few hours ago. He was stabbed to death in the parking garage of his office building."

Chapter 10

Krista struggled to keep the phone from slipping through her suddenly numb fingers. Her whole body went cold as all of the blood seemed to drain to her feet. She put the phone back to her ear and forced herself to put her emotions aside for the moment and get as much information from Cole as she could. "What happened?"

"It's not my case, but since Stew is friendly with the department, the details got around. You've heard about the knifepoint muggings going on in that neighborhood?"

"Several people have been wounded but no one's been killed."

"They're looking at Stew as the first fatality."

Krista sank down into a chair as her knees threatened to give out under her. "Do you buy that?"

Cole was silent a few seconds, torn between loyalty to his fellow officers and his deeply ingrained streak of skepticism. "All the other victims were stabbed from the front."

"Stew wasn't?"

"They haven't done the autopsy, but the initial report indicates that Stew appeared to have been surprised from behind. He had his gun on him and it was partially out of its holster when he was found, but otherwise there were no signs of struggle. The knife went up under his ribcage, straight through his diaphragm, and into his heart."

Krista swallowed back a surge of nausea. "That sounds like a professional hit."

"If I wasn't suspicious before, I sure as shit am now. Who knew he was working with you?"

Krista pressed the heel of her hand into her head. "I didn't tell anyone, but we weren't careful. If whoever's doing this can buy off a dirty cop miles outside of the city, they're probably capable of hacking into phone and e-mail records."

Cole bit out a curse.

Krista hesitated before asking the next question. She didn't want Cole—and by extension Megan—getting pulled into another mess stemming from Sean's case, but without Stew, Cole was her only reliable source of information. "Stew was following up on Jimmy Caparulo's death," she said. "Is there any way you can get me an update on that without putting yourself at risk?" For the most part, the Seattle Police Department kept close track of evidence and case files. It wasn't impossible, but it might be difficult for Cole to do any nosing around without attracting notice.

Cole's mirthless laugh crackled through the phone line. "Funny you should ask that. I just got an update yesterday morning. I was curious, for obvious reasons."

Krista's stomach knotted and she wondered if Cole had already inadvertently put himself and his fiancée in danger. What Cole said next made her jaw drop.

"The case has already been ruled a suicide and the body has been released for cremation."

Krista shot to her feet. "After less than three days? That's ludicrous. They can't have even performed an autopsy."

"They didn't."

"Who's in charge of the investigation?"

"Jorgensen."

Cole's former partner, who had been with him the night they'd arrested Sean. "I guess we know who we can't trust."

"Don't be so sure," Cole said. "Nick was beyond pissed when he found out, and if he wasn't, he gave an Academy Award–worthy performance. It came from the chief himself—he wants this case and anything remotely related to it closed up tight. Says the department's reputation has suffered enough and we don't need to give the press any more blood."

Krista rubbed at the back of her neck. "The PA's office is the same way. Benson considered the case closed and refused to reopen it. They just want it all to go away. I thought if Stew found something I could convince him otherwise."

"I'll get you whatever information I can on Caparulo. And if they're looking at Stew's death as a mugging, there's no reason to take anything from Stew's office as evidence. I could get in there, see if there's anything in his files—"

"Absolutely not," she said, though she knew it would mean nothing if Cole was determined to launch his own investigation. "I know you want the truth—hell, right now you're the only one besides me who wants to get to the bottom of this—but Sean's right. You've already been through hell, and I've seen what these people are capable of. They won't hesitate to come after you and Megan. You have to get her someplace safe."

"I don't like the idea of checking my balls and slinking away with my tail between my legs."

Krista looked at Sean and caught him staring at her with a thoughtful expression on his face. "I imagine you'd like it even less if something happened to the woman you love. Nate Brewster almost killed Megan once. Don't let the assholes he worked with finish what he started."

"Right," Cole bit out. "Now how do I get you whatever information I do have?"

Krista handed the phone to Ibarra, who went over a series of convoluted steps for Cole to follow to ensure he transferred the information in a way that would leave no digital footprints.

Krista moved in front of the glass wall and stared out over the mountains. Pink and purple streaked the sky as the sun fell behind the peaks, and she could see the first blinks of stars as the sky darkened.

As she took in the harsh beauty, the vast wilderness empty of humans, it seemed impossible to believe that there were people out there who were searching for her at this very second. Plotting to find her so they could silence her forever.

"Thank you," Sean said beside her.

"I can't imagine what for."

"Reminding Cole to keep his nose out of this and remember what's important."

"I don't want anyone else to get hurt. Especially not your sister."

"We're set," Ibarra said, coming to stand between them. "Your friend should have the files to me in a few hours, and I shouldn't have a problem tapping into the Seattle PD's network. And if Stew's computer is still in his office like Detective Williams thinks, as long as it's still connected to the Internet I'll be able to get in there and see if he knows anything the cops don't."

"Tapping into the PD's network?" Krista asked uneasily. "That sounds an awful lot like hacking into a law enforcement network, which is definitely a felony."

"So is stealing cars," Sean pointed out.

"That was necessary," Krista said through gritted teeth. And even knowing that didn't chase away the guilt clawing at her stomach.

"So is this," Sean said. "We need to know everything the police know, and since the only cop we can trust better be packing his bags as we speak and getting my sister somewhere safe, we have to be a little more creative about how we get it."

"Don't worry," Ibarra said. "I won't get caught. No one will ever know I was in there."

"Getting away with it isn't the point! The point is that you'll be breaking the law and we'll be accessories."

"And no one will ever know unless we tell them," Sean pointed out.

Ibarra settled in behind his computer and got to work. Krista slumped down on a chair and wrapped her arms around the rapidly growing lump in her stomach.

"I don't like this any more than you do," Sean said. Ibarra shot him a glare and made a *shushing* sound. Sean rolled his eyes, and when he spoke again his voice was pitched lower. "If you remember, I was minding my own business and being a law-abiding citizen before you showed up."

Like she needed that point hammered home again.

"Whatever these people started, Krista, we have to end it. Even if that means breaking the rules."

"My whole life is the rules. Don't you get it? I work hard. I try to do the right thing—I've never stolen so much as a pack of gum! I follow the letter of the law and work the system to put the bad guys in jail. I don't like having to be the bad guy!"

"Sometimes the system fails. And sometimes you have to break the rules to get what you want."

Sean watched Krista as she sat across the table picking listlessly at the sandwich she'd assembled from Ibarra's impressively stocked kitchen. The man might live in the middle of nowhere, but that didn't mean he subsisted on what was available at the local Stop & Shop.

But Krista had taken about half a bite before she put the sandwich down. Sean knew exactly what she was feeling. No amount of gourmet deli meats and artisanal bread could get past the lump that had no doubt formed in her gut or keep any morsel of food from turning into dust before she could choke it in.

He'd felt it, too, the first time he'd been in heavy combat. Felt that sick pit in his stomach that came from the knowledge that death was all around. He'd quickly learned, like everyone else in the battalion, to compartmentalize and not let the horror of whatever he'd been through interfere with attending to basic bodily needs like sleep and eating.

Despite the stress, Sean had no trouble polishing off two sandwich rolls piled high with real roast turkey, roasted red peppers, provolone, and some kind of fancy mustard and chased them down with a bottle of beer from a microbrewery in nearby Coeur D'Alene.

As he looked at Krista, her face pale, eyes shadowed with grief and regret, he felt another surge of unwanted sympathy. She liked to think her line of work had given her a tough hide, but right now she looked like she'd fall over if he so much as touched her.

"Why don't you go get some rest?" Sean said. "You look like you're about to collapse."

"There's one guest room, down the hall, first door on your left. Nothing fancy but the sheets are clean," Ibarra said around the last bite of his sandwich as he keyed something into his laptop. He shot a look at Sean. "You can take the couch, unless you want to share."

A hint of color rushed to Krista's cheeks. "Couch is fine," Sean said.

"Williams sent the police reports on Caparulo," Ibarra said as he turned the laptop around so they could see the screen. Sean uttered a silent prayer that Ibarra's subterfuge worked and Cole wouldn't get busted for sending electronic copies of the files.

"There's nothing there I don't know already," Krista said, disgust and disappointment barely edging out her fatigue. "The crime scene report doesn't even mention that the window to his bedroom was open." She let out a soft curse. "Maybe Stew found something else. How long will it take you to access his computer if it's online?"

"I've already done it," Ibarra said, "but it's going to take me awhile to sort through everything on his hard drive. Same thing with the queries I'm running on the bank accounts." He looked first at Krista and then at Sean.

"It's late. No reason for any of us to stay up and wait for the data to churn."

"I don't think I can sleep." Despite her obvious fatigue, her voice was laced with nervous tension.

"Then rest," Sean snapped. "Your body needs to recover. You won't do anyone any good if you collapse."

"Fine." Krista straightened up with a sigh and stretched so her hair tumbled down her back and her T-shirt tightened over the round fullness of her breasts.

Sean tore his gaze away and caught Ibarra staring at the same thing. His friend shrugged at Sean's glare.

Krista, oblivious, poured herself a glass of water at the kitchen sink and ambled down the hall, "Come get me if anything happens."

"That is one damn good-looking woman," Ibarra said, loud enough for Krista to hear if she cared to listen.

"She'd eat your balls for lunch," Sean snapped as he gathered up the empty plates and took them to the sink.

"Don't worry, man. I wouldn't try to horn in on your territory."

"For fuck's sake, did you forget that that woman helped put me on death row?"

Ibarra cocked a thick eyebrow at him. "You're gonna try to tell me that that mark on her neck came from the car accident?"

Sean's blood heated as he had a sudden, vivid memory of closing his lips and teeth over the delicate skin of her throat.

"People fall for each other across enemy lines all the time. Hell, I wouldn't be here if my great-grandfather had gone along with his father's plan for him to marry a nice Basque girl."

Somewhere in his tired, overstimulated brain were a thousand arguments to shut his friend down, but at the moment all he could come up with was "Shut up, Ibarra."

His friend laughed and clapped him on the shoulder. "Get some rest, man." His dark eyes turned serious. "It's good to see you, Sean. I'm glad you got in touch."

"You might change your mind if this gets you killed."

Ibarra shrugged. "Better to go out fighting than to keel over at age seventy from ass cancer."

"Hoorah," Sean said and smiled. The circumstances could have been better, but it was good to feel like someone had his back.

"There's some blankets in the hall closet," Ibarra said as he started down the hall to his room. "And if you change your mind about sharing with Krista, there's a full box of Trojans in the table by the bed."

"Fuck off," Sean called to Ibarra's retreating back. He kicked off his boots and stretched out on the couch. He closed his eyes, shifted around, but couldn't find a comfortable position. Krista's tight, drawn face haunted him.

He heard noises from down the hall. She was still awake, moving around. Now it sounded like she was pacing.

He pulled a pillow over his head, but he couldn't block out her restless movements. He got up from the couch, resigned to the fact that he wasn't going to get any much needed rest until she settled down.

Maybe he should check on her, try to get her to eat a little something, or better yet, bring her a drink to help her get to sleep.

He went over to Ibarra's bar and poured two glasses of bourbon. Krista was probably more of a fruity cocktail or a wine girl, but this would mellow her out a lot quicker.

Sean pushed open the door to the guest room and found Krista standing hunched over the small desk, scribbling madly as she muttered to herself.

She looked up, startled. "What is it? Did Ibarra find something?"

Sean shook his head. "You need to get some rest."

"How can I rest?" She gestured helplessly at the notebook on the desk. "People are trying to kill us. They got to Jimmy, they got to Stew, and it's my fault."

Her eyes were wide, haunted. Sean knew that look, knew she was imagining Stew Kowalsky's death, putting herself in his place, trying to envision what his last minutes must have been like.

"You're not going to do anyone any good if you burn out. Here," he said, pressing one glass into her hand as he cocked a hip on the edge of the desk.

Krista's nose wrinkled as she gave the liquid a delicate sniff. "Why are you bringing me bourbon?"

"I figured you could use some help relaxing."

"I guess it's worth a try." She shrugged and drained most of it in one gulp and set it aside with a little shudder.

He took a sip of his bourbon and tucked his free hand into his pocket so he wouldn't give in to the urge to comfort her. He didn't trust himself to touch her in any way, especially not when he was alone in a room with a goddamn queen-sized bed in it. Crap. He knew coming in here was a boneheaded idea.

But the lost look in her eyes wouldn't let him leave. He drained the last of his bourbon and set the glass down on the desk next to hers. "Don't dwell on it," he said quietly.

Her eyes narrowed on his face. "How can I not?" Her

hands came up to cover her face as he crossed the room to crack open a window. She gave a little shiver and wandered across the room and sat down heavily at the foot of the bed. She wrapped her arms around her waist and stared down at the floor. "We weren't very close, but Stew was a good guy, someone I considered a friend. I never imagined I would get him killed."

She swallowed hard and despite his better judgment Sean was compelled to cross the room until he stood in front of her, his big sock-clad feet almost toe to toe with her smaller ones. "I suppose you had to get used to this in the army, right, seeing friends die?"

"It's not something you ever get used to." He reached a hand out to her bent head and then thought better of it and yanked it back. She would be fine. There was no reason for him to sit in here while she wallowed. Best thing would be for him to leave her be and stretch out on Ibarra's couch for a few much needed hours of sleep.

He froze when she looked up at him with those big ocean-colored eyes, shiny with tears. Goddamn it, he hated how defeated and scared she looked. Krista was a tough chick. The kind of woman totally capable of taking care of herself.

But the last day and half had ripped away that tough-chick facade and shown them both exactly how vulnerable she could be. And God help him, but seeing her like this awoke the protective instincts Sean thought had been mostly beaten out of him over the last three years. He reminded himself that whatever trouble she was in was her fault, and his only worry should be getting himself out of the mess she'd put him in.

Still, it was almost impossible not to pull her into his

arms and tell her he'd do everything he could to make sure she got out of this in one piece.

"I don't guess you do." She shook her head and dropped her gaze back to the floor.

She stood up and reached for his hand, and Sean reflexively gave it. An action he immediately regretted when the protective urges roaring in his blood were joined with a jolt of lust so intense it almost made him forget who she was, where they were, and why it was beyond stupid to give in to the need screaming through his body, demanding he lay her down on that bed and claim her once and for all.

He stifled a groan as Krista's fingers curled around his. Yeah, he was hard up, but this was ridiculous. One touch of her hand on his, plus the memories of that hand on other parts of his body, and he was as hard as a spike, almost shaking with the need to yank her into his arms.

She tilted her face up to his, and he had to strain to hear her over the roaring in his ears. "I'm sorry," she said, and then shook her head. "I feel like that's all I ever say to you, but I am. I'm sorry I dragged you into this and I'm sorry Megan has to go into hiding. I'm sorry I got Stew killed and us shot at. I know it doesn't seem like it, but I was trying to do right by you. I just wanted to make sure anyone who had a hand in what happened to you and those women got what they deserved."

Sean felt like something was cracking open in his chest as he pulled her to him, unable to resist taking her into his arms. He was just comforting her, he told himself firmly, determined to ignore the thick heat pulsing through his veins. He knew what it was like when you tried to do the right thing and somehow managed to fuck it up for everyone.

Hell, his urge to protect Evangeline Gordon had helped get him into this mess in the first place.

And where do you think protecting Krista Slater will get you? whispered a sinister voice in the back of his head.

He shoved it aside. Like it or not, he was hip deep into her trouble, and no way was he hanging her out to dry.

Krista buried her head against his chest. He felt the press of her breasts against his ribs, the heat of her breath through the thin fabric of his shirt. He tipped his head until his nose was nuzzling her head and inhaled the floral scent of her hair, and under that, the warm fragrance of the woman herself.

She tipped her head back from his chest and his breath caught when he looked down to meet her gaze. Her pallor was gone, her cheeks as rosy and pink as her plump little mouth.

Sean wasn't even sure how it happened. One second he was looking at her, and the next he was covering her mouth with his, thrusting his tongue between her lips like he would die if he didn't get a taste.

She made a startled sound and froze with her hands on his shoulders, and that was enough—barely—to pull him back from the edge.

He jumped back, propelling himself halfway across the room as Krista backed up in the opposite direction, her hand held to her mouth, eyes wide with shock.

"Shit, I didn't mean for that to happen again," Sean said. "It's not—"

Krista held up a hand. "It's not personal. You were just being nice and trying to make me feel better. I get it," she interrupted. "And I know that what happened last night wasn't personal either, so don't worry that I'm reading too much into it."

Sean put his plan for a hasty retreat on the back burner and cocked his head. "You had your hand on my dick. I'd say that's pretty personal."

The pink in her cheeks darkened to fuchsia and she swallowed hard. "That's—that's not what I mean..." Her voice trailed off.

Sean never thought he'd see the day when clever, articulate Krista Slater would be at a loss for words. "Then what do you mean?" He took a step forward.

"I mean, I get what happened then, just now, isn't about me specifically." She wrung her hands in front of her, her fingers twisting and untwisting. Sean's blood warmed at the memory of how those long, slender fingers had circled his cock. "You said yourself, you weren't with a woman for over three years, and I imagine even with some...uh, relief...from, uh...other women..."

Sean forced himself not to smile at the way she struggled with the euphemism and wondered what she'd say if he told her there hadn't been any relief since he had gotten out of prison.

Not until last night, anyway.

"You're young, and obviously, uh,"—another swallow—"virile. You probably have a lot pent up and are not as discriminating as you might be otherwise..."

"You think I'll fuck anything with a pulse? Is that what you're getting at?"

Krista's brows pulled into a frown. "I wasn't going to put it that crassly, and I'd like to think I have some appeal. But let's face it, under normal circumstances, given our history, there's no other reason for that to have happened, right?"

He studied her face carefully, saw the uncertainty in her eyes. He knew exactly what she wanted. She wanted him to tell her she was right. It was nothing about her, nothing but him scratching an itch that had been three celibate years in the making.

Wanted him to brush it off, tell her it meant nothing so she could convince herself it meant nothing to her.

But after everything she'd put him through, no way was he going to let her off that easy.

Three steps had him across the room, mere inches from her, so close he could feel the air around her heat up. She took a step back but was hampered by the small desk, where she sat perched, her eyes darting around him as she searched for an escape.

Sean leaned down and planted his hands on either side of her hip bones. "So what's your excuse?" he rasped.

"What do you mean?" Her voice was high, breathless.

He bent down his head until his mouth was right next to her ear. "You know exactly what I mean. You were as turned on as I was. Don't try to tell me you weren't. And I can't imagine you have three years of celibacy to explain it."

Her breath caught and then sped up as she tilted her gaze up to his. "Not quite that long, but no, I don't." Her face was pink before. Now it was crimson, her light eyes standing out in stark contrast as she looked at him with embarrassment and resentment.

That wasn't the look he wanted to see on her face, not by a long shot.

He slid one hand up, under the silky fall of blond hair

to curve around her neck. He leaned in, widening his stance until her legs were bracketed by his. "So it's really me you want, not just a hard dick and a warm body?"

Her nostrils flared at the crudity, but she didn't deny it. "It doesn't make any sense, does it?" She kept her hands tightly fisted against the desk, like she was fighting the urge to slide them around his waist. "But I felt something . . . even before you got out of prison."

"So what are you saying? You're curious to see what it would be like to be with a convicted murderer? Don't feel bad. Lots of women like the idea of a man who's been behind bars. The caged beast who could snap at any second. All that danger—"

"Stop it," she snapped through gritted teeth. "Don't act like that. I know you would never hurt me. I know you're a good man."

The impact of those words was so powerful he actually took a step back. That, and the absolute conviction and deep regret in her greenish-gray eyes hit him like a fist in the gut. *I know you're a good man.* He shouldn't care about her opinion, or anyone else's for that matter. He knew he was a good man. He knew what he was and wasn't capable of, so he shouldn't care what people thought of him in the past or present.

But the way she was staring at him, really seeing him for the first time . . . He felt like the lead blanket he'd been wearing for the past three years was finally falling away.

Her lids dropped under his intense stare and her tongue came out to lick her lips.

He bent his head, calling himself a thousand kinds of idiot as the last thread of his resistance snapped. He sucked her plump bottom lip between his teeth and ran his tongue over the curve. Jesus, he thought, groaning at the way her lips parted so easily beneath his, the way her tongue slid out to meet his. Blood roared in his head as he struggled not to thrust his tongue down her throat.

Jesus, if only he could write off his response to her as just an overreaction to stimulus—any stimulus—after being locked up. Deprive a healthy young man of female contact for three years, put him in the room with a woman who was attractive and receptive, and what did you expect? Of course his dick was going to get hard.

But that wasn't the truth, not even close. And for reasons he couldn't put his finger on—not with every bit of blood dropping from his brain and heading for parts below the waist. He wanted her to know she wasn't alone in her crazy, inexplicable reaction to someone completely inappropriate. "I wish I could tell you this was all just because I'm desperate and horny, making up for lost time after being locked up." He slid his palm under the hem of her T-shirt, groaning at the feel of warm, smooth skin. "It would be so much easier if that was all this was." He cupped a breast and flicked a nipple through the silk of her bra, loving the way it jumped to immediate attention against the pad of his thumb.

"There hasn't been anyone," he said between kisses. "I haven't wanted anyone. I've been walking around like I'm dead inside and then you show up." He couldn't keep the edge out of his voice, angry at his own lack of control. Like she needed anything more on him, but he couldn't keep himself from spilling his guts. "All of a sudden all I can think about is how you smell, how you might taste." He sucked her tongue into his mouth for emphasis. "How soft your skin would feel." He whipped her shirt over her head and slid his hands down the smooth line of her back, down the curve of her waist and hip.

"I go from not even thinking about sex to driving myself crazy thinking up ways to make you come." He bent his head and swept his tongue over her silk-covered nipple. "And then I finally get the chance and I blow it, literally."

The sound of her soft chuckle went straight to his balls. "I was willing to wait for you to recover," she said as her hands came up to his head, pressing him more firmly against her breast. "You were the one who jumped off the bed like I was a leper."

He licked and nipped his way up her neck, back to her mouth. Sure enough, there was the faint purple bruise Ibarra had noticed. Sean paused to taste it. "You willing to let me make it up to you?"

Maybe this was what he needed, just one night to give in to whatever chemical imbalance made him respond so strongly to her. One night to scratch the itch and get her out of his system for good.

She froze, looking up at him with wide eyes. The moment of truth. Seconds stretched like an eternity as he absorbed every detail of her flushed face, kiss-swollen lips, pulse pounding in her throat. He was leaving it in her hands, a deliberate choice so there would be no excuses later about getting swept up in the moment and giving in to their raging lust without a thought.

She bit her lip, nodded. Her mouth moved, her lips shaping an almost inaudible "Yes."

Chapter 11

Sean didn't realize he was holding his breath until it came out in a rush. He lifted her around the waist and carried her to the bed. He stripped off her jeans and took her socks with them. He shoved his own pants and underwear to the floor and froze with one knee on the bed, mesmerized by the sight of her.

He hadn't had a chance to really look at her the night before. He'd been so crazed, almost blinded by his lust, that all he'd taken away were impressions of her smooth skin, pink nipples, and soft lips. Now he drank in the sight of her like a man who'd just crawled out of the desert.

Her skin was milky white against the navy-blue bedspread, the silk and lace of her bra and panties making her look somehow almost more naked the way they covered up just the bare minimum. He could see the peaks of her breasts, beading against the fabric like they were begging to be sucked. Her stomach was a smooth, flat plane, her legs long, smoothly muscled, ready to wrap around him and hold him tight.

And in between...Jesus, that was the fucking promised land. His cock strained and jerked with a mind of its own.

Krista's eyes traveled down his body, drinking him in as he had her. He saw her lips part as she sucked in a breath at the sight of his erection. The thought of her closing those lips over the tip, sucking him into her mouth had him gritting his teeth as he struggled not to come right then and there.

Not this time. Not until he'd made up for last night's premature performance about a dozen times over. He settled on the mattress and pulled her to him, hooking one knee over his hip so she was flush against him, breast to chest, sliding against the soft skin of her stomach. He yanked the straps of her bra down her shoulders and undid the clasp with all the finesse of a fourteen-year-old getting his first shot at second base.

Krista didn't seem to mind as she tugged the bra off and pressed herself against him, the whole time making those eager little noises in the back of her throat as her mouth consumed his. Her leg shifted, drawing him closer and he groaned at the feel of her smooth inner thigh rubbing against his naked hip. He wanted, *needed* to taste that silky skin, almost as much as he needed to taste the wet heat that soaked the silk of her panties as she ground her hips against his stomach.

He rolled her onto her back and hooked his fingers into the waistband of her panties. The rich scent of her arousal fogged his brain as he slid the scrap of fabric down her legs and positioned himself between her thighs.

God have mercy. Krista was a natural blonde.

"Shouldn't we get a condom or something?" Krista said through panting breaths as Sean sucked first one and then another nipple in his mouth.

"Eventually," he said against the soft skin of her stomach, loving the way her fingers tangled in his hair and held him close as she arched into his mouth. "But we're not going to need it for a while."

He bent his head to the dusting of gold curls on top of her mound and without hesitation spread her open with his thumbs. Her entire body tensed and she gave a surprised "Oh!" Her fingers tightened in his hair, almost as though she wasn't sure if she wanted to yank him away or shove him closer. "Oh God, you don't have to do that if you..." Her protest trailed off in a low, throaty moan.

Not do this? Was she insane? His tongue traced tight circles around her clit, the salty sweet taste of her flooding his mouth. He sucked her into his mouth, lashed her with his tongue as he slid first one and then two fingers into her.

He ground himself against the bedspread, fighting not to come, forcing himself to focus on her, her pleasure, the way she was rocking herself against his face as he fucked her with his fingers and his tongue like he was dying to fuck her with his cock.

Through the blood roaring in his head he could hear her moans, feel her tightening around his fingers and knew she was close. He wanted to slow it down, wanted to make it last, but more than anything he wanted to feel her come, wanted her to experience the searing wave of release he'd felt last night when he came in her hand.

One last lick, one firm thrust of his fingers and she shuddered hard against him, her muscles convulsing around his fingers like a tight, wet vise.

He didn't stop kissing her until her tremors had faded to quivers, and even then he couldn't stop himself from burying his mouth against the slick skin of her inner thigh, hot and smooth and soaked with the evidence of her need.

Her hand brushed his shoulders and the light contact sizzled through him as though he'd been struck by lightning. Jesus, he felt like his world had been rocked and he hadn't even come yet.

He wanted to linger down there, give Krista another orgasm or six, but his body wasn't having it. Straining, demanding, aching to sink into the wet heat of her sex. He rocked back onto his heels and leaned over to open the drawer of the bedside table.

Ibarra better not have been shitting him when he'd said he kept a stash of Trojans in there. He pawed through the contents of the drawer and did a mental fist pump when he found half a dozen foil-wrapped packages. He kept one and scattered the rest across the table, unable to stifle a smile as Krista's pleasure-blurred look turned wary.

"Three years," he reminded her.

Sean rolled the condom down the length of his cock and positioned himself against her entrance. He gripped himself hard, squeezing his eyes shut as that first contact threatened to send him over the edge. Hot, tight, wet, stretching around the broad head. He heard her answering cry as he pressed his palms against her inner thighs, holding her open to receive him as he shoved himself, inch by agonizing inch, inside her body.

Oh God, it was too much, Krista thought as she squirmed against the invasion. She was still shaking from an orgasm so powerful she almost blacked out, and her body felt swollen and tight as he pushed himself inside.

She tried to retreat, but there was nowhere for her to

go. And he knelt between her legs, palms pinning her thighs wide as he pushed deeper, rocking his hips past her body's resistance.

Relentless.

Jesus, she was insane, giving in to him like this. But there was no stopping him. No stopping the need that had hit her full force from the moment she'd laid eyes on him yesterday.

And now there was no doubt he felt the same way. *I haven't wanted anyone. I've been walking around like I'm dead inside and then you show up.*

With any other guy she would have brushed that off as a line of BS—every woman wanted to think she was the one and only.

But Sean had no reason to use a line, not with her, the last woman on earth he should want to have sex with for any reason other than to get some kind of twisted revenge. And even knowing that, Krista couldn't stop herself. She was as out of her mind as he was, sucked up into the vortex of sexual heat and chemistry that had been snapping and crackling between them for months.

If this was revenge, she never knew it could feel so good.

She ran her hands up his arms, felt the corded muscles jump under her touch. She'd never had sex like this: primitive, raw, needy. Never been with a man like Sean, tough, powerful, but gentle when he needed to be.

He wasn't gentle now. Pleasure danced on the edge of pain as her body struggled to accommodate him and she let out a little gasp. It had been a long time since she'd had sex, sure, but there was no getting around the fact that Sean Flynn was a very big man, in every way.

"God, you feel so good, Krista," he murmured. The low rumble of his voice sent a shimmer of pleasure through her. "So wet and tight around me. I don't think I've ever felt anything this good."

She opened her eyes and caught his gaze, green eyes narrowed, blazing with such heat she felt their sizzle on her skin.

He rocked his hips forward, sinking in another inch as he held her stare. The look in his eyes, dark, possessive, the primitive pleasure on his face made her clench around him, sent another rush of moisture from her to ease his way. Then his thumb was between her thighs, rubbing, circling her clit until she was running hot and wet and dying for him to come all the way inside her.

She slid her hands to his ass, urging him forward as she rocked her hips from the mattress.

He threw his head back and thrust all the way inside, so deep she could feel him at the base of her spine. The last pinch of pain gave way to mind-blowing pleasure as he began to thrust in slow, steady strokes, sinking deep, withdrawing nearly all the way before squeezing back in as the firm strokes of his thumb sent her spiraling out of control.

She called his name and let out a choked cry as her orgasm exploded through her. Jolts of pleasure coursed through her, making every nerve ending from the top of her head to the bottoms of her feet sing.

She heard his answering groan as she drifted back down to earth. Sean hooked her legs over his elbows and pumped his hips, driving into her in hard, pummeling thrusts. She thought he was relentless before. Now she realized how much he'd been holding back. She rested her hands on his shoulders and hung on for the ride.

She felt him freeze against her, every muscle tight. He swelled impossibly larger inside her, and then he was coming, his body jerking, shuddering against her as he held himself buried as deep inside her as he could go, his hands gripping her hips almost desperately.

Krista felt a rush of power and pleasure as he collapsed against her, knowing that she was the one who gave him such pleasure, that she was the one to break him out of the sexless cocoon he'd wrapped himself in. She stroked her hands down his back, sank her fingers into the now-softening muscles, and turned her face into the crook of his neck.

He smelled like sweat and sex and Sean, a potent combination that made her want to hold him here inside her and never let him go.

Unease rippled through her at the thought. She was never one to get all gooey after sex and start getting all carried away with thoughts of happily ever after. And Sean Flynn was the last man who should make her start.

But God, it was hard to remember that when he smelled so good and felt even better. Still buried deep inside her, his thundering heartbeat echoing her own as it pounded against her chest.

After a few moments, he took a deep breath and propped himself up on his elbows. He cupped her face in his hands and captured her mouth in a kiss that started out as a tender thank-you and then went hot and wild as his tongue slid in to tangle with hers.

He was still rock hard inside her, buried deep, and as his hips ground against her, she couldn't stop her body from clenching around him. "I thought you were kidding about making up for three years in one night," she gasped as he bent his head and sucked her nipple between his lips.

His chuckle rumbled through his chest, rippled through her body. "I don't think I could do that without killing us both, but I'm going to do my damned best at taking the edge off."

Krista's edge had been worn down to a soft curve, but that didn't seem to matter as Sean stroked, kissed, sucked, and licked his way over her breasts, up her neck, and back again, all the while holding himself deep inside her, gently grinding in lazy circles, touching bundles of nerves she hadn't even known existed.

She barely recognized herself as the woman who was lucky if she got one orgasm a night with past lovers, and that was with a lot of coaching, directing, and heavy concentration on her part.

Now she lay back and gave herself over to her intense, powerful lover who seemed to know exactly how to touch her with those big hands, where to kiss her with those firm, full lips to bring her right back to the brink for the third time tonight.

Sean was changing the game on her, making her call into question and throw out everything she thought about her own needs and desires. He did it with everything else. Why should sex be any different?

Jesus, how could he have ever looked at Krista and thought she was an ice queen? Now she was molten hot, melting around Sean like a pool of honey.

He wanted to lose himself in her, get so deep inside of her he could disappear and never come out. It was messed up, the effect she had on him, and he was sure he'd get up in his head about it later. But right now it felt too good, better than he ever could have imagined.

He struggled not to lose control, not to pound into her like an animal as he had at the end there. Slow, steady, the edge was off now. He could take his time.

At least that was the theory, but his body had other ideas.

He felt his body tighten, knew his climax was close. Some still-functioning part of his brain reminded him he was still wearing the same condom.

Shit. Even as an evil, selfish voice urged him to forget about it, keep going, it was a dumb-ass move and he tried not to be a dumb-ass when it came to risky sex.

Like sex with Krista isn't the riskiest move of all?

He shoved the thought away and slid out, squeezing his eyes shut at the way her body clenched at him as she cried out in protest. As though she couldn't stand to let him go. "One sec," he said, rolling onto his back as he fumbled for another foil packet. He'd no sooner rolled on the condom than he was pulling Krista on top of him.

She settled her knees on either side of his hips and locked her gaze with his. Her lips parted on a long moan as she sank down, all the way down on him. Sean had the crazy thought that being with Krista like this took the sting off having people wanting him dead.

Krista jerked awake at the sound of a fist pounding on the door. Disoriented at first, it took her several seconds to remember where she was and whose muscled, hair-roughened arm was wrapped around her waist.

Holy Christ, she'd had sex with Sean Flynn. She

closed her eyes but that didn't help to shut out the memory of what had happened. Multiple times. She'd never experienced anything like it.

His hands and mouth everywhere, stroking, licking, sucking, thrusting. Him on top, her on top, him buried so deep inside her that he touched bundles of nerves she never knew existed.

She came so many times she lost count, and Sean wasn't that far behind as he made up for his years of celibacy. And she'd been equally insatiable, unable to get enough of the taste of his lips, the feel of his hot, smooth skin stretched tight over acres of muscle, the heavy thrust and drag of him moving inside her.

She'd finally fallen asleep, exhausted, vaguely aware of Sean's arm wrapped around her waist, one hand possessively cupping her bare breast. She was shocked to realize they hadn't moved an inch from that position in— she squinted at the clock—six and a half hours.

Hell, she was shocked she'd slept at all, since she could barely tolerate sharing a bed with a lover much less with a guy spooning her so hard you couldn't even get a slice of daylight between them. It had gotten so bad that her last boyfriend had nicknamed her Prickly Pear.

It was the exhaustion brought on by lack of sleep and continual adrenaline rushes and crashes, she told herself. That was the only explanation for how she had slept so soundly. It had nothing to do with the warmth of Sean's chest against her back as he curled around her, almost like he was trying to protect her from the rest of the world even as he copped a feel.

He was awake, too, and had been since the first knock. She could feel the change in his breath, the subtle stiffening of the muscles against her back and wrapped around her waist.

That wasn't the only thing that was stiff. She could feel him against the curve of her backside, hard as a club and burning hot. Amazing he still had the ability after last night. Even more amazing was the answering tightness she felt low in her belly, the clutch of her body as it yearned to take him back inside.

Ibarra knocked again. "I found something interesting in your friend's files if you two ever want to leave your love nest."

Krista shifted in Sean's embrace and felt her face heat with embarrassment, over the fact that Ibarra knew exactly what had gone on in his guest room or over his use of the phrase *love nest* Krista wasn't sure. All she knew was that what had happened between them in this room had absolutely nothing to do with love.

At least for Sean it didn't. Me? I'm not so sure.

Krista shoved the unbidden thought away. Yes, she had discovered more to admire in Sean Flynn in the past couple of days than she'd discovered over the course of a year-long relationship with her last boyfriend, but when it came down to it, she'd succumbed to a mixture of chemical attraction, overactive hormones, and an adrenaline-fueled emotionally charged situation, same as Sean.

Nothing more than that.

"Quit pounding on the door," Sean called. "We'll be out in a minute."

Krista started to pull away but Sean's arm was still locked around her waist like a vise. He whispered a curse and gave her breast a little squeeze, almost like he couldn't help himself, and released her.

He rolled off the other side of the bed, treating her to a visual orgy of mile-wide shoulders and a muscular back that tapered into the tightest ass she'd ever seen.

Or touched.

She squeezed her eyes shut and clutched the sheet to her chin.

"You can take the shower first," he said, his sleep-roughened voice sending a shiver of awareness pulsing to all the spots he'd touched and kissed just hours before. "I'll go see what he uncovered."

Krista waited until she heard the doorknob click before she opened her eyes. Satisfied she was alone, she threw back the sheet and sat up, wincing in discomfort as muscles she didn't even know she had protested from overuse.

Jesus, who knew great sex could do so much damage, she thought as she headed for the shower. She was sore and achy inside and outside, but even that couldn't stop her blood from heating at the memory of her body being so well used.

She took stock of her injuries and let the hot water of the shower soothe her tight muscles. Some of the aches and pains were a result of being thrown around the car during the crash.

Others, like the tight pulling of her inner thigh muscles and the faint bruise along her hip bone, were a result of being thrown around the bed by Sean. Jesus, what was she thinking, letting herself indulge in the overwhelming attraction she felt for him?

What was it about him that made him so damn irresistible that she would go to bed with him? Especially knowing that, sexual chemistry aside, she was pretty sure Sean didn't have much regard for her.

But then, guys didn't have to like a woman to sleep with her, and Krista was too much of a realist to indulge in any illusions of his affection for her.

She, on the other hand, had never gone to bed with a man she didn't care about. For her, sex wasn't enjoyable without genuine affection, plain and simple.

But nothing had ever come close to what had happened with Sean.

There was no question she liked Sean. A lot. What had started as admiration all those months ago when she'd realized the truth about the man she'd once viewed as a cold-blooded killer had morphed into something more in the past day and a half.

She'd seen through the cracks in his tough, emotionless facade enough to catch glimpses of the man he used to be. Warm and caring, a born protector. But there were scars there, too, new pieces to his personality that hadn't been there before he'd been so devastated, not just by prison but his friends' betrayal.

She couldn't blame him for the wariness and reluctance to trust anyone. He'd been wounded, and even though she knew she could never heal him, something inside her urged her to try.

Is that was this is about? Martyring yourself to Sean as though a night of hot sex could ever make up for what happened to him?

She ducked her head under the spray to rinse away the last of her shampoo and acknowledged that her reasons for sleeping with Sean were far too complicated to untangle right now.

Once this was all over, she'd have time to ruminate and dissect her motives. Right now, she had to focus on finding out who was behind all of this and getting her and Sean out of this alive.

She got out of the shower and toweled off. She pulled on her jeans and a new fresh-from-Walmart T-shirt. It had a picture of a panda with a pink Mohawk on the front. Not her usual style, but she'd been half dazed with shock when she'd done their shopping.

She ran a brush through her hair and stared at her reflection. The solid six plus hours of sleep had done her good—the circles under her eyes had abated so she no longer looked like a prizefighter. Her cheeks were pink and her lips were redder and puffier than usual.

And just in case anyone looking at her would have any doubt about what she'd been up to that night, there was a rosy scrape along her jawline from Sean's stubble and two faint purple bruises on either side of her neck. Christ, she hadn't had a hickey since high school.

Come to think of it, she was pretty sure she hadn't had a hickey then either.

She rifled through her bag, pulled out a cosmetic case stocked with the basics, and did her best to cover up the damage.

She took a deep breath and opened the bedroom door. She dreaded walking down the hall to face Sean and Ibarra more than she'd ever dreaded facing down anyone—even her father—in the courtroom.

They weren't in the kitchen or great room, so Krista helped herself to a cup of coffee on her way to the office. Ibarra was seated behind the desk, Sean standing to his right. Both men were focused on one of the LED monitors mounted on the wall across from them.

"Morning," Ibarra said when he heard her footsteps on

the hardwood floor. His gaze briefly flicked to her and he gave her a quick nod. If he and Sean were indulging in locker room talk about what had gone on, she wouldn't have known it from either of them.

Sean nodded curtly, his face blank of emotion.

Krista tried to ignore the adolescent pinch of hurt in her stomach. This was real life and they were in real trouble. No time to get all teary because the boy she liked hadn't smiled when he passed her in the hallway.

She moved to stand on the other side of Ibarra. Even with the other person between them, Krista could feel every nerve jump in awareness. She risked a glance in his direction, taking in the hard lines of his profile. He kept his gaze locked firmly on the monitors across the room.

"What did you find?" she asked, forcing her voice into the firm, professional tone she used in the courtroom. She squinted at the monitors. One was just the shot of Ibarra's desktop; the other was a grid showing a variety of bank transactions. Her heart skipped a beat only to slow to a normal pace when she realized it was the same report she'd already seen and told Sean about.

"I connected with Kowalsky's computer," Ibarra said, and as he opened several files Krista realized the monitor showed a remote display of Kowalsky's desktop, not Ibarra's. "He kept his case files well organized, but I couldn't find anything related to Brewster or Caparulo."

Krista felt like a lead weight had settled on her shoulders. "Someone must have deleted them and left the other files intact so no one would get suspicious."

"Good guess," Ibarra said. "And whoever did it knows their shit. They didn't just trash the files."

"They used some kind of shredding program," Sean said.

Krista nodded, her mouth pulling into a frown. It wasn't enough to delete files. She'd worked on several cases where data recovery experts were able to retrieve supposedly deleted files—e-mails, pictures, you name it—it was almost impossible to permanently get rid of anything in the digital age.

Unless, like whoever killed Kowalsky, they knew exactly what they were doing. "I suppose it was a good one?" Krista sighed, the restorative effects of sleep washing away in the face of her disappointment.

"As good as anything I've ever seen," Ibarra said.

Krista uttered a soft curse. "If nothing else, I guess this confirms Stew's murder was no random mugging. Not that we'll be able to convince anyone of that." So much for Ibarra's great find. She felt a throbbing at the back of her neck and knew a full-fledged tension headache was waiting in the wings.

"Lucky for us, whoever did this forgot to delete the activity logs," Ibarra said.

Krista's hand froze in the act of kneading the knot at her nape.

"Kowalsky transferred everything to an online backup site less than fifteen minutes before he was killed," Sean clarified.

"Tell me you're able to access it."

Ibarra nodded. "I just finished downloading them right before you walked in."

Chapter 12

He paged through the open files, and Krista shook her head. "That was all in the last report he gave me. Wait." She held up a hand and Ibarra kept the document up on the screen.

She took a few steps closer to the monitor as she read. The header read *Caparulo Suicide (?)* It wasn't a formal report, more a collection of notes about what Kowalsky had uncovered.

According to source, powder burns and angle of entry consistent with self-inflicted gunshot. No sign of forced entry into house. Bedroom window unlocked and ajar. Source indicated ground beneath window was slightly disturbed but no discernible footprints. Fingerprint dusting revealed only victim's print.

Canvassed the neighborhood. A Mrs. Elanor Vicks claims to have seen someone "lurking around Angela's place" on and off for several days before Caparulo's apparent suicide. No other claims of anything unusual. Vicks known to suffer episodes of dementia—unreliable witness. Claims police questioned her briefly but no follow-up questions asked.

There were a few spaces as if Stew had taken a break,

and the next paragraph was just two days before, the day Krista had gone to talk to Sean, and Jimmy Caparulo's case was closed and his body released for cremation.

WTF? Caparulo case closed, body released, no autopsy. Source in SPD has closed up tight, no one giving up anything. Why close ranks around apparent suicide if nothing to hide?

Why indeed, Krista thought.

Detective Jorgensen in charge of investigation gave no further info than official statement, but was extremely agitated when I tried to ask him about decision to release the body. Action items: follow up with E. Vicks, contact client to discuss how to proceed.

Krista swallowed hard. She was the client Stew had never had the chance to contact.

Ibarra cycled through the rest of the files. "That's the only new information as far as I can tell," she said and blew out a frustrated breath. "I don't suppose you've managed to hack into the SPD's network and find the official report?" she asked, almost dreading the answer. She was now a knowing accessory to cybercrime—against the Seattle Police Department, no less.

Hell, compared to two boosted cars and a suspected cop shooting, this was nothing, right?

"Here it is." Ibarra pulled it up in on the opposite monitor, hiding for the moment the list of bank transactions.

"Is it just me or does that look a little light?" Sean asked as Krista scanned the two-page document.

Krista shook her head and drained the last of her coffee. "Like Cole said, the chief wanted the case closed, and fast."

"But why?" Sean asked.

"It's impossible to tell. The coroner's office had to sign off on it, but they could be getting pressure from any number of the higher-ups to close the investigation."

"Like who?"

Krista shrugged. "A judge, the mayor..."

"Or someone from the PA's office?" Sean bit out.

Krista took a deep breath and bit back a retort. "What happened with you and the Slasher case got a lot of people upset and now a lot of people feeling like they need to cover their asses." She could feel the anger vibrating off Sean and instinctively lifted her hand but stopped short of touching him. "It's no surprise they wanted to make anything even remotely related to the case disappear quickly." The thought of anyone she worked with being involved in the cover-up made her sick, but she knew this wouldn't be the first time something related to a controversial case was pushed under the rug.

"So you think it's okay?" Sean snapped. "You and the people you work with fucked up and that gives them the excuse to make sure no one questions the fact that Jimmy committed suicide?"

His accusation, his fury, blindsided her. She felt like she'd been punched in the gut. "How can you possibly think I'm okay with that? Would I be here risking my life to find out what really happened if that were the case?"

"Kids, can we quit with the bickering?" Ibarra broke in. "You're keeping me from getting to the good stuff."

Sean snapped his mouth shut. The fury had dimmed from his gaze, but hot color stained his cheekbones.

"What?" Krista said, focusing on Ibarra, feeling heat stain her own cheeks. It was humiliating how easy it was for Sean to make her lose her cool.

"I looked at that bank statement Kowalsky recovered," Ibarra said, closing the police report. There was a reason they wanted the case closed so quickly, a reason that went beyond worrying about the public's view on how they'd handled Sean Flynn's case.

But who was really behind it, she wondered as she watched the document disappear from the screen.

Someone who had something to hide, someone who had enough weight to lean on both the coroner's office and the detective running the investigation—or his superiors—to get the investigation expedited and the case closed before it even made headlines.

Six months, a year ago, Krista would have looked on the act with disapproval, but she wouldn't have made any waves or gotten overly suspicious of the motives. Of course she believed everyone was entitled to a thorough investigation, even if all of the evidence pointed in the direction of suicide.

However, she'd accepted that not everyone thought or worked the way she did and decided the best thing she could do was keep focused on her own cases, fight her own battles. It wasn't worth it to raise a ruckus when they all knew what the results would be whether the case took six days or six weeks to close.

But with Jimmy Caparulo dead and his case closed so quickly...no way she could ignore that. And now she couldn't help but wonder how many other cover-ups had she missed as she kept her eyes on her own paper, convincing herself she was above it.

Sean was right. She had sat silently by while others around her cut corners, made compromises, accepted their excuses for not doing everything by the book.

"I ran a query on that account as well as Nate's business account and found something interesting."

Krista's pity party faded to the background.

"So there's this account that Kowalsky found, right? It's a money market account registered under a bogus business name."

"Right," Krista said. "A deposit for fifty thousand dollars was wired in the day after he killed Bianca Delagrossa, and there was another one before that, which might link to the death of one of the earlier victims, a Jane Doè killed last year."

Krista couldn't help but shudder at the memory of the gruesome videotapes that had emerged of not only those two women, but of Nate Brewster's other victims. Including a recording of him murdering Evangeline Gordon, a video made all the more haunting as it showed Sean slumped in the background, unconscious and helpless as Brewster brutalized and killed her.

"Those aren't the only accounts, or the only deposits."

Krista looked at Sean, but his expression was carefully blank.

"I was able to link this account to three others, all under fake LLC names."

"How did you do that?" Krista asked uneasily, sure that it was highly illegal.

"Better you don't know. But I wouldn't expect it to stand up in court."

"I already told Sean that this is about the truth, not a conviction."

"Fair enough" His fingers clicked on the keyboard and three other documents appeared on the screen.

Sean noticed the pattern before she did. "The dates match the deaths of four other victims," he said grimly.

Krista squinted up at the screen but couldn't scan through the numbers fast enough. "How do you know?"

"When I first got out, I didn't sleep a whole lot," Sean said, "so I did a little light reading on my friend the Slasher. Look, he got two deposits into that account in the Caymans, one on June twenty-fourth, which coincides with the first victim—well, if you don't count Evangeline Gordon. Then on January seventh, when the third victim was killed."

Ibarra helpfully highlighted on screen while Sean rattled off dates and victims, all of whose deaths coincided with a hefty deposit to a secret account linked to Nate Brewster.

"Someone was paying him to kill them," she breathed. Even when she'd showed the single transaction to Mark and then to Sean, she hadn't really believed Nate was being paid for what he'd done to those women.

Murder for hire was one thing. Paying a brutal monster like Nate Brewster to do what he did to those women...

That was diabolical.

"Can you tell who? Can you tell where the deposits are coming from?"

"Not yet," Ibarra said. "I've traced a few of the deposits back to one account. I'm still working on the others."

"What about the others?" Sean asked. "He had a lot of money moving in and out over the past—how far do these records go back?"

"The most recent one was opened a couple months ago, the oldest...huh, that goes back almost five years."

Ibarra turned away from the screen to look up at Sean. "Looks like it was opened up right before we did that op in Mogadishu."

"Does that mean anything?" Krista asked.

"Hard to tell," Ibarra said. "But there were several deposits made into that account. The last one was after Colombia."

"Both Nate and Jimmy were injured on that op," Sean said. "They both got out on medical discharge a few months later."

"And you stayed in another year," Krista said. "You too?" she asked Ibarra.

He shook his head. "I went to para-rescue training. I didn't get out until last year."

Neither man seemed inclined to say any more. "Is it significant that they both were discharged after that mission?"

Sean shook his head slowly, not so much in denial but as though he were trying to clear out the cobwebs. "Didn't seem like it at the time."

His eyes took on that dazed, thousand-yard look that told her he'd shifted his focus out of this room. She started to question him again and thought better of it. Sometimes it was better to let a person parse all the information before she went after them with both guns blazing.

She shifted her focus back to Ibarra. "What about the dates of the other deposits? Seattle doesn't have a huge homicide rate. How difficult would it be to match homicides in the Seattle area with the dates of the deposits?"

Ibarra shrugged and tapped a few keys. "The fastest way would be for me to get into HITS."

The Homicide Investigative Tracking System was a statewide database of information about homicides and other violent crimes.

"Are you sure you're okay with that?" Ibarra asked.

With every step, she was getting herself into deeper and deeper trouble. God, she hoped it would be worth it. Her gaze snagged on Sean, who had moved in front of the open window to take in deep lungfuls of cold mountain air. A warrior to the core, they hadn't been able to break him, but the scars ran deep. If she had any doubts before, she knew in that split second she'd do whatever it took to expose everyone responsible for hurting him, and to erase any doubts Sean had about her. "Do it," she said, her gaze never leaving Sean.

He didn't look up, but the tension coiling through his broad shoulders eased a degree. It wasn't much, but she'd take it. Krista didn't know when or how it had happened, but at some point in the last two days it had become very, very important what Sean thought of her.

"You might want to do a check in northern California and Oregon too," Sean said. "That's where Nate said he was headed the last time I talked to him."

"When was that?" Krista asked.

"After I was arrested, he came to visit, asked if there was anything he could do to help," Sean said, his upper lip curled in a snarl. "I thanked him. Dumb fuck that I am, I never realized he was coming to gloat." He shook his head. "Anyway, who knows what the hell else he was up to before he came back up here."

Another thought occurred to Krista. "Is it possible to flag any suicides that were rushed through?"

"No problem," Ibarra said. "And in the meantime I'm

going to keep following the money thread and see what we come up with."

Even with the window wide open and chilly air flowing into his lungs, Sean couldn't shake the tight, confined feeling. Ibarra's office was huge, and the door was partially ajar, but Sean couldn't convince his brain that the door wasn't about to slam shut, lock itself, and trap them all inside.

He forced himself not to look at Krista, who had positioned herself back behind Ibarra's desk. Over the sound of his heart pounding in his head, he could barely make out their quiet conversation. He snuck a glance, snapped it back to the window, and told himself he didn't care that she was standing so close to Ibarra, that every few seconds or so Ibarra's attention wandered from his computer screen to the firm curves of Krista's thighs and ass in those form-fitting jeans.

And now he knew exactly how soft the skin was that was hidden underneath, knew exactly how she tasted between those long, sleek legs...

And that was exactly why he had to stay over here in his corner and push her back into hers. He'd hurt her with his accusations. She was used to taking hits in the courtroom, but she hadn't been able to mask the pain when he'd lashed out and questioned her integrity.

A month, hell, a week ago, he wouldn't have felt a lick of remorse for tarring her with the same brush as those she worked with. But having spent the last forty-eight hours in constant, too close contact, he didn't believe her sincerity was false.

And after last night, it was hard to dismiss the notion that she was starting to care about him.

The thought filled his head with a rush of possibilities that he had no business entertaining. He tried but couldn't shut any of it out, his tangled-up feelings for Krista, the pain over Nate's betrayal, oozing like a fresh wound after what Ibarra had uncovered.

He'd always been able to shut everything out when he needed to, first in the army when he was on an op and his life depended on it. Then in prison, when he closed up in on himself, the only way to stay sane when every bit of power was taken from him.

But now he couldn't keep a lid on anything, and it was all hitting him at once in a giant tidal wave of suppressed emotion. The muscles in his chest tightened, making it hard to breathe.

He had to get a grip. It was the only way to make it through. He moved closer to the open window and tried to calm his rapidly increasing heart rate as cold sweat misted his face. He couldn't submit to the anxiety, not when he needed all of his brainpower to process what Ibarra had uncovered.

Someone had paid Nate to kill those girls. It was so hideous that Sean wanted to believe those deposits were a coincidence. But he'd been in some bad places in the world, and he'd seen firsthand the kind of horror that human beings were capable of inflicting on each other.

So no, he wasn't exactly surprised. He was sickened. At Nate, for the horrible way he'd tortured those women. Not to mention whoever was paying him to do it. At Jimmy, who, though they'd never know for sure, might have had an idea of what Nate was up to but kept his mouth shut, even though it meant sending his best friend to prison.

That was the kicker, the most nauseating thing of all. That he had stupidly trusted them. He'd always considered himself a good judge of character, but he hadn't had even an inkling of what kind of twisted soul lived beneath Nate's too handsome, all-American facade. And he and Jimmy had had their differences, but never in a million years had he thought his friend would not only stand by while Sean was framed for murder but give him a good hard shove through the prison doors.

Now Ibarra had found that bank account, and while it might lead nowhere, it opened up the possibility that Nate and Jimmy were up to something even before they had left the army.

And once again, clueless Sean had no fucking idea.

He knew he was no rocket scientist, but Sean had never questioned his intelligence and especially not his street smarts. But ever since he'd found out what had really happened the night Evangeline Gordon had died, he'd started to wonder if he had no sense of people or if he was just stupid in general.

He sucked in another breath and caught a whiff of something fresh and almost fruity, like sliced apples. *Krista's shampoo.* He shook his head and told himself he was imagining it and looked over just in time to see Krista doing that twisty thing with her hair like she did when she was thinking hard, squinting at one of the monitors.

Talk about stupid. He'd had some major missteps in his life, but sleeping with Krista had to be right up there in the top five.

One night to scratch the itch? Yeah, right. More like one night to send him into overdrive, to conjure up the lust and God knew what else to mingle with everything that was blowing up inside him.

He'd been trying not to look directly at her. Sort of like being afraid of looking into the sun for fear of being blinded, Sean was afraid that if he let himself look at her, the last logical brain cell in his head would die and he wouldn't be able to stop himself from hauling her back to Ibarra's guest room and spending the next month or so making up for the last three years of celibacy.

Right. He only wished he could chalk his crazy attraction to something so simple. Now, as he watched her stare at the monitors, brows knit over the delicate bridge of her nose as though she could force the data to give up its secrets, awareness sizzled through him, chasing away the impending panic attack.

He might be able to remind his brain why she was a systematic threat to his sanity, but his body didn't have a single reservation about picking up right where they'd left off in the wee hours of the morning.

Christ, it was a miracle he could even get it up after last night, and yet heat pooled in his groin and he shifted his weight in his suddenly too-tight jeans.

Somehow she'd yanked him from one extreme to the other, forcing him from the cold comfort of numbness into wanting, needing, feeling with a ferocity that was too much for his overloaded system to handle.

She looked in his direction then, as though she could feel the heat of his stare. He wondered if she had any inkling what was going on in his body right now. But he couldn't indulge, no matter what.

She drove him crazy, and he'd had his one slipup. Now it was time to pull himself back under control.

When she met his stare, her frown relaxed and she gave him a tentative smile. Just that gentle curving of her lips cut straight through the haze of lust and made his chest twist with something. Something that carried a hell of a more powerful punch than lust.

He dropped his gaze and backed away from the window. Without a word he made a break for the door, not stopping until he was outside on Ibarra's deck. He looked out onto Ibarra's semimanicured lawn that ended in the heavy stone wall that ringed the perimeter. Sean knew the wall was at least fifteen feet high, but from this vantage he could see over the barrier and into the open grassland that stretched for miles before giving way to the rugged peaks of the mountains.

It took some doing, but eventually the roaring in his head quieted and he could feel himself coming back from the edge. The anxiety had fled, but it left him with a restless energy that made questions bounce around his head like a flurry of rubber balls and made his own skin feel like it was two sizes too small.

Footsteps sounded on the hardwood planks. Sean didn't even have to turn to know it was Krista. He had a bad feeling that in fifty years he'd still be able to pick her out by feel in a crowded room.

"Are you all right? You looked like you were having a... moment there for a second."

He almost laughed at her terminology. "Nothing a little fresh air can't cure."

"This has to suck, finding out Jimmy might have been working with Nate."

His muscles jumped at the light brush of her fingers on his arm. He wanted her to stay; he wanted her to go. He wanted to go back to the place where a slight touch of her fingers didn't send him skyrocketing out of control.

He wanted to lean into her touch like a scruffy stray who had just received the first gentle pet of his life. He wanted to lose himself and his pain. It had happened last night. With her, he'd forgotten about everything.

With her hands running over his skin, her mouth on his, her legs wrapped around his hips as he drove endlessly, he'd lost himself inside her until his satisfaction had moved beyond the realm of mere pleasure and morphed into pure joy.

It would be so easy to lose himself again. Which was exactly why he had to be on guard at all times.

He stepped away and out of the corner of his eye he could see her shove her hand into the pocket of her jeans. "What's hard is knowing what a fucking idiot I was. That I couldn't see what kind of people they were when I was with them practically twenty-four seven for months at a time."

"Can you think of anything that was happening back then, anything that might have given you a clue that they were up to something?"

Sean stared out at the rugged peaks of the mountains, but in his mind he was back five years, in the jungles of Colombia. He started to talk, almost as though to himself. "That last mission, we were brought in as security to support the rescue of two American doctors who had been taken hostage by FARC troops—that's the Colombian revolutionaries," he said for clarification. "Me, Nate, and Jimmy were on the advance team with two Delta Force guys to watch their backs while they tried to pinpoint the hostages and map out an extraction plan.

"We split up, Nate flanking the group on the left, Jimmy the right, and I took up the rear. Within a few steps they had melted in to the jungle. You couldn't see more than a few feet in front of you. The only contact was over the radios. The Delta team had just gotten eyes on the hostages when all hell broke loose.

"Gunfire everywhere. I dove for cover and looked to return fire but it was impossible to get an eye on anyone through the trees. Then I heard Jimmy screaming over the radio. He was hit and taking heavy fire, and some of it was from our own guys—no one could see what the hell they were shooting at. The Delta guys called in for air support but it would be several minutes before they could get the helicopters in the air. Jimmy was pinned down. I didn't even think about it before I ran for him.

"I went for the last place I'd seen him. He was behind a tree in a clearing next to a little jungle hut, and FARC troops were firing from a hut about ten yards away. I heard the bird coming and got Jimmy over my shoulder, somehow managing to avoid fire and get Jimmy out."

"So you saved his life and he screwed you over," Krista said quietly.

"Oh, it gets even better. Right as I get to the bird, Jimmy says, 'Nate went down too. I saw him on the other side of the clearing.' We're all calling and he's not responding." Sean shook his head, disgusted at the memory of how worried he was, how sick he was at the thought of his friend dying at the hands of some teenage guerilla in the rot of a Colombian jungle.

"I went in after him too. He'd taken one to the chest and somehow his radio got damaged. Got him back to the bird. Jimmy's knee was fucked and they had to rebuild

Nate's shoulder and they both took their get-out-of-the-army-free cards."

He met her gaze, bracing himself for her pity. Dumb fuck who couldn't tell enemy from friend. To his shock, all he saw was the warm glow of admiration. "And you were totally unharmed?" Krista said.

"Not totally," he lifted the hem of his shirt up a few inches and indicated the pucker of scar tissue that striped his right side.

"I was wondering how you got that," she said, and then blushed as though remembering how she'd come across it.

Heat pulsed in his veins at the memory of her hand skimming over the sensitive flesh, pausing to trace it again, taking note of the unevenness. "I also got a Silver Star out of the deal," he said, yanking himself back to bitter reality. "One of the highest honors you can get in combat, and I got it for saving the guys who ruined my life." He shook his head.

Then he felt something, like a finger tapping at the back of his brain, like it was trying to get him to remember something.

He'd had that feeling often in the past three years, especially when he let himself think about the night Evangeline Gordon was murdered. He remembered going into the club, finding Evangeline. She'd tried to blow him off, told him she was too busy to talk to him until after she finished her shift. Sean had said he'd wait. He'd sat himself in an empty seat at the bar and ordered a beer.

And that was it. He didn't remember anything until he'd woken up, sixteen hours later, Evangeline lying in bed with her throat cut and her blood all over him.

He'd tried desperately to break through the concrete wall that seemed to have come down in his brain, tried to respond to the tapping finger to remember what had happened. He'd learned the hard way it only led to excruciating headaches and even more frustration that he couldn't remember something, literally, to save his own life.

Now he had that same niggling feeling as he remembered back to that mission. Something bothered him that he hadn't thought to question until now. "It never made any sense, how he and Jimmy ended up so close together. When we spread out, Nate was supposed to go twenty meters to the south, Jimmy was supposed to go to the west, and I was supposed to keep up the rear. Nate said he got turned around in the underbrush and had gotten off course. He was always kind of shitty at navigation so no one ever questioned it. But now..." Sean thought back to that night. "Even if he had gotten off course, it's too much of a coincidence that he ended up just a few yards away from Jimmy."

"You think they planned something?"

Sean blew out a frustrated breath. This was a waste of time. "Fuck if I know. Fuck if I'll ever know, now that they're both dead."

Krista cocked her head. "Maybe there was something in that building."

"Maybe," Sean said and shrugged. "Could have been drugs, weapons, even cash. Wouldn't be the first time someone in the military tried to get their hands on some spoils, but smuggling it by hand out of the jungle would be a damn stupid way to do it."

Krista's brow knit but before she could ask the question clearly forming in her brain Ibarra came out onto the deck.

"Any hits on the deposits into Nate's accounts?" Krista asked.

Ibarra made a noncommittal noise. "Still parsing the data. But I did find some interesting connections. Have you ever heard of a company called West Hall Security?"

"That's who Jimmy used to work for," Sean said.

Ibarra said. "Right. Well as far as I can tell that makes you the only person who can confirm a single employee of that organization. After Nate was killed, it was like the company was dissolved and all past employee records seem to have disappeared. There isn't even a record of Jimmy's employment."

"What about the people who worked at Club One? We have a list of everyone from the initial investigation," Krista said.

"Unless someone has destroyed it," Sean bit out. "So fine, yet again, critical information has either disappeared or is inaccessible. How does that help us?"

"Hey, I'm working with what I've got here. As much as I hate to admit it, someone has been very good at covering their tracks, and I have to be especially cautious in my methods so I don't tip anyone off that I'm snooping on your behalf."

"Sorry," Sean said. "I just feel like I should be doing something instead of hiding up here like a pussy waiting for something that will point us in the right direction."

"I feel you," Ibarra said. "He was always the brawn of the battalion while I was the brains," he said with a little wink in Krista's direction. "The shell company that owned West Hall was also processing payments to Jimmy

Caparulo up until last week. So even though he techni-
cally quit, he's been working for the same people the
whole time. And that's not the only thing. This company,
JD Partners LLC, transferred ownership of Club One to
Hexacorp just nine months ago."

Sean struggled to remember why the name Hexacorp
name struck a familiar chord. Krista answered before he
could ask.

"That's the company we traced back to Nate. The one
he used to hide the fact that he owned Club One."

Chapter 13

Krista held up her hand. "Okay, let me make sure I have this straight. Up until nine months ago, JD Partners owned Club One before ownership was transferred to Hexacorp, which we've already traced to Nate Brewster. But JD Partners effectively owned West Hall and also paid Jimmy as an independent contractor?"

"Yep." Ibarra nodded.

"And West Hall has since been dissolved, and other than Jimmy, we can't find any records of anyone else who ever worked for them?" Krista rubbed her thumbs against her forehead as though that could put a dent in the headache that was building beneath her skull.

Krista closed her eyes as she struggled to process the confusing web of shell companies and hidden transactions. "So even before Nate's death, someone was trying to cover up any connection they might have had to Club One." She let out a sigh. Something was niggling at the back of her brain. Why did the name JD Partners jump out at her? "What about Jack Brooks? He was working as head of security for Club One—can you tell if he was hired through West Hall?"

A few minutes later, Ibarra replied. "Not by name, but

looks like the same bank account was paying him up until just before the club was closed."

"Okay," Krista said. "We have two confirmed employees of West Hall, both of whom worked at Club One and both of whom were involved with Nate somehow."

"What about the other people who worked at Club One?" Sean asked. "Maybe they knew something."

Krista shook her head. "Stew tried to track several of them down in the last few months. He didn't get anywhere. Certainly nothing to indicate a connection to Karev." She paced, pausing at the office's huge picture windows to stare out at the jagged peaks of the mountains, struggling to get the pieces to slide into place.

Then it hit her like a fist in the gut. "Holy shit," she whispered. "JD Partners. I know that name."

"What?" Sean asked. "How?"

She turned to Sean. "From my father's files. He's an attorney," she explained for Ibarra's benefit. "I interned for him after my freshman year of college, and I know I saw that name in some documents."

Sean reached out and brushed her arm. "Are you sure? Your father's firm dealt with a lot of clients. You could be mistaking the name—"

Krista shook her and tried to swallow back the lump in her throat. "I wish I wasn't so sure, but I remember now. It was something he wanted me to keep really quiet, some kind of property transfer or something." She shook her head. "He had me handle all of the administrative stuff because he didn't want anyone else in the office to see it." At the time she'd felt so special, like her dad had let her in on some little secret. God, what an idiot.

"So who was the client?" Sean asked.

"I have no idea," Krista said, her shoulders slumping in defeat. "None of the paperwork I saw had names associated with the company. One of his partners is heading up Karev's defense team. Karev wasn't a client back then, but it could be connected." But somehow all of this secrecy and maneuvering didn't seem to fit with Karev's style.

"There has to be something, a signature page for the contract," Sean said impatiently.

"I'm sure there was," Krista snapped back, "but I never saw it." She brought her hand to her forehead and tried to massage away the headache forming behind her eyes. "I'm sorry," she said softly. "I wish I had more specifics, but all I know is that by some freaky coincidence, my father has somehow ended up in the middle of all of this. I'm so sorry, Sean."

She turned to face him, but instead of the anger and accusation she expected, she could see the sympathy in his eyes. "You had no idea what these people were involved in. Hell, there's a chance your father doesn't either."

Krista huffed out a laugh. "Nice of you to give him the benefit of the doubt, but I'm not optimistic." Hurt and disappointment coursed through her. God, after everything her father had put her through, it seemed impossible that his behavior still had the power to disturb her. But deep down inside, there was a part of her who was the girl who'd adored and idolized her daddy before everything went to hell.

She shook it off, forcing herself to regroup and focus. "So we have a lead on JD Partners. Now we need to get a hold of my father's files." She watched as Sean and Ibarra exchanged a look.

"You don't want to try to contact your father directly?"

Krista shook her head and swallowed down the bitter taste in her mouth. "If we can't trust Mark, we definitely can't trust my father." It seemed ridiculous that she couldn't simply call her father directly to find out what he knew. But despite his emotional reaction to her supposed kidnapping, there was no way she could fully trust her father not to tip off his clients.

"I can tap into the corporate network," Ibarra said.

"You can try," Krista said, "but my dad is totally old-school and doesn't trust network security. If he was that determined to keep his dealings with JD Partners quiet, he wouldn't have kept digital copies. We'll have to search for hard copies."

Sean sighed and ran a hand through his hair. "Breaking into an office building is a lot harder than it sounds."

"My father keeps duplicates of everything in his office at home," Krista said. "And if it's something extremely confidential, I don't think they even make it to the office. We'll search the house first. In the meantime, let's find out everything we can about what kinds of business JD Partners has been up to."

Ibarra was able to pull up several transactions, many of them to accounts at banks implicated in money laundering scams, and two to accounts they could directly link to Karev.

"You think the shell company is just a way for Karev to transfer money back and forth to himself?" Sean asked as he stood behind her to look up at the monitor.

He was so strong, so solid next to her. Krista wanted nothing more than to turn and bury her head in his broad chest and to absorb some of his heat. She forced herself to focus. "That's the easiest explanation, but why go to such lengths to keep their connections to Nate Brewster a secret?"

She seized on the problem, momentarily putting her father's involvement aside. "I've been going after these guys my entire career, and they don't really give a shit whom they're associated with, or even about their ties to the mafia being exposed. Trust me, they like the notoriety. Thugs like Karev wear the veneer of legitimate business-men, but they want the world to know they're gangsters and that they know how to work the system. Thanks in part to lawyers like my father," she said bitterly. "Who-ever is really behind JD Partners isn't just afraid of losing business or getting on the cops' radar. Everything we've found is circumstantial, not enough to pose any real legal threat to anyone."

Sean nodded. "I get what you're saying. This is some-one worried about scandal. Someone who stands to lose big if his connection to Nate and the girls at Club One is exposed."

But who? Krista's mind churned. She could only pray that her father's files would reveal the truth.

"If we leave soon we can get to Seattle by late after-noon."

"Fine," Krista said and sighed. "I'll go get my stuff."

"Wait," Ibarra said. "You're going to need to do some-thing about that hair."

"My hair?"

"Tommy's right," Sean said, his expression tinged faintly with regret. "You're known in the city, and with all the news coverage about us, people are going to be on even higher alert. That hair . . . it's too distinctive."

"Why can't I just do like a ball cap and sunglasses?" She knew she was being vain, but her thick, straight, naturally pale-blond hair was one of her physical points of pride.

"No way," Sean said. "Hat plus sunglasses, especially on a woman wearing clothes that don't fit," he said, gesturing at her baggy jeans and borrowed sweatshirt, "pretty much screams 'I'm incognito,'" Sean said. "Don't you ever read those celebrity magazines, where the actress is supposedly trying to be inconspicuous, but all you see is Britney Spears in a giant hat and sunglasses?"

"I'm a little too busy to read gossip rags, but yeah, I see your point," Krista conceded. Forty-five minutes later, thanks to a pair of kitchen shears and a box of hair color Ibarra had scored from his mother's house down the road, Krista's shoulder-length pale-blond hair had been transformed into a chin-length brunette bob. She stared wide eyed at her reflection, reminding herself it was just hair even as she wondered if she'd ever be able to get her natural color back.

"It doesn't look that bad," Sean said, as though reading her thoughts.

She lowered her hand self-consciously. "It's a stupid thing to worry about how bad I look considering..."

"Don't worry," he said. "It would take a hell of a lot more than a bad dye job to make you look anything less than amazing." He frowned as though angry at himself for saying it out loud. He was recognizable enough, but with his hair cut in a buzz so short she could see his scalp and his three-day stubble shaped into a goatee, he might slide by if no one looked too hard. Especially with his vivid green eyes hidden by dark contacts.

Krista had also traded her baggy jeans and fleece for a pair of skintight leggings, a thigh-length sweater, and flat boots taken from Ibarra's college-age sister's closet. "She has so many goddamn clothes, she won't ever notice they're gone," he muttered. Combined with her dark, blunt cut hair, the look was distinctly edgier than anything Krista normally wore.

An hour later, they were packed and ready to go. In addition to Krista's overnight bag and the odds and ends they'd bought at Walmart, they'd acquired several more pieces of baggage courtesy of Ibarra.

Krista's jaw had dropped when Ibarra led them to the underground storage area. Canned food and dry goods— enough to last months—lined the walls. He slid a can of coffee aside to reveal a panel. "What's that?" Krista asked, and before she could answer, Ibarra leaned forward and looked directly into a beam of light.

Sean let out a low whistle. "You must have some serious shit if you have a retinal scanner security system installed."

Ibarra shrugged. "Nothing special. I just like to play around with innovations myself before I recommend anything to clients."

Nothing special. Krista begged to differ. Ibarra had a fully stocked armory down here. "This is enough to make the ATF wet their pants."

"Good thing they won't find out," Sean said sharply.

"Not from me," Krista assured him. As long as Ibarra was on their side, he could have a Scud missile down here for all she cared. Nevertheless, she couldn't shake her uneasiness in the presence of so much firepower.

Unlike Sean, who held a semiautomatic pistol as

though it was an extension of his own hand, Krista didn't think she'd ever be totally comfortable around guns. It was one thing to know how to load and shoot a gun at a shooting range. It was another to be surrounded by high-caliber weapons that could tear a hole through not just herself but the concrete wall behind them.

She supposed she should count herself lucky that after a brief discussion Sean and Ibarra decided to limit their arsenal to several handguns, mainly because they were easier to conceal and because Krista wouldn't be completely useless with one.

Sean handed her a Glock 9mm. She checked the safety and tucked it into the back of her waistband like Sean had his. Sean didn't seem to notice his, but Krista could feel the metal biting into her lower spine and reached back to adjust it. No amount of shifting or tugging eased the discomfort, reminding her with every breath that she had a loaded weapon in her pants.

"Here," Sean said as he tossed a small canvas backpack at her. She caught it in midair and nearly keeled over from the weight.

"Sorry," Sean said. "Should have warned you that that was heavy. There are ten extra magazines in there, which should be more than enough."

"I should say so, since I'm hoping not to shoot anything if I can help it."

"Not if I can help it either," Sean said as he tucked a pistol into his own waistband. "But the way things have been going, I'm not sure we'll have much control over the situation."

While Ibarra pulled ammo off the shelves and put it into a carrier, Sean finished packing half a dozen handguns into a steel case. He snapped it shut and leveled his stare on her. "What do you think? If it came down to it, do you think you have it in you to pull the trigger? Because if not, you're better off sticking with pepper spray and a Taser than with a weapon you're not willing to use."

Krista swallowed hard as the weight of Sean's question fully sank in. Images flashed in her head. The explosion, the bullet tearing through the deputy's chest and head in an explosion of blood, bone, and flesh.

Jimmy Caparulo, lifeless on his blood-soaked mattress, the wall behind him spattered with gore.

Could she do that? Pull the trigger to launch a bullet through another person's body in an attempt to cause that kind of damage?

Then she remembered kneeling with a gun to her head, sick with fear as she waited for a bullet to rip into her own skull. Then running through the dark with Sean, his grunt of pain, the bloody gash in his leg that hadn't slowed him down in his mission to get them to safety.

I would kill for him.

The thought was so shocking, so visceral, it made her stomach flip. But in that flash, she knew down to her very core, she wouldn't hesitate to pull the trigger if it meant keeping Sean safe. Sean watched her, still waiting for her answer. "If it comes down to us or them, you don't have to worry."

"Good girl," he said, smiling a little at her fierce tone. He reached out and the feather-light brush of his fingers on her cheek was enough to make her knees wobble.

"Here, take this," Ibarra broke in. Sean dropped his hand and muttered angrily under his breath as Krista hastily stepped away. Sean accepted the wicked-looking knife from Ibarra along with a black nylon sheath. He ran his thumb along the edge and nodded in approval. He hitched up his pant leg, strapped the sheath to his uninjured calf, and slipped the knife inside.

She followed Ibarra and Sean out of the weapons cache. While Sean carried the cases full of guns and ammunition, Krista struggled not to list under the weight of her own ammunition.

"You can take one of my cars," Ibarra said as he led them out of the underground storeroom and up through another passage that opened up into a three-car garage.

Krista prayed he didn't mean the open-top Jeep, or she'd be a Popsicle by the time they reached Seattle. Then again, maybe it would serve to cool down the hormones that had gone berserk after nothing more than a touch on her cheek and the glint of amusement in Sean's eyes.

And, okay, the endless loop of what they'd done last night running constantly in the back of her mind wasn't helping matters any.

"You can take the Subaru," Ibarra said, indicating the blue station wagon parked in the spot farthest from them.

Krista let out a sigh of relief when she saw it had a completely enclosed cab.

"You sure it's going to get us there?" Sean asked skeptically, noting the dent on the front fender and the rust spots on the rear panel. "Looks like that thing has seen better days."

"She's not much to look at on the outside, but my cousin kept it in perfect running condition."

"I'm just happy we get to use a key to start it," Krista muttered. "One less felony to add to my list," she said as she walked over to the car, opened the passenger door, and set the backpack of ammunition on the floor.

"But you are carrying concealed without a permit," Sean said, a ghost of a smile crossing his face as he regarded her over the top of the car. "But don't worry, that's just a little misdemeanor."

Chapter 14

The car ride was torture, trapped in the small space with Krista mere inches away. At least had the distraction of the reports Ibarra had pulled, cross-referencing the larger deposits into Nate's accounts with suspicious deaths, which Ibarra expanded to include not just suicides but accidents as well.

He'd loaded everything up on a mini laptop with security features that would render their communications invisible to anyone who cared to monitor. He also outfitted them with a secure satellite phone that would both provide them a direct line to Ibarra—who was staying put for now—and enable them to make untraceable outgoing calls—finally, a secure connection to the outside world.

As Sean drove, Krista sifted through the data and found a possible hit.

His name was Steven Amstel, a customs official who had died in a boating accident while on a fishing trip in the San Juans. According to the official report, he was intoxicated and had fallen off his boat, hitting his head in the process. He's slipped unconscious into the water and drowned.

But according to the toxicology screen, his blood alcohol content was a mere .085, barely above the legal limit, enough to indicate a few beers but not enough to make a man of his size sloppy drunk.

And interestingly, at the time of his death, he'd been investigating a trafficking ring where goods and people were allegedly being smuggled over the Canadian border.

"There's nothing that links them directly," Krista said, "but this has Karev written all over it."

And buried deeper in the files, yet another connection to the omnipresent JD Partners.

Jesus, how deep did this shadow corporation's influence go?

And would John Slater's files provide the clues?

She sent Ibarra a text with the information to see if he could dig up any more details.

He was amazed at her focus and ability to stay on track, especially after the discovery of her father's involvement with JD Partners. She'd been visibly upset, taking it like a physical blow. But shaken to her core, she hadn't fallen apart.

As a man who had seen some of the toughest guys in the world crumble, he couldn't help but admire her strength.

Yet another damn thing to drive him crazy. As though the chemistry radiating between them wasn't distracting enough. Even with the discovery of possible additional evidence, Sean found it hard to keep his focus where it should be: on analyzing the information they'd found and pulling all the threads together to see if they could connect the bank accounts to the real live human or humans who were behind the killings.

Jesus, he'd been through years of some of the most

grueling training on the planet, designed to keep him focused and on task, so that when the world was literally blowing up around him he didn't waver from his mission.

Turned out that to him at least, Krista was more dangerous than a nuclear bomb. Everything about her was a distraction. The warmth of her skin, the scent of her flooding the car so thickly, even the cold air blowing through the open windows offered no relief. He knew it was his imagination, but he swore that with the new dark hair, her own scent got darker, richer, and even more mind-blowing.

Which was ridiculous, because he of all people knew she was still blond where it counted.

He rolled his shoulders and told himself to get his mind out of the gutter and made himself a silent promise: When and if they got out of this mess, somehow, some way, he was going to work Krista Slater out of his system once and for all.

As they drove, he entertained thoughts of taking her back to his cabin, caveman style, and keeping her there for a week, a month—as long as it took.

But for now he needed to put a lid on all this craziness, get his head off of Krista and back on the task of getting them out of the mess that had them running for their lives.

Five hours later, Sean parked the car along a curb in Seattle's ritzy Washington Park neighborhood. He pulled a cap over his closely shorn hair and slipped on a pair of mirrored sunglasses.

Despite the cloudy day, Krista followed his lead and put on oversize shades as they climbed out of the car. With the haircut and the wardrobe change, she looked nothing like her usual self. No one, not even a neighbor who had known her all of her life, would match this urban fashion victim to cool, classically beautiful Krista Slater.

Unless that person was intimately acquainted with her body, Sean thought, shifting uncomfortably as his eyes drifted to the long line of her legs, the muscles flexing and shifting under the clingy fabric of her pants. Others might not know her, but he'd recognize the curve of her neck, exposed now by the new haircut, across a crowded room.

He gave himself a mental shake and forced his brain back to the mission.

Sean followed Krista around the block and up the walk to an imposing iron gate. The main gate was wide enough to allow access to cars, and there was a keypad with a built-in speaker that would be level with the driver's side window if you came in by car.

Krista bypassed the keypad and went for the smaller gate to the right. She pulled her key ring from her purse and, *click, click*, they were inside the ten-foot-high, ivy-covered brick wall that surrounded the house.

Sean let out a low whistle as he got his first glimpse of Krista's father's house. It looked like someone had transplanted a miniature French chateau to Seattle, complete with a cobblestone circular drive featuring a fountain in the center. To the right of the main house, Sean saw what looked like a four-car garage. "Nice digs."

Krista shrugged. "Pays well to defend rich scumbags," she said.

Sean gave another quick look around as she walked straight up to the front door. A place this big—Sean couldn't tell for sure from the front but he'd bet the house was at least six, maybe seven, thousand square feet, not including the grounds—needed a decent-sized nearly full-time staff to stay on top of everything. Sean had expected maybe a nice craftsman, not a sprawling mansion potentially crawling with staff. "You sure we're not going to run into anyone? A housekeeper, a gardener?"

She gave a quick shake of her newly dark head and opened the door with her key. "It's May."

"So?"

"Elinor—my father's wife—is in Maui until June, which means my father spends most of his time at the office or on the golf course, and staff works on half time." The hard soles of her flat boots sounded against the marble floor of the entryway.

Sean followed her inside, his nose picking up the scent of furniture polish and traces of expensive perfume. The entryway was dominated by a sweeping staircase, the curved kind Sean had only ever seen in hotels or in movies. "You grew up in this house?"

"Since my mom and dad divorced."

"Which was when?" Sean asked.

"When I was six," she replied.

"You split time between both parents?" he asked, and then told himself he shouldn't give a crap how Krista grew up. Yet for some godforsaken reason he was intensely curious about Krista's past.

"No," she said as she locked the door behind her. "My mom wasn't really into parenting," she said with little air quotes around the last words. "She moved down to Southern California to find herself. Last I heard she was playing sugar mama to a guy who's my age."

She tried to play it off like it was no big deal, but beneath her flippant tone he sensed it still stung a lot more than she wanted to let on. He felt a pinch deep in his chest and had to force himself not to pull her into his arms.

It was clear from her posture she didn't want to walk any further down memory lane, so Sean took a moment to take in the details of the cold, imposing mansion. To the right of the staircase he could see a large, formal living room, and behind it an archway that looked like it might lead to a kitchen. Krista turned right and started purposefully down the hall. "Office is this way."

He followed at a slower pace, trying to imagine what it must have been like to grow up in this mausoleum. Not fun, judging from the few pictures of Krista, her father, and the dark-haired woman who must have been her stepmother.

Unlike the informal and sometime goofy snapshots of him and Megan that had covered nearly every surface of his grandparents' walls, the only pictures of Krista were formal and so tightly posed that her smiles almost looked like grimaces of pain. In the pictures of the three of them, Krista stood slightly off to the side. He leaned in to study a portrait where she couldn't have been more than eight or nine. Her father and stepmother sat shoulder to shoulder, hands clasped so Elinor's massive diamond ring caught the light, self-satisfied, almost smug smiles on their faces. Off to the side with her pale-blond hair and wide, solemn eyes was Krista, as though she understood even at that young age that she wasn't really part of the main unit.

"Are you coming?" she called. "No one's here now but I don't want to hang out any longer than we have to."

Even as he told himself Krista's poor-little-rich-girl upbringing wasn't his concern, it hurt him to think of that sad-eyed young girl. He could only wonder how the recent discoveries about her father might be chewing her up inside.

He continued down the hall and found her in what had to be her father's office, with its massive desk, heavy leather club chairs, and shelves and shelves of leather-bound books.

Krista stood in front of a wall lined with wooden filing cabinets. She tugged at one drawer, grunting when she found it locked.

"I got it," Sean said. He pulled out his lock pick and knelt down on the floor. As he slid the pick in, he felt her shift and then she was kneeling next to him.

"Careful not to scratch the lock," she said, close enough for him to feel her breath against the skin of his neck. His hand shook a little and he mentally listed the top ten reasons it would be really bad to turn around, pin her down on the thick, no doubt woven rug, and have her right there in her father's office.

Come on, give her one happy memory in this ice chest of a house, his dick argued. The big head won out, barely. He slid the pick in and opened the lock with a soft *click*. She started to flip through the first drawer while he continued down the rows of drawers, unlocking as he went.

Not finding what she was looking for in the first drawer, she moved down to the next, and then the next.

"There's a bunch of stuff for Karev, but nothing for JD Partners," she muttered and continued to sift through the manila files. "Damn it," she swore. "If he kept any files, they should be here."

Sean swallowed back his own disappointment and started to shut the drawer he'd been looking in when something caught his eye. His jaw started to clench as he pulled the thin folder out. He opened it up and found it held what looked like a business contract. "Do you have any idea why your father would have a file for Nate?"

Krista gasped and rushed over to peer at the contents of the folder. "I have no idea." She flipped through the papers. "It's a transfer of ownership document," she murmured. "And there again, JD Partners is involved. They transferred ownership of a piece of land up in Bellingham to Nate." She flipped through the pages, her mouth pulling into a tight line when none of them revealed the identity of the company's owners. "No signature pages"—frustration made her voice tight—"but there are a few handwritten notes."

Sean looked over her shoulder at the yellow-lined paper full of handwritten scrawls. Nothing but a few notes about the deal. Nothing interesting except—"'Ref. D.M. Strictly confidential.' What does that mean?"

"Could be a note on who referred Nate as a client or maybe D.M. is one of the parties involved in JD Partners." Krista looked up from the documents, her face grim and pale. "I thought nothing he could do would surprise me," she said, her voice shaking so hard Sean couldn't stop himself from covering her hand with his. He threaded his fingers through her icy ones as she clung for dear life. "It's one thing that he represented JD Partners, but to knowingly do business with that psycho..." She swallowed hard. "When the truth came out, Nate's name was all over the papers. There's no way he didn't remember—"

A loud thump sounded outside the door. Sean's stomach jumped and in the next breath he wrapped his arm around her waist to pull her down behind the heavy leather couch. From here, he had a bead on the door so he could see who was coming. No idea yet how they'd get out if whoever that someone was decided to plant it for a while, but he'd jump off that bridge when he came to it.

With his chest pressed against Krista's back, he could feel their hearts thudding against each other and he struggled to slow his breath. He kept his gaze pinned to the doorway, barely breathing as he heard the whisper of movement.

A small white paw appeared in the doorway, followed by a black-and-white face dominated by green eyes. Then a sleek black body ending in a long, white-tipped tail entered the office.

Krista let out a relieved groan. "Goddamn you, Boots, you almost gave me a heart attack."

Boots turned at the sound of Krista's voice, flattened her ears against her head, and bared her teeth in a menacing hiss.

Sean rose to his knees to let her up and she pushed to her feet. "Yeah, feeling's mutual, you stupid cat," Krista muttered as she checked to make sure nothing had fallen out of the files she swiped.

As she crossed the office, Boots held up a threatening paw, claws exposed. "I take it you two aren't friends?"

"If I didn't know better, I'd say she always knew I resented her for not being an Australian shepherd, but she hates everyone. Even Elinor, who got her when she was six weeks old."

As she said it, Boots turned her attention to Sean and trotted over, her tail whipping a salute. She stopped at his boots and looked up at him with a meow, and the next thing he knew, the damn cat was weaving her way in and out of his feet.

He looked at Krista, who was staring, open mouthed, and shrugged. "Animals tend to like me." He bent down to absently scratch the cat's ears and he felt its purr rumble up his leg.

He felt a smile tug at his mouth at the suspicious look she gave the two of them, almost like she thought he'd somehow put the cat up to it. He bent and gave the cat a scratch between the ears. "We should get out of here. Let's take Nate's file and whatever he has on Karev to Ibarra's and figure out our next move."

She tucked the files under her arm and headed to the front door. She shut and locked the door and they headed across the drive, back to the pedestrian gate at the top of the driveway.

The wrought iron creaked as the gate swung open, and he could hear the crunch of gravel under her booted feet. As Sean stepped onto the sidewalk next to her, he did an automatic scan of the street.

His stomach nearly bottomed out when he saw the squad car heading down the street toward them.

"Shit," he whispered. He grabbed her hand and started walking down the sidewalk toward it.

"What are you doing? Our car's the other way."

"And the last thing I want to do is lead the cops to it."

"But they saw us come out of Dad's place."

He kept walking, his pace brisk but not rushing. He tucked his chin into his collar against the wind and hoped the cop would take them for a couple walking down the street, away from the giant mansion neither of them lived in…

The cop tweaked the siren just as they passed him. "Fuck," Sean muttered and picked up the pace.

Behind them a car door slammed. "Hey, can I ask you a couple questions?"

Sean took off in a flat-out run, adjusting his pace to make sure Krista stayed with him. He heard the squawk of a radio, the sound of a car door, and the squeal of tires as the squad car whipped around.

The siren pealed through the cold air as they sprinted around the corner.

"This way." The squad car screeched around the corner just as Krista pulled Sean between two houses and through a back yard that opened into a heavily wooded area that bordered one end of the neighborhood park.

Branches slapped his face as he followed Krista, who seemed to know where she was going despite the lack of any trail. He could hear sirens coming from two different directions now. The first officer on the scene must have called for backup.

They came out of the woods about a block from where they had parked the car, near the park's playground. Fortunately the park was deserted, no curious eyes to wonder what they were doing as they squatted behind a Dumpster and watched one of the squad cars go screaming by.

"Do you think they recognized us?" Krista asked, panting from the run.

"Either way, if they pick us up we're screwed." He waited a couple of seconds. He could still hear the sirens in the distance, but they didn't seem to be coming any closer. "You ready to make a run for it?"

Krista nodded, and on his signal they both took off flat out across the park and down the block to where Ibarra's vehicle was parked between a Saab coupe and a Volkswagen station wagon.

The sirens were getting closer—the cops must be doing a loop through the park, but with no cover and the car only a dozen yards away there was nothing to do but run. He skidded to a stop and unlocked the car. He and Krista both scrambled inside.

The sirens were blaring now.

"Go, go," Krista whispered, frantic.

"Wait," Sean said and scrunched himself down on the floor, ignoring Krista's cry of pain as she banged her hand on the gear shift when he yanked her down.

"What—"

"I'm pretty sure they didn't see us get in the car." But "pretty sure" wasn't a hundred percent and he was taking a big goddamn risk. "If we go screaming out of here like a bat out of hell, they'll know it's us. And whatever you've seen in movies, a high-speed car chase in a populated area is no fucking picnic."

"What if they get out to check the car? We're sitting ducks."

As she said it, the sirens abruptly silenced and blue-and-red light flashed through the interior.

Sean could hear the low rumble of the squad car's engine and the intermittent static of the radio.

"Keep driving," Krista whispered, echoing his thoughts.

Sean watched the lights bouncing off the interior and tried not to think about the fact that the doors were shut and the windows rolled up tight. A bead of sweat trickled down his neck and his chest started to go tight.

"I think they're going," Krista said.

The lights moved through the car and finally faded. Sean closed his eyes and forced himself to stay on the floor for another minute before checking. As soon as he was sure the cop car was gone and another wasn't about to come hurtling around the corner, he turned on the ignition and opened the driver's side window wide.

Krista opened her window too.

Sean sucked down half a dozen lungfuls and then forced himself to roll the windows up until there was only an inch-and-a-half crack in each to let in air.

At Krista's cocked eyebrow, he said, "It will look a little strange if we're driving around with the windows down in this kind of weather." Sure, native Seattle-ites were used to the cool spring weather, but most didn't drive around with the windows wide open when it was barely sixty degrees and threatening rain. "And the windows will help obscure us from the traffic cameras."

In case the cops decided to monitor the cameras in the vicinity, Sean pulled a ball cap over his short hair. He picked his way carefully back to the house Ibarra owned in Seattle's Rainier Beach neighborhood, avoiding as many stoplights and busy intersections as possible.

Krista stared nervously out the window, but after several minutes with no cops following them down the side streets, she relaxed a few degrees. Her face was still grim, her eyes shadowed as she stared sightlessly out the window.

Sean couldn't help but try to comfort her. "I know it's a blow, finding out your father's messed up in all of this, that he was working with Nate..." Though he knew it led to danger, he couldn't stop himself from reaching across the gear shift to put his hand on her leg.

She let out a mirthless laugh and covered his hand with her own. "It shouldn't be, but it is."

"I get it. He's still your father. No matter what your differences, it has to hurt."

"You'd think I'd be immune by now, and yet, in the back of my mind, I'm always hoping..." Her voice trailed off. She shook her head and a hard glint appeared in her stare. "Let me tell you why nothing my father does should surprise me anymore."

She closed her eyes and swallowed hard. She didn't know if Sean would even care, but she had to make him understand what had happened, make him see she was nothing like her father or any other stereotypical scumbag lawyer. "When I was a junior at U-Dub, my college roommate and I went to a party after the Washington-Oregon game. It was at the Delt house, which is the football fraternity, so things got pretty wild. But Nicole and I didn't go too crazy, at least not compared to some people."

Sean kept his eyes on the road, but his curt nod told her he was listening.

"We were drunk, no doubt about it, but not sloppy, not to the point we were going to do anything stupid." Krista let out another little laugh. "Nicole hated to throw up. *Hated* it. So she was always really careful when she drank not to push it too far. I wasn't always as smart," she said, watching her finger trace a circle on her leg. "But lucky for me, the couple times I got out of control I had Nicole there to hold my hair."

"Nice," Sean said with a faint smile.

"Anyway, it was the usual. We were drinking, dancing, flirting with the guys. Eventually the players showed up, and Jason Worley came over to dance with Nicole." Just saying his name made her feel like acid was being poured down her throat. "He was the wide receiver for the Huskies and his father is a big-shot software mogul."

"Ted Worley?" Sean asked, recognizing the name of the billionaire who'd only recently retired as CEO of one of the largest software companies in the world. She could tell from Sean's face that he knew exactly where this was going, that maybe he even remembered some details of the case that had been splashed on the covers of the local papers.

But to his credit, he didn't interrupt or try to speed her to the conclusion, as though he knew she needed to spew it all up at once before the black bile of what happened that night threatened to poison her. "That's the guy. Handsome, rich, star football player. Who wouldn't want to date him, right?

"Then"—she broke off as a lump in her throat threatened to cut off her oxygen. This was when the story got hard. "This guy I liked from my political science study group showed up. We went outside to talk. One thing led to another, and when I went to tell Nicole I was leaving with him I couldn't find her. Another friend said she'd seen her go upstairs with Jason.

"So I took poli-sci guy home, and we fooled around a little bit until I decided it was time to send him on his way. Nicole still wasn't back, but I just figured she was having a good time and would come home in the morning."

She closed her eyes against the memory of what happened next. "She came home around ten-thirty the next morning, and right away I could tell something was wrong." Nicole's face had been gray, which could have been attributed to the usual hangover pallor had it not been for the haunted look in her big brown eyes.

"I asked her what happened and she just shook her

head. But then she went to take her shirt off I saw... She had all these marks on her back and above her bra. I got closer and realized that he'd *bitten* her, hard enough to break the skin in a couple places. He'd also choked her. I could see the marks on her neck."

The guilt gnawed at her, as fresh and bitter as it had been that morning.

Sean must have seen it. "You couldn't have known that was going to happen."

Krista shook her head. "We had an agreement. We were supposed to look out for each other... I knew enough about rape cases that I didn't let her take a shower. So we packed up her clothes and went to the clinic. They did a rape kit and the police took her report. I thought that would be it."

She shook her head, marveling anew at her naïveté. Now, after seven years in the PA's office and dozens of rape cases, she knew firsthand how incredibly difficult they could be to prosecute. Especially cases of acquaintance rape.

But what Jason had done, the brutality he'd inflicted, had been so extreme, Krista couldn't see how anyone could ever imagine that that was consensual.

"The police arrested Jason later that day." Her one bright moment in the horrible ordeal. "And he retained my father as his lead counsel two hours later."

Sean's breath left his lungs on a harsh curse. "I had just gotten out of Ranger school right around then, so I only heard bits and pieces from the news. But I didn't remember that part."

"Yeah, it's pretty screwed up, right? I begged him to drop Jason as a client." She smiled bitterly as she remembered that exchange. Her sobbing, pleading with him on the couch, getting more hysterical by the second as she listed in gruesome detail exactly what Jason had done to Nicole. Looking back now, she realized it was the last time she'd ever lost control in front of her father. "He didn't even bother feeding me the line that everyone has the right to an attorney. He just told me that Ted Worley had called him personally, and he couldn't refuse such an important opportunity regardless of how I felt about the matter."

"Selfish bastard," Sean bit out and then clamped his mouth shut. "Sorry, I know he's your father and all, but that's stone cold."

Shame at what came next made Krista drop her gaze to the polished hardwood floor. "He tore Nicole apart. I don't know why I was so shocked when Jason got off. I mean, even then without any experience, I knew enough about acquaintance rape cases to know how it went. But what he did to her—" She swallowed hard, squeezing her eyes against the sting of tears. "The bites, the bruises. Sean, he tore her inside. How could anyone in their right mind ever think Nicole would have *wanted* that? But my father got all these witnesses to say how they'd seen her drinking and dancing with him, and how she'd followed him upstairs willingly. Even I couldn't deny that."

"He made you testify?" Sean's voice was equal parts shock and fury, his knuckles white as he gripped the steering wheel. "What kind of fucked-up sociopath does that to his own kid?"

Krista shook her head. "I volunteered as a witness for the prosecution before my father could get to me. And to be fair, he wasn't nearly as tough on me as he'd been on some of the other witnesses. But it didn't matter.

"He didn't even make it to trial," she continued. "The judge dismissed all the charges after the evidentiary hearing."

"What happened to Nicole?" Sean asked.

"She dropped out and I heard she transferred to the University of Montana. The last time we spoke was the day she moved out of our apartment. She didn't keep in touch, for obvious reasons."

Sean's hand gave her thigh a gentle squeeze. "What happened to her wasn't your fault," Sean repeated. "You couldn't have known what he was going to do."

Krista turned her hand so it was palm to palm with his, savoring the feel of callused skin and the warmth that traveled up her arm. "Logically, I know that's true, but I can't help but feel I should have seen or sensed something to clue me in to what he was capable of. But I didn't. You want to know something sick? I was actually a little jealous that he chose her over me. Part of me wanted to be hooking up with Jason Worley that night instead of the guy from my poli-sci class." She'd never admitted that out loud before. "I still wish he'd chosen me, but for different reasons."

"That's ridiculous and you know it," he said with a firm squeeze of her hand. "What happened to her wasn't her fault, and it sure as hell wasn't your fault."

Krista shook her head. He was never going to convince her. "Whatever. But do you get now why I shouldn't be shocked that he's up to his neck in all of this?" Hell, for all she knew, he knew who was trying to kill her.

Yet she couldn't get the memory of her father's devastated face in the news footage out of her head.

He was capable of many things, but he wouldn't stand

by and let her get murdered, would he? She swallowed thickly, tears stinging her eyes.

As though reading her thoughts, Sean said, "Maybe we should talk to him. If he knows that people he's working with are behind all of this—"

Krista shook her head. "I'd like to think his loyalty would be with me, but I can't take the chance that it's not. We have to find another way to get to the truth of this." She stared out the window for a few minutes, wishing she could call on Mark, depend on his wisdom and connections to figure it all out. But whoever was after them would be keeping an eye on Mark, as they were no doubt watching Cole and Megan. They would expect them, once backed into a corner, to reach out.

They'd hit a dead end, and for the life of her, Krista couldn't see a way out of it without endangering the people she and Sean loved.

"Who is Talia Vega?"

At Ibarra's question, Krista's head snapped up from the files on Karev she'd taken from her father's place.

"She was the star witness during my trial," Sean said, and though he kept his gaze locked on Ibarra, she felt a guilty flush rise in her cheeks. "Why?"

"It looks like she received several deposits from JD Partners over a period of four years," Ibarra said. He'd left his mountain fortress shortly after she and Sean had, and started poking around in JD Partners' money transfers again as soon as he'd arrived.

Sean strolled over to get a closer look at the screen. "What do you know? She got fifty grand the day of my conviction." His green eyes glittered as his expression hardened.

Fresh shame coursed through her at the thought of how thoroughly she'd been played, and the horrible consequences that had on Sean. "I was supposed to have a meeting with her about two months ago, but Nate got to her first. I wonder if this was what she was going to tell me."

"Then why the hell haven't we been talking to her?"

"We can't find her," Krista said, exasperated. "She disappeared from the hospital and no one has seen her since. The last I heard, she and her sister were in Canada, but after that there's been no trace."

"You think they got to her, finished what Nate started?" Sean asked grimly.

"It wouldn't surprise me. But if we can find her..." Krista paced. "There was a guy, Jack Brooks, who worked security with her at Club One. He was the one who convinced her to talk to me, and he showed up at the scene with Cole when Nate took her and Megan..."

Sean's hands clenched into fists as though he was imagining closing them around Nate Brewster's neck.

"Anyway, I tried to get in touch with him, but he's another brick wall. He worked with these guys in California, Gemini Securities—"

"I know those guys," Ibarra interjected. "Family business. Head of it is a former Green Beret," he said to Sean.

"Jack contacted them to get Talia's teenage sister Rosario someplace safe. That was the condition of Talia giving me a statement—we have reason to believe she initially testified against you in order to gain custody of Rosario from foster care. But when I called Gemini's offices to find out if they had any information about Talia and her sister, they shut me down and told me that if I wanted any information I'd need a warrant."

Ibarra stroked his chin. "I've worked with them before. Let me see if I can pull any strings."

He picked up the phone and placed the call, but it was clear from the side of the conversation they could hear that Ibarra wasn't getting any further than Krista had.

"Danny says he can't help. All of their client information is confidential."

"I don't suppose you could find a way into their files?" Krista felt dirty even asking the question, but desperate times...

"Hell no."

"Don't tell me you've suddenly developed a conscience!"

"With people I like and respect and hope to continue working with, hell yes, I have a conscience," Ibarra said, offense written all over his darkly handsome face. "And even if I didn't, their tech security specialists kick my ass all over the place," he said, the admiration clear in his tone. "With the systems she'd have in place, Toni Taggart would sniff me out before I even breached the firewall. However," he said as Sean let out an irritated grunt, "he did let it slip—likely on purpose—that Jack has been doing some work for them here in Seattle and might have some pertinent data if we manage to track him down."

"Let's go find Jack Brooks then," said Sean.

It was a little easier said than done. Jack Brooks didn't exactly have his info posted on his Facebook page. But with a little digging Ibarra was able to get the info for Brooks's last known residence, which was the Lake Union Marina where Jack rented a houseboat.

At this hour in the early evening, the parking lot was

about half full. Many of the boats were probably used only recreationally, and many of those who lived here full time were most likely at work.

"Good, he's not home," Sean said when he noticed that the parking spot that corresponded to Brooks's slip number was empty.

"Why is that good?" Krista asked. "The sooner we talk to him, the sooner we have a chance of making any sense of this."

"Like you said, he wasn't interested in talking to you before. He sees us coming, he's likely to bolt."

He started to climb out of the car.

"Where are you going?"

"You don't think we're going to wait in the car?"

Krista sighed and followed.

He quickly scanned the parking lot, which didn't offer much in the way of security. A couple cameras were mounted to light posts, but they were the stationary kind that maintained the same angle. Anyone who noted their position could easily avoid getting captured on camera.

He led Krista around to the far end of the parking lot, well out of range. The ramps down to the houseboats were accessible by locked gates, but nothing a basic pick couldn't get past.

Krista's head darted around like a bird's.

"Quit it," Sean hissed under his breath as he slid the pick into the lock.

"What?"

"Keep still."

"I'm keeping a lookout."

"The only person I've seen is two docks down, and as long as you don't keep scurrying around like you have something to hide, I don't think they're going to pay us any attention."

"Sorry, I'm still not used to this whole 'acting casual while we break the law' thing," she whispered. "And in case you forgot, if someone calls the cops, they're not going to be on our side."

"Thanks, I got that about three years ago." A faint *click*, and the metal gate swung open.

He took Krista's arm and led her down the dock. She managed to shrug off the nervous air, pulled her shoulders back, and strode down the walkway to Brooks's place like she had every right to be there.

Sean did a quick sweep to make sure no one had taken any notice of them and then checked the front door. Locked with a sturdy dead bolt, which was doable but would take time. He was pretty sure there was an easier entry. "Stay here," he said. "I'm going around the back."

"Be careful," Krista said unnecessarily as Sean slipped into the space between Brooks's place and his neighbor. Sean had no desire for a dunk in the fifty-degree water, so he was careful as he balanced himself along the edge of Brooks's boat and skirted his way around the back.

Like all of the other places, Brooks's house featured a water-level patio extending out from the main living area, accessed from the interior by glass sliders whose flimsy locks posed no challenge.

Brooks hadn't even bothered to upgrade the easy-to-subvert latches with sturdier bolt locks.

Interesting.

He ducked inside and let Krista in through the front door. She stepped into the foyer, slipped off her shades, and looked around, her darkened brows pulled into a V above her small nose. "Does it strike you as weird that a guy in the security business doesn't have any kind of serious security himself?" she asked, echoing Sean's thoughts. "Or have I spent too much time with Ibarra?"

Sean gave a little smile. Ibarra was definitely on the extreme side, but thank God he had their back. "It is a little weird," Sean said, but he had an idea of what might be going on.

He'd seen it in a lot of the guys in his company. When you entered the Special Forces, the military spent hundreds of hours and millions of dollars turning you into a highly trained fighting machine. When you saw regular combat, even if it fucked you up, it was easy to get a little addicted to the adrenaline rush of the fight, the intense surge you got from being in a situation that meant life or death for you and the men fighting beside you.

So when you were sent home and tried to resume civilian life, it was hard for a lot of guys to settle into the regular day-to-day of life in America where, for the most part, life was pretty cush and a firefight wasn't likely to erupt outside your front door.

It was why so many guys ended up working private security, some domestic and a lot overseas, doing contract work that paid a hell of a lot better than the army and put you virtually right back into that life, but without the pesky rules and bureaucracy. A lot of people thought guys did it for the cash—and no doubt it was good, but most did it because on some level they were still itching for the next fight.

Sean suspected Brooks had some of that going on. Granted, he hadn't hired on with an outfit like Blackwater or another firm that would have sent him right back onto the front lines. Instead, the work he'd chosen focused on stopping any violence in its tracks. But that didn't mean he wasn't still itching for a fight.

If he was worried about someone coming after him for meddling with Talia Vega, it didn't show. Instead of tucking tail and heading out of town, he'd stayed put behind a pair of flimsy locks a five-year-old could pick with a bobby pin.

It was like an engraved invitation. Brooks was just waiting for someone to come mess with him.

He shared none of this with Krista. She was already jumping around like an exposed nerve. No need to ratchet her paranoia up any higher. As they waited for Brooks to show, Sean kept himself on high alert.

Krista nervously perched on the edge of Brooks's couch. "Now that we're here, maybe we should wait outside," she said. "I met Brooks only once, but he doesn't seem like a guy who will react well to finding us waiting in his house."

"What, you think I can't take him?" Sean asked.

Krista rolled her eyes. "I couldn't even speculate—all I'm saying is that if we want him to cooperate, maybe surprising him in his house isn't the best plan."

"I get what you're saying, but better to get him in here than risk him spotting us and taking off before we get a chance to talk to him." And right now, the element of surprise was their only slight advantage.

A soft *thud* sounded from the back of the house. Shit. Maybe they'd lost their advantage after all. Krista's eyes went wide as Sean pulled the Glock from the back of his waistband and pressed himself up against the wall. He motioned for Krista to stay silent and directed her to the small alcove by the front door, which Brooks used as a doorless hall closet.

Wait here, he mouthed. She nodded, eyes wide as she burrowed silently between two huge jackets that hung from metal hooks.

Sean slipped into combat mode like it was a second skin as he crept silently along the wall, waiting for Brooks to round the corner. Like Sean, the former Green Beret had years of training drilled into him that allowed him to ghost in and out of places undetected. Despite his size, Brooks didn't make a sound as he came down the short hall, and it was only a slight disturbance in the air that alerted Sean that he was about to round the corner.

Brooks scanned the room, gun gripped in both hands as it followed the path of his gaze. Sean took two silent steps back and raised his Glock.

Sean knew the second Brooks sensed his presence, and in that split second he shoved the muzzle of his gun into the back of Brooks's neck. "Drop yours," Sean said.

Brooks grunted and did as he was told.

"Kick it."

The gun skittered along the hardwood.

"My name is—"

Before Sean could finish, Brooks whirled around and launched a fist into the center of Sean's chest. Sean jumped to the side at the last minute, taking the blow in the meat of his pec instead of dead center. A blow that, delivered with enough force, could have stopped his heart in his chest.

Still, Brooks's fist landed with considerable force, enough to make him grunt and loosen his grip on the Glock enough so that when Brooks's next blow landed against his wrist it was enough to send the gun out of his hand and across the room.

"Brooks, I just want to ask you some questions," Sean said as he blocked a blow to the face.

Brooks wasn't interested in what he had to say. His sole focus was on beating the shit out of the guy who had dared to invade his home.

It took all of Sean's concentration to keep Brooks from pounding the shit out of him, and within a few seconds the adrenaline kicked in. They were well matched in size and skill, and soon Sean had nearly forgotten why he was even here, he was so caught up in the rush of the fight.

Brooks swept out with his leg and Sean jumped back, barely avoiding being taken to the ground. Brooks rushed him, slamming him into the wall with enough force to knock the wind from him and crack the plaster. Sean could see the heel of Brooks's hand rushing to his face and quickly ducked his head.

Shit, if that blow had landed it would have sent pulverized bits of bone straight up into his brain.

Fucker was seriously trying to kill him.

The primitive urges Sean had kept so carefully in check for the past several years surged, straining to break free, urging him to give as good as he got. But the steady, rational voice inside him reminded him that they needed Brooks to talk—they needed him on their side. If they weren't fucked enough already, they would be if he accidentally killed or maimed their one possible connection to a key witness.

He forced himself to pull his punches and he tried to push Brooks past the red haze of combat to get him calm enough to talk.

Sean grunted as a blow glanced off his temple, flooding his head with pain and making him see stars.

The wound on his head opened up, sending blood coursing down his face, quickly blinding him in one eye. With his depth perception all fucked up, he couldn't move fast enough to avoid a kick to the chest. It sent him reeling into a low table. He keeled over backward, felt the wood splinter under his weight as he went down like a ton of bricks.

Brooks came over him, his face a mask of cold rage.

Krista. Desperation flooded him with a surge of power. Brooks was in full-on fight mode, in no mood to listen. No matter that Ibarra's friend vouched for him—in the place Brooks was in, there was no telling what damage he might do to Krista.

Sean was vaguely aware of her screaming as he brought his knees up to his chest and shoved his feet into Brooks's stomach. The other man stumbled a bit and reached out to grab something from the floor.

The yelling got louder as Brooks swung what looked like a table leg at Sean's head. He heard the whoosh of the bludgeon as he ducked at the last second.

Blam blam!

"Knock it the fuck off!"

Both men froze and turned in the direction of the dark-haired woman standing at the front of the room like some refugee from *La Femme Nikita*, feet in a wide, bracing stance, forearm muscles corded as she gripped a pistol in both hands and pointed it straight at Jack Brooks's chest like she meant business. Bits of plaster still fell from the bullet holes she'd shot in the ceiling.

Brooks's eyes narrowed on the gun and Sean could see the other man's muscles coil as he prepared to spring.

"Don't you fucking touch her," Sean growled. "Even if she doesn't manage to shoot you, I'll fuck you up if you touch so much as a hair on Krista's head."

"Krista?" Brooks's head cocked to the side and Sean could sense a little of the tension melting out of him. "Krista Slater?"

Krista nodded, but kept the gun raised and aimed at Brooks. *Good girl*, he thought as he moved to stand beside her.

Brooks eased back off the balls of his feet and held his hands up. He turned his focus to Sean. "So you must be Flynn."

Sean nodded.

"I take it she's not your hostage."

"And he didn't kill a cop, either," Krista said. "We were set up, and we're hoping you can help us figure out who's behind it."

"I'm not sure how I can help," Brooks said. "Do you mind putting that down?"

Krista's hand was cramping at the weight of the pistol but she didn't lower the gun. "You'll have to forgive me if I'm a little nervous after the way you tried to kill Sean with your bare hands."

Both men were breathing hard, muscled chests heaving up and down. Krista was afraid that if she breathed too deeply she'd sprout hair on her chest, the air was so thick with testosterone.

The room itself was a wreck, furniture splintered, cracks in the plaster coating the walls, and blood—probably from the oozing cut on Sean's forehead—stained the pine planks of the floor.

"I didn't notice him holding back," Brooks said, lifting his fingers to the cut on his lip. His right cheekbone was red and already swelling, and he winced as he probed the left side of his ribs. "And how do you expect me to react when my alarm goes off in the middle of the afternoon and a guy jumps me in my own living room?"

"Sorry about that," Sean said, "but your boss indicated you might be reluctant to talk to us, and since we can't exactly get to you in public, we had to improvise. So you have a remote monitoring system?"

"Sends an alert to my cell phone if the perimeter is breached."

"Nice," Sean said, admiration evident in his voice. Krista could see them relax a degree as they took each other's measure.

Each must have found something they liked because their faces lost some of the hardness and they gave each other nearly imperceptible nods.

Krista took it as manly man speak for *we're cool.* She thumbed the Glock's safety back on and tucked it into her waistband. "Does it alert the police?" If so, they had about five seconds before they needed to get out of here.

Brooks shook his head and gave her a look like she was crazy. "Just me. I don't like dealing with the cops." He pulled the couch back to its original position and sank down. Krista followed suit, taking a seat in the armchair across from him. Sean went to the kitchen to retrieve a towel for his head and positioned himself behind her chair as though he was standing guard. "Although I can't make any promises if any of my neighbors heard you tear up my ceiling," he said to Krista.

Krista felt guilty heat rise in her cheeks and she shot Sean an apologetic look.

"Let's get right to the point," Sean said. "We need to get in touch with Talia Vega."

Only a subtle shift in Brooks's facial muscles gave a clue that the name had meaning to him. "What makes you think I can help you?"

"Spare me the bullshit, Brooks," Krista said. "Talia went missing from the hospital after her attack. The way I see it there are two options: Either someone finished what Nate started or someone helped get her into hiding. If that's the case, I'd lay odds you had something to do with it."

Brooks was silent, his blue eyes unreadable.

"We know you helped her before, that you brought in Gemini Securities to get her sister to safety." She blew out a frustrated breath. "Before she was attacked, Talia was supposed to meet with me to give me details about Sean's case. I know she was pushed to testify in Sean's trial by someone other than Nate, and we think whoever that is, is trying to shut us up before we find out. We need to know who."

"What makes you think I have an answer?" Jack said curtly.

Sean cocked a doubtful brow. "You were one of the last people to talk to her before Nate got the drop on you and took her," Sean said bluntly.

Krista could see the guilt flash across Brooks's face. He was still beating himself up for that. After examining the scene and seeing photos documenting Talia's injuries, it wasn't hard to see why it still ate at him. "I find it hard to believe she didn't tell you anything," Krista said.

"You can believe what you want. But Talia was dead set on telling only you." He shook his head.

"If that's the case, then we need to talk to her," Sean pressed. "What little we've found so far—it's not enough. We still don't know who's driving this boat and if we don't find out, more people are going to die."

"I promised I'd keep her safe, and I let her down. I fucked up big time and it almost got her killed with your sister," he said to Sean.

Krista exchanged a look with Sean. Did he know for certain someone hadn't finished what had Nate started?

"I know you want to nail these assholes," Brooks continued, "and believe me, if I knew who they were, they'd be too dead to be fucking with you right now." He scrubbed his hand over his short-cropped hair. "But it's like I told the cops, aside from the little bit Talia let slip, for all I know everything started and ended with Nate Brewster."

Krista exchanged a look with Sean, who gave her a quick nod. "That's obviously what someone wants us to believe, but based on some financial transactions we were able to dig up, it's pretty clear there was someone else paying Nate's bills."

Jack's brows pulled into a frown that grew darker as Sean and Krista shared their theory that Nate was in fact a knife for hire for a much bigger fish.

"Some sick fuck paid him for what he did to Talia?" Brooks said. Krista could see a vein start to throb in his forehead.

"We don't know about Talia specifically," she said, cautiously watching Brooks's fists as they clenched and unclenched. Next to her, she felt Sean subtly shift into readiness, poised to spring if Brooks lost it. "But we can connect some deposits to the murders of the other girls, as well as to the murder of a U.S. Customs agent."

Brooks wrestled himself back under control and blew out a shaky lungful of air. "No names?"

"Nothing but bank accounts and multiple dummy corporations," Sean said, "including the one that ran your former company. That's why we were hoping maybe you could help."

Jack shook his head. "I heard about the job from a friend of a friend, and I was low man on the totem pole. Guys who were more senior got moved out into the private sector, working high-end jobs for corporations and executive muckety-mucks. What I did at Club One was basically glorified bouncer work."

"You seem a little overqualified for that," Krista said.

"With my record, I had to pay my dues before they'd trust me with the big jobs."

Sean heaved a frustrated sigh. "And if any of the big jobs are connected, we'll never know because the company and its records evaporated into thin air. What's up with that?" he asked Brooks.

"Hell if I know," Brooks said. "I gave the police my statement, and next thing I know the club is closed and I can't get in touch with anyone in the company. All I got was a cashier's check for my last week of work."

"You didn't keep in touch with anyone you worked with?" Krista asked.

"We weren't exactly a tight-knit group of guys," Brooks said. "I didn't ask too many questions." He gave his broad shoulders a shrug. "I figured it made sense for me to lie low for a little while and not go nosing around. But, shit, if I'd had any idea how fucked up this all was..." He got up abruptly and went to stand in front of the windows, gazing out into the marina.

"When's the last time you saw Talia?" Sean asked.

"As she was loaded into the ambulance," Brooks said, and Krista thought she detected a subtle stiffening in his shoulders. "I wanted to ride with her, but Williams wanted me to stay and talk to the cops."

"And you haven't seen her at all since?"

He gave his head a definitive shake, but Krista wasn't buying it.

"The company you're working with now—Gemini Securities—they're no longer protecting Rosario? Maybe they helped Talia too?"

Another negative. "I saw them load Talia into the ambulance, and the next thing I heard she disappeared. I was afraid someone had gotten to her, but apparently she picked up Rosie at one point and headed over the border." He turned and hit Krista with a challenging stare. "Unless you've heard different."

Crap. This was going nowhere, exactly what she'd been afraid of. Whatever he knew, he wasn't giving it up any time soon, and they didn't have the leverage to force it out of him. She sank back into the cushions of the armchair. "No." Then: "I know this is a long shot, but do you know of any connection Nate might have had to a man named Roman Karev?"

Brooks's eyes narrowed. "I've seen him in the news. Russian mobster, you were trying to get him for murder?"

Krista couldn't stop a wry half smile. "He likes to call himself a restaurateur, but yeah, that's the guy."

Brooks's eyes got a faraway look. "He came in only

once the whole time I worked there, him and three of his guys. I thought it was weird at the time, because those guys usually keep to their own territory."

The tiny hairs on the back of Krista's neck stood on end. "Was there trouble?"

"Talia asked me to keep an eye on them and told the staff to make sure they got everything they wanted. They made her nervous. They headed straight up to the VIP room and got a bottle for the table." He frowned as he tried to call up the details. "They kept to themselves and didn't try to get any girls. I remember it was kind of weird—like they weren't there to party but to check out the scene."

Krista looked to Sean as she tried to sort it out in her mind. "Maybe they were there to check out their operation?"

"Or the competition," Sean said.

"You think they paid for the murders?"

Krista shrugged. "It wouldn't be their regular MO. If Karev wants someone dead, he has plenty of heavies on his own crew. But all of this has gotten so convoluted, I wouldn't be surprised at anything."

"Me neither," Brooks said. "The night I saw them, they left after an hour and one bottle, and didn't speak to anyone but each other."

The only way to get to the bottom of this was to get to Karev, and if he was behind the hits, it would be suicide to take him on directly.

There had to be another way. She rose from the chair and grabbed a pen and piece of paper from the kitchen counter. "If you can think of anything else that might help, you can call us on this number or send an e-mail to this address." She handed him the slip of paper with their contact info.

"Both are completely secure and untraceable," Sean said. "So don't get any ideas about trying to turn us in."

"I know we're all on the same side here," Brooks said as he idly flicked his thumbnail along the edge of the paper. "Whoever the fucker is, he has to go down." Krista could tell from his expression that Brooks was deeply disturbed by the idea that someone had paid Nate to kill those women, knowing what kind of torture he would inflict. Knowing that it would send a terrifying message to the others. "Problem is, if his influence goes as deep as Talia said, we're going to have to be damn careful," he said, almost to himself.

Krista's ears pricked up. There was something about the way he'd said "we."

He gave his head a little shake as though trying to clear it. "I'll let you know when I hear anything."

Krista cocked her head to the side and shot Sean a look. Yep, he'd caught it too. Brooks's use of *when*, not *if*.

He didn't seem the type to out himself with a simple slip of the tongue.

Brooks offered his hand first to Sean and then to Krista. "I hope to hear from you soon," she said.

Talia Vega answered Jack's call, assuming he would give her an update about how her younger sister Rosario was faring living under her temporary secret identity. After he told her about his visit today from Krista Slater and Sean Flynn, she wished she hadn't.

"Just tell me who Nate was working with, and it will

finally be over." She could hear the frustration in Jack's voice, imagined his big hand gripping the phone till his knuckles turned white.

"We've been over this a hundred times, and I told you, it's not going to do you any good. You'll never get to him, and you'll only put yourself in danger." It was a sore spot with Jack that she'd never given up David Maxwell's name in all this time. She didn't know all the details, but she knew Maxwell's reach went deep, deeper than Jack ever could imagine.

After all Jack had done for her and her sister, she wasn't about to risk his life by squealing. "You've already done so much to help me and Rosario," she said, feeling her anger at his sneak attack ebbing. "This is my part to keep you safe."

"You let me worry about myself. This is about nailing this asshole—whoever he is—for good so that you and Rosario can get on with your lives."

At the mention of her sister, Talia had to ask, "But Rosario's safe, right? Nothing has happened to her?" Her heart thudded against her ribs. Maxwell could do whatever he wanted to her, but the thought of him getting to Rosario terrified Talia.

"She's fine. But this isn't good for her, and it isn't good for you."

"As long as Rosie's safe, that's all that matters," Talia said as she ran a frustrated hand through her hair. But she knew Jack was right. Safe or not, Rosario shouldn't have to live under the shadow of maintaining a secret life, of worrying that she was going to slip up and use her real name. Of knowing that if she did, there were people out there waiting to hurt her.

"And what happens if she slips her cover?" Jack said, feeding into Talia's fear. "She's sixteen, not an age known for keeping secrets. I already had to warn her twice to take down her Facebook page."

Talia's stomach flipped over. "Please tell me she didn't post any pictures."

"I wish I could. Luckily we were able to get them down and erase any trace, but she's a kid. No matter how closely we watch her, there's a huge risk she'll spill her guts to a friend. You know there's no way we can keep this arrangement long term. All you have to do is give us a name."

"There's no way to get this guy, no matter what I tell you."

Jack bit out a curse. "There's no way we'll know unless you tell us!"

"He will do anything to protect himself, no matter whom he hurts. If he thinks his cover's at risk, he will hurt you—"

"I'll take that risk."

"He will hurt your family. He will hurt your friends— they know you work with Danny Taggart and they'll go after the whole company—"

"They're professionals. They can take care of themselves."

"What about me? You have no idea what he'll do to me—"

"How would it change anything for you? You're already in hiding now and you'll stay there until this plays out. I can keep you safe—"

"You made that promise before," she snapped and fingered the raised scar just beneath her ribcage.

Several seconds of dead silence hung on the other end of the line. It was a cheap shot, and part of her felt ashamed. But there was no way she wanted to back a desperate David Maxwell into a corner. There was no limit to how far he'd go to get even.

"Danny and his whole team will keep you safe," Jack said, practically spitting out the words. "You trust them with Rosario, and they've kept you safe this long."

Talia didn't respond.

"Why are you protecting him?" Jack finally shouted. "Do you care about him? Is this some twisted shit where you love him even though he wants you dead?"

"No!" But she had once, and she shuddered in revulsion at her own stupidity. "I'm not protecting him. I'm protecting everyone else."

"Krista and Sean don't feel that way. Neither does Cole Williams, who had to take his fiancée into hiding because of her connection to this case. And I bet Rosario doesn't either, having to be in a strange town, strange school, reminding herself every morning to use the right name because her life depends on it. You keep hiding, he wins. He lives his life and gets away with everything. We can end this right now, Talia. One phone call. One name. And I will make sure you and Rosario go so deep underground, I won't even be able to find you. When this is done, you and your sister will be free."

Chapter 15

Between traffic and taking back streets to avoid traffic cameras and the police, the drive to Ibarra's took nearly an hour. Sean didn't say much, though Krista caught him looking at her a couple times with a thoughtful expression on his face.

Her brain was too busy stewing on what they'd discovered about her father and what Jack Brooks might reveal—if anything—to dwell on what might be going through Sean's mind behind those pensive looks.

Sean pulled into Ibarra's garage. After he disarmed the alarm system, they entered through a door that connected to the house's small living room. She tossed the files they'd taken from her father's house on the low coffee table while Sean updated Ibarra on the scant information they'd gleaned from Brooks.

"So far he's a dead end, but that could change."

Just like the files, Krista thought morosely as she stared down at the thin pile of manila folders. Other than revealing that her father was involved with people willing to kill her to keep their secrets safe, she didn't think they'd offer up any great clues.

Krista scanned through Nate's file one more time as

she rubbed her temples. On the surface it was a business transaction, completely clean and for all intents and purposes seemed aboveboard. But her stomach churned as she wondered how much her father knew. Did he have any knowledge, even an inkling, that when he was working with Nate he was representing a cold-blooded killer? Did he even think, for a second, that after Nate was exposed as the Seattle Slasher, he should reveal his dealings with him?

"That's good at least, but who knows how soon before they put two and two together?" Krista followed his voice into the office where Sean was talking to Ibarra. They were side by side by the open picture window, their massively powerful frames silhouetted against the late-afternoon light. Sean turned, showing her his profile. His hand lifted to his chin, his fingers brushing back and forth against the grain of his goatee.

For a split second Krista had a memory of those long, strong fingers brushing over her skin, delving between her legs, sinking deep...

As though he felt her stare, his eyes flicked to her face. After the day they'd had, this was so not the time to let her hormones take over.

Again.

"What's up?" she said, turning her attention to Ibarra. Handsome as he was, for whatever reason she didn't lose herself in daydreams of tying him to his bed every time she looked at him. She kept her eyes pinned on Ibarra's face to keep herself from getting distracted by Sean.

"A little good news," Sean interjected. "The cops showed up at your father's house because the neighbor's housekeeper called it in."

"Esmerelda," Krista gave herself a mental asskicking. It was a measure of how fried she really was that she didn't remember the Johnsons' hypervigilant housekeeper. "She busted me both times I tried to sneak out after curfew."

"Only twice?" Sean cocked a dark eyebrow and gave her a look like she was the biggest nerd on the planet.

Krista shrugged. "I got busted both times and cut my losses. Why is that good news?"

"She wasn't able to identify either of us."

Krista felt a little tension leave her shoulders. "Hopefully our luck will hold, because I'm afraid our next move is going to be breaking into my father's office."

"You think he has the files there?" Sean said. "I thought you said he keeps anything sensitive at the house. Why would he change that?"

"I don't know!" Krista said, exasperated. "Maybe he's changed up how he does things. God knows I've discovered things I never expected about my father today."

Sean and Ibarra exchanged a look.

"I'm going to make myself a sandwich," Ibarra said, giving Krista a sympathetic pat on the arm as he passed her on the way to the door.

She closed her eyes against the sting of tears. But God, she was so tired, so wrung out by everything. "I know it's probably just another dead end, but I don't know what else to do—"

Her voice caught in her throat as strong hands slid over her shoulders, thumbs kneading at the tension as hot tingles shot down her spine. "Hey, why don't we take a breather, relax and give ourselves a minute to think on our next move?" Sean said, so close she could feel the warmth of his breath ruffling her hair.

Before she could open her mouth to protest, he continued. "You've had a hell of a day, finding out that shit about your dad and standing up to a bad-ass like Jack Brooks."

Despite herself, Krista felt a smile pulling at her lips. "He wasn't that bad."

Sean gave her shoulders a firmer squeeze. "I have a bruise on my back that proves you wrong. I've never run from a fight in my life, but I even I have to admit the dude's intimidating. But you stood up to him like you were channeling Wonder Woman."

She tipped her head back to look at him. "Amazing how desperation can motivate you."

A smile quirked his full lips. "Whatever it was, I was impressed. That's some spine you have."

"Thanks," she murmured, unable to take her eyes off that full mouth, more sensual now that it was framed by the whiskers of his goatee. Dark and thick, she wondered how they would feel brushing against her skin.

And then she didn't have to wonder, because Sean was turning her in his arms and bringing his mouth down on hers. He whispered something at the last second that sounded like "Idiot." Probably aimed at himself, but it applied to both of them. That's what this was. Idiocy, craziness. Yet as his tongue stroked hers and the brush of his whiskers against her cheek sent a thrill straight to her core, nothing had ever felt more right.

The sat phone shrieked, and Sean gave a frustrated groan as he reluctantly untangled his tongue from hers. As though he couldn't help himself, he pressed one last, lingering kiss on her cheek before he reached for the phone.

Sean studied the display, his face grim. "It's not a number I recognize."

The heat from Sean's kiss was gone in an instant. The only person besides Ibarra who had the number was Jack Brooks.

Unless... *Don't panic.* Even if someone else had gotten hold of the number, the phone was untraceable. And if they'd somehow made the connection to Ibarra, well, Krista had all the faith that he could take care of himself.

Still, her stomach flipped over as Sean pressed the ANSWER button and held it to his ear. "Yes." His shoulders relaxed a little. "Hold on, let me put it on speaker."

Sean placed the phone on the desk and pressed a button. "Are you there?"

"Yes." Jack's deep, familiar voice filled the office. "And I have Talia Vega on the line."

Chapter 16

W ait, that's not possible," Krista said, snapping straight and stepping back from the desk as she reeled from the bombshell Talia had just dropped. "David Maxwell?" Krista felt like she'd taken a blow to the stomach. "Is this some kind of joke?"

"Honestly, after having my diaphragm perforated and my liver almost cut in half, I don't have much of a sense of humor left," Talia's voice crackled over the line.

"I told you this was stupid, Jack," Talia said. "No one will ever believe that it's him."

"Talia," Krista said, trying to keep her tone less combative. "I know you've been through a lot and I'm sorry if I don't sound sympathetic, but it's just hard for me to believe that a member of one of the city's wealthiest and influential families could be a part of this." She tried to make sense of it. Thanks to her father's dealings, she'd known Maxwell since she was a teenager.

His wife, Margaret Grayson-Maxwell, came from one of Seattle's most prominent families, which had made their fortune in manufacturing but had since branched out into everything from financial services to electronics. The family had been involved in local and state politics for decades, and now Margaret was trying to make her mark in a run for the state senate, funded by the millions David had made through his own business ventures.

Somehow she just couldn't picture the roughly handsome David Maxwell, with his shrewd blue eyes, being involved in something like this.

"Maxwell is known as a philanthropist and his wife is running for state senate, for God's sake," Krista said.

"Yeah, well the money for all that has to come from somewhere, and I'm telling you, most of David Maxwell's is dirty."

Hours later, Krista was still reeling from Talia's revelation that David Maxwell was behind everything that had happened to Sean. The biggest issue was that Talia had no evidence to back up her claims about Maxwell. Talia knew only two things with total certainty. First, that she had been David Maxwell's mistress for four years, up until the day she was kidnapped and attacked by Nate Brewster.

Second, that David Maxwell had pulled strings in social services to get Talia custody of her younger sister, who had been in foster care up to that point, and had given Talia a big fat promotion and a raise at Club One in exchange for one simple thing: come forward as a witness and testify in a court of law that Sean Flynn had been stalking Evangeline Gordon in the weeks before she was murdered and that she'd seen Evangeline leave with Sean the night of her death, not entirely voluntarily.

But impossible as it all seemed, Brooks's colleagues back at Gemini Securities headquarters had been able to connect Maxwell through banking transactions to the maze of shell corporations they'd uncovered.

"He must have covered up Nate's murder of Evangeline Gordon because he knew it could be tied back to him," Krista said with a shiver. "But it still doesn't explain how he got started working with Nate in the first place." As far as they could tell, Maxwell's dealings with Nate had predated Maxwell's relationship with Talia by at least a few years. Both Ibarra and Jack's colleagues at Gemini Securities were digging for links but hadn't been able to uncover anything.

Outlandish as it sounded, it looked like Talia was telling the truth. She might not have been privy to all the details, but she alone could provide the missing link to get them pointed in the right direction.

Which had led them here, in the industrial section of Seattle, breaking into a warehouse adjacent to a shipping lot owned and operated by Maxwell's transportation company, where they hoped to find more information to back up Talia's claims.

"Okay, what you want to do now is key in this combination." Krista could hear Ibarra through her earpiece as he talked Sean through resetting the building's alarm system.

She looked over her shoulder at every little creak and scuffle that rang through the darkness, listening for any sign that the handful of security guards who were monitoring the shipping lot were alerted to their presence.

Talia had claimed that the transportation and shipping company was one of Maxwell's last legitimate businesses, and while it brought in hefty revenues, it hadn't been nearly enough to pull Margaret out of debt and build their bank accounts back to the current levels.

For that, David had had to get creative, Talia claimed.

And even though the shipping business itself was legit, many of the activities and transactions that went down in the shipping yard, she suspected, weren't.

Despite what they'd uncovered, for Krista it felt like a gigantic leap of faith to take the word of a questionable witness and use that as her excuse to break into private property.

Again.

And this time it wasn't owned by Jack Brooks who would call it good after a few punches. Unlike her father's house, she couldn't rationalize this away with the excuse of if she used a key, it wasn't really illegal.

This time they were breaking into a place owned by one of the wealthiest, most influential men in the Pacific Northwest. A man who would ruin her life and her career if they didn't find what they needed to nail him to the wall.

Oh, who are you kidding. After everything you've gotten yourself into in the past three days, you'll barely get a chance to kiss your career good-bye as it swirls down the toilet.

"I can't believe it," Sean said as he keyed in the combination Ibarra gave them. "It's been fifteen minutes and you haven't whined once about committing another felony."

"I'm too busy calculating how many years I'll be doing when all this is over," she snapped.

There was a high-pitched beep and a click. "Door alarm should be disarmed," Ibarra, who was parked near the lot entrance to keep watch, spoke to them through the earpieces both she and Sean wore. Talia had briefed them on the security systems installed at the warehouse in an earlier phone call.

"He always thought I was stupid," Talia had said, bitterness evident in her tone. "But I watched everything. Unless he's changed the codes, you should be able to get in."

Ibarra assured them that even if that was the case, he would have no problem working around the security system. Still, no plan was foolproof, and Krista held her breath as Sean turned the handle, bracing herself for the shriek of an alarm.

The door swung open.

"Looks like the codes Talia gave us are still good. Stay close to the front of the building," Ibarra's disembodied voice commanded. "You've still got the internal motion sensors to contend with."

Sean swept the interior of the warehouse with the beam of his flashlight. Though it was completely dark, from what Krista could see, the warehouse was exactly as Talia had described. What looked like a beaten-down abandoned warehouse on the outside was a fully finished, luxuriously furnished space.

"Go to the east wall and walk about ten paces," Ibarra's disembodied voice commanded.

"Stay right with me," Sean said. In the darkness, his gloved hand sought hers and he placed it on his shoulder. Only inches separated them as Sean moved carefully along the wall. Though the warehouse was cavernous, according to Talia the downstairs had been partitioned to make a sitting area combined with a kitchen and a private office.

Up the spiral staircase Krista could just make out in the darkness a master bedroom suite.

"A secret lair worthy of a James Bond villain," Talia had said wryly.

From the little that Krista could see, it looked a lot like any number of warehouses that had been converted into luxury work/living spaces, although those spaces were all clumped together in newly gentrified neighborhoods, not supposedly abandoned spaces next to a trucking lot.

"There should be a panel along the wall," Ibarra said. "Can you see it?"

They carefully sidestepped a low couch and Sean flashed his light along the wall. No panel, but there were two massive abstract acrylic canvases on the wall above the couch. Sean handed Krista the flashlight and took first one and then the other canvas down off the wall and propped them on the back of the couch. "Bingo."

Ibarra repeated the information Talia had provided, and Sean had the motion sensors deactivated in a matter of seconds.

Sean carefully rehung the paintings and said, "According to Talia, the office is in the back right corner of the warehouse."

They walked more quickly now that they didn't have to worry about the motion sensors. Krista still held onto Sean's shoulder, not so much because she was worried of losing him in the dark, but because that slight contact took the edge off the anxiety pumping through her, the awful feeling that something was about to go horribly, irrevocably wrong.

They came to a closed door. As Sean's hand reached slowly for the knob, Krista's heart leaped to her throat, and as Sean turned the knob she fully expected alarms and sirens to sound and for a trap door to open and send them hurtling down to a deep dark cave.

Instead, the door opened without issue. There wasn't even a simple button lock to keep a person out.

Sean closed the door and switched on the light. Even if someone happened to walk by the warehouse, no light would leak from the windowless room. The room was dominated by a huge mahogany desk topped by piles of paper and a large computer monitor, and the wall behind the desk was lined with custom cabinets built from the same material as the desks.

Krista flipped on the computer as Sean went to work on the cabinet locks. As the machine hummed to life, Talia's words rang in her head.

He used to brag that he had secrets there beyond what anyone could imagine, secrets that could take down the entire state from the top down.

If that was true, those secrets were in this room, hidden in those locked cabinets or stored on his hard drive. Krista crossed her fingers and prayed for the dozenth time that Talia hadn't steered them wrong.

A few minutes passed, and Ibarra whispered, "Okay, I'm in." By simply turning on the computer and ensuring it was connected to the network, Krista had opened a back door for Ibarra to hack his way in, just as he had Kowalski's computer and the police department's intranet. Krista didn't understand the methods or the technicalities, but she promised herself that when this was over, she was never leaving her sensitive information on a networked computer.

"He's got a lot of data on here," Ibarra said, almost to himself. "It will take me a few minutes to copy this."

There was a loud thud behind her. Krista jumped, gasped, and then gave a little laugh when she realized that Sean had just dropped the heavy flashlight. "You scared the—" Her voice stuck in her throat when she saw Sean.

He was standing at the end of the cabinets, his hands braced on the narrow counter jutting out from the wall. Krista could hear the breath soughing in and out of his chest, see the sweat bead on his forehead.

"Sean?"

He straightened abruptly, his eyes frantic as they bounced from her to the closed door behind her to the thick, windowless walls.

"It's okay," she whispered, approaching him slowly, as she might a nervous animal. "We're going to be out of here in just a few minutes."

He nodded jerkily. She didn't know what else to do, so she put her hand on his back, half expecting him to jerk away from her touch as he had before. She winced at the tremble of muscles under the damp fabric of his shirt. To her shock, instead of turning away, he turned toward her. She instinctively wrapped her arms around him, lifted one hand to his neck to pull it into her shoulder, and held him as tightly as she could.

His breath whistled heavily in her ear—in, out. Maybe it was her imagination, but he seemed to calm a degree. No, he was settling down, his breath slowing as his arms held her in an almost desperate grip.

Krista whispered reassurances and molded herself against Sean as though she could pull the anxiety from his body to hers.

"We're almost finished. Shit!" The alarm in Ibarra's tone snapped them both back to attention.

"What?" Krista whispered.

"I've got two cars headed in your direction, heading down Marginal from the north."

"How do you know they're coming here?" Sean asked, his voice steady but tight as a bowstring.

"I don't," Ibarra snapped. "But they've passed the Boeing complex, and there's not much else around here to interest anyone at this time of night."

"How much time do we have?" Sean asked.

"About forty-five seconds."

"How much longer to finish copying the files?" Krista asked.

"About thirty seconds."

"That doesn't give us enough time to re-arm the alarm system and lock up," Sean said grimly. "They'll know we were here."

Krista shook her head. "We can't tip him off. Not until we know exactly what we have. But if we go now—"

"If you stop the transfer process now, some of the files will be corrupted on his end," Ibarra said grimly.

Krista blew out a frustrated curse. "We'll have to come back—"

But before she could finish Sean had opened the office door. "Make sure the transfer finishes clean." He headed for the door.

"Sean wait—"

"I'm going to reset the alarms."

"You can't do that, we'll be...trapped," she barely breathed the last word, because Sean was already halfway across the warehouse.

Sweat beaded on her own brow as she went back to the computer. "Come on, come on," she muttered as the status bar seemed to pause interminably at ninety-eight percent complete. She looked toward the door, but the meager glow of the computer cast just a small halo of light. Only the beam of Sean's flashlight glowed in the inky darkness beyond.

Sean finished resetting the alarms, and Krista felt her stomach drop to the floor as he hurried through the dark warehouse. "What about the motion detectors?" she hissed.

"I re-armed it but left the motion detectors off," Sean hissed back through the darkness. "Unless he tries to set them off himself, he shouldn't notice."

"I no longer have a visual on the vehicles," Ibarra said. At that moment, Krista heard the sound of car tires crunching in the gravel outside. A few seconds later, the doors slammed.

"They just parked," she whispered into her collar.

"You need to kill the light, Sean."

Her heart thudded in her throat as Sean's flashlight went dark and she looked frantically at the glowing computer monitor. She could turn off the screen, but if they came into the office, they would notice it had been turned off with the tower unit still on.

"Copy is complete. Kill the computer. Be sure to use the proper shut down procedures," he cautioned.

Krista quickly powered down the machine, feeling the sweat bead under her shirt as it seemed to take an eternity for the screen to go black.

She waited by the door and thought her heart was going to crash through her chest as she heard muffled voices outside and then the beep of the door alarm being disarmed. A metallic scrape, and the door was opening...

A large hand caught Krista in the chest and pushed her back into the office. She barely stifled her squeal of alarm as Sean quietly shut the door behind them.

Light showed in the crack under the door, and footsteps sounded. The voices got louder.

"I don't know why you insisted on this meeting," she heard a male voice say.

A nudge on her arm pulled her attention back to Sean. He aimed his light at the ceiling, clicked it on and off twice, pointed at himself, her, then up at the ceiling, and then handed her the flashlight.

Was that supposed to be some kind of signal, she wondered frantically.

Sean moved quietly as a cat on top of the desk. "Light." His whisper cut through the stillness. "Up," he snapped, squinting angrily as the beam hit him full in the face.

Realization dawned as he reached up and carefully, quietly popped a ceiling panel from the frame and shifted it to the side. He beckoned her up onto the desk.

"Careful," he whispered and she nodded, gently shifting her foot away from the jar of pens stacked in the middle of the desk top.

She raised her hands up but was barely able to curl her fingers around the edges of the panel. Strong hands gripped her hips and lifted her. She smothered a grunt as she got her elbows up over the edge and used them to help pull herself up. Sean's hands moved to her butt and finished boosting her through the hole.

She rolled to the side and heard a *thunk* as Sean put the flashlight up through the opening. In the pitch black, every sound was magnified. As Sean reached to pull himself up after her, Krista swore the sound of plaster shifting echoed like a bullet in the room below. She held her breath, expecting the door to burst open at any second.

But so far, so good, and Sean reached for the light and shined it on the opening long enough to make sure he placed it back squarely and securely. "Let's hope they don't notice the plaster dust on the desk," he whispered. The panel slid into place, and Krista thought of the wall of cabinets whose contents they hadn't had time to search.

They had the contents of Maxwell's hard drive, she consoled herself. It had to be enough.

For what? a doubtful inner voice taunted her. *You broke into his private property and stole the information. No matter what he's up to, you'll never be able to use it against him in court.*

It didn't matter, she reminded herself. She had started this quest in the name of truth, and if that was all she got, that had to be enough.

But will it be enough to put an end to all of this? Will it be enough to save you and Sean?

She didn't have time to contemplate the question as Sean's hand found hers in the darkness. "Let's move."

Chapter 17

Sean focused on keeping his breathing steady as he inched along the crawl space on his belly. The crawl space spanned the area of the office and the bedroom suite below it, but it was only about twenty-four inches high.

And completely enclosed.

He positioned the flashlight in front of him and did a quick three-sixty scan of the space. The good news was that there was room for them at all, that the ventilation and plumbing for the master bath required the space between the two floors for all the tubing and piping.

Bad news was there was no easy way out, not into the bedroom anyway. While the ceiling of the office below them was done in modular paneling, the floor of the master suite above them was solid, either hardwood or carpet on solid flooring. In any case, no easy way to pop up out of the crawl space like they had out of the office.

A bead of sweat trickled down and dripped off the tip of his nose. He wrapped his gloved fingers tighter around Krista's, cautioning himself not to hurt her in his desperation to drown the panic that was trying to burst free.

On one end, about fifteen feet away, was a roughly

two-foot-long-by-one-foot-high opening covered by a slatted vent. The overlapping slats were closed, but if the panic hadn't totally fucked up his orientation, if he popped it off, it would open out to the south side of the building.

He focused on that opening to the outside and started inching toward it.

There was a low rumble of voices in a foreign language—Russian—drifting in from the other side of the space.

"Stop," Krista breathed and dug her fingers into his arm to emphasize her point.

"I call this meeting because I think you are about to try to—how you say—squelch on this deal?"

"Welsh," an angry male voice replied. "And it's welsh on a bet. And I haven't given you any reason to think the delivery won't go down on Tuesday as expected."

The vent opened out over the main room and a faint glow of light came in from fixtures mounted on the high ceiling. In the faint glow, Sean could see Krista's hand pointing at that opening. Away from freedom.

She hitched up on her elbows and started to combat crawl for it. Every instinct in Sean screamed to go the other way, toward freedom, but one last rational cell in his brain knew they needed to stay on top of David Maxwell and whoever was working with him so they could find out exactly what the fuck they were up to.

He fought to keep his breathing quiet as he followed, though he was sure they'd be able to hear his heart thudding on the panels below him.

From their vantage, he could see seven in total. A tall broad-shouldered man with slicked-back hair, cold gray eyes, and flat, Slavic features and three men who were variations on the same template. They all wore expensive-looking tailored suits over silk shirts. No ties.

"Who are the suits?"

"Karev, and three of his men," Krista breathed in his ear, and though he knew he was picking one poison in favor of another, he focused on the way her lips felt moving against the sensitive skin of his ear, remembered how good they had tasted earlier at Ibarra's house.

To his surprise, it actually worked, and the surge of raw lust took the edge off the panic. Who knew that two primal, irrational forces would serve to cancel each other out? Already close in the cramped space, he inched close enough to feel the vibration of her pounding heartbeat as it rattled through her.

He wasn't the only one struggling with his fear.

He could see three other men, including Maxwell, whom Sean recognized from his pictures in magazines and newspapers. In contrast to his gangster companions, he was dressed in khaki pants, loafers, a V-neck sweater pulled over a collared shirt, and a beige trench thrown over his arm.

Like he'd been pulled away from another night at the yacht club.

Next to him was a dark-haired, wiry man, similarly dressed and younger than Maxwell by quite a bit. It wasn't until the man turned more fully that Sean saw the scar that bisected the man's face. It was Carl Grayson, Maxwell's stepson and publicly acknowledged heir apparent to Maxwell's business empire.

Evidently, Grayson was involved in all of dear old stepdad's business ventures.

Next to Grayson was a tall man with a crew cut and a goatee, his jacket shoulders straining the seams of his black trench. Obviously Maxwell's muscle, with his at-the-ready stance and his hands hanging loose beside him, poised to grab a weapon at a second's notice.

It was a sign of how much the anxiety scrambled his brain that Krista recognized the thug before he did.

"Holy crap," she breathed. "I think that's one of the guys who shot the deputy and tried to kill us."

Now that she said it, Sean saw it. Sure enough, that was the motherfucker who had shot him in the leg.

All of the people in the room below were responsible for trying to have him killed. Worse, they'd tried to hurt Krista, the thought of which sent a tsunami of primal rage roaring through him, startling him with its intensity.

And Sean could do nothing but wait here like a fucking rat, helpless for the moment to do anything to hurt the men who would have killed Krista without a second thought.

The anger tipped his agitation into overdrive. He took another breath, the air starting to taste stale and close in his lungs. Despite the feel of Krista next to him, he felt suddenly like a thousand ants were crawling on his skin, like a rhino had just taken up residence on his chest.

A female voice rang through the room. "We have to suspend all shipments until we know Slater and Flynn have been taken care of."

"Guess that answers our question about the wife knowing what's going on." Krista's breath warmed his neck.

And holy shit, there she was, complete with the blond helmet of hair and a gray knit pantsuit that probably cost more than his truck. An icon of Seattle old money, a grand dame of local society so renowned that even Sean, a jock who grew up in a middle-class neighborhood in Kirkland, knew her name.

Standing here in a warehouse with armed guards, arguing with Russian gangsters. It was so jarring, it pulled him back from the edge.

Maxwell hit her with a dark look. "Goddamn it, Margaret, this isn't your decision to make." He turned on his stepson. "I told you she shouldn't have come."

"Fuck you, David," Margaret snapped. "We're just getting momentum in my campaign. I will not let you risk it because you've crawled into the sewer with these lowlifes—"

Like a striking snake, Karev's hand lashed out and caught the queen of Seattle society's cheek in a vicious backhand.

Margaret staggered back with a cry and would have fallen if the bodyguard hadn't caught her.

"What the hell was that?" Maxwell asked Karev.

The Russian shrugged, the flat, reptilian expression never wavering. "You don't handle your woman, I do." He nodded at his thugs, who stepped forward and seized Margaret from the bodyguard's arms. Too busy trying to hang onto Margaret, he couldn't get to his weapon before Karev's three had their semiautomatics out of their waistbands and trained on the woman.

"Now, let me make this clear like crystal, yes?" Karev said. "We do shipment Tuesday as planned, and next one after that, and next one and you get the idea, no? You use this power you say you have to take care of attorney and keep cops out of my business. If no, I pump her full of lead and leave her on front lawn for world to see."

"You can't—"

"Of course I can. Look at it like this: You either have money, your regular cut—I even up commission on next delivery, it's that valuable. Or you can have dead wife and people wondering what you do to get her killed by Russian gangster."

Sean sure as hell hoped Krista was listening carefully, or better yet, that Ibarra was taping this, because Sean was too blown away by the surreal scene to take it all in.

"It was never my intention to cancel the shipment," Maxwell bit out.

"Good, then we are on same page," Karev said with a cold smile. "In the meantime, you get the cops off my ass. They are watching me like hawks."

Maxwell shook his head. "You got yourself into that mess when you did the Salvatores. I told you it was a bad move. I did my part when I got the evidence dismissed."

Beside him, Krista stifled a gasp.

"The cops have to look like they're at least doing something," Maxwell continued, "or the whole charade falls apart."

Karev shrugged. "I'm not asking for opinion. Cops are cramping my style, and I don't want to have to kill any for sniffing in my business. Makes complications. So you have power to get them to back off. Use it."

Maxwell gave a begrudging nod, his expression like that of a dog who knows he's been beaten by the alpha but wants nothing more than to tear out a throat or two.

Karev left, and sure enough, as soon as the door slammed behind him Maxwell turned on his wife. "You fucking idiot! What the fuck are you thinking, getting in the middle of this?"

To her credit, Margaret Grayson-Maxwell was no

shrinking violet. "I'm the idiot? What about you, getting in bed with that, that ghoul!" She gave her head a violent shake. The hair didn't budge.

"You sure as hell weren't complaining when the money rolled in fast enough to cover up the fact that Carl's father drained you dry."

"You have to admit," Carl chimed in, "the events of the past few months have left us exposed."

"I told you he would only bring trouble. You should have left him to rot after he murdered that whore," Margaret hissed. Through the haze of his mounting anxiety, Sean realized she was talking about Nate. "I always told you he was a bad seed and helping him was going to cost us."

What was the connection with Nate? It had to be more than financial.

"Shut up." David put his hands to his head as though he was trying to keep it from blowing apart. "Everything is under control, as long as we're careful and don't attract too much attention—"

"Under control?" Margaret raged. "Despite all of your influence, you haven't even been able to eliminate the two people who could annihilate everything we've worked for!"

Krista felt like a grenade had gone off in her brain. She was right. It hadn't ended with Nate, not by a long shot. Karev, David and Margaret Maxwell, even Margaret's son Carl were in on it too.

Not just guilty by association, accidentally involved in some questionable financial transactions or even know-ingly involved in something more white collar like money laundering. No, they were absolutely ass deep in all of it, their hands stained as darkly with blood as Nate's had been.

And the blood they were gunning for now was theirs. How many times had she chatted with them over cocktails at some party she'd been forced to attend for work? Hell, she'd even shared her father's dinner table with the Maxwells a time or two, back when she was in law school and her father had some harebrained idea about hooking her up with Carl.

And now that man was trying to kill her, to kill Sean. A tremor shook through her at the realization of how powerful their enemies truly were.

"We need to stay calm," Carl stated, his tone soothing as he looked anxiously between David, whose face had gone past florid to purple with rage, and his mother, whose normally patrician, camera-ready features were twisted beyond recognition.

"That's what you said when he died! You said we had nothing to worry about! But she found something, goddamn it—he left too many loose ends. They're alive. They're looking. They're a threat. And if even a whisper of the truth comes out, if you think for a second you're going to take me down with you—"

Maxwell moved so fast, grabbing Margaret around the throat and pinning her to the wall, Krista jerked and stifled a cry. Sean squeezed her hand in warning. She squeezed back, hanging on for dear life as she wondered if David Maxwell was going to murder his wife right before her eyes.

Horrible gagging sounds erupted from Margaret's throat as she struggled, her feet kicking and her nails clawing at her husband's hands. Carl leaped at his step-father and tried to pull his arm off, but Maxwell threw him off like he was a pesky gnat.

Carl fell back and fumbled under his coat.

"No you don't," the bodyguard said. A *click* echoed through the room as he released the safety from the gun in his hand, now pointed at Carl's face.

No question where the thug's loyalties were.

David seemed oblivious as he screamed at his wife. "You will not interfere in any way, you understand? And if anyone is stupid enough to ask questions, you will keep your mouth shut about everything." He let her go and she dropped to the floor, gasping for air, and then he whirled on Carl. "Get her the hell home and make sure she stays there."

Though he was still glaring daggers at the bodyguard, Carl nodded. "How do you want me to follow up with Karev?"

"Meet with him tomorrow as planned and work out the details as usual. But I want extra security, at every level." He turned to the bodyguard. "I want the systems in all facilities upgraded, and I'll need men watching the trucking lot and this building until next week. And for fuck's sake, find Slater and Flynn. We know they're back in the city. I don't care what you have to do, take care of them." To Carl he said, "Get Karev to send some of his men. Make it sound like we need his help. It will make him feel better."

Carl took Margaret by the arm and started toward the door. As soon as it closed behind them, Maxwell turned to the bodyguard. "Go get her."

Her?

"You shouldn't be here alone. I'll call one of the others—"

A sweep of his arm knocked the magazines and coasters from the low coffee table to the floor. "Has everyone suddenly gone deaf? Why the fuck is no one listening to me tonight? I have perfect, fucking control of the situation."

The bodyguard didn't say anything, his expression carefully blank.

"What I need right now is a goddamn moment to myself, and for you to get the girl over here."

The man shrugged. "Half hour."

"Twenty minutes," Maxwell bit out.

Krista thought Maxwell was out of control before, but as soon as the muscle left, he really let loose. Screaming, throwing furniture, kicking in the doors of the kitchen cabinets. Like all the years of pretending to be the perfect high-society husband had finally taken their toll.

"What the fuck is going on in there?" Ibarra whispered in her ear so suddenly it made her jump, kicking Sean in the process. Must have been something sensitive, because he couldn't quite stifle the strangled grunt.

It had to have been impossible for him to hear over his own screaming, but Maxwell paused, his laser blue gaze locking on the opening of the vent.

They both froze, not even daring to breathe as Maxwell stared at the vent for several long seconds.

Then he shrugged, muttered something to himself as he went over to a cabinet and pulled out a half-empty bottle of what looked from here like scotch. He removed the stopper and didn't even bother with a glass as he drained the bottle in several deep gulps.

He wiped his mouth and coughed a little. The bottle dropped from his hand with a hollow *thunk* and rolled from side to side on the hardwood floor.

Maxwell walked out of view, but they could hear him thumping up the stairs to the master suite. Footsteps sounded over their heads. If Krista punched through the floor she'd be able to grab Maxwell's ankle.

A squeal, followed by the metallic roar of water rushing through the pipes around them.

"That's our cue," Sean said through clenched teeth. "Are we clear on the outside?" he asked Ibarra.

"For now."

"Let's go."

David Maxwell splashed water on his face and willed his hands to stop shaking, though the rage still pulsed hot and fierce through his blood.

Control. He had to maintain his control. When you lost control, that's when you fucked up, as shown by his nephew before him.

David shook his head and stared at himself in the mirror, bloodshot blue eyes, his blunt features heavily lined. Nate had aged him a fucking century in the last four years.

He should have pulled some strings, made sure Nate stayed on active duty for a few more years. Kept him overseas, out of his hair, more likely to get killed on one of the missions that had taken him to the most dangerous parts of the world.

It had been a hell of a lot less stressful, keeping Nate at a distance, confident he was getting the fix for the blood-lust that ran through his veins in dark, faraway corners of the globe where a whore who turned up dead didn't raise an eyebrow on either side.

And lucrative, too, when Nate and his buddy Jimmy had used their missions as a cover to direct Maxwell's men to hidden caches of weapons, drugs, people...whatever treasures that particular armpit they were operating in had concealed. All for the taking if you just knew the right strings to pull.

But Nate had wanted to come back home, and so had Jimmy. Like an idiot, Maxwell had given in, half afraid of what Nate might do if he didn't get his way.

Idiot. He should have known then, listened to that first tremor of unease, gotten rid of Nate at the first inkling that he might not be one hundred percent under his control. But he'd never forgiven himself for abandoning his sister on his way to a better life.

It was shortly after he'd conned his way into Margaret's bed that he'd gotten the news of his sister's murder at the hands of her boyfriend, and the tragic death of his niece—her death from heat stroke in the trunk of a car as she hid from the boyfriend's abuse on a scorching summer afternoon.

The only survivor was his nephew, Nate, who had lived because he'd killed the boyfriend in self defense. Apparently there was still feeling in his dark, twisted lump of a heart, because it had ached at the last memory David had of Nate. At seven, he'd been a remarkably handsome—not just cute—kid, with his thick wheat-colored hair and clear blue eyes. He was already almost frighteningly intelligent, reading and doing math far beyond his grade level. Absolutely devoted to his younger sister.

He'd been the son David always thought he wanted.

Unfortunately—at least, he'd thought so then—he was never able to claim Nate publicly. But he'd been able to protect him, support him, and steer his baser needs into more productive directions.

As Margaret, and now Carl, was now eager to tell him at every turn, it had been the biggest mistake of his life. Far from being able to control Nate, David had realized after many years that he was being manipulated. He was the one bending over backward to clean up Nate's messes and keep him out of trouble.

And at the end, they were so deeply entwined, David was afraid that any trouble Nate got into was bound to suck David down with him.

When it came out that Nate was the Seattle Slasher and was killed by that cop, it could have been the end of it. Nate was dead, and no one ever had to know about David's failed attempt to channel his nephew's sick impulses into something more productive.

But too many traces, too many ties were left, just waiting to be revealed.

Damn it, if only Nate hadn't gone after Sean Flynn, no one would even give a shit. But take a war hero, wrongfully accuse him of murder, and put him on death row, and people—especially compulsive do-gooders like his sister Megan and that goddamn Krista Slater—got damn anxious about making things right.

And the hell of it was, once he got over his anger at Nate for taking matters into his own hands and killing Evangeline Gordon, Maxwell had been on board with taking Sean down in the process. Nate had convinced him that Sean was on the verge of discovering the truth about the scouting work Nate and Jimmy had been doing on some of those far-flung missions.

He didn't have to die, but he had to be taken out of action, and why not kill two birds with one stone? Evangeline, whom Nate claimed was about to start spilling about the prostitution ring and exactly whom the girls were servicing was silenced. Sean was locked up, too busy worrying about his next appeal to make any more trouble for them.

But come to find out Sean was in no position to make trouble and never had been. After Sean was tried, convicted, and locked up, Jimmy Caparulo revealed that Sean had no idea about the deals Jimmy and Nate had done for him. He knew nothing of the weapons and drugs that had ended up in his network instead of the hands of the U.S. Army.

Of course, not until after Sean was tried and convicted, but better late than never.

No, Sean, big sap, was honest and ethical to the marrow of his bones, and believed his closest friends were too.

So trusting, he'd stumbled right into the trap Nate had laid for all of them.

Based on what they'd found, Nate had been poised to blow Maxwell's entire operation wide open while he rode off into the sunset with Megan Flynn. He'd been killed before he could execute his plan, but that didn't stop the little leaks from creeping out like so much toxic waste.

And of course there was the huge leak, in the form of Talia Vega, who had somehow managed to make it out of Nate's dungeon alive.

There was a time when David would have done anything to protect her from the sick needs of his nephew. Now, when David wasn't fantasizing about killing her himself, he had fantasies of conjuring Nate back to life for the sole purpose of hunting her down and killing her in the manner she deserved.

Three months and not a word from her, as it should be. She knew goddamn well what would happen to her— not to mention her sister—if she tried to expose them. For anything to happen, she'd have to talk to the police, and, well, they would talk to him.

One peep, and she'd be his. He hoped she was keeping that in mind as she cowered in whatever corner she'd scurried off to.

He paced the length of the bedroom and checked his watch. He still had fifteen minutes, at least.

The floorboards creaked under his feet and he took a step back, bouncing as he tried to locate the faulty board.

Nothing.

A chill crept up over his neck as he remembered the muffled *thump* a few minutes ago. In that instant, he'd chalked it up to the blood roaring in his head as he gave vent to his anger.

No, it wasn't possible. No one knew this place, and anyone who did was deep enough in the shit with him not to make any trouble.

Talia. Her face swam in his brain. Her knowing dark eyes, the glow of adoration long since replaced with disdain. Red full lips and their faint curve of revulsion.

She knew.

But how could they have found her when no one—not his contacts in the SPD, not the FBI, not even the fucking Canadian Mounted Police who'd been discreetly hunting for her ever since he'd been alerted by border control she'd crossed over—had picked up a single whiff of her trail.

He flew down the stairs as though compelled by an invisible hand on his back. He unlocked his office and switched on the light. Cold sweat beaded on his forehead and every hair on his body stood on end.

He did a slow circle around the office. The computer was off. The cabinets that lined the wall behind it were closed and locked. As far as he could tell, the notes and papers on his desk were in the same disarray as he'd left them. He had a sudden, fervent wish that he was one of those meticulous types that kept everything exactly in its place, making it obvious when anything was even a millimeter out of order.

Now he kicked himself for growing too soft, too accustomed to having others clean up his messes to keep his own shit straight.

He shook his head. There was no way they could know about this place, the deal set to go down on Tuesday.

He went back out to the bar and took another slug of scotch. Felt the warmth seep into his tissues and let it overtake him. Sank into the cozy confidence the liquor always provided.

He took the bottle upstairs with him, kicked off his shoes, and stretched out on the bed to wait. So what if she told anyway? What good would it do? Like anyone would believe her.

And if Slater took it in her head to come sniffing around, if she suspected what he was really up to, what was the worst that could happen? The investigation would be killed faster than she would. They were cut off, working without a net, and living like fugitives. With the police on high alert and his and Karev's men ordered to kill on sight, the chances of them finding anything, much less talking, were slim to none. And no matter what they uncovered, Maxwell had his hooks so deep in this town, no way an ex-con and a rogue prosecutor could pose a risk.

There might be a brief public scandal before the story died in the papers. Not enough to bring them down, but probably enough to kill Margaret's political aspirations.

His smile morphed into a sneer. That might not be a bad thing—his bitch of a wife was getting a little too loose in the saddle for his liking, and he was starting to question how she might wield her power once she got it.

So what if Slater and Flynn were back in the city?

Still, he knew the gut-churning sense that everything could blow apart at any second wouldn't disappear until he got the news that both Slater and Flynn were dead.

Chapter 18

Krista held her breath as she watched Sean twist his shoulders to squeeze through the vent. After Margaret, Carl, and Maxwell's thug left, Krista and Sean had made slow, careful progress across the length of the crawl space, aiming for the vent cover that opened to the outside of the building.

She'd nearly had a heart attack when her knee pressing up had made the floor squeak and the heavy footsteps above her had frozen right above where her head was. He'd stayed there a good five seconds while Krista held her breath, half expecting him to riddle the floor with gunshots like something out of a Tarantino movie.

But Maxwell had continued his pacing and they used the sound of his hard leather soles to muffle the sound of their slow but steady shifting. Krista held the light as Sean quickly unscrewed the vent cover and carefully laid it inside.

The relief on his face as the cold night air washed across it was palpable, and Krista felt some of the anxiety in her body wash away along with his.

Only to come roaring back when she saw the drop, which had to be at least twenty feet. "Do we have, like, a rope or something? Or maybe Ibarra could bring us a ladder?"

She knew the idea was ridiculous before Sean answered. "Way too risky, and not necessary, not at this height," Sean said as he turned his body so he aimed feet first. "I'll go, so I can help soften your landing. Just make sure when you jump, don't pitch forward or you'll fall on your head. Keep your knees soft, your body relaxed, and try to land on the balls of your feet."

The next instant he dropped, and Krista heard him land with a soft crunch of gravel. She peeked out and saw him straighten from his crouch and brush his hands on his thighs as though he'd jumped from a park bench and not a second-story window.

He beckoned her silently with his hand, but Krista felt her legs go all noodly. She didn't have a fear of heights, exactly, but Sean's whispered lesson on how to fall safely wasn't exactly reassuring. She wouldn't have minded an air bag or a crash mat or, hell, a bunch of clowns with a blanket stretched out to break her fall.

Sean beckoned her again, pointed at his watch, and then at the front of the building. Right. Maxwell's thug would be back soon with whatever hapless woman Maxwell had commandeered for the night. It went against her conscience to leave the unseen woman here with Maxwell in the mood he was in. After what they'd learned tonight, who knew what he was capable of?

But right now, she had to stay focused on the big picture, on exposing the truth about Maxwell and nailing his ass to the wall.

And to do that, she had to get the hell out of this warehouse.

She turned and positioned her feet toward the opening and squirmed back until her legs dangled down the side of the building. She eased her shoulders out and looked over her shoulder, down at Sean.

Sean was under her, arms outstretched. She could barely make out his features in the dim light, but she could see his lips move. *I've got you*, he mouthed. *Trust me.* She nodded and pushed back, trying to remember Sean's instructions in midair.

She felt his arms close around her in the split second before she landed and heard his breath whoosh out at the impact. He rolled to the side, released her, and she scrambled to her feet.

Sean lay still on his side, his breathing labored. Krista's stomach bottomed out. She knelt beside him and ran her hands frantically up and down his legs, ribs, neck, any part of him she could reach that she could have injured. "Sean, are you okay? Say something."

He rolled his head in her direction. Even in the dim light she could see his skin was so pale it was gray, and he looked like he was fighting not to throw up. "Landed wrong," he wheezed out.

"What did I hit? Is it your leg? Did I break something?"

She started to roll him to his back and then remembered from CPR class that you weren't supposed to move someone. But it wasn't like they could call the EMTs. "Ibarra," she whispered, tears of fear and frustration clogging her throat. "I need help. I can't move him by myself—"

"Just need a minute to catch my breath," Sean interrupted. "I think I caught a knee or an elbow when she hit."

Ibarra's voice crackled into her earpiece. "Racked you pretty good, huh?" Krista could hear the sympathy in his voice along with...amusement?

"This isn't funny! He's really hurt. I—"

"Kneed my balls halfway up my chest when you landed on me," Sean whispered tightly.

Krista's jaw dropped in horror. "Oh God, is there anything I can do?" Her face went hot and she reached out awkwardly, stopping short as she saw Sean cupping his hands between his legs.

Sean stared at her, one dark eyebrow cocked.

"Yeah, Sean, why don't you have her kiss it and make it better?"

It was hard to tell in the dark, but she was pretty sure Sean's face was as red as hers.

"Let me help you up," she said simply and rose to her feet, pulling Sean up with her.

He rose gingerly and they skirted along the back of the warehouse and picked their way carefully through the dark until they reached the van where Ibarra had set up shop. They drove in silence back to Ibarra's house as Krista's brain churned on everything she'd learned tonight.

"What kind of delivery do you think they're waiting on?" Sean asked as they gathered in the office in Ibarra's place.

"Could be anything if he's in bed with Karev," Krista said, rubbing her eyes tiredly as Ibarra connected the hard drive with Maxwell's files to his computer. "Drugs, weapons, people. We've been trying for years to get him but haven't been able to make anything stick."

"I guess now we know why," Sean said. "He's got Maxwell in his corner, lining the right pockets—"

Krista shook her head. "Maybe. But it feels like there's something more than bribery going on here. Something bigger—" Her jaw-cracking yawn cut her off and brought tears to her eyes. She rose up on her tiptoes and reached for the sky, trying to work out the kinks from being stuck in the crawl space as Ibarra stared intently at his screen, fingers flying over the keyboard.

"What?" she asked at his incomprehensible grunt. On the screen was a list of what looked like gibberish, a mishmash of meaningless letters and symbols. Ibarra didn't answer, and to her surprise he powered off his monitor and pushed back from the desk.

"Aren't you going to look at his files?" Sean said around a yawn of his own.

"Nothing we can do with them right now," Ibarra said. "Everything's encrypted, pretty sophisticated program."

"You'll be able to get around it?" Sean asked.

"It'll take a few hours, but yeah," Ibarra said, offended. "So I vote we all get some shut-eye and start fresh on this in the morning."

"I'm going to go over the files we got from my dad's house one last time. See if there's anything he worked on for Karev," Krista said. Sean's hand on her arm stayed her as she started for the door.

"Get some rest. You need it. We all do."

She was used to pulling all nighters on her cases, sleeping at her desk for days if needed until she had what she needed. It went against every instinct to throw in the towel—even for only a few hours—with so much still hanging in the balance.

As though he could read her mind, Sean said softly, "Whatever's happening, it's not going down until Tuesday. That gives us at least thirty-six hours to figure something out. This is going to be tricky, you know? We need to do whatever we can to make sure we're firing on all cylinders."

She nodded. "Speaking of which, are you okay?"

"I was fine as soon as I got in the fresh air. As long as Ibarra lets me keep the windows open, I'm cool."

"Good. And the other?" Krista felt her face heat and could have kicked herself. Had she really just asked about his balls?

His teeth flashed white in a sheepish smile that sent a curl of warmth to her center. "I think I'll recover with no permanent damage."

"Oh, good." She forced the words from a mouth gone suddenly dry. She whispered a quick good night and practically flew down the hall. She took a quick shower to rinse away the dust and grime of the crawl space, brushed her teeth, and fell face first onto a pillow.

She was asleep within two breaths, her heightened anxiety and crippling embarrassment no match for her body's exhaustion.

Krista woke several hours later to find a hint of blue sky peeking through the curtains of the guest room. The clock confirmed it was after nine a.m. What day was it, she thought as she struggled to shake the cobwebs from her brain.

Monday. Which meant that whatever delivery Maxwell and Karev had planned was happening in the next day and half. Hopefully they would find something in Maxwell's computer files that would help them nail him before it happened.

Or at the very least, information about what the delivery involved so they could pass the tip-off to the police.

Wait, she reminded her addled brain, going to the police wasn't an option. Aside from Cole, they didn't know one hundred percent who they could trust, not just in Seattle but across the state.

Benson. She had to call Mark. She knew Sean wouldn't like it, but she was past the point of caring. No matter what they'd overheard between the Maxwells and Karev, until they knew who their allies were, she and Sean were still backed into a corner and unable to come out of hiding or take any action against Maxwell that might stick.

But Prosecuting Attorney Benson had as good a line into the Seattle PD as the mayor or chief of police, maybe even better, because he had an in with the judges and politicians as well.

She was sick of skulking around like a scared rat, waiting for the other shoe to drop. Now that they had their target, it was time to fight back, get the truth out there once and for all. She passed the open door of the guest room Sean had claimed. The room was empty, the bed made with military precision, the only sign Sean had even slept in there was his bag at the foot of the bed.

She heard voices from the other end of the house. The guys must be in the office. She headed that direction, making a quick detour into the kitchen for some much needed caffeine. As she got farther down the hall, the sounds coming from the office got more distinct.

And more bizarre. The door to the office was partially open and she could hear something, but it wasn't Sean and Ibarra talking.

It wasn't conversation at all but…moaning? Almost like…

She pushed the door open. "Are you guys watching *porn*?"

If it was, it wasn't very good, because both men's faces were set in grim lines as they stared at the computer monitor.

"If only it were that simple," Sean said as his shadowed gaze met hers.

"What is it? Let me see," she said as she came around the other side of the desk.

"We can just give her the list," Ibarra said as he started to move the mouse. "She doesn't need to see—"

"Don't talk about me like I'm not here," she snapped. "I'm thirty years old, Ibarra. I've seen porn—oh my God, is that Chief Ormond?" She didn't even feel the hot coffee sloshing over her hand as she stared transfixed at Seattle's chief of police having sex with a woman who was definitely not his wife.

"I think we found the source of Maxwell's influence," Sean said. "There are more than two dozen recordings like these. I recognize only a few of the faces—you probably know more, but as far as we can tell, Maxwell set the men up with prostitutes and recorded them having sex."

"Who else is in there?" Krista asked. Ibarra looked at Sean, who nodded and then opened up another window. Krista recognized Judge Terence Phillips. "That's the judge who threw out the eyewitness testimony in Karev's pretrial hearing," she said, swallowing back a surge of nausea.

She did a quick scan down the printed list of file names. Along with the chief of police, the mayor, Christ, the goddamn governor, and several high-ranking members of the police department, Krista recognized the last names of at least half a dozen judges who worked in the King County criminal court system.

She thought she also recognized the names of some prominent businessmen and financial types. It was impossible to be sure without looking at the video footage, and she wasn't sure she had the stomach for it.

With a little digging, she was sure they'd discover that the names corresponded to other influential men whose scope went far beyond the city of Seattle and King County. She thought about the customs official, the one whose death corresponded with a fat deposit into one of Nate's bank accounts. Had he refused to give in to temptation? Or was the threat of blackmail not enough to dissuade him from his investigation?

They would never know.

"You were right," Sean said, pulling Krista from her spiraling thoughts. "You said that whoever was behind this was someone with a lot to lose, not just money, but reputation too. That's not just Maxwell, but every one of the men in these videos."

Krista nodded and turned away from the lurid image on the screen as she scanned the second page of the list.

M. Benson.

She shook her head. It had to be someone else. "Show me," she said simply. As Ibarra clicked on a file and typed in an access code, Krista could feel her heart beating from her throat to her stomach as she told herself there was no way Maxwell had footage of Prosecuting Attorney Mark Benson having sex with a prostitute.

Her heart skipped several beats when she saw that not

only did Maxwell have footage of Benson having sex with a prostitute, but that Krista recognized the woman in the video. With her short blond hair and petite stature the girl was almost fairylike.

Stephanie, the girl called herself. And the last time Krista had seen her was in a photo taken from a crime scene, where she was crumpled on the floor like a broken doll after Nate Brewster snapped her neck.

There was no way Benson hadn't recognized her, hadn't known the dead girl was the same one he had sex with.

Krista's breath seized in her chest and there was a roaring in her ears. She felt like someone was sitting on her ribcage, and she wondered vaguely if this is what Sean felt like when they were stuck in the crawl space together.

She wondered if he felt this same devastating, soul-wrenching feeling when he realized his friends had betrayed him.

Maybe he could tell her how to survive it, because right now she felt like she'd been hit with a shotgun blast. She looked down, surprised not to find herself split wide open and bleeding.

She gripped the list in her shaking hand and tried to focus on the remaining names swimming in front of her. She struggled to keep it together, even as she felt like she was splintering into a million shards of glass. She couldn't afford to fall apart. Not yet.

Even the discovery that her father had worked with Nate hadn't made her feel like this, like the earth was about to open her up and swallow her whole.

Mark Benson was on that list. Mark Benson knew Maxwell was working with Karev. Mark Benson knew Maxwell was behind this.

Mark was the only person who knew she planned to visit Sean.

Her coffee cup slipped from numb fingers to shatter on the hardwood floor as she turned and left the office. She walked mindlessly on wobbly legs back to her room. She needed quiet. She needed to *think* but she could barely get her thoughts to form through all the questions swirling in her head.

Had he known all along that Sean was innocent? Had he watched her, working so intensely during the trial, knowing they were going after the wrong man?

Had he looked across the courtroom into Sean's haunted eyes and known he was no murderer?

Had he known Maxwell would kill her if she kept digging? He must have, because he'd tried to warn her away. He'd tried. She supposed she should be grateful for that. A small sound escaped her bloodless lips, not quite a laugh, not quite a sob.

She saw a large shape in her peripheral vision and turned to look at Sean. Harsh lines carved his face—no doubt he was as shocked as she was by some of the names on that list. After a few seconds, she realized his mouth was moving but she couldn't hear him through numbing dread that seemed to have dulled all of her senses.

She shook her head and squinted. "I'm sorry, what?"

"I said I know how much of a shock it must be—like I've said all along, I know better than just about anyone how it feels to be stabbed in the back...first your dad, and now this."

Krista shook her head helplessly. "My father..." There were no more words. "But Mark..." The lump in her throat swelled to the size of a grapefruit, making it hard to choke the words out. "He understood why I chose the path I did. He hired me right out of school, mentored me. I always thought of him and his wife, Rae, as the parents I was supposed to have."

Her eyes closed against the memories of obligatory appearance at her father and stepmother's chilly mansion in Washington Park for holidays before she'd escape to the Bensons' house in Medina. "I spend Christmas day at their house every year," she said. "I went to his daughters' high school graduations. Oh my God, his wife, the girls, they're going to be devastated."

She tried but couldn't keep the tears from slipping down her cheeks.

"Come here," Sean whispered.

It was the goddamn tears that got him. The final straw that broke his vow to keep his hands off her. But he couldn't stand to watch her cry.

Maybe because he understood her particular brand of heartbreak so well. Or maybe because he'd spent the last twelve hours wondering what would have happened had Jack Brooks's call not interrupted their kiss.

Idiot, he'd called himself then and again now. But stupid or not, there was something about Krista Slater that ripped a hole in the wall he'd built around himself, making him feel like his heart was going to bleed out of his chest if he didn't stop her from hurting.

The tears that soaked his shirtfront were like acid on his skin, and he would do anything to ease her pain. He didn't know exactly when it had happened, but despite all of his efforts to shut her out, Krista had worked her way inside him the way no woman ever had.

Against all reason, she'd created a crack in his shield, one that widened with every second he spent with her.

As he pulled her close, buried his face in her hair, and held her while she cried, he felt that all too familiar squeezing in his chest, that burning ache that told him he was starting to care way too much.

And damn it, he was tired of fighting it. Stupid, crazy, or both, all he cared about right now was making her feel better.

"I know it hurts," he said, rubbing his hands in long strokes up the slim length of her back.

"I guess you do." She sniffed and lifted her head from his chest. Her eyes were puffy, her pale skin blotchy, but the way she was looking at him made his heart twist in his chest.

It was unsettling, like she was peering into his soul, like she could really see him like no one else ever could.

As though their shared betrayal had bonded them somehow.

He shied away from the notion. But he couldn't tear his eyes from her face. "How do you stand it," she said, "knowing you were so wrong about people you loved?"

He shook his head. "I stand it because I have to. You got past what your father did to you, you'll get past this too." But that was bullshit and they both knew it. What her father did changed her, drove her down a path she might not have otherwise followed. Just because she'd found a functional way to deal with it didn't mean it didn't still eat at her at some level.

And what had happened with Mark—Sean understood all too well the scar that would leave behind. It was bad when your family fucked you over, but you didn't choose to bring them into your life. When you got screwed by someone you chose, it was hard to get past the fact that on some level you'd screwed yourself.

It was one thing not to trust others, but it was pure hell when you couldn't even trust yourself.

"I always prided myself on being such a good judge of character," she said with a teary chuckle. "When I worked a case, I thought I knew who was guilty, who was lying, who was telling the truth. But I've been so clueless."

"Don't beat yourself up about it. Believe me, I've been there and it doesn't do any good."

Easier said than done, he knew all too well. Krista shook her head. "How could I have not seen what was right in front of my face? How could I have worked so closely with Mark for so many years and not had an inkling that he was involved in something like this?" Her hands fisted against his chest and he could feel her whole body tighten with anger.

"You're an honest person, Krista, and you took it for granted that the people you trust are being honest too."

Another shake of her head and the short wispy ends of her hair tickled his chin. "It's so screwed up—the people I've trusted. And the people I haven't." She raised her hand to his face and her eyes filled up again. "I thought you were a *murderer.* I looked at you and thought you had raped and killed a woman. That kills me—"

"Krista, you were doing your job and you got snowed just like I did—"

"No, let me finish. This isn't about me feeling guilty about making a mistake or even feeling bad about sending an innocent man to prison. Believe me, I do, and I will beat myself up for the rest of my life for that. What I want to know is what's wrong with me that I could look at you and believe for a second that you could..." She choked on a sob and he pulled her back into his chest.

"I looked at that creep Jason and saw a guy I wanted to date, for Christ's sake, and I looked at Mark like a second father," she said, the despair in her voice settling somewhere in his chest. "Although," she sniffed wryly, "knowing my father, I suppose it's appropriate I found someone deceitful and self-serving." She swallowed hard, sniffed. "I'm so angry at myself that I believed the lies about you, that I couldn't see— "

His arms tightened around her and his hand splayed across her back. "It's okay, Krista—"

"No, it's not! I should have believed your sister and seen the kind of man you are."

She blinked and looked up at him, her thick lashes clumped together around her ocean-colored eyes. Her eyes were full of guilt, admiration, and something else that made his skin prickle like his whole body was blushing. "I'm just a regular guy, Krista."

"No, you're not," she said, fisting her hand in the fabric of his T-shirt. "You are anything but regular. You're strong, and you're brave, and you take care of the people you care about, and even some of the people you don't." Her lids dropped for a split second, hiding her eyes.

I care.

But her gaze flicked back to him and the words stuck in his throat under the ferocity of her stare. "And it makes me sick to my stomach that I didn't see it soon enough. You're one of the only people in the world I can trust, and I didn't even see it." She closed her eyes with a grimace.

He held her so tight you couldn't get a beam of light

between them. But somehow he pulled her closer. "Sometimes shit has to go really bad before you can see who's on your side."

"I should have been on your side all along, Sean," she whispered through tears. "I should have—"

"You have my back now," Sean whispered, "and that's what matters." He realized that somewhere in the past few days, the resentment he'd felt for Krista had disappeared. He didn't know when it had happened, but somewhere along the way it had been replaced with admiration, and God help him, affection—he wasn't prepared to call it anything else yet. "And I have yours. Don't doubt that."

She whispered his name and rose up on her tiptoes to close that last millimeter of distance between them. It got out of control fast as Krista's grief transformed to passion in the space of a breath. Sean groaned against her soft, parted lips and he sucked her tongue into his mouth. Her taste, hot and salty from tears, rushed through him. Part of him knew she wasn't totally in control, that the emotional trauma was drowning out common sense.

He was taking shameless advantage, but he, better than anyone, understood her need, the need to forget, to drown herself in pleasure to block out the pain even if it was only for a short time.

The little sound of pleasure she made in the back of her throat obliterated any nobility or restraint he might have had. A jolt of lust shot through him, and his cock strained against his fly and his fingers shook as he pulled her shirt over her head.

Mine. The word started as a whisper when his palms met the silky bare skin of her back and built to a roar when Krista pulled his shirt up his torso and bent her head to lick the skin of his chest. He tossed his shirt onto the floor next to hers and stripped off her bra. He pulled her to him, the silky slide of her skin against his making his muscles jump like he'd been electrocuted.

Her scent and taste flooded his brain, every little noise she made echoed in his ears, and every nerve in his body jumped at her slightest touch. He wondered if it would always be this way, if he would always be so tuned in, keyed up, so hyperaware of everything about her that one touch from her made it impossible for him to think about anything else.

Right now, there was nothing but her, the silky heat of her under his hands, the soft moans into his mouth that grew sharper when his hands slid from her back to cover her breasts, cupping and kneading as his thumbs whisked across the rock-hard tips.

He moved them to the couch and pulled her down to straddle his lap. His hands went down her back, over her hips to cup her jean-clad butt. Firm, full curves filled his hands and he pulled her against him. She was on fire, the heat of her radiating through her clothes, searing him as she rocked against the bulge of his cock.

She cupped his face in her hands and kissed him like her life depended it, hard and fierce, sucking at his tongue like she was starving for the taste of him.

Like he was starving for her, drinking her in, sucking her up, every nerve on fire as he sprang to life in a way he hadn't felt in at least three long years.

Hell, maybe ever.

Her tongue licked like a flame down his neck, dipped into the hollow of his throat. Her lips sucked and teased their way down his chest, sending a surge of lust through him so powerful it became a physical ache. His jeans were suddenly about three sizes too small at the crotch as she kissed her way down, down...

And then, holy God and hell yes, she slipped off his lap to kneel between his spread knees. The soft press of her breasts against his stomach as she slid down was one of the best things he'd ever felt. Nimble fingers flicked open the button on his jeans and carefully worked his zipper down.

She tugged his boxers down and pleasure slammed through him at the feel of those slim fingers curving around him, and Jesus, the sight of her pale, feminine hands stroking the throbbing length of his cock.

He was pretty sure he could be ninety years old and on his deathbed and the memory of this moment would still give him a hard-on that could cut glass.

"I guess this means you've recovered from your injury," she said, her eyes gleaming hotly at him from beneath her lashes. His back arched and he groaned as she stroked him from root to tip.

"I'd say everything is in perfect working order," he said, his voice strained with need.

"Still, I better kiss it better, just to be sure," she said in a teasing, impish tone he hadn't heard from her before but wanted to hear again.

Her hot breath wafted over him a split second before her lips closed over the sensitive tip. A groan ripped from his chest at the sweet, hot suction. He watched her through slitted lids.

With her hair cut short, there was nothing to obscure his view. Pink, plump lips surrounding his cock, sliding down his shaft as she took him into her mouth. Sliding back up, leaving him wet and slick, making him pulse against her lips and tongue.

She squeezed him in her fist, pumping as she sucked, sending him to the edge. He cupped her head in his hands, closed his eyes, and felt the silk of her hair slip through his fingers.

"Krista, Jesus, that feels so good." He gritted his teeth, holding onto his control by a thread. "You need to stop. I'm not going to be able to—"

"I don't mind if you come in my mouth." The frank tone and carnal words nearly made him do exactly that.

God, it would be so easy to be that selfish, but this was about both of them. About sealing the bond they'd forged against all odds. About helping them both forget, even for a few minutes, that the world as they knew it was falling apart around them.

He forced himself to pull her face from his lap and up to his mouth and scattered kisses across her cheeks and fought to get himself under control. "Inside you," he whispered. "I need to be inside of you."

Her only response was a muffled moan as he lifted her from the couch and carried her over to the bed. He laid her back on the mattress and stripped off her pants and panties in one move. His were next, shoved down his hips to crumple at his feet.

He came down beside her and pulled her to him, hissing when his cock brushed the soft skin of her stomach. Though every beat of his heart urged him to take her, fast and hard and now, he forced himself to slow down, take his time, building her up with slow, deep kisses as his hands memorized every inch of her skin.

All too soon, her breath was coming in quivering

pants. One smooth leg hooked over his hip and he could feel her wet heat as she strained against his thigh.

She pulled away suddenly and rolled to her stomach, reaching for the bedside table. "Please let Ibarra have stocked this room too," she muttered and Sean would have laughed had the undercurrent of desperation in her voice not perfectly mirrored his feelings.

She gave a triumphant little shout and passed back a foil packet. She started to roll onto her back but Sean stayed her with a hand in the slim hollow of her back, his mouth gone bone dry at the view she was giving him.

Long, pale thighs topped by the firm curve of her ass, the deep dip of her waist, and the flare of her hips... Sean had always considered himself a breast man, but Krista Slater on her stomach, hips tilted up and legs spread just enough to provide a glimpse of the hot sweetness between was enough to fuel his fantasies for the next millennium.

He bent his head and trailed hot kisses over her shoulders, down her back, loving the way she shifted and sighed and squirmed against the sheets. His cock jerked and bobbed against the curve of her ass, and she arched her back and ground herself against him. Then his shaft slipped between, and she let out a moan as he slid against her wet heat.

God, it felt so good, her slick heat against his hardness. God, how would it feel to slide inside her, with nothing between them?

The one remaining brain cell not consumed by lust reminded him to be practical and he retrieved the foil packet from where he'd dropped it on the bed.

His hands shook so hard as he rolled on the condom

that he nearly dropped it twice. Finally it was firmly in place. Sean guided Krista to her knees with one hand and grasped his cock in the other.

This time there was no resistance, no hesitation as he guided himself inside her. One stroke and he was buried deep, captured by the tight clutch of her body as she rocked back against him.

He established a hard, steady rhythm that quickly had her fisting her hands in the sheets as the pillow muffled her moans.

"Oh God, Sean," she whispered "Sean, I can't."

Her voice broke off and he felt her stiffen around him. She was close, so close he could practically see the steam rising from her as every muscle pulled tight in pleasure.

He slid one hand around and between her legs until he found the slippery bud of her clit. Stroking, circling, he gritted his teeth against his own pleasure, determined to give her hers.

Then she stiffened on a long moan, a tremor running through her as her body squeezed and pulsed around him. He held her hips, keeping himself buried deep until the last quivers drained from her body.

She collapsed forward onto the bed, panting and limp.

Sean was about to give himself a mental high-five when she burst into tears.

She tried to be quiet about it, muffling her sobs in the sheets, but there was no mistaking the quivering breaths and the shudders racking her body that had nothing to do with pleasure.

"You don't have to stop," she said when he pulled reluctantly from her body. "I'm sorry. I don't know what's wrong—"

"Total fucking emotional overload," Sean said gently as he lay on his side and rolled Krista to face him. "Completely understandable, with everything that's happened."

"I'm sorry," she said again. "It has nothing to do with— I mean, you were— I—"

Her already blotchy face went even redder as she struggled to speak through the tears. "I know you came," he said, softening the blunt words with a kiss on her nose.

"Oh."

It was funny, he thought as he stroked his thumb over the curve of her cheek, to see confident, tough-talking Krista so at a loss for words.

She sniffed a few times, swallowed hard, and blinked tear-reddened eyes. "I don't know what I was thinking. This is a disaster—"

"Krista, I'm not complaining." He pressed his lips to hers, licked away the salt of tears.

"You don't have to stay," she continued, almost like she hadn't heard him. "I'm used to handling my emotional breakdowns on my own."

"I don't have anywhere else I need to be," he whispered.

And more to the point, he didn't have anywhere else in the world he *wanted* to be other than right here, his body in an agony of frustrated desire, holding Krista Slater while she cried.

He had a weird, twisting sensation in his gut, kind of like he had the first time he'd jumped out of an airplane into a combat zone.

Big, gray-green eyes searched his, looking for any sign of BS. Satisfied that he meant what he said, she curved her lips in a watery half smile. She stroked his cheek with slender fingers and gave another little sniff. "I wish—" She cut herself short.

"What?"

Her eyelashes flicked down, hiding her eyes from his. "Nothing. It's stupid."

"Tell me," he said with a little squeeze of her hip.

"I just—" She licked her lips and hot color flooded her cheeks. "I wish it could have been different, the way we met. Something normal, like through friends, or even at a cheesy singles bar."

He tried to imagine what that might have been like, watching cool, classy Krista walk into a bar. How he would have mustered up every ounce of his very limited game and approached her. She probably would have taken one look at him, fresh out of the army and barely civilized, and given him an icily polite "thanks but no thanks."

Not that he would have taken no for an answer.

He tried to make a joke about it, but as he stared at her beautiful, tearstained face, he got the strange feeling that regardless of how he met her, no matter the circumstances, they would have ended up together like this. All he could croak out was, "Me too."

He pressed his cheek into her hand and squeezed his eyes shut, and suddenly it was like she was comforting him instead of the other way around. She kissed him, softly at first, and then with more force as his lips parted under hers.

He splayed his hand on her back and pulled her tightly against him, close enough she could feel him, still rock hard and unsatisfied, against her stomach. She hooked one leg over his hip and reached between them to grip him in her warm palm. Jesus, it felt so good, but she was just seconds from her crying jag and he didn't want her to think he was a totally selfish asshole.

Didn't want her to think sex was all he wanted from her, even if it was probably better in the long run if she did.

"I'm okay," he said. "You don't have to—"

"Shut up," she said, and rocked her hips so she could rub the tip of his cock against her hot core. Her breath hitched and started to come a little faster, all traces of her tears gone. "I want you," she said against his mouth. "I need you," she gasped as she guided him into her body. "I—"

Whatever she was going to say was lost in a long moan as he sank all the way in. His eyes locked on hers as he thrust, not wanting to miss a second of her pleasure. He could feel it in the way she clenched around him, see it in the way her eyes got that blurry, faraway look as he rocked himself harder and deeper inside her.

He could feel it, rippling through her in waves. He could feel his own orgasm building at the base of his spine, feel every muscle tense as he struggled to hold on for just a few more strokes.

She clung to him, her fingers digging into the muscles of his back, and that little sting was all it took to send him hurtling over the edge. Her moans echoed his as her body milked him to a climax so intense he felt like he was blown apart into a million pieces.

The pieces came back together, almost in their right places but just slightly off. And as Sean came back to himself, he felt a wave of unease as he realized there was no going back to life as he'd known it.

Chapter 19

Krista buried her face in the naked skin of Sean's chest. She breathed him in, his scent, his heat flooding her, chasing away the cold that threatened to crystallize every cell in her body. He was still inside her, and she wrapped her leg tighter around his hips, held herself even tighter to him in a last ditch effort to close out the world.

He didn't seem any more inclined to let her go, with his big hand splayed possessively on her lower back as he held her lower half tightly to his.

Why, she wondered again, couldn't they have met like two normal people? If things had gone differently, maybe they would have met years ago through Cole, or at a bar, or maybe he would have walked into the courthouse to contest a traffic ticket and made her look past the end of her nose for once.

Anything would be better than this. Clinging to each other as they tried to keep reality at bay for a few more precious seconds. "We could run away," she said, the words slipping from her lips before the thought had fully formed. But it could work. "Ibarra could get us fake documents. Hell, I bet he could even steal some money from one of Maxwell's bank accounts, or better yet, from my dad. We could go to an island off the coast of Central America where no one would even think to look for us…" Her voice trailed off as she realized how far gone she was. Was she really talking about living as a fugitive, off stolen money to boot?

And did she really think that just because he was the kind of guy who would hold her patiently while she cried, that Sean Flynn would really consider running off to an island with her?

She felt the press of Sean's lips on the top of her head. "As much as I love the idea of sipping umbrella drinks on a beach with you, we both know that's not an option. You've come too far, risked too much, to turn tail and let those motherfuckers win now."

"I know," she said and sighed. "But what now?"

Be careful what you wish for. She'd gone into this on a quest for truth. Mission accomplished, but so what?

She could practically hear Jack Nicholson screaming in her head. She had the truth, but she wasn't at all sure she could handle it.

Worse, she didn't have a goddamn clue what to do now that they'd found it. Maxwell's fingers were sunk so deep into the fabric of the system, there was no move they could make that would go undetected. If they tried to confront Maxwell in public, they'd be arrested. And if that happened, she didn't have any hope of either of them making it to the arraignment alive, much less through a hearing.

And if by some miracle either of them made it to trial, Maxwell was sure to use his influence to make sure nothing fell in their favor.

She headed to the bathroom for a quick shower and Sean followed her like it was the most natural thing on earth. It seemed ridiculous to be embarrassed after what they'd just shared, but Krista felt her face heat from more than the water as Sean joined her under the spray.

With the water and soap running in rivulets down his body, Sean was sex personified. However, he seemed all business. And the fact that he didn't make any overtly sexual moves and seemed so comfortable to share the space with her made the experience somehow more intimate. Almost like they were a couple, easy together, and though wildly sexually attracted, didn't need to jump each other's bones every second because each knew the other was going to be around for a good long time.

It was like a glimpse of some impossible future. And Krista felt the burn of tears and the crushing weight of regret at the realization of just how impossible it was, for so many reasons.

I'm falling in love with him. It hit her with such force she felt her legs crumple underneath her.

Sean caught her and kept her from falling. "Careful, it's slippery in here," he said and gave her an affectionate kiss on the forehead as he traded places with her to rinse off. He tipped his head back under the spray and a burst of warmth coursed through her.

The touches, the kisses, holding her while she sobbed, and oh God, the sex . . .

Maybe it wasn't all so impossible after all.

She forced her brain away from mooning over the gorgeous naked man in the shower with her. There would be no future for them of any kind if they didn't figure out how to get to Maxwell. Still, she felt the buzz of optimism for the first time in days as she shared her fears with Sean as they dried off and got dressed.

"He's too well connected," she said as she ran a brush over her damp hair. "I just don't see how we get to him—or Karev for that matter—without running into the same walls. Unless maybe we can turn them against each other—"

"Or better yet, turn everybody against *them*," Sean said.

Krista shot him a puzzled look.

"Once we figure out what's in the shipment Maxwell and Karev are waiting for, we use Maxwell's biggest weapon against him."

Realization dawned. "Once we get the goods on Maxwell and Karev, we use the recordings as leverage to make sure Maxwell can't bury it." Her mouth pulled tight in distaste. "Feels like it's our own form of blackmail."

"You're thinking too much like a prosecutor. But sometimes you need to bend the rules and fight a little dirty."

Krista cocked an eyebrow at him. "Between the stolen cars, cyber hacking, and breaking and entering, I think I've shown I can fight as dirty as I need to."

"And now you'll add blackmail to your list," he said. "You going to be okay with that?"

Krista waited for her moral compass to start spinning out of control, prepared herself to stifle her gut when it screamed that this was wrong, that there had to be a way to work within the law, a way to manipulate the system to turn this around.

But Maxwell had changed the game, capitalized on men's weakness, and injected the system with his poison. Now they had no choice but to use his own poison against him.

She thought of all the names on the list, all of the videos on that computer. Too many for her and Sean to get to in time.

"We're going to need more help."

"Jesus, I'm glad you guys called." Detective Cole Williams's voice crackled over the speakerphone. "Sean, your sister is about to kill me, so I hope you have some news I can pass on."

Sean knew his sister had to be bouncing off the walls with worry, resentful as hell that she'd been dragged into hiding and forced to stand on the sidelines for her own safety. He could only imagine what she was putting poor Cole through. "I'm glad I'm not the one stuck up in a cabin with her," Sean said with a grim smile. "And yeah, I think you could say we have some news."

Cole listened quietly as he and Krista laid out everything they'd discovered about Maxwell's operation and his work with Karev.

"Son of a bitch," Cole muttered.

"We have just enough time before whatever delivery is scheduled gets all the players on board," Krista said. "Think you can help us out?"

"Absolutely," Cole replied. "I can be back in the city in two hours, and I'll handpick a team to make contact and handle the bust—"

"What about Megan?" Sean broke in. "I don't want her left alone, and I don't want her anywhere near this."

"Of course not," said Cole. "We'll have to make arrangements. You know, she thought we were overreacting until my partner called to tell me our house had been broken into. According to Petersen, whoever did it tore it all to shit."

Sean's tension ratcheted up a few more notches. He clenched and unclenched his fists, not knowing what to do with everything swirling around in his brain. Jesus, what would have happened if his sister had been home when Maxwell's thugs showed up? He struggled not to let his brain spiral out of control and tried to focus on the fact that Megan was totally safe, but he couldn't keep a lid on the anger and anxiety welling up, threatening to send him over the edge.

From the second he and Krista had left the cocoon of the bedroom, he'd been bombarded on all sides with everything he'd been trying so hard for so long to keep shut out. He wasn't used to this—to feeling so much, to walking around the world with every one of his senses turned up to eleven. Moments like this, it hit him so hard, so fast, his brain short circuited.

"I'm sure we can figure something out. We need whatever help we can get, Sean," Krista said.

He whirled on her, her cavalier response to the potential threat to Megan snapping the final thread on his temper. "I could give a fuck what happens to any of us," he yelled, "but I won't leave my sister vulnerable."

"I understand—"

"No, you fucking don't understand," he yelled. Krista's eyes got wide, and even though some logical part of his brain knew she didn't mean anything by it, he couldn't stop the fury from spewing out. "All I wanted— all I want—is to be left alone, to pick up what's left of my life. I never asked to be dragged into any of this, and my sister sure as fuck didn't either! You almost got her killed once because you locked up the wrong guy. I don't want her anywhere near this!"

It was like that time when he'd gone after the prison guard, like he'd stepped outside of himself and couldn't stop what was happening even though he knew it was the wrong thing to say. He could see himself: face dark with rage, the vein pulsing in his forehead, his mouth pulled into a snarl.

And Krista, the woman who had turned to him so trustingly, whose pain he wanted nothing more than to erase, was looking at him, her eyes wide with hurt, and worse, guilt.

The room was dead silent. "We can send Megan to my folks' place," Ibarra said, stepping warily between them. "They live right down the road from me outside of Sandpoint."

Krista retreated to the opposite corner of the room and kept her gaze locked on the floor. His own guilt was a fist in his gut, but he didn't know where to start to undo the damage. For now, he needed to focus on Megan and keeping her out of this. "She'll be safe there?"

"Safer than she'd be with us, and no offense, Cole, but safer than she is with you right now. You know they're looking hard for you but no one knows I'm in on this." He turned to Sean. "Trust me, Sean. I designed their security system myself, and it's as bulletproof as my own. She'll be okay there."

Sean wasn't totally sold, but Ibarra did have a point. No doubt Maxwell's minions were trying to track down Cole to either find out if he was helping them, or worse, get to Megan to use her to flush out Sean. Megan would be safer someplace that no one would even know to look.

"What do you think, Cole?"

"You trust this guy, Sean?"

Sean looked up and caught Ibarra's stare. *Trust.* Such a simple word, with so much weight. It could be lost forever in a heartbeat. He dropped his gaze. "He's helped us stay alive and off the radar so far. That has to count for something."

Sean listened quietly as Ibarra gave Cole the details on the quickest way to get Megan out there. "My dad will get a huge rush out of this. He was military police before he took over the ranch and he can still kick major ass," Sean heard Ibarra say. "Megan will be in good hands, I promise."

Sean looked up and saw that Ibarra was still staring at him and nodded in silent acknowledgment.

"Who else can we count on, Cole?" Krista said in a tight voice.

"With the chief and so many others compromised, we need to play this really close," Cole said. "My partner, Petersen, is rock solid, no doubt. And Jorgensen too— he's going to want in on this after the shit they pulled with Jimmy Caparulo's suicide."

"Only two people you can trust in the entire department? That's pathetic," Krista bit out.

"I'd call Agent Tasso—he's local FBI, Sean. My gut tells me he's okay, but I think this Maxwell shit shows us we can't really be sure about anyone."

"I can't argue with that," Krista said, almost but not quite managing to kill the tremor in her voice. "I say we call Brooks too. He's a wild card but he gave us Talia Vega, who gave us everything."

Sean nodded. "And I get the sense he's still beating himself up over not being able to stop Nate from getting to her. I think he'll be more than willing to do his part to take these fuckers down."

They quickly went over the game plan with Cole and then got in touch with Brooks to bring him up to speed. As predicted, Brooks didn't take much convincing. They went over the list and decided who the primary targets were and how they should make contact, and once Cole confirmed the others on board, Ibarra started to send video clips out over an encrypted network.

As he looked at Krista, tense and fragile as she hovered over Ibarra's shoulder, Sean's anxiety ratcheted up a few notches.

I could give a fuck about what happens to any of us. Nothing could be further from the truth. Not when it came to Krista. "You should go with Megan," he said abruptly.

Both Ibarra and Krista looked at him, confused.

"This could get really ugly. If you go with Megan, you'll be safe."

He didn't even realize how important that was until he had said the words out loud. Feeling protective was nothing new—that was part of his makeup. Added to all the old stuff bubbling to the surface, what he felt for Krista was new, different. Almost too intense to put into words, this bone-deep, terrifying knowledge that if something happened to Krista, if she got hurt, or God, he didn't even want to think about it, killed on his watch, it might be nearly as bad as losing Megan.

He was starting to care for her. No, scratch that. Was falling—he cut the thought off before it could fully form and he gave himself a mental shake. On top of everything else, it was too much. No way he could go there, not now, if ever. If he even tried to scratch the surface, it was going to send his brain into permanent overdrive.

The best solution was to just get her the hell away where he knew she would be safe.

Krista shook her head. "Absolutely not—"

"It makes the most sense," Sean said, cutting her off. "Everyone else is a cop or a trained soldier. You'll just get in the way."

He knew he'd used the wrong approach even before her mouth pulled tight and her nostrils flared. But it wasn't like he could tell her the truth—that as impossible as it seemed, the idea of losing her was enough to push him straight over the edge.

"I may not have the training you guys do, but I think I've managed to hold my own. You don't have to worry about me. Like you keep reminding me, I'm the one who dragged you into this mess. So if anything happens, it's on me, not you."

"Krista—"

"Shut up. This topic is closed. I started this and I'm going to finish it."

After a fitful night's sleep, Krista spent most of the next day doing whatever she could to help carry out their plan to stake out the delivery site and do the bust when the deal went down. Now she listened, stomach in knots, as Cole went over the plan one more time to make sure everyone was crystal clear on every single detail. She was strung tight, like a rubber band stretched so far it would snap at any moment.

"We've tapped into the security system monitoring the shipping lot," Cole said, "and Ibarra has placed additional surveillance equipment around Maxwell's warehouse." With Maxwell's influence so deeply felt in local law enforcement, they knew they needed incontrovertible evidence of what he was up to.

Sean stood across the room, his mouth grim behind the goatee. He'd barely said two words to her since she'd flat-out refused to join Megan in her mountain hideout. She'd been circling around him like a nervous cat, unwilling to brave the tension emanating off him in waves to try to break through the fortress he'd built around himself.

What good would it do to talk, anyway? Despite the passion, tenderness, even admiration he'd shown in the last few days, fundamentally his feelings hadn't changed.

Had it been only yesterday that she thought for one fleeting moment that maybe he returned some fraction of the feeling she had for him? Now he'd shut down, cut himself off from her. *I could give a fuck what happens to any of us. All I wanted was to be left alone.*

It shouldn't hurt so much, but it did.

How had she, usually so levelheaded and by the book, gotten so carried away over a man who would have happily lived his life never setting eyes on her again?

She didn't think she'd ever know the answer to that question, and it wouldn't do her any good to miss details of Cole's plan because she was moony and distracted over Sean.

She kept quiet, absorbing the intricacies as Cole went through each step. "We should have major backup and a SWAT team involved," Krista muttered even though she knew that wasn't possible.

Their plan wouldn't have a snowball's chance in hell of working if they broadcast through the Seattle PD that they were planning a bust at Maxwell's shipping lot in the next twenty-four hours.

Instead, it was a team of seven: herself, Sean, Ibarra, Brooks, and the skeleton crew from the Seattle PD homicide department consisting of Cole, Petersen, and Jorgensen against a crew of who knew how many Russian thugs and cutthroat guns for hire.

The odds were so not in their favor, but they didn't have any choice but to push through.

"Petersen, Jorgensen, what's happening on your end?"

"Karev's still at his restaurant," Jorgensen's voice said over the speakerphone. He'd been tailing Karev, while Detective Petersen was keeping tabs on Maxwell.

"Maxwell's still at the fund-raiser," Petersen said, "but they just started serving dessert, so it's probably going to wrap up pretty soon."

Krista looked at the clock. It was nine o'clock on Tuesday night. They'd spent hours strategizing and, not knowing when exactly the delivery would happen, had been monitoring Maxwell and Karev's movements since midnight the night before.

Now everyone was tired and jumpy from too much caffeine and amped up to finally get this thing over with.

With only three hours left in the day, it had to be soon.

"All right, then, call us back with an update—" Cole started to say but Jorgensen cut him off.

"Wait—Karev's on the move. He's heading to his vehicle with three of his men."

"Maxwell too," Petersen said. "He's leaving the event. He's with his wife and stepson. Looks like they're arguing. She's pissed. Okay, stepson is dragging her to a separate vehicle. Valet just pulled up in a Mercedes and Maxwell's getting in. He has three guys with him as well."

"Seven against eight," Brooks said quietly. "I'm liking these odds."

"Let's load up," Cole said. "Petersen, Jorgensen, you have everything you need?"

"Yep," Jorgensen said. "We have our full gear, including vests."

"That reminds me," Cole said, catching Krista's eye. "I dug up an extra one that should fit you."

"Good," Sean said, and Krista told herself not to make anything of the unmistakable relief in his voice.

So he was happy she'd have a Kevlar vest that fit instead of one of Ibarra's oversize flak jackets that would weigh her down and become a liability if there was any running to do. That didn't mean he regretted a single thing he'd said.

It didn't change the fact that as soon as this was over and Maxwell and Karev were behind bars, Sean was going to walk away from her and never look back.

Metallic *clinks* and *clicks* filled the air as everyone geared up. Between Ibarra, Brooks, and Cole, along with the weapons Sean had poached from their would-be assassins, they'd amassed quite an armory.

The others gathered up at least one handgun apiece as well as the larger assault rifles along with round upon round of ammunition.

She accepted the pistol Cole offered, along with the belt and several extra magazines. It felt heavy and foreign as she checked the clip. Even though the safety was on, she handled it gingerly as she slipped it into the holster.

"We need to get moving. We've got a fifteen-minute advantage on them if they head straight to the shipping lot and we need the time to get in position," Sean said as he slipped another clip of ammo onto his belt.

The others nodded and headed to the door. Krista trailed behind, struggling to hook a Taser onto her belt.

"Let me."

Krista looked up, startled as his big hands covered hers.

"You need to clip it like this." He hooked the Taser in one of the loops. "Now make sure you can get it off and back on quickly, and get your thumb on the trigger as you pull it off. And don't zap me," he said almost as an afterthought.

It was the first time he'd spoken directly to her in nearly two days, and now he was so close that the heat of his breath, the scent of his skin made her a little dizzy.

"And I saw you having a little trouble with the Glock." He reached for the gun and she tried not to flinch as his hand brushed her waist. She closed her eyes and tried to get a grip. She was holding herself together with dental floss and Scotch Tape at this point, and she was afraid the slightest touch would blow her into a million pieces.

He slipped it in and out and wiggled it around in the leather holster and then slid it in and out a couple times to make sure it came out more easily. "Keep it unsnapped," he said, flicking his thumb over the little strap at the top. "Now practice reaching for it."

"Sean, we need to go. You said yourself—"

"And I need to know that if anything happens, you'll be able to keep your head and get your gun out," he said harshly. "It's going to be even more awkward once you have your vest on."

She jerked the gun out, took up her stance, and slid it back in, more smoothly this time.

He rubbed his hand over his face, obviously unimpressed with her technique. "You don't have to go tonight. You can stay back here—"

She drew up, insulted. "I know I'm not exactly Dirty Harry, but I can handle a gun and you need me as another set of eyes on the scene if nothing else. I know you think I'm selfish and ego-driven, but I'm not so selfish I'm going to hide back here and leave you short a woman."

"Damn it, it's not about you being selfish. It's about you being safe!" he shouted. He grabbed her by the shoulders and gave her a little shake. "If anything happens to you—" He broke off and squeezed his eyes shut. When he opened them, she saw fear in their green depths. For her. And along with the fear, something dark and stormy that looked a hell of a lot like regret.

"Look, if anything happens and this starts to go south, I want you to run like hell and find a place to hide, okay?"

"I'm not—"

"Don't argue. Just promise me you'll do whatever it takes to stay safe. This plan is dicey as it is and I can't waste any energy worrying about you getting into more trouble."

"Fine," Krista snapped. "I promise."

"Good," he said, his eyes hinting at a smile. "Because once we do this, we're going to need you around to make sure these assholes get what they deserve."

They loaded into Cole's unmarked car. Jack's shoulders spanned nearly the width of the front passenger seat, while Krista found herself in the back sandwiched between Sean and Ibarra. On the drive over, she was distracted from obsessing over Sean as he, Ibarra, and Brooks traded stories of their most insanely far-fetched operations. It was comforting to hear that tonight's bust was a relative cakewalk to, say, a team of six guys sent in to secure a weapons cache that was protected by fifty armed guards.

Yet even if they succeeded tonight, the aftermath was bound to get messy. It would take a lot of legal maneuvering to keep Maxwell and his cohorts in custody and brought up on charges, much less getting them to trial.

For her, surviving the attempts on her life was only the beginning. The real work hadn't even started.

They parked in an alley about a quarter of a mile from Maxwell's trucking lot and the nearby warehouse. Sean double-checked his weapons and communication unit. He, Ibarra, and Brooks slipped into the flak jackets Ibarra just happened to have lying around while Cole and Krista strapped on their Kevlar vests.

As quickly and quietly as possible, they took up their positions. Sean slid into the shadows between two big-rig engines. Ibarra and Brooks flanked either side of the warehouse.

Though, like the rest of them, Krista was dressed from head to toe in black, Sean could still make out her outline as she disappeared into the darkness across the way. Cole was with her to watch her six, and he tried to take comfort in that. He reassured himself that Cole was a damn good cop and more than capable of keeping Krista out of trouble.

His impulse when they'd formed the plan was to keep her with him, but rationally he knew he'd be too distracted by her, and as in any mission, to be successful he had to keep his head fully in the game.

So when Cole had automatically put him and Krista together, Sean had interrupted and asked for Krista to be paired with Cole.

The flash of pain on her face, on top of everything else he'd already put there, almost brought him to his knees. But there in the middle of Ibarra's living room with all the guys as they worked out the details of the bust was not the time to try to explain how fucked up he was, how little control he had over these eruptions of rage that seemed to come out of nowhere. Bubbling up, spewing like lava and destroying everything in its path before he even realized what he was doing, the damage he was inflicting.

There was no excuse, no explanation he could offer that would undo the hurt he'd caused. The hurt he would continue to cause, intentionally or not, the longer he stayed around her.

No matter how he felt when they were alone together, shut away from the rest of the world, Sean couldn't escape the fact that he wasn't normal. It didn't matter that he forgave Krista for her part in his conviction, and it didn't matter how hard he'd fallen for her, prison had rewired him. There was no telling when he would snap, when he would lose his shit, potentially putting them both in danger.

So he'd sat there, quiet, with the guilt over the way he'd lashed out eating through him like acid, and he let her think it was because he didn't want to be near her.

Jesus, that couldn't be further from the truth. Right now he was the farthest he'd been from her in four days and it was like his body was going through withdrawals.

Tense, anxious, and resentful that he couldn't reassure himself with a quick look, a touch, that she was safe, if only for that moment.

And if you want to make sure she's safe for good, you need to get your fucking head together and focus on nailing these assholes.

He settled back, willing himself to calm down, forcing away the uneasiness gripping his spine from not having Krista right here where he could see her. He needed to get into the zone, that place of supreme focus that allowed you to sit motionless in a steamy jungle for days while the bugs chewed off your face.

Tonight, the wait would be short, easy. Within minutes they should get confirmation from Jorgensen and Petersen that Maxwell and Karev were headed this way.

"Karev just turned down Marginal," Jorgensen said. The voice popped through his earpiece before he'd finished the thought.

"Maxwell's about a half mile behind," said Petersen.

"Cameras are up and the feed is live," said Ibarra.

"Let's get this party started," Sean said.

"Hooah," Ibarra and Brooks said on cue.

Sean grinned into the darkness. It had been a long time since he'd felt anything close to the brotherhood he'd felt in the army. Nice to know he could still get a glimmer of it even after being screwed over by Nate and Jimmy.

He willed his pulse to keep steady as a black Mercedes pulled into the lot and came to a stop several yards from the front of the warehouse. The driver got out, his hulking figure draped in an overcoat, and opened the back door.

Sean recognized Karev's tall, rawboned frame as he emerged, along with three others.

"Confirming visual on Karev," Ibarra said.

Sean watched as the driver popped the trunk. He heard them muttering but couldn't quite make it out as the bear-like driver extracted several large guns from the car.

"Good thing we have the vests. We're going to need them when the Kalashnikovs start spraying."

"If all else fails, we can get them on weapons charges," Krista said.

Sean hoped to hell Karev hadn't invested in armor-piercing ammo, which would rip through Krista's Kevlar vest like it was made of tissue paper.

No need to go there, he reminded himself, especially if she stayed good on her word to get her ass out of there if things got ugly.

Which, as he took in Karev and his thugs, he was pretty sure they would. Somehow when Cole and the other detectives flashed their badges, Sean didn't see Karev and his goons meekly laying down their guns like good little gangsters.

But they were solid cops and he, Ibarra, and Brooks were used to facing worse odds than this. They might get a little dinged up, but they were going to be fine.

"Second car's coming in," Cole said over the comm.

Another dark Mercedes. It had to be Maxwell's. Within a minute the Mercedes parked and Maxwell emerged, along with his own thug league. All three carried what looked like mini Uzis and Sean was willing to lay odds they had more toys tucked under their coats.

"Hey, Krista, it's our friend from the mountains," Sean said quietly. Karev and Maxwell were speaking. Sean inched forward a few feet to hear.

"I am glad you are here," Karev said.

"I told you I would be," Maxwell's voice was tight with irritation. "I don't go back on my word."

"Is good," Karev said. "Has been a very successful partnership. Would hate to have to end it by cutting out your liver and serving it as an appetizer to my customers."

"Remind me not to eat at Café Kiev until it's under new ownership," muttered Jorgensen, who along with Petersen had ditched his car and was on the approach.

"Don't try to intimidate me, Karev. The only reason you're still in business is because of me and we both know it. The feds and the local cops were breathing down your neck before I came into the picture."

"You smooth a few wrinkles, *da.*" Sean couldn't see Karev's face but he could hear the disdain dripping from the Russian's voice. "But I think you overestimate your importance."

"You think whatever you want, but after tonight, we need to close up until we take care of our mutual problem." He widened his stance and straightened up like he was bracing for a fight.

"*Ya soglasen.* I agree. I see reason. I understand if you are exposed, you are no use to me."

"He's threatening him, isn't he?" Krista said, the sound of her voice sending an electric current through him.

"Definitely some bad blood brewing," Sean said, and then went quiet at the sound of a truck approaching.

He shrank back from the glow of headlights as what looked like a ten-foot truck emblazoned with the Maxwell Trucking logo turned into the lot. The driver parked next to Maxwell's Mercedes, obscuring Sean's view of the group.

The driver climbed out and went around the side of the truck. "Brooks, Ibarra, what's going on?" From their vantages they should be able to see what was happening.

"Maxwell and Grayson are talking to the driver. They're headed to the back of the truck," Ibarra said.

Sean heard the sound of metal clanking as the door slid open.

"Karev's coming over to take a look," Brooks said. "Grayson just handed the driver an envelope."

Payment for getting whatever was in the truck to the delivery point without incident. "Can you see what's inside?" Krista asked.

"Hold on, let me…Oh fuck," Brooks breathed. "It's girls."

"How many?" Cole asked.

"Light's bad and I can't make it out."

"We need to rethink our original plan," Cole said. "We're dealing with a potential hostage situation."

Petersen's voice came over the wire. "They're planning to use the warehouse to hold the girls. We wait till the girls are securely inside and—" Her voice suddenly broke off, replaced by a high-pitched squeal that threatened to pierce his eardrum.

He popped the earpiece out, but his relief was short lived when he realized the sound wasn't just coming through the earpiece.

"What the fuck is that?" Sean heard someone—Maxwell maybe—from the other side of the truck.

"We're going in!" Cole said.

"Krista, you stay put!" Sean palmed his Glock and took off at a dead sprint, as did the other men and Petersen. He saw Cole out of the corner of his eye and was relieved to see that Krista had kept good on her word to stay out of the line of fire.

The Russians were screaming profanity, and then Karev shouted in English, "You fuck me over!"

Cole shouted, "Stop, police!" just as the first shots sounded.

And all hell broke loose.

Chapter 20

"Karev is down," Brooks shouted into his mic. As Sean raced to the truck, he saw a small figure make a wild dash across the lot and into the dark maze of cargo trailers and truck engines. One of Maxwell's thugs gave immediate pursuit, spraying AK-47 rounds as he ran.

Sean ducked and rolled to avoid getting hit. He squeezed off a few rounds of his Glock, but couldn't get a clean shot.

It was a total clusterfuck. Karev was not just down but dead from the bullet one of Maxwell's heavies put in his head. Grayson was on his side, alive but bleeding as he gasped for air while both Karev's and Maxwell's men fired wildly at anything that moved.

The driver was huddled next to the wheel well, hands in the air. Clearly just a stooge who wanted no part of it.

"Where's Maxwell?" Sean asked.

"Scurried off like a rat," said Ibarra. "I'm on him."

"This is the Seattle PD," Petersen shouted from behind a truck. "Put down your weapons."

"Fuck you," Maxwell's bearded goon, the one who had tried to take out Sean and Krista, shouted as he turned to open fire in Petersen's direction. Brooks leaned around the edge of the building and took him out with a shot to the chest. Blood bloomed on his shirtfront as he fell to the ground.

No vests. At least they had that advantage over them.

Another shot rang out from the shadows.

"Fuck," he heard Jorgensen wheeze. "I'm hit. It went right through my vest."

Armor-piercing ammo. There went that advantage.

"Put your fucking gun down, Maroney," Grayson gasped at one of his security force. "Are you crazy, shooting at goddamn cops?"

Karev's driver wheeled around and finished Carl Grayson off with a close shot to the chest. He saw Cole come around the other side of the truck and caught one of Maxwell's guys in the chest. The guy dropped his gun as he went down clutching at the bloody wound.

Cole went to kick the gun and Karev's driver turned to take aim and then screamed when Sean's shot went straight through his elbow, while Cole's caught him in the abdomen.

"Drop your weapons," Cole repeated to the three left standing—two of Maxwell's and one of Karev's men realized they were outgunned and decided not to push it. They dropped their guns.

"Face down on the ground," Cole said.

The driver was already there, babbling into the dirt about how he was just the delivery guy. "You didn't know you were delivering a truckful of underage girls?" Petersen asked.

"I want to talk to an attorney," the driver said.

"Ibarra, do you have Maxwell?" Sean asked as Cole and Petersen cuffed the driver and the other men who were still alive and Mirandized the ones who were conscious.

"Not yet."

"One of the girls took off from the truck and another one of Maxwell's men went after her," he said to Cole. "That means we're missing two, and that girl's still out there."

"Come back in, Ibarra. Once I call it in, we'll get squad cars to canvass the area. They'll turn up."

Sean shook his head. "You and I both know he can disappear for days. Hell, in the time it takes the cops to get their shit together, he could probably flee the country."

Cole's jaw clenched. "Since we know Maxwell got to the police, I'm going to let that dig slide. I don't like letting him slip through any more than you do, but right now my priority is these girls."

As Cole got on his radio to call in for ambulances and backup, Sean went around to the back of the truck. There, cowering from the beam of the flashlight as Petersen tried to coax them out, were eleven girls. Skinny, scared, and dirty, none of them looked a day over sixteen.

When they caught up with Maxwell, Krista was going to nail him to the fucking wall. "Party's over, Krista. You can come on out now. You're going to want to see this."

He'd been caught up in the firefight, but now he realized she hadn't said anything since the shooting stopped. "Krista, answer me. Are you hurt? Tell me where you are." Dread settled over him like a wet blanket when she didn't respond.

But the voice that answered him wasn't Krista's.

Sean saw his own dread reflected in the others' faces

as they recognized the deep male voice that replied, "She's with me. And now she's going to find out firsthand what happens when you try to fuck with me."

It had been torture for Krista to hunker in the dark like a coward. The shooting went on for only a couple of minutes, but to Krista it had been endless. When Jorgensen confirmed that some of the men were using armor-piercing bullets, she'd gone cold with fear and guilt.

She should be able to help. She was the one who'd dragged them all into this and she was hiding like a coward because Sean didn't want to worry.

To be fair, Cole had also cautioned her to stay behind and watch for anyone else when the shooting started, but she felt lower than dirt, watching as he and the others ran into the thick of it while she stayed behind.

"Karev's dead." Relief mixed with anger at the news Maxwell's thug had shot him. He was a disgusting, violent psychopath and the world was better off without him.

But she'd wanted Karev to have his day in court, for the murders of Nico and Aurelia Salvatore and for making money peddling underage girls.

But there was satisfaction in knowing Maxwell would have to suffer through a trial, watch his empire crumble as the truth of who he was and the atrocities he'd committed were revealed to the world. Margaret would get her due as well. Since she'd knowingly conspired with both her husband and Maxwell to traffic in young girls and used the money to finance her political campaign...Krista was thinking a hefty stay in a federal prison would be in order.

After the scene she'd witnessed in the warehouse, Krista had no illusions about the Maxwells presenting a united front. It would be fun to watch them go after each other like a couple of rabid wolverines.

But they needed to make it out of here first. She was frozen in place, listening so intently to the gunshots and the shouting that she didn't even hear Maxwell until his gun was pressed to her head.

She started to yell but Maxwell's hand clamped around her throat. He yanked off both her earpiece and her mic and fisted them in his hand. Krista struggled as he dragged her deeper into the shadows, away from the others.

Away from Sean.

She struggled and kicked, and landed a blow to his knee that made him stumble. She wrenched herself free of his hold and staggered as she tried to get her feet under her, and waited for the punch of a bullet hitting her in the back.

But it wasn't a bullet that froze her in her tracks.

"Stop, or he'll shoot her."

Krista looked up and saw that a man—the big, bearded goon who tried to kill her and Sean before—stood just a few feet away, his arm locked around the neck of a terrified girl.

"Careful." Maxwell's whisper sent a tremor through her. "Safety is off, and Cushman has an itchy trigger finger."

She felt the barrel of the gun in the base of her spine. "Walk," he ordered. "And you," he snapped to the whimpering girl. "Shut the fuck up."

The girl's whimpers faded to the occasional sniffle.

In the distance the gunfire went silent. She heard the tinny sound of a voice yelling into the earpiece Maxwell still held in his hand. As they walked, he held it up to his ear and chuckled. Krista cringed as he shoved the ear-piece into her right ear. "He sounds worried. He should be."

Tears stung the backs of her eyes when she heard Sean's voice. "Krista, where are you? Answer me!" He was in control, not giving in to fear yet, trying not to think the worst. She tried to reply, but Maxwell already held the mic to his lips.

"She's with me. And now she's going to find out first-hand what happens when you try to fuck with me."

Maxwell threw the earpiece and mic off into the darkness and forced Krista into a fast walk while Cushman kept hold of the girl. Maxwell kept the gun buried in her spine as he dragged her behind a building whose peeling sign read JENSEN FORGE, and made a phone call. "We need a pickup. Now. Behind the Forge office building."

Krista tried to slow him down without being obvious. They weren't far from the others, and they would be combing the darkness for any sign of her.

They traveled deeper into the maze of empty buildings and Krista kept her gaze straight ahead, as her brain wrapped around the fact that David Maxwell, who'd sat across a dinner table and asked her high school self about her college plans, was now marching her through the darkness at gunpoint. She prayed for the sound of foot-steps, a shout, any sign that Sean and the others were close.

An engine roared as a car approached. *Please let it be them.* Her meager hopes died a swift death as a dark sedan screeched to a halt in front of them. The trunk popped open and Maxwell, surprisingly strong and solid under his cashmere coat, muscled her over to it.

She had a random flashback to a self-defense course she had taken in college after Nicole's attack. *Never get in the car.*

If she had been alone, she might have tried to make a break for it. But Maxwell's goon was squeezing the girl's neck, the muzzle of his gun pressed tightly to her head.

She didn't resist as Maxwell shoved her into the trunk. The girl started struggling in earnest.

The thug tumbled the girl in on top of her and slammed the lid shut. The girl's soft whimpers filled the dark space. Krista reached out and found her hand in the tangle of arms and legs. Thin fingers clutched Krista's hand in a desperate grip.

"It's going to be okay," Krista said. "They're going to find us."

She didn't believe it for a second, but there was nothing else she could think to say.

Sean took off at a dead run in the direction of Krista's last known position. He heard shouting behind him, but he couldn't make out the words over the roaring in his head. All he could think of was Krista with that slime bag.

She's going to find out firsthand what happens when you try to fuck with me. God, Sean didn't want to think about what that might mean, but that didn't stop the horror show in his head.

Please let her be okay. It was like a mantra in his head as he ran his flashlight beam through the darkness, looking for any sign of them. Footsteps crunched behind him and Brooks and Ibarra joined him to search the immediate area.

"Footprints," Brooks said, illuminating where the gravel

had been disturbed. "Looks like he dragged her a little here." Sean saw the grooves in the dirt where Krista's feet had slid.

"Someone else is with them," Ibarra said as his light picked up another set of drag marks.

"It's the girl," Sean said grimly. "The one who ran off from the truck."

They took off in the direction of the footsteps. Maxwell had only one man with him—better than decent odds if they could find an angle to get a clear shot. He heard voices up ahead and picked up his pace.

Sirens wailed in the distance, signaling the approach of the paramedics and crime scene techs. All they had to do was catch up.

There was the roar of an engine, a car screaming to a stop. A female voice crying, pleading in Russian. *"Please don't put me in there. Please not in the dark again."*

They switched direction, toward the street and pounded as fast as they could go. "They're on Marginal Way. They're being forced into a vehicle," Sean gasped.

He heard the unmistakable *thunk* of a trunk slamming closed and willed his body to go faster.

Tires squealed as he rounded the side of a building. Sean drew his Glock but the Mercedes was going so fast he knew that if he managed to hit the driver or blow out a tire the ensuing accident would kill Krista as easily as a bullet would have.

He watched helplessly as the taillights disappeared into the darkness.

"Driver is in a black Mercedes headed north on East Marginal Way." Ibarra's voice snapped Sean out of his inertia. He had to get his head back into the game. Detach himself as much as he could and treat it like it was any other mission.

He summoned up that layer of calm, used it to muffle the panic screaming inside him at the thought of where Maxwell was taking Krista and what he was going to do to her.

"I need to get down to the station to get the girls processed," Cole said over the earpiece, his voice grim. "Petersen, take a team out to Maxwell's house and I'll send another team to his downtown offices."

"He knows we're onto him. You really think he's going to take her to his house?" Sean snapped as he, Ibarra, and Brooks took off at a jog toward their car.

"No," Cole said calmly, "but if we can get a hold of his wife or any of his associates, they might be able to provide a lead. Until we nail down the car's location, it's our only option."

"The three of us will head out—" Sean started, only to be interrupted by Cole.

"No, take my car and meet me down at the station. You need to let me handle this, Sean," Cole said. "There are going to be enough questions and problems with what happened tonight. When we take Maxwell, I want to make sure it's by the book."

"Fuck that. While you're following the rules, you're going to get Krista killed," Sean snapped.

"Don't forget you're still wanted in connection with the murder of that deputy. I'll lock you up in a holding cell if it's what I have to do to keep you from interfering."

They reached the car. Good thing Cole wasn't riding with them. Sean didn't think he'd be able to resist the urge to pound the shit out of his sister's fiancé. His jaw pulsed as they climbed into the car, Ibarra driving, Sean shotgun, Brooks in the back.

"I care about Krista too, Sean," Cole said. "I don't want to see anything happen to her any more than you do."

Sean ripped the earpiece out of his ear, feeling like his head was going to explode. He wanted to scream at Cole not to fucking patronize him. He had no idea what Sean was feeling right now. How Krista had somehow ripped away the fog of numbness he hadn't been able to escape from since his release from prison.

How just being around her had dragged him kicking and screaming back to life and now he was afraid he'd lose his fucking mind for good if he lost her.

How he was nearly paralyzed with terror at the idea of that monster getting his hands on her, at the idea that she might die and he'd never have the chance to tell her that everything he'd said in anger was bullshit. That really he thought she was the most beautiful, brave, amazing woman to ever barrel into his life. That while he'd never been in love before, as crazy as it sounded, he was pretty sure if he ever did it would feel a hell of a lot like this.

When he brought his hand to his face it was shaking. He rolled his window down several inches and sucked in a lungful of cool night air. "I don't like this. Sitting on our asses waiting for the police to handle it when we're ten times better prepared to handle something like this."

"True," Brooks's voice came from the back seat. "But there's nothing we can do until we get a lead on her location. And for now, the cops are the best resource."

The darkness closed in on Krista like a fist, the air thick as the sound of panicked breathing from both herself and the girl filled the trunk. Where was he taking them? She was totally disoriented, had no idea what direction they were headed, and was already having trouble figuring out how long they'd been driving.

Five minutes? Fifteen? Impossible to tell, as her body struggled to process what was happening to her.

The way they were smashed together, Krista could feel the girl's heartbeat pounding as fast as her own. She wondered where she was from, how she had ended up on that truck to be delivered to Maxwell and Karev. "What's your name?"

The girl sniffed and said, "Nadia."

"Are you from Russia?"

Another sniff. "*Respublika Gruziya*, Georgia," she said in English. "From Sukhumi, small city on the Black Sea."

"Your English is really good."

"We learn in school," she replied. It wasn't much but the small talk somehow managed to calm them both, adding a dash of normalcy to this entirely messed up situation.

"How old are you?" Krista said, almost afraid to hear the answer.

"Fifteen." The same age as Mark's oldest, Hannah. But instead of private schools and beach houses, this girl was going to be sold like a farm animal.

"How did you end up on that truck?"

"In my city I go to special music school. A woman, she come in and say she is auditioning students for special trip to come perform in the U.S. Is great opportunity, she says and if we do well we can even get scholarship to go to school."

"Are all the girls from your school?"

"No, from my school there are only two, me and my friend, Olga. Our parents, they were so excited, they have big party before we go."

Krista could hear fresh tears in the girl's voice. Her stomach curled as she thought of Nadia and her friend being so excited for the so-called opportunity, having no idea what kind of monsters they were putting their trust in.

"But instead of going to U.S., we fly to Canada. And when we get off the plane we go to hotel and they take our passports. They tell us if we run away, they will kill our parents back home."

Though it could have easily been an empty threat, Krista knew it wasn't uncommon to keep tabs on the families of the girls they trafficked. Threatening their loved ones was one of the easiest ways to keep the girls under control.

"I have a little brother, Georg. He is twelve. They tell me if I run away or tell anyone, they will sell him to *izvrashchenets*, a *pedofil*. But I couldn't help it—we were in that truck, in the dark, for so long—"

"Shh," Krista said, squeezing Nadia's hand harder. "The police here will make sure nothing will happen to your family—"

She broke off as the car came to a stop and the engine turned off. Doors slamming sent vibrations through the car. She could hear footsteps and muffled conversation. Krista strained to listen but could make out only every few words.

"Need to hurry . . . have . . . sunrise."

What happened at sunrise?

The lid of the trunk popped open. Fresh air rushed in and Krista took a greedy inhale, as did Nadia.

Her relief was short lived as Maxwell's angry face

loomed over her. Even in the darkness his ice-blue eyes glittered with an unholy light. How had she not recognized the evil lurking so close beneath the surface?

He reached in and grabbed her by the front of her shirt and dug the gun into the tender underside of her chin. Krista registered the smell of salt air and the sound of lapping water. They were at a marina. A wild look around registered slips full of luxury yachts.

The other man dragged Nadia out by the arm, and she stumbled and fell.

"Easy with her," Maxwell snapped at the other man.

"Sorry, boss," Cushman muttered and seemed to take a little more care when he pulled Nadia to her feet.

"What—" Stars exploded in her head as Maxwell hit her across the cheek with enough force to spin her head to the side.

"You keep your mouth shut."

Krista's cheekbone throbbed in time with her heartbeat. "Or what? You'll kill me?"

"No, but by the time I'm done with you, you'll be begging for it."

He grabbed her by the collar of her shirt, and with his gun held squarely against her chest, he bent his head to hers. Krista held his gaze and forced herself not to flinch as his hot, sour-smelling breath hit her face. "You want to know why I told him to be careful? She's a virgin. And the buyer Karev lined up won't be happy if she comes to him all banged up."

So Maxwell had been bluffing when he had threatened the girl. If he and Karev already had a buyer lined up, he'd be out thousands if anything happened to the girl. Nadia was too valuable to kill.

The marina was dark, deserted, but it was possible people were sleeping on the boats. Maxwell wouldn't hesitate to hurt her, but she had to take the chance. She knew that if she and Nadia got on that boat they'd both be lost forever.

She jerked back with all her strength, catching Maxwell off guard enough that she broke his hold. She opened her mouth and screamed at the top of her lungs. "Help us! Somebody please—"

Pain exploded through her skull with such force she fell to her knees. A rough hand clamped over her mouth, the fingers digging into her cheeks. Her lips ground against her teeth and she tasted blood.

Her vision tunneled and she fought for consciousness and felt herself thrown over a hard shoulder. She wanted to fight, but she couldn't seem to get the message to her legs and arms. Her head throbbed and she realized the warm tickling sensation on her cheek was blood. His shoulder dug into her stomach so hard she thought she was going to be sick. *Maybe if I throw up he'll drop me.*

Maxwell threw her onto the deck of a huge yacht and dragged her into a stateroom. She was thrown on the bed like a duffle bag, the impact jarring her head hard enough to make her vision start to waver again.

"Nosy bitch," he muttered. Krista held her breath. What was he going to do now? Kill her? Rape her?

Bile rose in her throat at the thought.

But to her shock, Maxwell quickly bound her hands and feet with zip ties, pulling them so tight they dug into her wrists and ankles, and sealed her mouth with a strip of duct tape. Had he fantasized about doing this while he practiced his golf swing at the country club? A bubble of hysterical laughter lodged in her throat at the thought.

Nadia landed on the bed beside her and Karev's thug bound and gagged her too.

Maxwell leaned over Krista, his leering face penetrating her fog. "I have some things to take care of before we go. But don't worry. We're going to have a lot of fun together." He reached out and covered Krista's breast with his hand and gave it a painful squeeze, smiling at the way she whimpered behind the duct tape. "I've had my eye on you since you were sixteen, Krista." His voice was rougher, the cultured tones giving way as he shed the final layers of civility. "I'm gonna enjoy every second. And when I'm finished with you, thanks to Karev I know some guys in Turkey who will pay me good money for you. You know Middle Easterners and their taste for the white women. Even the ones who are all used up."

Chapter 21

Sean paced the conference room that had become the center of operations. Though it was nearly ten p.m., the Homicide wing of the Seattle PD was humming with activity as they worked to track down Maxwell and Krista before it was too late.

Though there was still a statewide APB out on Sean and a warrant for his arrest for the shooting of the police deputy, Cole wasn't about to turn him over to the authorities in Chelan County. Fortunately, no one else present seemed inclined to challenge him on that, especially after Cole made a few well-placed phone calls to some of the subjects of Maxwell's lurid videos.

As expected, Maxwell wasn't at home, his office, or any of the other obvious places. Petersen had been sent to pick up Margaret Grayson-Maxwell for questioning.

Maybe she could shed some light on where her husband had taken Krista. Sean wasn't holding his breath.

They'd been back at the station for half an hour, and still nothing. Sean tried not to dwell on the fact that half an hour was plenty of time to rape and kill a woman. "This is ridiculous. There has to be a way to find this asshole," Sean said. "Traffic cameras."

"City hasn't installed them in that area." Cole shook his head as he looked at the map they had posted. There was a red dot that represented where Karev's driver had picked them up, and concentric circles outward to show the radius they might have traveled. "If they head this way," he said, indicating the south end of the city, "we might be able to pick them up on the cameras. I have an APB out on them. Every cop in the city is looking for that car."

"And in the meantime that fucker is doing God knows what to her," Sean bit out. "We have to do something. I can't just wait around here." He started for the door, but Cole caught him by the shoulder.

"Believe me, Sean, of all people, I know what's going through your head right now."

Sean met Cole's dark stare. Right. Just a little over three months ago, Cole had been going out of his mind trying to figure out where that sick fuck Nate Brewster had taken Megan. He of all people knew how it felt to know the woman you loved—

His brain slammed into that word like a brick wall. No way. It was just the insanity of the last few days combined with a burst of a psychotic amount of chemistry. And now wasn't the time to go all Dr. Phil on his feelings for Krista.

"Do these windows open?" Sean asked as he stalked to the ones that lined the wall across from them. He needed air. He needed to think...He managed to get one cracked open a few inches. "What about in-dash GPS, cell phones—"

"We're trying to get in touch with all the service providers—"

"Do you mind?" Ibarra, who along with Brooks had remained mostly silent other than to answer questions from the other cops brought in on the case. "This kind of thing is right in my wheelhouse."

"What are you going to do?" Cole said. Ibarra pulled a laptop out of his bag and flipped it open.

Ibarra started typing. "Probably best if I don't give you all the details. Let's just say I'm bending a few rules and leave it at that."

Cole shrugged. "Whatever it takes."

Within minutes Ibarra had a hit. "I've got an outgoing call, about four hundred meters from the warehouse at ten oh two. " Ibarra said and ran off the number. "Another call five minutes later."

There was a commotion outside the room as Margaret Grayson-Maxwell arrived. "This is a travesty," she shouted. "I refuse to speak to anyone until my attorney arrives." For a woman who had been dragged out of her house in the middle of the night, she was remarkably put together.

Then again, Sean thought as he felt disgust curl his lip, she was probably wide awake waiting to hear from David that the delivery had gone as planned and she was about to receive another infusion into her campaign fund.

"I'm here, Margaret." A tall, athletic-looking man in his late fifties hurried in carrying a briefcase. The guy looked familiar and suddenly Sean realized why. It was John Slater, Krista's father.

"John, thank God you're here," Margaret said, confirming Sean's fears and offering her cheek to kiss.

"Of course," he said, and then spun to pin Cole with a cold stare. His eyes were a familiar shade of grayish green. "What's the meaning of this, detective? You drag my client down here in the middle of the night for no reason."

"We need to ask her some questions about her husband," Cole said.

The guilty flash in Margaret's eyes was immediately hidden by indignation. "David is away on business. He left right after the fund-raiser tonight—"

Rage bubbled up in Sean's chest at the lie that came so easily. "He's in town. His goons killed Karev," Sean snapped, ignoring Cole's warning look.

Slater turned at Sean's words. His head snapped back as he recognized Sean. "You! Where is Krista? What did you do to my daughter?"

"I didn't do anything to her. Your fucking slime-bag client Maxwell has her. He kidnapped Krista after we interrupted the delivery of their truckload of girls."

Margaret's face went white. "I don't know what you're talking about. Who's Karev? I have no idea—"

Sean ignored her and turned to Slater. "He shoved Krista into the trunk of his car. That would be an interesting trial, watching you defend the man who kidnapped your daughter."

Slater's golf-course-tanned face went gray. "Where did he take her? Where is she?"

"That's the million-dollar question," Cole said. "Maybe you two can shed a little light."

Slater looked like he'd been kicked in the chest. For all that Slater was a sleazebag, it was clear he still cared about his daughter. He didn't seem to hear Margaret's loud protests as she was led to an interrogation room, and his hands shook as he fumbled with the clasp of his briefcase. "My files—he has several properties in the area that he didn't want traced to him. I can get you a list—"

"Did you help him buy a boat?" Ibarra broke in. "Because the last call I traced was fifteen minutes ago at the Corinthian Yacht Club."

"That place is huge," Brooks commented. "Could take us hours to locate if we don't know what we're looking for."

"*The Eva Marie.* I helped him with a transfer of ownership from a business associate who wanted to keep it quiet." Sean understood why when Slater named a well-known software company executive whose name was included on Maxwell's list. "If it's still at the yacht club, it hasn't moved from the original owner's slip."

Slater quickly passed on the information. "I had no idea... I thought I was just helping David move money around..." he said, his voice tight. "Please don't let her be hurt." He said it like it was a prayer.

"I'll do everything I can," Sean vowed, though as he waited, muscles coiled tightly, for the cops to move out, he feared it wouldn't be nearly enough.

Cole was barking orders, calling in requests for a helicopter, a hostage response team, a dive team, and assistance from the U.S. Coast Guard if needed.

But everyone seemed to be gearing up in slow motion. They didn't know if Krista was dead or alive and they were all acting like they had minutes to spare.

He looked around the room and caught Ibarra's eyes, then Brooks's. All it took was a slight nod, and Sean made a grab for Cole's keys on the table and the three went sprinting out of the building, ignoring Cole's warnings to stop.

"If this goes wrong, it will be on you," Cole said as the three flew out the front door.

It had been on him since the second he'd ignored his instincts and let Krista out of his sight, Sean thought as they jumped into the car. And now he just prayed he'd make it to her in time to set it right.

The stateroom where Maxwell had put her and Nadia was nearly pitch black. The lights along the docks had been shut off for the night, offering no illumination through the portholes.

Nadia was next to her, and Krista could feel the tremors of fear racking her body. Or they could have been her own. Krista was tight as a spring, every muscle tense and quivering.

She tried to stay present, to not let her fear-fueled imagination spin out of control. But bound and gagged in the dark, her only company a terrified, whimpering girl, it was hard not to think about what was likely to happen when Maxwell decided to return.

According to the glowing red numbers on the digital clock, they'd been on the boat just shy of forty-five minutes. Long enough for her legs to cramp and for her hands and fingers to swell and throb from the tight bindings.

She wondered what Maxwell was up to, but in the time they'd been here, all she'd heard was a lot of stomping around and unintelligible conversation. At one point she'd heard him shout, and then what sounded like people on the docks outside. Someone going? Someone arriving?

Maybe by some miracle, Sean and the others had figured out where Maxwell had taken them and were here to stage a rescue.

She let herself indulge the fantasy of Sean charging in like her personal knight in shining armor for about five seconds before allowing it to slip away. *Sean*. Her eyes stung with tears at the thought of him, his shadowed eyes that couldn't hide the sparks of humor and passion that lurked beneath that hard surface.

His warrior's soul and protective instincts that wouldn't die no matter what had been done to him.

And the anger, too, bubbling inside him. She would never begrudge him a second of his rage, even though it had felt like a knife to the chest when it was finally aimed straight at her.

Now she was desperate to see him one more time and tell him she understood his anger. That she loved him whether he could ever forgive her and love her back or not.

A low rumble jerked her from her thoughts of Sean. Was that the engine? Every cell in her body went cold as she realized that, yes, they were moving.

The door flew open and Krista shrank back from the glare of the overhead light that was switched on. Her stomach rolled when she saw Maxwell in the doorway, a glaze of lust in his icy eyes and a smirk on his face. She couldn't believe this leering monster was the same man whose ruggedly handsome face had graced the pages of the local society pages.

There was another man with him, not the thug who had grabbed Nadia. Maxwell stepped into the stateroom and shrugged out of his jacket to neatly drape it over the back of a chair.

He nodded at the thug, who grabbed Nadia around the

waist and pulled her off the bed and out of the room.

"Now let's have some fun." He closed and locked the door behind him.

Sean could hear the wail of sirens in the distance as Ibarra screeched to a halt in the marina's parking lot. There was Maxwell's yacht, exactly where Krista's father said it would be. The main cabin was illuminated and from here he could see lights on and dark figures pacing around, but he couldn't see Krista.

Sean, Brooks, and Ibarra jumped out of the car to gear up, and Sean heard it immediately. The unmistakable rumble of an engine. The yacht was already pulling away from the dock.

He didn't stop to think. He just ran. He didn't know if the others were behind him or not as he scaled the gate and thundered down the dock. The boat was already several yards off the dock.

Brooks and Ibarra shouted, catching the attention of one of Maxwell's men who was on the deck. Shots rang out on both sides, but the bodyguard was shooting at Cole's car and didn't seem to realize there was a third man in pursuit.

Sean did a shallow dive, gasping as the frigid water hit him.

He didn't have time to be cold. He forced his arms and legs to churn through the water as he chased the boat. It was traveling fairly slowly now as it maneuvered through the crowded marina but once it got past the docks it would pick up enough speed that Sean wouldn't have a chance in hell of catching it.

One more stroke and he was even with the stern. He

could see the gleam of the chrome ladder hanging down and he reached for it.

At that second, the yacht cranked into higher gear, jerking through the water as it picked up speed. Sean's fingers, stiff from the cold, threatened to slip their grip. He threw his arm over a rung, hooking it with his elbow as the yacht sped past the end of the docks.

He hung there for a minute to catch his breath, listening to see if he could hear any footsteps over the engine noise. When no one appeared above him to shoot him in the face, Sean was satisfied his desperate grab had gone unnoticed.

He hauled himself up the ladder as quietly as possible and became aware of a new snag, one he hadn't considered in his desperate dive into the frigid waters of the marina.

He was cold. Shaking, shuddering, fingers stiff, he was in no shape to take on Maxwell and at least one, but probably more, of his men. He thought longingly of the arsenal he'd left in the trunk of Cole's car. Sean hadn't even taken the time to strap his knife to his calf, not that he would trust himself not to drop it right now, the way his hands were shaking.

Fuck. He'd never considered himself an impulsive person. He had gone into each mission with every move planned out and contingency plans to deal with the snarls that inevitably emerged.

But when it came to Krista, all bets were off and the rules went out the window. Trampled to dust by his overpowering need just to get to her, protect her, and keep her safe.

And make sure the fuckers who dared to go after her paid dearly.

All of which might be tricky in the situation he found himself in now.

He closed his eyes and cleared his head. As much as he wanted to go busting in on them and send some heads rolling, in the condition he was in, he'd be dead in an instant. First, he needed to get his body warm so it could do what he needed it to do. He could already feel his brain getting muzzy as all his energy was channeled into shivering.

How? He kept himself flat on the deck and to the right of the door that led into the cabin. He couldn't just stroll in and ask for a blanket. He found his answer in the rumble underneath his body.

The engine room. The engine itself would throw off plenty of heat. He might even find something to use as a weapon.

It would also be dark and enclosed. His heart started to pound and his breath shortened as every cell in his body rejected the idea.

But he didn't have a choice. Odds of saving Krista were already slim. If he didn't warm up and get his shit together they'd dwindle to zero.

He forced his body into action, ignoring the screams of protest in his head. It was like he pulled out of his body and was watching himself with dread as he opened the hatch to access the engine room.

He climbed inside and pulled the hatch down, enclosing himself in absolute darkness.

It was worse than his cell. The noise from the engine was deafening, the vibration so strong it shook his teeth.

The smell of diesel fuel made his stomach roll and his head pound.

But that was nothing compared to the suffocating pressure in his chest, so strong he felt like he was going to die.

He couldn't do this—he couldn't stay here. His hand was reaching up through the darkness when he heard the footstep above him and froze.

Krista. He had to think of Krista. He couldn't let this stupid phobia get the best of him. Not when it would cost her life. He closed his eyes and imagined her, the way she'd been in Maxwell's office, how she'd been in the crawl space. Pulling him close, wrapping her arms around him, tangling her fingers with his and sending a calming wave through him that blew all the relaxation exercises his therapist had given him out the window.

The sound of the engine faded as he replayed her voice in his head, telling him to calm down, that everything would be okay. The smell of the diesel fuel disappeared as he summoned up the scent of her hair, her skin.

Within moments, the panic receded and Sean felt the heat from the engine penetrating his wet clothes, easing the stiffness in his hands and limbs. His shudders slowed, his mind cleared, and he waited impatiently for his body to get back up to speed.

Forced to wait, he used the time to prepare any way he could. He felt around in the darkness, smiling when his hand brushed across what had to be a toolbox. He opened it up and searched around until his hand closed over a screwdriver. He tucked it into his waistband, reached around some more, and experienced a burst of satisfaction when he found a good-sized wrench as well.

He put the wrench next to him on the floor and flexed his fingers experimentally, swearing as another shudder rippled through him. Weapons secured, he scooted as close to the engine as he could without getting burned and waited to make his move.

Krista yelped as Maxwell ripped the duct tape off her mouth in one cruel jerk, taking what felt like several layers of skin with it. She tried to scramble away but there was nowhere to go, and then she was pinned up against the headboard with Maxwell standing at the foot of the bed.

He put one knee on the bed and jerked her toward him. A switchblade appeared in his hand with a metallic *snick*, and Krista held her breath as the blade slashed down.

The ties on her ankles slackened, and she winced as the sudden rush of blood made her feet tingle painfully. Minor discomfort was nothing to the horror that flooded through her as Maxwell pinned her down with his knees on her hips and the wicked blade came arcing down to her chest. Fabric ripped and she realized he was cutting her shirt down the middle, and her bra too.

Goose bumps prickled as cold air hit her bare skin. Every muscle shrank back in revulsion as the icy-cold tip of the knife skimmed down her belly, up under her breasts.

Krista's head flooded with images of Nate Brewster's victims, the bloody slashes he'd cut into their bodies. "Please don't," Krista whispered.

"Don't worry. I don't share Nate's taste for blood. But I'll cut you if you make me."

He rested the blade of the knife against her throat and covered her breast with his other hand. A cruel twist of her nipple made her cry out. "You're a beautiful woman, Krista, even though you tried to hide it under those suits. Most of the people I deal with like the younger girls, but you'll do well, I think. But we will have to do something about this hair." He moved his hand to her head and gave the short strands a sharp tug. "They like to fuck the blondes, you know. I always liked brunettes, myself."

Even with the knife at her neck, Krista couldn't stop herself from struggling as Maxwell reached for the waistband of her pants. She kicked and tried to wrench free of his hold. He kept the knife in his fist and laid his forearm across her neck so hard she could feel her windpipe start to give as she struggled for breath.

She was going to pass out, her vision darkening around the edges. Suddenly Maxwell let up with a violent curse. As the buzzing faded, Krista realized it was oddly silent.

The motor was out.

"Don't move," Maxwell said as he turned and left the room.

Krista threw herself off the bed and looked around frantically for anything that could be used as a weapon. She kept one eye on the door, knowing she could have only a few seconds to save herself.

Sean smiled into the darkness as the engine gave a choke and then died completely. He heard the click and whine as someone tried to restart the engine, and then muffled angry shouts as they realized the engine was dead.

His body warm and his brain mostly in check, he held the wrench in one hand, ready to strike when they came to investigate.

He didn't have long to wait. Within a minute the panel that covered the engine popped open and a man climbed inside. Sean struggled to keep his breathing quiet and steady when all he wanted to do was suck in the fresh air as he ducked from the glow of the flashlight.

"What is it?" a voice called down.

"Give me a minute," the man snapped back.

"You need to fix it now," the thug said.

"For fuck's sake, you can't just drag a guy out of bed in the middle of the night and expect him to be firing on all cylinders. My brain isn't even awake yet."

He moved closer to the opening. Sean could see the thug looming overhead. The thug took a draw on his cigarette, muttered something under his breath, and started to pace. The second he stepped clear, Sean made his move on the guy working on the engine.

Pouncing from behind, he locked his arm around the guy's neck and pressed with his opposite hand. The guy struggled, choking, but Sean had at least five inches and forty pounds on him. In seconds the man slumped to the floor.

Sean quickly patted him down but found no weapons. He shoved the guy into the corner just as the thug paced back over.

"Simpson, you fix it yet?"

When Simpson didn't answer, the thug leaned over to peer into the engine room. In one swift move, Sean aimed the flashlight right in the thug's face, blinding him. Sean reached up and grabbed the guy by the collar and toppled him into the engine room.

The guy went down on his knees, disoriented as he fumbled under his coat. One blow of the wrench to the side of the head sent him to the floor. Sean gave him one more whack for good measure.

The flashlight revealed the thug to be the one who got away from the warehouse with Maxwell. A quick pat down scored Sean a semiautomatic pistol and a pocketful of flex ties that he used to bind the thug and the guy called Simpson.

Two down. Sean wondered how many more there were besides Maxwell himself. The engine block was covered in thick black grease. Sean palmed a handful and smeared it down his face and the backs of his hands to cut any glare on his skin before he climbed out of the engine room. He listened for any sign of movement as he carefully closed the hatch.

Krista was searching the stateroom's adjoining bathroom to no avail when Maxwell returned.

He was less than pleased when he saw that she wasn't where he had left her.

Krista cried out as he grabbed her by the hair and pulled her out. He threw her down on the bed, a savage look on his face as he came over her. "You never listen, Krista. If you'd listened and kept your nose out of it, none of this would have happened."

"Is that what you told Talia? That she better listen or you'd hurt her and her sister?" Krista swung her doubled-up fists at his head and felt a sickening crunch as she miraculously managed to hit him in the nose. "Is that what happened to those other girls? They didn't listen so you sent Nate to kill them?"

Blood spurted and he held his hand to his face as he fell back. He staggered a bit and charged at her like something out of a horror movie. "I'll make what Nate did look gentle by the time I'm done with you."

Krista kicked out with her legs, caught him hard in the chest, and sent the knife clattering to the floor.

She dove after it, scrambling to get her legs under her as her bound hands strained for the knife.

Maxwell landed on top of her with a roar, fisted his hand in her hair, and slammed her head into the floor. Dazed, Krista felt herself being dragged back to the bed, landing face down this time. Maxwell secured her bound hands to the headboard and she kicked wildly as he dragged her pants and underwear down her hips. Pain throbbed in her head.

"You just couldn't leave it alone, could you?" he said and grunted as he jerked her legs apart. "Nate's dead, Flynn is out of jail, you got what you wanted, but you had to keep digging."

Even through her terror, one question demanded an answer. "Why Sean? Why did you frame him?" The sound of her own voice made her head throb harder.

Maxwell let out a little huff of laughter. "Because Nate needed a scapegoat for Evangeline Gordon, and he wanted it to be Sean. I had no beef with him. As far as I was concerned, he could have lived the rest of his life in peace until he decided to try to come after me."

Oh God. Sean hadn't been in any danger until she'd put him there. As fervently as she'd prayed for him to come rescue her, she started to pray he'd stay away, stay safe. She couldn't live with the guilt if anything else happened to him because of her.

But the way things were going, she might not have long to live with her guilt, period.

Maxwell wrapped something around her ankle and bound it to the bed. He then did the same to the other until she was bound facedown and spread-eagled on the bed.

Helpless.

Sean crept quietly up the stairs that led to the main deck, keeping to the shadows as he determined how many he was up against. He listened in the distance for the sound of a motor indicating Ibarra and Brooks were in pursuit, but as of yet, nothing.

He quickly found the first man, stationed on the outside of the main deck, at the stern. Not wanting to draw attention, Sean took him out with a blow with the wrench and secured him as he had the others. He sifted through the guy's pockets and used the roll of duct tape he'd lifted from the engine room to gag him. He took the guy's AK-47 and slung it over his shoulder.

Gun cocked and ready, the screwdriver tucked into his waistband, Sean crept along the side of the main cabin. Inside, he could see one of Maxwell's men pacing restlessly as his AK lay on the table of the dining area. No sign of Maxwell, Krista, or the other girl.

Sean forced himself not to dwell on what Maxwell might be doing to them and focused on taking down Maxwell's muscle.

He ducked below the window line and combat crawled his way to the front of the boat. There were two men up here, both smoking and speaking in low voices. They were speculating on how many days it would take to meet up with their contacts, and how much their cut of the sale of the women would be.

Women. Definitely plural. Sean's relief at the evidence that Krista was still alive was tainted by horror at what Maxwell had planned for her.

Sean struggled to keep a rein on his temper when one of the guys said, "I get first go at the woman after Maxwell's finished."

"No way, you got first go last time," the other thug said.

"Yeah, and she was worthless after that."

The other guy shrugged. "It's not my fault she couldn't handle me."

"Yeah, well, your needs are likely to kill her before we even hit international waters."

The thug laughed, remorseless. "Ah, just as long as I get a taste of that before we dump her off the side."

Sean's blood exploded to a boil and he pounced from the shadows, catching one thug with a blow from the wrench as he rolled to the side as the other thug fumbled for his gun. Gunfire peppered the deck as Sean took aim, hitting the thug who'd talked about dumping Krista over the side with a shot straight to his face.

The other woozily reached for his pistol, screaming as Sean blew a hole right through his chest.

Sean took the thugs' guns and charged inside, diving behind a couch as the guy grabbed his semiautomatic from the table and opened fire on the room, shouting for reinforcements that would never come.

Sean stayed down and groaned like he'd been hit. Sure enough the meathead came to investigate. Sean opened up and the guy went down, clutching his throat.

Angry shouts came from the opposite side of the cabin. Through the walls he heard a woman scream.

Krista!

He took the inside staircase down, the screams getting louder as he got closer to the staterooms.

Then silence.

Heart in his throat, Sean pushed through a door that opened up to a sitting room, and all he could think was that he'd fucked up. He'd lost control and gone out guns blazing, tipping his hand to Maxwell.

Who no doubt was still with Krista. And there was nothing to penetrate the eerie silence to give evidence she was still alive.

Krista felt the bile rise in her throat as rough hands grabbed her hips as Maxwell ground himself against her.

He was fumbling with his fly when the first shots rang out. He froze and then gave an enraged shout when the shooting continued.

Someone was here! Maxwell sliced the tie that bound her hands to the bed. He went to work on her ankles, and Krista gave a scream as the knife slipped and sliced into the skin of her leg.

"Shut up," he shouted and punched her in the back of the head hard enough to make her see stars.

Maxwell grabbed her by her bound hands and wrapped a blanket around her and pulled her to her feet. He positioned himself behind her, knife to her neck, and backed her toward the adjoining bathroom.

The door burst open, and there was Sean, his face blackened with grease and a wild look in his green eyes, but the most beautiful thing she'd ever seen.

"One move and I will cut her," Maxwell whispered, and Krista felt the sting of the blade biting into her neck.

She saw Sean's gun hand lower and felt the pressure of the knife ease. "Now drop it."

Sean let both his pistol and the rifle drop to the floor.

"Kick them over here."

Sean did. Maxwell snatched up the gun and opened fire as he backed Krista out of the room.

Krista cried out as Sean's head jerked from the impact and he fell backward in a heap.

Maxwell dragged her through the bathroom and out a door that led to the deck. Sean appeared to be alone, but if he'd gotten a location on the boat, his friends and the cops couldn't be far behind.

Maxwell obviously did the same math as he forced her into the dinghy attached to the boat and fumbled with the rope. Krista huddled in the blanket, head throbbing, feeling like a hole had been blown open in her chest.

Sean had taken a shot to the head. No way he could survive that.

Because he'd come after her.

Even if she survived Maxwell, her guilt and grief would consume her.

She numbly wondered how long it would take for the others to find the yacht, how long Nadia would remain helplessly bound and gagged wherever Maxwell's thug had put her. And if they managed to escape, how long he would keep her as a hostage before he decided she was no longer useful.

Maxwell struggled to untie the Zodiac from the yacht. Once he finally had it free, he jerked at the starter, swearing when all he got was a pathetic sputter.

Then there was a steady rumble, but not from the Zodiac. Motorboats were approaching.

A siren sounded and a spotlight shone in the distance. The police were here.

An instant later, Sean burst from the door. Blood

streamed from his shoulder as he thundered onto the deck.

Maxwell made a grab for Krista as a swell hit the Zodiac, sending him careening to the side. Krista kicked out hard and sent Maxwell to the other side of the small rubber boat. A heavy shadow and then a *thump* as Sean's weight hit the Zodiac.

There was a cry of pain as the men grappled, but in the darkness Krista couldn't see who had the upper hand.

She got on her knees and fumbled with her bound hands to find a weapon. Her hands closed over something smooth and cylindrical. An oar? She raised it over her head just as a swell tilted the Zodiac at a precarious angle and a heavy body slammed into her. Krista didn't have time to even take a breath before she was hurled into the frigid sea.

"Krista!" Sean realized what had happened the split second before the splash of seawater hit him in the face.

Maxwell took advantage of his distraction and punched Sean in the head, glancing off the deep furrow the bullet had left in his scalp. Shooting pain stabbed at his head and blood seeped into his eyes as he staggered back. Maxwell seized the opening to pounce. The knife slashed down and Sean hissed as it sliced through the muscle of his forearm as Sean raised it to ward off the blow.

Maxwell raised the knife as Sean struggled to heave him off. Maxwell was surprisingly strong despite his age and soft life, and he had the advantage of not being wounded. Blood from the wound mingled with sweat to pour down Sean's forehead. Another swell hit the boat as the rumble of approaching engines grew louder. The high beam of the police boat hit them with blinding strength.

Maxwell hesitated only for a second. It was all Sean needed.

The screwdriver arced up and ripped into Maxwell's throat, tearing through the skin of his neck, ripping a jagged hole in the carotid artery.

He dropped the knife and fell back clutching his neck. Wet gurgling sounds filled the air.

"Shine the light on the water," Sean screamed, wiping frantically at his eyes as he ignored the throbbing in his head. Could they even hear him, he wondered as he frantically searched for Krista. She'd been in the water for less than a minute, but with her hands bound and injured from Maxwell's blows, she wouldn't last for much longer in the frigid ocean.

His eyes scanned and saw nothing. He waved his arms and pointed frantically at the water and they finally found something. The spotlight skimmed the surface of the ocean, and there it was: a glimpse of pale skin just underneath the surface.

He dove in, the saltwater stinging his head wound like a thousand burning needles as he felt frantically for her in the dark, frigid water. She was limp when he grabbed her, unresponsive when Brooks and Ibarra hauled her up on to the speedboat they'd commandeered. They averted their eyes and covered her naked body with their jackets as Sean put his ear to her mouth.

"She's not breathing." He put his fingers to her neck but he was so cold he couldn't feel anything.

Brooks's hand gently brushed his aside. "She's got a pulse," Brooks said.

Sean nodded, pinched her nose shut, opened her mouth, and covered it with his own to breathe air into her lungs. "Come on, baby. Don't leave me," he whispered. Her chest expanded—one breath, two breaths, and on the third she sputtered and choked. Sean rolled her quickly to her side as she coughed up about a gallon of seawater.

"Sean?" she whispered weakly.

"Yeah, honey, I'm here."

She lifted a shaky hand to his face. "I thought you were dead," she said. "Thank God you're not dead—" She broke off as another wave of coughing racked her.

Sean gathered her into him as the spasms shook her body. "It's okay, honey. I've got you," he murmured over and over, squeezing his eyes shut against the tears of relief. "I've got you, and I'm not letting go."

Chapter 22

Fuck," Sean said, wincing at the way his head throbbed behind the thick white bandage when he bent to pick up his bag. As injuries went, the half-inch-deep groove Maxwell's bullet had gouged on the right side of his scalp wasn't much, but it still hurt like a son of a bitch when the blood came rushing to his head.

Megan, who was packing up the last of his stuff, rolled her eyes. "Let me help you."

"I got it," he snapped, wincing at the pain that stabbed through his head when he lifted the bag off the floor.

"Stop being an idiot," Megan said under her breath and took the duffel from him.

Sean forced himself to stay still, clenching his teeth against the nausea as he waited for the worst of the pain to subside and bit back a complaint about having to ask his baby sister to carry his luggage for him.

"Could be worse," Megan said as though she'd read his mind. "Another inch to the left, and you wouldn't have enough brains left to get annoyed with me."

"Believe me, I know how lucky I am," Sean said, wincing at the bite he couldn't quite keep out of his voice.

"I'm going to go get your prescriptions filled," Megan said. "And then I'll meet you back here?"

Sean nodded. "I need to go say good-bye."

Megan paused, studying him. "You sure that's all you want to say?"

Sean looked away from his sister's too-probing gaze. As though she would be able to read all of his secrets with one look. He didn't want Megan to see that his system was rocked by the sensation of having every emotion, every fear, every desire he'd been suppressing from the day he was locked up come roaring back to life in the space of three days.

Didn't want to admit that Krista was the woman who had ripped off the cover and brought it all screaming back.

And he sure as hell didn't want to admit that he thought he might be in love for the first time in his life with a woman who was his destruction and salvation all wrapped up in one classically beautiful package.

He was already pretty sure he was crazy, but admitting out loud that he was in love with Krista Slater would be the closer. "What else is there?" he said.

Megan muttered something under her breath and then walked over to him and leaned up to peck him on the cheek. "I'll be back in a few."

Sean listened to the door of his hospital room click shut behind her as he braced himself for what he needed to do. God, he wanted to be a coward and slink off without a word. But Krista deserved better than that.

She deserved better than him.

For two days he'd been haunted, day and night, by thoughts of Krista, beaten, scared, lips blue with cold. And it didn't stop there. As if reality wasn't sufficiently traumatizing, his brain was clever enough to come up with all kinds of scenarios of what might have happened to her had he not shown up in time.

Sean didn't know the extent of Maxwell's depravity, but his too-vivid imagination had gone to the outer limits.

For a moment there on the dock, holding her in his arms, he'd felt a peace like nothing he'd ever felt before. If only he could hold onto that feeling, he could get through anything. *They* could get through anything. But to Sean's dismay, the moment they got to the hospital, the moment Krista was safe and their lives weren't in danger, Sean came out of combat mode.

And in that instant, all of his old demons came out to play. Lights were too harsh; people were too loud; the softest touch made him want to jump out of his skin. It was like the first few days after he was released from prison, the full-on sensory overload, the whole world too big, too overwhelming to deal with. His fear of being trapped came back with a vengeance, to the point where he'd pissed off the hospital staff by moving his bed directly under his wide-open window.

Even then, on the few occasions when he'd slept, he'd woken up soaked in sweat, gasping for air, convinced he was back in his cell or inside the engine room of Maxwell's boat.

Before Krista had come stomping back into his life, he'd found peace in numbness, where everything stayed muted, distant, as though he was three steps removed from everything happening around him.

Now he longed for that same numbness but was afraid he'd never find it again, not without some serious pharmaceutical aid.

So in the two days since he'd pulled Krista out of the ocean, he'd come to a realization.

He had to let her go.

But Jesus, the idea of saying good-bye for good, face to face, made him feel like he had an anvil on his chest.

He walked the short distance to her room, and when he raised his hand to knock, he realized his hand was shaking. Grimacing, he curled his fist tighter and gave the door a sharp rap.

"Come in," she called, and just the sound of her voice was enough to make his nerve endings buzz.

He pushed the door open and found her sitting up in bed. Her dyed-dark hair stuck up a little in the back, and her skin was a shade too pale.

"Hey," she said softly. The joy in her clear eyes and the smile that swallowed up the bottom half of her face when she saw him just about made his heart explode. "I was starting to wonder why you hadn't come to see me."

Oh, he'd seen her plenty of times. Krista just didn't know it. Several times when the nightmares ripped him from sleep he'd slipped down the hallway to her room. He'd hovered outside her door, face pressed against the tiny window, and taken a small degree of comfort in the steady rise and fall of her chest.

She was alive. She was okay.

"I figured you needed your rest," he said, barely able to form the words as it felt like his heart was about to bust out of his chest.

He stood frozen in the doorway. It was too much. It was all too much.

Her smile faltered. "Aren't you going to come in?"

Torn between the desire to turn tail and run in the opposite direction and the equally strong urge to snatch her up in his arms and never let go, he forced himself to take a few steps closer.

"How are you doing?" she asked.

"I'm okay," he said. "Head still hurts. You?"

"You can pretty much see for yourself," she said with a little upward twist of her mouth.

The bruises on her face and the angry red marks on her wrists made him want to kill Maxwell all over again. "They told me nothing's broken, so that's good."

"I should be able to get out of here tomorrow." She looked him up and down and seemed to just notice he was dressed with his coat on. "Are you going now?"

"Yeah, Megan's waiting for me downstairs," Sean replied. "I wanted to stop by and say good-bye first."

Krista's brow knotted in that confused, slightly pissy way he'd come to adore. "Just good-bye?"

"No, not just good-bye," he said. But with everything swimming in his head, the lights too bright, the room too small, and God, the scent of her skin over the hospital antiseptic smell, he didn't really know where to start. "Do you mind if I open your window?" he asked abruptly.

"Of course not."

The fresh air cleared his head. *Tell her the important stuff. Tell her that you're sorry.* He sank into the chair next to her bed. "I didn't mean what I said, back at Ibarra's place. About not caring about what happened to you, wishing you had left me alone. I needed to know the truth about what had happened. And it feels good, knowing that we saved those girls and everyone got what was coming to them."

Her hand was lying on top of the covers, just a few inches away, and it seemed natural to take it in his. Warmth washed through him at the first touch of her skin, and with it came a sense of peace, quieting the demons that had been raging inside of him for the past two days.

His destruction.

His salvation.

And then it hit him. What if he just held on tight? If he kept her close, he would never lose this feeling he got when she touched him—that everything was all right, no matter what was going on around them.

No, he had to let her go, he was still too messed up, too close to the edge of crazy to be the kind of guy Krista needed. The kind of guy she deserved. The way he'd lashed out at her, tearing her to shreds before he even realized what he was saying was proof of that.

But he held on, stroking the back of her hand with his thumb, savoring the feel of her for a few more minutes before he had to let her go. "And I never would have had that closure without you. You're brave, smart, and beautiful on top of that. I know what I said was awful, but I want you to know I think you're pretty incredible."

A soft smile curved her lips and her fingers squeezed his hand. "I think you're pretty incredible too. I just wish there had been a better way for you to come into my life."

Sean gave a short smile. "Me too. I know this is going to sound crazy, as fucked up as everything was, but I'm glad I know you."

There was a sheen in her eyes, along with an expectant, almost hopeful look. "I'm really glad I know you too, Sean."

Sean swallowed hard, telling himself he needed to let

her go now. That it was better this way, he told himself, not to let either of them get too caught up in what had happened in three short, adrenaline-soaked, emotionally heightened days.

He had no right to drag her down into his abyss of emotional turmoil. He could barely keep his head in check. He needed quiet. He needed alone. He needed to get away from her and back to the place where he didn't feel anything anymore. He opened his mouth to tell her good bye.

"I love you."

Krista's heart stopped in her chest as the words popped from Sean's mouth without warning.

She shook her head, sure she must have hallucinated it. She'd been bracing herself to get her heart crushed. Despite every tender word, everything in Sean's manner told her that's where this was going.

Not...

"Excuse me?" she said.

To his credit Sean looked as shocked as she felt at what he'd blurted out. His eyes were wide, his mouth hung slightly open. "Oh, fuck, I didn't mean to say that."

He dropped her hand like it was burning him and brought his own to his head as though he was in pain.

Krista pushed herself up against the back of the hospital bed. "Do you mean it?" Her heart thundered in her ears as she waited for his answer. It was irrational, absolutely insane to even entertain the idea of trying to take what had happened to them in three crazy days and turn it into something more permanent.

She was not naïve. She was not a romantic. She knew

that the chances of this going anywhere good were infinitesimal at best.

But right now, she felt like she was going to live or die based on his answer.

"I'm a fucking mess," he said. "I lose my temper all the time. I'm still trying to figure out what normal life even feels like." He paused and looked at her, and what she saw in his eyes would have sent her to her knees if she hadn't already been in bed.

She reached out her hand to him. He came to her warily, like a wild animal sniffing her out to decide whether or not he'd be safe. He perched on the side of the bed and slid his big hand into hers. At the first touch, the tension leaked out of him and his fingers tightened around her so tightly it was almost painful.

"I don't know how to handle this. I can barely deal with my shit myself, and I don't want to hurt you too—"

Krista brought her hand to his cheek and looked him square in the eye. "Did you mean it?"

The answer was there in the glittering green of his eyes. But she still felt joy pulse through her, warm and fierce and staggering in its force as he whispered, "Yes. I meant it. I mean it. It's probably another sign of just how batshit I am, but yeah, I love you, Krista."

"I guess that makes me batshit too," Krista said, not even realizing she was crying until a fat tear dropped onto their clenched hands. "Because I love you back."

His mouth came over hers, soft, tender, and so sweet it brought the fresh burn of tears to her eyes. Her lips parted eagerly under his, and even the prickle of pain from her bruised lips couldn't stop her from sucking his tongue into her mouth. He groaned against her lips, pressing her back against the pillow as he threaded his fingers through her hair. "You better mean it," he murmured against her lips, "because I'm going to hold you to it, no matter how jacked up on pain medication you are right now."

She grinned, the pain of her injuries disappearing at the warmth of his touch. "I haven't had any for twelve hours. This is all on me."

He kissed her nose, her cheek, her lips again before he pulled back, his expression serious. "I can't promise I'll be any good at this. I came in here today to tell you good-bye. It would be better for both of us if I could just leave you in peace." As she opened her mouth to protest, he held up a hand. "Everything's crazy and is going to stay that way for a while. I don't want to be the one who drags you down with me."

His arms unconsciously tightened around her. "I thought if I left you I could go back to where I was before you showed up. Numb and not feeling much of anything. You yanked me out of that and it's scary as hell to feel everything at once after not feeling anything for so long. But the idea of leaving you to go back to that…I've got a lot of shit to work through, stuff you shouldn't have to deal with, but I can't let you go."

Krista felt an odd twisting in her chest, as though she had just stepped off the side of a cliff and into a free fall. But then she looked into Sean's eyes, which mirrored all the fear and hope and love welling up inside her, and she knew that with him there to catch her, everything would be okay. She stroked her thumb along the whiskers of his goatee, loving the way he nuzzled into her hand like some big jungle cat craving a loving stroke. "I don't know if you noticed, Sean, but I'm not exactly a shrinking violet."

Sean chuckled. "You're a certified badass," he said, turning to press an affectionate kiss into her palm.

"So are you. And I think two people who are badass enough to take down the biggest criminal network this city has ever seen are strong enough to overcome anything, as long as we have each other."

Three Days Later

"You sure you don't want me to go in with you?" Sean asked. They stood outside an interrogation room in the Seattle Police Department, and even Sean's strong, steady presence and his hand on the small of her back wasn't enough to banish the sickness twisting her stomach into knots.

Krista shook her head. "I need to talk to him, one on one. I need to try to understand." As though there were any acceptable explanation for why a man she had admired, trusted, and loved like a father would go along with a plan to have her killed.

She looked up at Cole, whose harsh features were nearly as grim as Sean's, and nodded for him to open the door.

Mark Benson looked up at the sound of the door closing, the click of the latch echoing through the small space like a gunshot. He'd aged a decade since she'd seen him barely a week ago, his face drawn and haggard.

He paled when he saw her, guilt flashing across his face as he took in the bruises that still marred her face.

Any illusion Krista might have clung to that somehow Mark wasn't really involved, that maybe the recording of him with the blonde was somehow doctored or manufactured had died the day before when Mark had been picked

up at the airport with little more than his passport and a
ticket to Jakarta in his possession.

Still, Krista felt like a huge fist was squeezing her heart
at the thought of how Mark had thrown her to the wolves.

"Krista, you have to know I never meant for you to get
hurt by any of this," Mark said without preamble. He half
rose from his chair, cuffed wrists raised in supplication.

"But you did tell him, didn't you? You told Maxwell I
was trying to find out more about Nate?" She knew, but
she needed to hear it from his lips, once and for all.

Mark nodded, his gaze locked on the table as though
he couldn't bear to look at her.

"Did you know all along that Sean was innocent? Did
you help Maxwell cover up for his nephew?" After
Maxwell's death, they'd made a startling discovery.
David Maxwell wasn't actually David Maxwell at all.
He was born Mark David Allen. His sister was Elizabeth
Allen Brewster, Nate's mother.

The information hadn't been made public yet, and
judging from Mark's reaction he was just as startled as
Krista had been at the news. "His nephew? Brewster was
his nephew? No, I had no idea. I swear. All he said was
he didn't want anyone connecting him to Brewster—I assumed he meant they had business dealings together. I
had no idea Brewster was his nephew, and I had no idea
he was paying Brewster to kill anyone."

"You knew he would try to kill me though, didn't
you?" Krista felt the sting of tears behind her eyes when
Mark didn't even try to deny it.

"He was going to ruin me," Mark said, his voice
sounding choked. "My career, my family."

Krista let out a mirthless laugh. "I'd say you did that

yourself when you couldn't bother to keep your pants zipped."

"I made a mistake," Mark said grimly, "and I didn't want Rae and the girls to pay for it."

"Public humiliation wasn't worth my life?"

"It wasn't that simple," Mark said tightly. "He didn't just threaten me. He threatened them too."

Krista sank down into the hard plastic chair opposite him. "You could have come to me. We would have figured something out."

Mark shook his head. "I was in too deep, and he'd made himself untouchable. Karev too."

"No one is untouchable," Krista said. "You of all people taught me that."

"And so what?" Mark said angrily. "You got Maxwell—good for you. But did you think for a second about everyone else who's going to suffer? The whole system is going to collapse. Convictions will be overturned, cases will be thrown out, and we'll be without leadership in nearly every public office. Krista, you've lived and breathed this job for nearly a decade. Because of what you've done, it's all going to dissolve into anarchy."

Disgust rose in her throat, threatening to choke her. What had happened to turn this man into the kind of amoral monster who could help send innocent people to prison and help a slime ball like Karev ooze back to the streets? The kind of man who could look the other way when Maxwell took out hits on Jimmy Caparulo and Stew Kowalski.

Who could sell her out, knowing it would result in her death.

"I don't know whom I hate more right now," Krista

said. "You for what you did, or me for actually believing in you all those years."

His skin paled to gray and his hands fisted on the table. "I never meant for any of it to go so far. I—" He shook his head. "I'm not going to offer explanations or try to excuse what happened. But you should know I've always cared about you, Krista. From the day you started working with me, I wanted my daughters to grow up to be just like you. God knows I've failed them."

Krista squeezed her eyes shut against the sting of tears and kept her voice steady. "You can redeem yourself by doing whatever you can to help clean up the mess Maxwell left behind."

His voice, when he spoke, was the calm, authoritative tone she was used to hearing in the courtroom. "I've kept detailed notes on the cases where Maxwell required my assistance. They'll be useful."

"Thanks," Krista said after he told her where to find them. "The fact that you're cooperating will help."

Mark let out a mirthless laugh. "Not enough."

Krista stood from her chair. "Good-bye, Mark." It felt like a death, letting go of him and everything he'd been to her over the years. Accepting that the man she knew didn't exist anymore, maybe never had.

She left the interrogation room, her eyes blurry with tears as she closed the door behind her.

"Hey, now, I've got you," said a familiar, deep voice. She turned blindly into his chest, gripping him around the waist as she sobbed. Sean didn't say anything, just stroked her back and held her up.

Finally she calmed down enough to look up and notice her father hovering behind Sean, looking uncomfortable at the sight of his no-nonsense daughter falling apart. "Hi, Dad."

"Hi, Krista," he said, leaning over to give her a kiss on the cheek and an awkward pat on the back. "We can do this later if you're not feeling up to it now."

The night Sean had rescued her, Krista had woken up in the hospital to find her father at her bedside, and since then he'd checked in on her at least twice a day and had become Sean and Krista's most vocal advocate in the media and to anyone else who would listen.

Though his representation of both Maxwell and Karev was widely known, John Slater claimed he had no idea the kinds of atrocities his clients were covering up. Odd as it seemed, Krista's gut told her that he was telling the truth. In a complete one-eighty from his past behavior he'd publicly fired himself as Margaret Grayson-Maxwell's attorney and announced he would be representing Krista and Sean in any lingering legal issues they might face in the fallout of Maxwell's death.

Today, he was supposed to take them to lunch to go through the details of getting Sean's arrest warrant for allegedly shooting the sheriff's deputy dismissed.

Krista looked to Sean. His face was lined with concern, and he looked so good, so strong, so beautiful standing there, it gave her the strength to push through anything, even the loss of someone she'd so dearly loved. She blew her nose and straightened up and slipped her hand into Sean's. "No, I'm fine. Let's do this. The sooner we clear all this up, the sooner I can get on with my life."

Sean cocked a dark eyebrow at her. "Our life," she quickly amended.

* * *

One Month Later

Thunk. Crack. Thunk. Crack. Sean lost himself in the steady rhythm of the falling ax. He breathed steadily, in and out, savoring the clean mountain air as the early-summer sun warmed the bare skin of his chest and back.

He heard the crunch of feet on gravel before a voice called, "Mail call."

Krista Goddamn Slater.

Sean couldn't have kept the goofy grin off his face if his life depended on it. He turned, propping the ax carefully against the splitting stump as he did. He reached for her with one hand and for his shirt with the other. "You're early."

"I was going to work a full day, but it was so insane I had to get out of there." Since the fallout, Krista had been working nonstop, the stress compounded by all the media attention the Maxwell case—not to mention Sean and Krista's unexpected romance—was receiving.

Sean hated all of it, the feeling of being cooped up in the house with nowhere to go, the feeling of being watched every time he did go out. The only thing that made it worth it was the time he spent with Krista, but it was taking its toll on both of them.

Luckily, she could already read him like a book and knew he was about to hit the wall without him saying anything.

They'd planned to come up to the cabin together for the weekend, their first trip up here together since everything had happened.

But a few days before, when Krista had come home from the office, she'd taken one look at Sean and said,

"You need to just go now. I'll drive up Friday after work." He'd left her with a kiss half an hour later, grateful for her understanding.

It had been a relief to get up here, to be out in the open and not worry about reporters hounding him, but goddamn he missed her.

He'd always thought the idea was corny, but he was pretty sure his heart actually did skip a beat every time he saw her, especially when it had been more than a few hours.

With her dark hair dyed back to its natural color, she looked once again like the icy blonde, remote, unattainable. Until he looked a little closer and saw the hot glow in her gray-green eyes as she eyed him hungrily, the heat of her gaze like a physical touch running up and down his torso. His own blood stirred, thick and heavy in his groin.

"No need to put that back on," she said, indicating the shirt in his hand.

He dropped the shirt, grinning even harder as he closed the distance between them. He pulled her close and vaguely heard the whisper of paper hitting the ground as his mail slipped through her fingers. But it didn't matter because she was in his arms, lifting her mouth to his, as hungry for him as he was for her.

"I missed you," she said, her voice going all breathy the way he loved as she sucked his tongue into her mouth and ran her hands up the sweat-slicked skin of his back.

"I missed you too," he groaned. His body roared to life at the first brush of her hands, desperate to touch her, taste her, get as deep inside of her as he could get. It felt like it had been weeks, not just days, since he'd been with her.

He lifted her off the ground, cradling her butt as she

wrapped those long, lean legs around him. His mouth never left hers as he carried her into the cabin, through the front room, and back to the bedroom. Within seconds, they were naked and he laid her out on the bed, groaning at the first contact of skin on skin.

Jesus, she was gorgeous, so much better than the heated memories that kept him up at night. Creamy skin, hard nipples pointing to the sky, begging to be touched. He sucked her into his mouth and slipped a hand between her pale thighs. She tangled her fingers in his hair and pulled his mouth to hers as his fingers thrust deep inside, stroking and teasing until she was rocking against him, every nerve pulled tight as she got closer to the edge.

He wanted to feel her come around him the first time, needed to feel the tight pull of her muscles, rippling and clenching around him like she was trying to pull him deeper inside. He let out a frustrated breath as he fumbled in the bedside drawer for one of the dozens of condoms he'd stashed there.

And then, Jesus, he was inside her, buried all the way in one slick thrust. It felt so good, the pleasure radiating out from his cock, coursing out to every nerve ending. Krista arched against him with a harsh cry and wrapped her legs around his hips, pulling him closer, urging him deeper, harder, as she sucked at his lips and tongue.

He squeezed his eyes shut and struggled not to come, but it felt too good, Krista's wet heat squeezing him with every stroke, the sting of her nails as they dug into the flexing muscles of his ass. And the way she was chanting his name in that high, breathless voice that never failed to send him soaring.

One last thrust and he couldn't hold back, but it didn't

matter because Krista was right there with him, grinding her hips against his as she pulsed and shuddered, her muscles squeezing around him, wringing him dry as he came so hard stars floated in front of his vision.

He held himself there, deep inside her as he propped himself up on his elbows and just stared at her. Her eyes were closed, her cheeks rosy pink, her lips swollen and parted in a soft smile of pure satisfaction. "I love you," she murmured.

Three words that never failed to hit him like a kick to the chest. "I love you too," he said, his voice suspiciously thick as he stared down at her.

They'd gone through hell to get here, been through shit two people could never expect to get past to be together. But here they were. To Sean, who'd once given up all hope on any kind of life, it felt like he'd been granted a miracle. Krista in his bed, loving him, needing him, her skin against his, a smile on her face that he'd put there. Completely his, body and soul.

All Talia Vega wants is
a quiet, normal life.

But a brutal killer from her past has
come back to haunt her—and Jack
Brooks, the man she swore she'd
never let herself depend on again, is
the only man she can trust...

Run from Fear

Available in March 2012

Please turn this page for a preview.

Someone was watching her. Talia could feel it. The tingling her in shoulders, her scalp, the way the hairs on the back of her neck stood on end. She pasted a smile on her face and kept her hand from shaking as she handed a friendly blonde in her forties another glass of chardonnay across the bar.

The blonde sidled aside and the feeling grew stronger. Her gaze scanned the bar of Suzette's. It was Sunday evening, never the busiest night of the week, especially not when March Madness drove a lot of the happy-hour crowd to the sports bar around the corner. But the bar was about two-thirds full, girlfriends catching a quick drink as they braced for a busy week ahead, couples having drinks and a light dinner, a few older students from the nearby university who craved something a little more sophisticated than the college bars.

No one stuck out as someone who should give her this feeling again. That feeling that had faded steadily over the past two years, to the point where she could imagine the day it would disappear entirely. But now it was back, that eerie sensation that had dogged her every day she'd been under David Maxwell's thumb, long years of always having eyes on her, knowing that nothing she did went unwatched, unnoticed.

Then she saw him.

And almost laughed out loud at her foolishness. Of course she was being looked at. As the only bartender working tonight in the decently crowded restaurant, people would be looking at her all evening, straining to make eye contact and get her attention.

The muscles in her face relaxed into a friendly smile as she greeted a man in his early fifties, salt-and-pepper hair swept back from his lined forehead. He was a regular enough customer for Talia to remember the face if not the name.

She poured him a vodka martini and made small talk, mentally reminding herself that just because there had been a fresh surge in the last couple weeks of news stories mentioning her name, that didn't mean she needed to let fear and paranoia once again rule her existence.

She had a new life now. She wasn't that scared victim anymore, living underground in a series of safe houses in northern California, always looking over her shoulder as she frantically tried to keep herself and her teenage sister safe from people who wanted nothing more than to see them suffer.

She was free, had been for two years, and she'd done pretty well for herself and Rosie if she did say so herself. All they'd needed was a fresh start.

Even after they'd been able to come out of hiding, Talia had no desire to return to the life they'd fled in

Seattle, so she'd convinced Rosario to get her GED a year early so they could spend some time traveling. Six months ago, Talia and Rosario had moved back to Palo Alto, so Rosario could begin her freshman year at nearby Stanford.

Through a friend of a friend—though to be fair, to call Jack Brooks a friend was both too strong and too weak a word to describe what he was to her—she'd secured a job as the beverage manager and bartender at Suzette's. It didn't exactly open the floodgates on her cash flow, but combined with the proceeds of the sale of her house in Seattle it provided a decent enough living while she paid for Rosario to go to school and saved what she could for her own education somewhere down the road.

All in all, it was a perfectly nice life, much nicer than she could have imagined or asked for two short years ago. Much too nice a life for her to let it be affected by a few news stories that dredged up a sordid past Talia wanted nothing more than to leave behind.

Still, it was hard to entirely shake off the prickles, and against her will, her eyes did another quick scan of the bar area. They snagged on a shadowy figure in the corner and for a split second the scars crisscrossing her back tingled as though electrified.

She shook it off. It was nothing. It was no one, just a lone male whose features she couldn't quite make out in the shadows, but whom she imagined to be young, in his early to mid-twenties. She could see the outline of a wool knit cap and guessed he was a grad student.

There was nothing about him to cause the spike in adrenaline that accompanied the paranoia that had snaked its dark tendrils around her in the past month. Ever since

Margaret Grayson-Maxwell had been released from prison in a wave of press that rehashed all of the sordid details of Margaret's involvement in her late husband David Maxwell's less than legitimate businesses of trafficking in people, drugs, weapons—whatever earned him the biggest profits, along with Talia's own role as the disgruntled mistress who helped to take him and his empire down.

Talia could have all the fresh starts she wanted, but she couldn't prevent her picture from appearing front and center on every newspaper in Seattle, as she was alternately portrayed as both the mercenary gold digger who looked the other way while her wealthy keeper used his monster of a nephew to carry out the murders of high-class prostitutes, and as the victim who had barely escaped with her life when that same nephew, Nate Brewster, known better under his infamous moniker the Seattle Slasher, had set his sights on Talia.

But what was big news in Seattle was nothing in a bustling Palo Alto, she reminded herself. Sure, the revelation of Nate as the Seattle Slasher had been a national story two years ago when it resulted in the release of Sean Flynn from death row. A few months later, it was revealed that David Maxwell, one of Seattle's most prominent citizens, a man who had married into a family often referred to as Washington state's version of the Kennedys, had not only been the shadowy force behind the Seattle Slasher but had also run a criminal organization that netted millions of dollars and was linked to the Russian Mafia.

At that point, there had been magazine articles, front-page stories, even features on news programs like *48 Hours* and *Dateline.* Though Talia had refused to be interviewed, her involvement with David Maxwell meant her name was dragged through the mud with his, and for about a week or so there, she was definitely on the country's radar.

But news moved fast, especially in the Internet age. Though Seattle-ites had clearly reveled in the opportunity to rehash one of the few lurid scandals to hit their comparatively white-washed city, as far as the rest of the world was concerned, Margaret Grayson-Maxwell's arrest and the nefarious activities of her dead husband were lost in the ether.

No reason for anyone to associate Talia's name with the ugly events of her past. Not unless someone was deliberately seeking, in which case nearly every lurid detail was on the Internet for anyone to find.

But so far no one seemed inclined to go digging, or to bring it up if they had. She shook off her unease. No matter what was going on in Seattle with Margaret Grayson-Maxwell or anyone else involved in the scandal, Talia had moved on. She was safe now.

She moved to the other end of the bar to clear away two wine glasses and a picked-over plate of calamari.

"Talia!"

A smile stretched over her face at the sound of the familiar voice. "Rosie, you're early," she said, turning at the sound of her younger sister's voice. She wasn't hard to spot in a crowd. At five-foot-nine, Rosario Vega was a good four inches taller than Talia, easy to spot in the mostly seated crowd.

But even without the height, Rosie would have stood out. At eighteen, she was finally growing into the huge brown eyes, long nose, and full mouth that had given her a mismatched look throughout her childhood. Now the bold features gave her a beauty that was as arresting as it was unique.

Something that didn't go unnoticed by a single straight man in the bar.

Except, Talia noted as she felt her smile fade, by maybe the boy-man to Talia's left, looking bored as he stood next to Rosario, hands stuffed in the pockets of his scruffy black hoodie. "Oh, and I see you brought Kevin," Talia said, trying to keep the acid from her tone, but failing if Rosario's warning look was anything to go by.

"Still cool if we have dinner here?" Rosario said as she plopped onto a bar stool. She motioned for Kevin to follow, who joined her with an eye roll.

It was on the tip of Talia's tongue to remind Rosie that the invitation to dinner on Talia's tab did not include shiftless twenty-three-year-old sixth-year seniors who should be out working for a living instead of sucking off their parents' seemingly limitless college fund while preying on hapless, wide-eyed freshmen.

Instead, she bit out a sharp "Sure." Sure, she'd forgo her share of tips tonight to pay for the extra forty or so dollars of food and drink Kevin would undoubtedly suck up. Sure, she'd do her best to ignore the way Rosario would tune out everyone, focus all of her attention on Kevin, bouncing around him like a puppy, while he mumbled monosyllabic replies through a mouth stuffed with food.

Because two years ago, when the tightrope she'd been walking had snapped out from under her, Talia had promised herself, promised Rosario, that she'd make a normal life for them. A life where Talia didn't have to hide out in a safe house, away from Rosario, who was forced to live under an assumed name with a family of well-meaning strangers. A life that didn't include living under the protection of full-time paid bodyguards.

And plenty of normal college girls had boyfriends, often directionless, disinterested, unworthy boyfriends like Kevin. Part of being normal meant getting your heart bruised by a guy who didn't deserve a second of your time, a lesson Talia fervently hoped Rosario learned sooner rather than later.

And really, who was she to judge? Kevin might be a shiftless douche bag, but at least he wasn't the force behind an international criminal organization that had resulted in the suffering and deaths of countless innocent women. Talia still held the gold medal in the falling in love with the absolute worst person on the planet award.

Talia swallowed hard and forced the memories of David's threats against herself and Rosie from her mind. David was dead. The truth was out.

He couldn't hurt them anymore.

She put menus in front of Rosario and Kevin and excused herself to fill an order for the main dining room. When she got back, she automatically put a Coke in front of each of them.

Kevin let out a little huff of disgust and pushed the glass back in her direction. "Can I get a bottle of Budweiser?"

"I don't think—" Talia started, only to be interrupted by her sister.

"God, Tal, why do you do this every time? He's legal, and you know it."

"You're not, and I don't think he needs to be drinking with you—"

Kevin started to stand. "Fine. I'm supposed to meet Sam at the Z-bar anyway," he said, referencing a bar across town that was popular with the students. A bar underage Rosario wouldn't be able to get into.

Rosie grabbed his arm in a vise grip. "No, she'll give you the beer!" As she spoke, she shot Talia a look that shouted, *Don't ruin this. You owe me. You owe me big time.*

Talia knew she could spot Rosario's boyfriend a whole truckload of beer and it wouldn't make a dent in what she owed Rosie for bringing a monster into their lives. She *thunked* the bottle in front of Kevin and started to ask what they wanted.

A low voice edged with menace cut her off before she could open her mouth. "You better not be driving her anywhere, punk."

Kevin whirled on his seat with a sullen glare. "Fuck off," he snapped. Then swallowed hard and shrank back when he got a good look at the man behind him.

Talia couldn't blame him. At easily six-foot-four with muscles on top of muscles, bristling with hostility as he stared down at Kevin with glacial blue eyes, to say Jack Brooks was intimidating was the understatement of the year.

Talia would have been scared, too, had she not been so shocked by the sight of him, here, in the flesh, after so long.

"Jack!" Rosario squealed, unfazed as she hurled herself in for a hug. Talia felt something in her chest twist as she watched those heavily muscled arms circle Rosario and give her a squeeze.

"Hey, kiddo," Jack said, as he shot another glare at Kevin.

Then Talia's heart did a strange flip as Jack met her eyes over Talia's head and he flashed her a grin that softened the harsh lines of his face and warmed the glacial blue of those eyes. "Hey, Talia."

"Jack," she replied with a nod, proud of the way the single syllable did nothing to hint at the turmoil his unexpected appearance was causing.

She held herself still as he released Rosario and did a quick scan of her face and body. There was nothing in his gaze that hinted at anything approaching lust or attraction—for which she was fiercely grateful. Still, Jack had a way of looking at a person that made them feel like he knew all of their secrets, even the ones they didn't know they were hiding.

Then again, she supposed of all people, Jack did know everything about her. The good, the bad, the horrifically ugly.

"You've been working out. You look strong."

Talia nodded, unsure if she should thank him, unsure it was a compliment. There was a time, a lifetime ago, when she would have come back with something snappy, shown some attitude, run her hands over her own body to make sure Jack got a good look at what she had to show.

Now her tongue stuck to the roof of her mouth, her brain spinning with a thousand things she wanted to say, wanted to ask.

And yet she remained tongue-tied, unable to make even the simplest small talk with the man who had saved her life.

Rosario was more than capable of taking up the conversational ball. "When I talked to you a couple weeks ago, you didn't say anything about coming down."

Broad shoulders shrugged under his jacket. "It came up last minute. Danny just landed a new client and they needed me to come down to help out." Jack managed the Seattle operations of Gemini Securities, a firm based in the San Francisco Bay Area that specialized in corporate and personal security. The firm was owned and operated by Danny Taggart, one of Jack's team members from his time as an Army Green Beret, along with Taggart's younger twin brothers.

"When did you talk to Jack?" Talia asked, wincing at the bite in her tone.

Rosario shot her an exasperated look. "A couple weeks ago?" She looked to Jack, who nodded in affirmation.

"We talk a few times a year, just to catch up," Jack said.

"Oh," Talia said. "I didn't realize you two were so close." Talia busied herself wiping down the already immaculate bar, telling herself there was no reason to feel this stab of hurt over the fact that Jack and Rosario were apparently BFFs when the only contact she'd had with him in the past year and a half was a terse one-line e-mail refusing any payment for the security services he and Gemini Security had provided while keeping her and Rosario safe from David's reach. Hadn't she breathed a sigh of relief at the sight of his retreating back, because it meant David was no longer a threat and she could finally move on with her life?

"He helped me with physics last quarter," Rosario offered. "Since that was his major in college."

Talia nodded and refilled another customer's glass of sauvignon blanc. She didn't even know Jack had gone to college, much less studied physics. She wasn't, she told herself, jealous of the fact that Jack apparently took the time to talk to Rosario on the phone when he didn't even bother to get in touch last month when the *Seattle Tribune* had rehashed the lurid details of Talia's past.

Not that she'd wanted him to, she reminded herself forcefully. Jack was a six-foot-four, two-hundred-plus-pound reminder of everything she wanted to leave buried.

And yet, seeing him here...it awakened something inside her, something struggling to dig its way through the rubble left over from the life she'd left behind.

"So, is this the guy you told me about?" Jack's voice interrupted her thoughts.

"Yes, this is Kevin, my boyfriend?"

Talia winced at the uncertainty in her sister's voice. She looked up and caught Jack's gaze. As their eyes met, she knew his thoughts echoed her own.

Douche bag. His mouth tightened in resignation and in that moment she felt a little crack in the wall that had always existed between them, even after Jack had pulled her out of a basement and saved her from a psycho killer.

Kevin, so sullen his bottom lip was practically protruding, reluctantly reached out his own hand to take the one Jack offered. His thin hand was swallowed up by Jack's massive palm, and Kevin winced as Jack gave it a firm squeeze.

"Kevin," Jack said, his voice scarier for its icy calm. "Let's get something straight, okay?"

Kevin nodded.

"These two have run into enough creeps for three lifetimes. I've taken it upon myself to keep an eye on them and make sure they don't run into any more. Got it?"

He released Kevin's hand, and the younger man glared sullenly as he absently rubbed his sore palm. "Yeah."

"Good," Jack said with a baring of white teeth that couldn't quite be called a smile. "I'm going to be in town for a few weeks, and while I'm here, think of me as their very big, very protective older brother, who will come after you if I find out you're giving either of them any trouble."

Kevin gave a grunt and heaved himself up from his seat. "Yeah, that's cool and all, but I think I'm out of here. Rosario, I'll catch you at school. It's getting a little heavy in here."

"No!" Rosario grabbed her coat and purse and started after him, shooting daggers at Jack.

Talia went after her and grabbed her arm. "Rosie, let him go. This is one of the only nights of the week I get to see you—"

Rosie jerked from her hold. "Damn it, Talia, let me go! Jack, you're as bad as her, thinking everyone in the world is out to get us. Just let me live my life," she said, whirling dramatically as she stomped after Kevin.

"Be back at my place by midnight," Talia called to her sister's disappearing back. She sighed and turned to Jack, whose usual poker face had cracked to reveal a faint sheepishness.

"I'm sorry if that was out of line," he began.

Talia waved him off as she went back behind the bar. The crowd was thinning out and it didn't take her long to refresh a handful of drinks. "It's okay. Kevin is a jerkoff but he's mostly harmless. But I can't say I don't wish she could find someone more motivated, not to mention someone who's actually nice to her," she said as she rejoined Jack where he was leaning against one end of the bar.

His full lips quirked into a rueful smile, revealing the

flash of a dimple in his lean cheek. "Why is it the good ones always go for the assholes who don't deserve them?"

"I don't know," Talia said and sighed with a tired smile. "But with my track record, I'm hardly in a position to question her judgment."

Jack's eyes darkened. "Don't tell me you're still blaming yourself."

Talia felt like a fist was squeezing her insides as the guilt and the shame over her own bad decisions tried to claw free from the dark corner where Talia had shoved them. "I really don't want to get into this right now," she said, faking a smile at a customer a few seats down. God, five minutes in Jack's presence and she was already back there, scared and powerless.

Guilty.

"Shit, Talia." Jack reached out a hand, stopping short of actually touching her. "I didn't mean to...I didn't come here to upset you. I'm looking after you too, Talia." There was something in his face that made her swallow hard and made her feel...something...she couldn't quite pinpoint. An ache, a curiosity—

"Hey, who's your friend?"

Whatever it was got pushed away in a wave of perfume and blond hair striding across the room, a glint of interest in her blue eyes and a toothpaste-commercial-worthy smile on her face.

"This is my, uh, this is Jack Brooks," Talia said. "And Jack, this is Susie Morse, the owner of Suzette's and my boss."

Talia watched Jack's huge hand swallow up Susie's much smaller one. She grabbed a rag and gave the bar a vigorous wipe down so she wouldn't see the inevitable flare of attraction on Jack's face. Who could blame him? With her thick, honey-colored hair, blue eyes, and tall, athletic body, Susie was a dead ringer for Christie Brinkley in her *Sports Illustrated* days. Normally, Talia didn't pay enough attention to her own looks to let the contrast bother her, but suddenly she felt like a small dark mouse in the shadow of Susie's blazing sun.

"Nice to put a face with the name," Susie said, though the way her eyes were raking up and down Jack's body, she was appreciating a lot more than just his face.

Something was odd though. "Why would you know Jack's name?"

Something flickered across Susie's face that looked suspiciously like guilt, but then her smile was back in full force. "Oh, Alyssa told me all about you."

Alyssa was Alyssa Taggart, married to Derek Taggart, who worked with Jack at Gemini Securities. Alyssa and Susie were childhood friends, and when Talia had moved to Palo Alto, Alyssa had hooked her up with Susie, who happened to be in the market for a new beverage manager at her popular restaurant. While Talia hated feeling like a charity case, she'd been happy for the introduction and had worked her ass off to make sure Susie never regretted the decision to hire her.

"Last time she and Derek were in, she said I had to meet you the next time you came to town, and I can see exactly why she was so insistent."

In her time at Suzette's, Talia had come to like and respect Susie a great deal and counted her as one of the few people she trusted enough to call a friend. But right now, watching as Susie looked at Jack like he was a juicy piece of meat, Talia had to squash the urge to smack her friend's hand away from where it lingered in Jack's.

Talia wasn't positive in the dim lighting of the bar, but she was pretty sure Jack was blushing. "Uh, thanks. It's, uh, nice to meet you too," he said and gently disengaged his hand.

"Dinner service is wrapping up," Susie said, "but I'm more than happy to set up a table for you and have the chef put something together—"

Jack silenced her with a raised hand. "Thanks, but I'm fine. I'll just sit here at the bar, if that's okay?" He quirked a thick brow at Talia as if asking for permission.

Which struck her as odd. In her short but intense interactions with Jack, he never asked her approval for anything. "Fine with me. What can I get you?"

Jack settled into a stool as she slid the requested beer in front of him. Talia saw another customer signaling her from the corner of her eye. "I need to—"

"Go right ahead," Jack said. "I'm good."

Talia got the customer his check, and as the crowd thinned, that sensation of being watched came back, ten times stronger now. But it didn't creep her out, having Jack's intense gaze track her. Instead of prickles on the back of her neck and between her shoulders, she felt a strange ache, almost like a yearning.

As she gathered up glasses from an empty table, she heard Susie's tinkling laugh from the main dining room and felt a sudden burst of envy. For the easy way her friend was able to smile at Jack, toss her hair, laugh, and make her interest clear.

Talia had been like that once. Friendly, flirty, ready and willing to use what she had to attract the attention of any man she set her sights on. She'd been normal once. She knew she had. Able to talk and banter and be attracted to a man as gorgeous and compelling as Jack.

But when she tried to remember what that was like, it felt as though she was parting the curtains on some distant, foggy past that belonged to another person. She'd tried to reclaim that part of herself in the past two years. She'd dated a few men, nice, normal men who took her out to dinner and *didn't* expect her to sleep with them. But none of them had been able to wake her body from its apparent coma. No one made anything that felt remotely like attraction spark in her belly.

Until now.

Of course. Because no matter how much she longed for a normal life, of course her fucked-up past and twisted psychology would make her yearn for the one man who knew exactly who she was, what she'd done, and what had been done to her.

The one man who'd made it all too clear he didn't want a damn thing from her.

THE DISH

Where authors give you the inside scoop!

♥ ♥

From the desk of Jill Shalvis

Dear Reader,

It's been a fun, exciting year for my Lucky Harbor series. Thanks to you, the readers, I hit the *New York Times* bestseller list with *The Sweetest Thing*. Wow. Talk about making my day! You are all awesome, and I'm still grinning from ear to ear and making everyone call me "N-Y-T." But I digress...

In light of how much you, the readers, have enjoyed this series, my publisher is putting *Simply Irresistible* and *The Sweetest Thing* together as a 2-in-1 volume at a special low price. CHRISTMAS IN LUCKY HARBOR will be in stores in November—just in time to bring new readers up to speed for book three, *Head Over Heels,* in December.

When I first started this series, I wanted it to be about three sisters who run a beach resort together. I figured I'd use my three daughters as inspiration. Only problem, my little darlings are teenagers, and they bicker like fiends. Some inspiration. But then it occurred to me: Their relationships are real, and that's what I like to write. Real people. So I changed things up, and the series became about three ESTRANGED sisters, stuck together running a dilapidated inn falling down on its axis. Now *that* I could pull off for sure. Add in three sexy alpha heroes to go with, and voilà…I was on my way.

So make sure to look for CHRISTMAS IN LUCKY HARBOR, the reprint of books one and two, available both in print and as an ebook wherever books are sold. And right on its heels, book three, *Head Over Heels*. (Heels? Get it?)

Happy reading and holiday hugs!

Jill Shalvis

www.jillshalvis.com

♥ ♥ ♥ ♥ ♥ ♥ ♥ ♥ ♥ ♥ ♥ ♥ ♥ ♥ ♥ ♥ ♥ ♥ ♥ ♥

From the desk of Margaret Mallory

Dear Readers,

Bad boys! What woman doesn't love a rogue—at least in fiction?

I suspect that's the reason I've had readers asking me about Alex MacDonald since he made his appearance as a secondary character in *The Guardian*, Book 1 of The Return of the Highlanders series.

Alex is such an unruly charmer that I was forced to ban him from several chapters of *The Guardian* for misbe havior. Naturally, the scoundrel attempted to steal every scene I put him in. I will admit that I asked Alex to flirt with the heroine to make his cousin jealous, but did he have to enjoy himself quite so thoroughly? Of course, if there had been any real chance of stealing his cousin's true love, Alex would not have done it. A good heart is hidden beneath that brawny chest. All the same, I told the scene-stealer he must wait his turn. When he laughed and refused to cooperate, I threw him out.

Now, at last, this too-handsome, green-eyed warrior has his own book, THE SINNER. I hope readers will agree that a man who has had far too many women fall at his feet must suffer on the road to love.

The first thing I decided to do was give Alex a heroine who was as loath to marry as he was. In fact, Alex would have to travel the length and breadth of Scotland to find a lass as opposed to marriage in general, or to him in particular, as Glynis MacNeil. Glynis's experience with one handsome, philandering Highland warrior was enough to last her a lifetime, and she's prepared to go to any lengths to thwart her chieftain father's attempts to wed her to another.

Alex has sworn—repeatedly and to anyone who would listen—that he will *never* take a wife. So the second thing I decided to do was surprise Alex partway through the book with an utterly compelling reason to wed. (No, I'm not telling here.) I hope readers appreciate the irony of this bad boy's long, uphill battle to persuade Glynis to marry him.

Helping these two untrusting souls find love proved even bigger challenge than getting them wed. Fortu-ely, the attraction between Alex and Glynis was so hot my fingers burned on the keys. The last thing I needed to do, then, was force them to trust each other through a series of dangerous adventures that threatened all they held dear. That part was easy, dear readers—such dangers *abound* in the Highlands in the year 1515.

I hope you enjoy the love story of Alex and Glynis in THE SINNER.

Margaret Mallory

www.margaretmallory.com

♥ ♥ ♥ ♥ ♥ ♥ ♥ ♥ ♥ ♥ ♥ ♥ ♥ ♥ ♥ ♥ ♥ ♥ ♥ ♥

From the desk of Cara Elliott

Dear Reader,

Starting a new series is a little like going out on a first date. I mean, doesn't every girl get a little nervous about meeting a guy who is a complete stranger? Well, I have a confession to make: Authors get the heebies-jeebies too. Hey, it's not easy to waltz up to a hunky hero and simply bat your eyelashes and introduce yourself! •

Okay, okay, I know what you're thinking. *How hard can it be?* After all, unlike in real life, all I have to do is snap my fingers (or tap them along my keyboard) and presto, as if by magic, he'll turn into a knight in shini armor, or a dashingly debonair prince, or... whatever my fantasies desire!

Strange as it may sound, it doesn't always flow quite so smoothly. Some men have minds of their own. You know... the strong, silent, self-reliant type who would rather eat nails than admit to any vulnerability. Take Connor Linsley, the sinfully sexy rogue who plays the leading role in TOO WICKED TO WED, the first book in my new Lords of Midnight trilogy. Talk about an infuriating man! He snaps, he snarls, he broods. If he didn't have such an intriguing spark in his quicksilver eyes, I might have been tempted to give up on him.

But no, patient person that I am, I persevered, knowing that beneath his show of steel was a softer, more sensitive core. I just had to draw it out. We had to have a number of heart-to-heart talks, but finally he let down his silky dark hair—er, in a manner of speaking—and allowed me to share some of his secrets. (And trust me, Connor has some *very* intriguing secrets!)

I'll have you know that I am also generous, as well as patient, for instead of keeping my new best friend all to myself, I've decided to share this Paragon of Perfection. I hope you enjoy getting to know him! (Pssst, he has two very devil-may-care friends. But that's another story. Or maybe two!)

Please visit my website at www.caraelliott.com to read sample chapters and learn more about this Lord of Midnight. •

Cara Elliott

♥ ♥

From the desk of Jami Alden

Dear Reader,

I first met Krista Slater in my first romantic suspense for Grand Central, *Beg for Mercy*. All I knew about her then was that she was tough, no nonsense, dedicated to her work and committed to right, even if it meant admitting she'd made an enormous mistake in sending Sean Flynn to death row. But it was only after I'd spent about a month (and a hundred pages) with her in my latest book, HIDE FROM EVIL, that I learned she's also an automobile expert who can hotwire a car in less than sixty seconds.

And I knew Sean Flynn was loyal and honorable, with a protective streak a mile wide. I also knew that when he was forced into close quarters with Krista, he'd fall and fall hard, despite the fact she'd nearly ruined his life when she prosecuted him for murder. However, I didn't know he listened to Alice in Chains until he popped in his earbuds and clicked on his iPod.

After I finish every book, I'm amazed at the fact that I've written three hundred plus pages about people who exist only in my head. For about six months, I spend nearly every waking hour with them. Even when I'm not actually writing, they're always around, circling the edges of my consciousness while I think up a sexy, scary story for them to inhabit.

When I first started writing, I read books that said I shouldn't start writing until I knew absolutely everything about my hero and heroine. And I mean EVERYTHING—

stuff like the name of their best friends from kindergarten and their least favorite food. So I would try to fill out these elaborate questionnaires, racking my brain to come up with a list of my heroine's quirks.

I finally came to accept the fact that it takes me a while to get to know my characters. We need to spend some time together before I get a sense of what makes them tick. It's like getting to know a new friend: You start with the small talk. Then you hang out, have conversations that go beyond the surface. You start to notice the little details that make them unique, and they reveal things from their pasts that have molded them into the people you're coming to know.

That's when things get interesting.

It was definitely interesting getting to know Sean and Krista in HIDE FROM EVIL. Especially finding out why, despite their rocky past, they were absolutely meant for each other. I hope you have as much fun with them as I did.

Enjoy!

Jami Alden

www.jamialden.com